Rescue Mode

BEN BOVA
LES JOHNSON

BAEN

RESCUE MODE

This is a work of fiction. All the characters and events portrayed
in this book are fictional, and any resemblance to real people or incidents
is purely coincidental.

A Baen Book

Baen Publishing Enterprises
P.O. Box 1403
Riverdale, NY 10471
www.baen.com

ISBN: 978-1-4767-3647-1

Cover art by Bob Eggleton

First Baen printing, June 2014

Distributed by Simon & Schuster
1230 Avenue of the Americas
New York, NY 10020

Library of Congress Cataloging-in-Publication Data

Bova, Ben, 1932-
  Rescue mode / Ben Bova and Les Johnson.
     pages cm
  ISBN 978-1-4767-3647-1 (hc)
  1. Astronauts--Fiction. 2. Mars (Planet)--Exploration--Fiction. I. Johnson,
Les (Charles Les) II. Title.
  PS3552.O84R43 2014
  813'.54--dc23
                                        2014009923
Printed in the United States of America

10 9 8 7 6 5 4 3 2 1

《 DEDICATION 》

To the first human being
to set foot on the planet Mars.

To strive, to seek, to find, and not to yield.
—Alfred, Lord Tennyson
Ulysses

(((foreword)))

Les Johnson

In 2012, NASA convened a workshop in Houston to "assess near-term mission concepts and longer-term foundations of program-level architectures for future robotic exploration of Mars." The event, NASA's Concepts and Approaches for Mars Exploration, was held at the Lunar and Planetary Institute and attended by several hundred scientists and engineers. Attendance was selective. Participants had to submit white papers describing some innovative or novel approach to Mars exploration that would either provide new science, save money or both. I submitted a white paper describing how solar sails could be used in support of a robotic Mars sample return mission and it was accepted for presentation at the workshop. I was thrilled. (My presentation is archived online at http://www.lpi.usra.edu/meetings/marsconcepts2012/pdf/4103.pdf).

During one of the plenary sessions in which all the participants were engaged, the age-old debate between advocates of future human exploration of Mars and those who believe that robots can explore more cheaply began to rage. And this was a venue in which it truly mattered. Being discussed as options for future robotic Mars missions were instruments that would help answer questions pertaining to future human missions—not fundamental science. If another human exploration-centric payload would be included on a future mission, then that would be one less science instrument on the flight. Payload space was at stake, and the funding that would be required to develop it.

1

Sitting on the front row, in a chair reserved for him and marked simply, "Buzz," was the second man to walk on the Moon, Buzz Aldrin. He had been quiet up to this point, but it was clear he could contain himself no longer. He stood up and waited on the room to notice and get quiet. It didn't take long. Once he had everyone's attention, he asked a question.

"How many of you would sign up for a one-way trip to Mars?"

In an audience comprised of mostly scientists and engineers, more than half raised their hands. I noticed that some who raised their hands were previously arguing for sending only robotic science missions to Mars—and not humans. That was certainly unexpected. I kept my hands at my side.

I was astounded at the response. Would these highly educated scientists really give up the blue sky and green grass of Earth to live forevermore in what amounts to a Winnebago on the fourth planet from the Sun? A good day on Mars is colder and more inhospitable than a bad day in Antarctica. Instant death would surely follow the first careless mistake and there would be no easy way to get help in an emergency. What were they thinking???

Apparently they were thinking of why they had studied science, space science and engineering specifically, in the first place. The dream of walking on Mars is powerful; perhaps more powerful than the logic used to justify one type of space exploration over another. And only the words of a person who walked on another world could jolt this group out of their parochial mindset and remind them of the wonder that is space exploration.

I later found out that most who didn't raise their hands were like me. They would love to go to Mars but not on a one-way trip. I would go on a round trip to Mars and back in a heartbeat. I would take a calculated risk in order to experience Mars firsthand but I would definitely want to return to my family and friends, to my yearly trip to the North Carolina mountains and to the simple walks around the neighborhood that I take with my wife each day. Fortunately, no one is saying that a trip to Mars has to be one way. But even if it is, there are many people who would volunteer. Consider Mars One and Inspiration Mars.

Mars One has the self-stated goal to "establish a permanent human settlement on Mars" by sending a habitat to the planet with people coming two years later, planning to remain permanently. Supplies would be sent from Earth to keep them alive until the colony becomes self-sufficient. They claim to be in discussions with several major aerospace companies and groups, including Lockheed Martin, SpaceX, and Thales Alenia Space.

Their plan is ambitious, audacious, and incredibly risky. The technical issues aside, what's interesting about Mars One has been the public's response. They claim that over two hundred thousand people have applied to take this one-way journey. These people have said they would risk their lives to be the first colonists on Mars. How many of them are serious and would get on the rocket if the plan becomes a reality? No one knows. But I would bet the number won't be zero. It might even be larger than the two hundred thousand they have today. If they actually can pull together the funding and support to make it happen, then more people will hear about it and possibly sign up. If and when launch day arrives, you can bet there will be people lining up at the door.

Less ambitious but no less audacious is Inspiration Mars. Led by millionaire Dennis Tito, who spent eight days in space aboard the International Space Station, paying the Russians for the trip and becoming the first real space tourist, Inspiration Mars would like to use today's technologies to send a man and a woman on a round-trip flight around Mars and back. The trip would last five hundred days and pass within 100 miles of the planet's surface. What a vacation that would be!

Is such a trip technically possible? Probably.

Can he pull it off? Why not? All it will take is money to buy good engineering — and more than a little bit of luck.

Would it change how we view deep space exploration and perhaps foster more ambitious future trips to the Martian surface? I certainly hope so and wish Mr. Tito all the success in the world!

We have the technology *now* to get people to Mars and to bring them safely back to Earth.

Mars awaits, and many of us are getting impatient.

—Les Johnson*
Les.mail@lesjohnsonauthor.com
www.lesjohnsonauthor.com

*The opinions expressed herein are my own and do not represent NASA.

I

Earth Departure

APRIL 5, 2031
EARTH DEPARTURE MINUS 4 YEARS
14:40 UNIVERSAL TIME
THE ROCK

The rock was tiny, barely a foot in diameter, with a mass of less than thirty pounds. It had been orbiting the Sun for nearly fifteen million years in an elliptical path that took it roughly from the distance of Mars to a little closer to the Sun than the heat-blistered planet Mercury.

It had been blasted off the surface of Mars by the impact of a much bigger meteoroid, the one that sent the famous Allen Hills Meteorite wandering through space until it crashed into the ice sheets of Earth's Antarctica some fifteen thousand years ago.

If the rock had reached Earth it would have never made it to the ground, but would have streaked across the night sky to burn up high in the atmosphere—a "falling star" to anyone who happened to notice its demise.

But that didn't happen. Instead, the rock continued on its long, looping trajectory, swinging through the vast, dark, silent emptiness.

Interplanetary space is not completely empty, of course. There were thousands of other meteoroids created by that single Mars impact so long ago. And millions more engendered by other impacts with different planets and the smaller bodies of the main Asteroid Belt, out beyond the orbit of Mars. They all quietly orbited the Sun, but they were very far apart, most of them too small to be seen even by the finest scientific instruments of humankind.

Looping around the Sun for millennia at an average velocity of 40,000 miles per hour, this rock was in a fairly stable orbit that would not bring it near Earth or any other planet for another ten million years. The chances of it hitting anything smaller than a planet were, well, astronomically small.

But astronomically small is not the same as zero. And humans were already planning to send explorers across the gulf of space to the planet Mars.

Steven Treadway stood in the baking desert heat, a microphone embedded in the stylish pin on his short-sleeved shirt. He gestured toward the twelve-story-tall rocket that stood on its steel launch stand, gleaming in the bright sunshine of a cloudless summer morning.

"This is the first of ten rocket boosters that will carry components of the Mars-bound *Arrow* spacecraft into a low orbit around the Earth," he was saying. The pin-mike picked up his words clearly.

"Over the next six months the *Arrow* will be put together in Earth orbit, then its crew of four men and four women will board the spacecraft and head off to Mars."

In the morning's heat, Treadway had dispensed with his usual studio "uniform" of crisp white shirt with navy blue trousers, and stood in an open-necked polo shirt and whipcord slacks. He was a handsome man, with finely chiseled features and cobalt-blue eyes. The latter were the gift of his parents, the former the product of cosmetic surgery.

This Mars program was Treadway's path to the top of his profession. Basically a science reporter, he had fought with every ounce of determination and cunning in him to have NASA select him as the one news media person who would "travel" with the astronauts all the way to Mars—without leaving the safety of Earth, thanks to virtual reality technology and the new three-dimensional TV system that the network was pushing so hard. And it didn't hurt that Treadway's cousin was a senator . . .

When they land on Mars, he thought, *I'll be with them. Everybody around the world will watch* me *standing on the red planet. In 3D.*

His voice deep and reassuring, Treadway continued, "The flight to Mars will take one hundred seventy-eight days—almost six months— and then the two astronauts and six scientists will spend thirty days on the surface of the red planet—the first human beings to set foot on Mars. During that thirty days, they will perhaps confirm the discovery that so rocked the world just six years ago when China's Haoqi robotic sample return mission found evidence of organic chemicals in the Martian soil. We may finally be on the verge of answering the question, 'are we alone in the universe?'"

Behind Treadway, technicians were at work up on the launch platform. A half-dozen white SUVs were parked around it. The rocket booster towered over them all.

"And I'll be going to Mars with them," Treadway said, with a dazzling smile. "Not physically, but through the wonders of three-dimensional virtual reality, I'll be digitally embedded with the crew, so I can report to you every day from the *Arrow* spacecraft."

"T MINUS TEN MINUTES," blared the loudspeakers set around the launch stand.

Technicians began to climb down the steel stairs and clamber into the waiting SUVs.

"The final minutes of the countdown have started," Treadway said into his mike. "Time for this reporter to go to the visitor center and interview some of the notables who have come to witness this historic moment."

"T MINUS FIVE MINUTES."

Inside the air-conditioned visitor's center, Treadway was standing between the two astronauts of the Mars crew. The center was crowded with luminaries: the governor of New Mexico, the head of NASA, several senators and congressmen, other dignitaries and glitterati, including two major Hollywood stars and a handful of pop musicians.

Coming up through the news media ranks as a science reporter, opportunities to meet with political luminaries such as this were microscopically small for Treadway. *This Mars program is my ticket to the big leagues,* he told himself, envisioning a new virtual reality global news series, with him as the immersive host, saturating the worldnet with viewership and downloads exceeding even the latest soft-porn reality shows.

Treadway smiled. *First things first*, he thought. He had a launch to cover.

Most of the visitors were gathered around the temporary bar the spaceport management had set up along the far wall of the center. The rest stood at the sweeping, ceiling-high windows, staring out at the rocket booster standing alone and seemingly inert more than a mile away.

"Quiet please!" shouted Treadway's producer, a plump round auburn-haired woman in jeans and tee shirt. "On the air in three . . . two . . ." She aimed a finger like a pistol at Treadway.

Standing before the hovering thumb-sized camera, Treadway smiled and introduced, "This is Benson Benson—or Bee, as he's called—the command pilot of the Mars mission."

Benson was tall, lean, almost regal in his erect posture and calm, austere expression.

"And this," said Treadway, swiveling his head slightly, "is the crew's other astronaut, Ted Connover."

Connover was a bantamweight, no taller than Benson's shoulder, a typical jet jock, wiry, bouncy, full of energy, his blond hair trimmed down to a military-style buzz cut. He was smiling lopsidedly, but in his intense, eager face the smile looked like a challenge, almost pugnacious.

Turning back to Benson, Treadway said, "I understand you're sometimes called Bee Squared."

Obviously suppressing distaste, Benson softly replied, "My parents had an offbeat sense of humor."

Obviously Benson's name was not a subject the man relished talking about.

"And you're the command pilot of the *Arrow*."

"That's right."

"And you're a Canadian."

A minimal nod. "That's right."

Making Benson commander of the mission had been a political compromise, Treadway knew. Although the United States had shouldered the major burden of funding the Mars mission, their

European, Japanese and Russian partners chafed at the idea of having an American in charge. So the Canadian Benson had been given the responsibility.

Treadway gave up on trying to get more than curt replies from Benson. He turned to Connover, and the tiny camera automatically pivoted to keep their images centered. Treadway asked, "And you will be the pilot of the vehicle that actually lands on Mars?"

"Yeah," said Connover, with a cocky grin. "I'll put her down on Mars and then I'll fly her back to the *Arrow* for the trip home."

"And you're an American."

"Like Mom's apple pie. Born in Nebraska, flew for the United States Air Force, got my doctorate in engineering from Caltech. How American can a guy be?"

Connover was much easier to interview than Benson. All Treadway had to do was ask a banal question and Connover rattled on happily.

"T MINUS THIRTY SECONDS."

Looking directly into the camera again, Treadway said, "The final seconds of countdown are here. Remember, this is an uncrewed launch, totally automated. Commander Benson, Pilot Connover, thanks for your time and your thoughts."

"You're welcome," said Benson.

"Anytime," Connover said.

The crowd surged toward the sweeping windows. Out at the launch pad, umbilical lines were disconnecting from the rocket booster. A thin cloud of white vapor issued from its lower section.

"LAUNCH VEHICLE ON INTERNAL POWER," the speakers in the ceiling announced. "ALL SYSTEMS ARE GO."

Treadway noticed that Ted Connover headed not for the windows, but toward a slim, good-looking woman and teenaged boy standing alone across the room. His wife and son, Treadway knew. The astronaut wrapped one arm around his wife's shoulders and pecked her affectionately on the cheek, then tousled the teenager's straw-colored hair.

They should have made him the mission commander, Treadway thought. NASA had wanted Connover for the top job; he was the veteran of a dozen spaceflights to the International Space Station and two flights to the International Moon Base. But the politicians had overruled the engineers.

Benson stood alone and seemingly aloof, no one within three feet of him. The Canadian was married, but his wife was not present for this launch. There were rumors that their marriage was on the rocks, but Benson refused to discuss his private life with the news media.

"T MINUS FIFTEEN SECONDS . . . FOURTEEN . . . THIRTEEN . . ."

The crowd seemed to hold its breath. Treadway felt their excitement. He had covered dozens of rocket launches over his years of reporting, yet the final moments of a countdown always clutched at his guts. It was as if his pulse rate synchronized itself to the ticking of the countdown clock.

"FIVE . . . FOUR . . . THREE . . ."

Despite himself, Treadway held his own breath. And felt foolish for it. He reminded himself that they'd launched this kind of rocket a hundred times. It was the most reliable booster on Earth. Still, he held his breath.

A burst of flame flashed from the base of the rocket, almost immediately blotted out by billows of steam from the launch platform's cooling water system. Standing tall in the midst of the clouds, the booster seemed unmoving, immovable.

Come on, Treadway urged silently. *Get your ass in gear.*

Slowly, slowly, the tall slender booster lifted out of the billowing steam, bright orange flame streaming from its base.

"Go, baby," someone shouted.

Then the noise hit them, the dragon's roar of the rocket engines, pulsing, throbbing, washing over them even through the thick, shatterproof windows. Treadway's innards went hollow; he felt as if he wanted to weep.

Up, up the booster rose. Slowly at first but then faster and faster, accelerating into the bright turquoise sky until it was no more than a bright star hurtling across the heavens.

Treadway turned to the huge screens that covered the visitors' center's rear wall. One showed a telescope's view of the booster soaring up into the sky. Another relayed the view from a camera on the booster's outer skin, showing the Earth falling away, the launch pad and spaceport buildings dwindling to dots on the desert floor.

Faster and faster the booster rose. The flash that separated the spent first stage brought a gasp from the crowd, but the gasp quickly turned into a cheer as the second stage's engines lit off and pushed the bird higher and higher until it was too distant to be seen by unaided eyes.

"THE *ARROW* SPACECRAFT HAS ACHIEVED ORBIT," the overhead speakers confirmed. "ORBITAL PARAMETERS ARE NOMINAL. THE LAUNCH IS A SUCCESS."

The crowd sighed, then cheered, and then rushed to the bar. Treadway looked past them, toward Connover and his little family, still standing by themselves off on the other side of the room.

Connover's eyes were fixed on Benson as the Canadian was pushed to the bar by the press of news media and celebrities.

But Treadway saw the expression on Connover's grim face. Silently, the American astronaut was saying to Benson, *You shouldn't be the mission commander. They should have picked me. I'm the better man for the job and we both know it.*

MARCH 30, 2033
EARTH DEPARTURE MINUS 25 MONTHS
14:55 UNIVERSAL TIME
EARTH ORBIT

"Steven Treadway reporting from four hundred miles above Earth's surface, thanks to the wonders of virtual reality."

He seemed to be standing in empty space, solidly three-dimensional, *real*. Behind him curved the massive bulk of Earth, heartachingly blue flecked with purest white clouds. To his right on the television screen hovered an ungainly-looking spacecraft, bulbous and bristling with piping, antennas, and a single cone-shaped thruster at one end.

"Today," Treadway intoned, "the centuries-old dream of using the energy of the atom to propel a ship into deep space will become a reality when the nuclear thermal rocket engine of spacecraft *Fermi* comes to life."

Treadway was actually standing in a TV studio in New York, in front of a blank green screen, reading his script from a teleprompter. He felt an urge to cross his fingers when he said so assuredly that the nuclear rocket would work, but realized that the viewing audience would see him do it.

"Within seconds," he continued, "*Fermi*'s propulsion system will begin pumping four hundred thousand pounds of hydrogen through the fuel rods in the core of the nuclear reactor. The fissioning uranium atoms will heat the hydrogen fuel to three thousand degrees, giving the nuclear thermal rocket twice the propulsion efficiency of chemical rockets like those that were used on the old Space Shuttle or the Apollo program's Saturn V."

On TV screens across the world, Treadway walked godlike on the face of the deep, explaining, "The *Fermi* lander is unmanned, completely automated. Its mission is to land on the surface of Mars, delivering enough supplies to keep the *Arrow*'s crew of eight men and women alive and well for thirty days, once they get there. The lander will also serve as rather Spartan quarters for the human explorers as they live and work on the surface of Mars."

Pressing one finger into the electronics bud in his left ear, Treadway announced, "Rocket engine ignition will take place in thirty seconds. Remember, there will be no sound. In space, there's no air to carry sound."

Treadway's image disappeared from the scene, but his voice continued, "There won't be much to see, either, since the ultrahot hydrogen gas expelled from the rocket's thruster will be invisible. But—*there she goes*."

It seemed that nothing much happened, but suddenly the huge bulk of the *Fermi* spacecraft leaped off the screen. The view immediately changed to a camera on board the ship, and the immense sphere of Earth dwindled noticeably.

"Godspeed, *Fermi*!" Treadway's voice called after the departing spacecraft. "On to Mars!"

Treadway's image appeared again. He was standing in the empty studio, looking slightly embarrassed after his burst of emotion.

"Steven Treadway reporting," he said.

The TV broadcast immediately switched to a scene of picketers marching in front of the main gate of the Kennedy Space Flight Center in Florida, some carrying signs proclaiming **NO NUKES IN SPACE** and others **HANDS OFF MARS**.

OCTOBER 4, 2034
EARTH DEPARTURE MINUS 6 MONTHS
16:05 UNIVERSAL TIME
MARSHALL SPACE FLIGHT CENTER, ALABAMA

"... and that's the NTR, behind the shadow shield," Benson was saying.

He and Treadway were in a huge, hangarlike building where the full-scale mockup of the *Arrow* spacecraft was spread across the concrete floor: a big rocket nozzle at one end, bulbous tankage, square panels the size of baseball diamonds, all connected to a long, metallic ladderlike central boom.

Four different TV miniaturized cameras were floating across the floor beneath toy-sized ballons of helium, automatically following their progress along the length of the mockup, with a fifth camera unit hanging up near an overhead truss that ran the length of the cavernous building.

Around the world, viewers who had the new three-dimensional home theaters didn't merely watch a screen, they could step into the scene along with Treadway and Benson, walk along the length of the spaceship beside them.

"NTR?" Treadway asked. He knew the initials stood for nuclear thermal engine, but the VR Net audience wasn't familiar with NASA's bewildering jungle of acronyms.

"Nuclear thermal rocket," said Benson, his voice flat, no trace of annoyance in it. "The nuclear reactor heats hydrogen gas to three thousand degrees Fahrenheit and the hot gas is fired through the rocket nozzles. That's what gives us the thrust we need for TMI."

17

"Trans-Mars Injection," Treadway translated the NASA acronym.

Looking halfway between embarrassed and irritated, Benson explained, "Right. That's when we break Earth orbit and head for Mars."

Making a slightly worried frown, Treadway said, "A nuclear rocket? Isn't that dangerous?"

Benson shook his head. "The Russians have flown dozens of nuclear power systems over the years. With the NTR we only have to carry half the propellant that we'd need with chemical rockets. It's got twice the specific impulse of the best hydrogen-oxygen rockets. It's actually a lot safer with the nuke, saves us months of travel time."

Suppressing a wince at the word "nuke," Treadway forced a smile as Benson pointed out the ship's propellant tanks, the payload section that held the smaller vehicle that would actually land on Mars, the square flat panels of the radiators that got rid of the ship's excess heat and the bigger, darker oblongs of the solar panels that would generate electrical power for the spacecraft.

"Why the solar panels?" Treadway asked. "Doesn't the nuclear reactor generate electrical power?"

With a shake of his head, Benson replied, "The reactor is for propulsion only. It's not bimodal. The engineers decided it would be too expensive and complicated to make it do both."

They slowly walked along the length of the spacecraft, the floating cameras following them, while Benson explained each segment of the ship.

"How long is this bird, anyway?" Treadway asked.

"Two hundred meters, from the end of the main thruster nozzle to the tip of her nose," said Benson.

"Two hundred meters . . ."

Benson's lips twitched in what might have been a smile. "That's right, you Americans aren't accustomed to the metric system." He frowned in silence for a moment, then said, "It's roughly six hundred and fifty-six feet."

"About an eighth of a mile." Treadway grinned, a trifle smugly. *I can do arithmetic in my head, too*, he told Benson silently.

Smiling back at him, Benson said, "Yes. Almost two and a half football fields."

As they neared the spacecraft's front end, Benson pointed to the metal gridwork boom that held the various attached components.

"The truss is the ship's spine," he explained. "It's got to be strong, yet light."

Playing the straight man, Treadway asked, "What's it made of?"

"MWNT," answered Benson. Before Treadway could respond, he explained, "Multi-walled carbon nano tubes. Four times stronger than the best metal alloys, yet lighter than any of them."

"Nano tubes?"

"Like Buckeyball fibers."

"Oh."

At last they reached the habitation module, a smallish cylinder near the front end of the spacecraft.

"Eight men and women are going to live in that little bubble for nearly two years?" Treadway prompted.

"It's not that little," said Benson. "There's a privacy cubicle for each member of the crew, plus a wardroom, control center, workshop and labs, and an observation blister."

"Can we go into the habitation module?"

On that cue, Benson replied, "Not the one in the mockup, up there. But we have another mockup of the module by itself, over there." He pointed across the floor. "We can go inside that one."

"Cut!" cried the director, from behind the monitor set up in the corner of the hangar. "Take ten and re-spot the cameras. We'll pick it up inside the module."

Treadway gave Benson a reassuring pat on the shoulder. "You're doing fine. Great."

Benson grimaced. "I'd rather have a root canal."

The director pressed his hand against the communications bud in his ear, then said to Treadway, "New York's happy. They think we'll get the biggest chunk of VR netviewers when this airs tonight."

Treadway broke into a genuinely pleased grin.

It was a tight squeeze inside the habitation module, with three of the cameras bobbing along with them. The director had squeezed into the module, too, telling them he wouldn't miss this opportunity—at least not for anything less than an Emmy award.

The module was compact, but efficiently laid out. Benson showed them the control center, with its consoles and display screens, the workshop and minuscule laboratory for the two geologists and their one biologist. Then they went a few more steps back, to the wardroom.

Treadway looked at the circular table and eight chairs.

"Chairs? They don't have chairs in the International Space Station. And the tables are chest height."

Benson explained, "That's because the ISS is in microgravity. Zero-gee, just about. You don't need chairs. You just stand at the table and hook your feet into the floor loops to keep from floating away."

"Won't the *Arrow* be in zero-gee?"

"Only while we're in Earth orbit. Once we start the TMI burn—" Before Treadway could interrupt, Benson explained, "Once we break orbit and start for Mars, the ship will rotate end-over-end to give us a feeling of one-third-gee during the trip."

"One-third gee?"

Nodding, Benson said, "That's the level of gravity on the surface of Mars. Rotating at one-third gee all the way out means that the crew won't suffer from muscle atrophy and calcium loss in their bones the way we would if we were in zero-gee all that time."

"And when you land on Mars you'll be accustomed to the gravity level there?"

Benson smiled slightly, like a teacher rewarding a student for a correct answer. "That's entirely right. You've got it."

Treadway beamed happily.

The individual privacy cubicles were about the size of telephone booths, big enough for an air-filled mattress fastened to one wall, a display screen on the wall opposite, and a modest closet on the third wall.

"There's a laundry further down the passageway, right beside the lavatory," said Benson.

Staring at the inflated mattress, Treadway asked, "You'll sleep standing up?"

Benson broke into an amused chuckle. "When we're in orbit and effectively weightless, the orientation of the bed doesn't matter."

"But when you're rotating to give you one-third gravity . . . ?"

Pointing, Benson said, "That 'wall' will become the 'floor.'"

"Oh," said Treadway.

Raising one long arm, Benson pressed his fingers against the springy surface of the habitat's curved ceiling.

"This module is made of fabric, coated with metal on the outer skin. It's double-walled, and filled with water for protection against radiation."

"Water?"

"Water can absorb radiation coming in from space. Even if the sun puts out a coronal mass ejection while we're in transit—"

"You mean a solar flare?"

Slightly annoyed, Benson replied, "That's the layman's term for it. A coronal mass ejection belts out a cloud of very high-energy subatomic particles. Plus gamma rays and x-rays. Very dangerous."

Poking at the slightly flexible wall, Treadway asked dubiously, "And this layer of water will protect you from that?"

With the ghost of a smile, Benson answered, "So the scientists tell us."

OCTOBER 31, 2032
EARTH DEPARTURE MINUS 5 MONTHS
12:00 UNIVERSAL TIME
JOHNSON SPACE CENTER, HOUSTON, TEXAS

The tension was palpable. Sixteen men and women sitting at their consoles, screens flickering, not a word spoken. In the visitors' gallery, above and behind them, sat four dozen NASA administrators, White House executives, senators and congresspersons, and a quartet of news media types.

On the ceiling-high wall screens an animated CGI image showed the *Fermi* habitation module descending toward the red Martian desert, tail first, its rocket thrusters firing fitfully.

Even José Aragon, NASA's official "voice of *Fermi*," was silent, nervously fingering his generous black moustache as the descent continued. A camera from the module showed the rock-strewn rust-red sand getting closer, closer.

Then the automated descent monitor intoned, "Five thousand meters. Trajectory nominal."

One of the mission controllers glanced up from her console for a brief peek at the wall screens. Before the chief of the monitoring crew could move or even speak, she focused on her console again.

"Four thousand meters. Trajectory nominal."

Bart Saxby, NASA's chief administrator and a former astronaut, wiped perspiration from his upper lip.

It all depends on this, he told himself. If *Fermi* doesn't land safely, the whole mission is ruined. The crew's going to live in that hab module for a month, once they reach Mars. No hab module, no humans on Mars.

"Two thousand meters. Final trajectory correction burn."

The view of the Martian surface from the ship-mounted camera blurred momentarily as the thrusters fired.

Saxby wished he were there, aboard the *Fermi*, personally guiding her down to the ground himself instead of the autopilot. *Look at all those damned stones*, he said to himself. *It's like a rock garden down there.*

He thought about Neil Armstrong piloting the *Eagle* to the first manned landing on the Moon. The bird was descending into a rockpile, so Armstrong took over manual control, jinked the lander over a few dozen feet, and put her down safe and sound.

Everybody knows Armstrong's first words from the surface of the Moon: "Houston, Tranquility Base here. The *Eagle* has landed."

But Saxby knew Houston's reply. "We copy you down, *Eagle*. You got a bunch of guys turning blue down here."

"One thousand meters . . . five hundred meters . . ."

The frozen sands of Mars were rushing up now. Saxby clenched his fists so hard his fingernails cut into his palms painfully.

"Touchdown," said the loudspeakers.

The whoop of relieved happiness was more heartfelt than any football crowd's.

The animation screen showed the *Fermi* module standing on the Martian surface, three stout landing legs supporting it. The camera on the module's outer skin showed plenty of rocks, but none of them big enough to upset the lander.

Everybody was jumping and shouting. Down on the floor of the control center the chief of the monitoring team was handing out cigars, even to the women. Saxby sat silently, unmoving in the midst of the uproar, his eyes misting, rubbing away the lump that he felt in his chest.

Fermi's made it, he thought gratefully. *Now we can send the human team and find where those microbes are hiding.*

NOVEMBER 8, 2034
EARTH DEPARTURE MINUS 5 MONTHS
20:00 UNIVERSAL TIME
THE WHITE HOUSE

President Harper never liked wearing a tuxedo; he felt much happier in a sweatshirt and dungarees. But Washington's inexorable social protocol demanded formal dinner wear so often that he had long ago surrendered to the inevitability of wearing "the uniform."

This evening he was to preside over a cocktail party in the White House's Blue Room in honor of the Russian ambassador's sixtieth birthday. The party's real purpose was to show the news media and the world that Russia and the United States were closer than they had been in decades. And the keystone to this newfound amity was the Mars project.

While there had been powerful opposition in Congress to revitalizing America's space program, even the narrowest minded politicians couldn't ignore that the Chinese rover had found powerful evidence that the chemicals of life existed on Mars. Washington politics simply wouldn't allow this historic discovery to belong only to China. Harper had put every ounce of the White House's prestige and power into the mission to Mars. The votes in Congress had been close, but one of the telling factors in favor of Mars was the obvious benefits of partnership with Russia—instead of distrust and tension.

The Cold War had been over for fifty years and if it took organic chemicals on Mars and the possibility of the discovery of life beyond

Earth being credited to China to bring the two world powers closer together, then so be it, thought the president.

Of course, Harper had offered a *proforma* invitation to the Chinese government to join the U.S. and its partners in the manned Mars mission. Beijing had refused, pointing out that China had its own plans for exploring Mars.

At the moment, Harper was sitting upstairs in the sumptuous Yellow Oval Room, a slim-stemmed martini glass in one hand. Sitting on the delicately ornate Louis XIV chair opposite him was Valeri Zworykin, head of Roscosmos, the Russian federal space agency. No one else was in the room; this was a strictly private meeting.

"I'm glad you had the chance to come early," said Harper, absently tugging at his tight collar with one finger.

"It was good of you to invite me," Zworykin replied diplomatically, in a deep bass voice.

Zworykin was built like a scarecrow: tall but very thin, all long legs and skinny arms. Harper was more like a hedgehog, short, thick, stubby limbs. Zworykin's hair was dark and long, tickling his collar; flecks of gray peppered it. Harper was silver-gray, his hair luxuriantly thick and carefully brushed back off his high forehead.

Raising his snifter of vodka slightly, Zworykin said, "I congratulate you on the safe landing of the *Fermi* module."

Harper smiled warmly. "Thanks, but the real congratulations should go to all the men and women who made the mission a success."

"Indeed."

"And to your nuclear rocket. It worked flawlessly."

Shrugging nonchalantly, Zworykin said, "A few dozen engineers won't be sent to Siberia, after all."

Harper felt a pulse of alarm, then he realized that the Russian was joking. "Your launch went well, I'm told."

Zworykin closed his eyes briefly, his version of a nod. "Extremely well. The propulsion module is safely in orbit, waiting to be mated with the other components of the *Arrow*."

"Good," said Harper. "Good."

The technical people's insistence on using nuclear rockets had given Harper the opportunity to create warmer relations between the United States and the Russian Federation. Seventy years ago the U.S. and the old Soviet Union had brought the world to the edge of nuclear

Armageddon. Even after the USSR was dissolved and the Cold War officially ended, relations between the two giant nations remained tense, frosty.

It was Harper's administration that realized the Mars program could create a bridge of cooperation and even trust between them—thanks to the Chinese.

Trying to build and launch a nuclear rocket in the U.S. was political suicide. The anti-nuke lobby was too strong, too vociferous, and Congress would knuckle under to their obstinate "no nukes" demand.

But in Russia, the anti-nuclear movement faced a government that either ignored or destroyed any opposition. Over the years, scores of Russian satellites had been powered by nuclear electricity generating systems. Although there were protests against these nuclear power systems in the United States and elsewhere, there were none inside Russia.

Building a nuclear rocket took advantage of decades of Russian experience. And there would be no demonstrators at the Plesetsk cosmodrome when the nuclear propulsion system was launched.

So serious talks began between Russian and American scientists and politicians at the very outset of the Mars program. The scientists had always gotten along well together. This time, even the politicians managed to find common ground.

The price was negligible, Harper thought. The U.S. paid most of the cost of developing the nuclear propulsion system. And one Russian scientist was included among the team making the journey to Mars.

With a genuine smile, President Harper raised his stemmed martini glass and toasted, "To a successful Mars mission."

"To Mars," Zworykin agreed.

Once they had drained their glasses, Harper put on a resigned face and said, "I suppose we should get ourselves downstairs and join the others."

Zworykin sighed dramatically. "Yes. It wouldn't be right to let the ambassador celebrate his birthday without us."

They got to their feet, the Russian towering over the American president.

Harper gestured toward the door, but Zworykin hesitated.

"May I ask a favor?"

With a mischievous grin, Harper replied, "You can ask."

Looking uncomfortable, Zworykin said, "My daughter is a fan of some musical group called Angels of Destruction."

"Never heard of them."

"Apparently they are quite popular among the young. My daughter is fourteen."

"Oh."

"They are giving a concert tomorrow evening in the baseball park. It seems there are no more tickets available."

President Harper pursed his lips. "I think we ought to be able to get her a ticket."

"Three tickets? I won't let her go without some security to protect her."

"Three tickets," said the President. "I'll see to it."

"Thank you very much. She is my only child, you know, and—"

"Think nothing of it," Harper said, gesturing him toward the door. "I have three kids. They were all teenagers once. I wouldn't go through that again for the world!"

McGillicudy's Pool Salon and Games Arcade was less than a half-hour drive from the main gate of Johnson Space Center. It was a strange place for a meeting of the team of scientists and astronauts who were to make the voyage to Mars.

Benson Benson took his responsibility as command pilot very seriously—so seriously that he had called this furtive meeting of the flight team in this unlikely place. No photographers, no news hounds—not even Treadway—and no NASA suits. Just the eight men and women who would be spending the next two years living together.

One by one they came in, looking puzzled, even suspicious as they stepped into the nearly empty poolroom. At ten in the morning, McGillicuddy's was almost devoid of customers: just a couple of truck drivers clacking balls across one of the pool tables, a lone pimpled teenager intently working one of the pinging digital game consoles, and three fairly disreputable-looking regulars drinking morosely at the bar.

Benson had come early enough to push a couple of tables in the restaurant area, so that all eight of them could sit together.

Catherine Clermont arrived first, looking as if she had just stepped off the pages of a sophisticated magazine—as usual. The French geologist had an impeccable sense of style. She was petite, fine-boned.

29

Her face looked almost ordinary until she began to speak: then it took on an animation and liveliness that sparkled.

She stood at the entrance, blinking at the unfamiliar surroundings, until she spotted Benson standing among the tables. With a slightly bemused smile, she headed swiftly toward him.

"Bee, am I the first?" she asked as she approached, her French accent barely noticeable.

"By a hair," Benson said, pointing toward the door. Virginia Gonzalez, their communications specialist, pushed the door open and came striding toward them. Tall and slim as a fashion model, as she passed the bar even the bleary-eyed regulars turned on their stools to stare at her.

Hiram McPherson, the team's other geologist came next, followed by Amanda Lynn, the biologist. A thickset African American, Amanda scowled at the barflies almost belligerently.

"Do you want something to drink?" Bee asked them as they sat along the table. "Or to eat?"

McPherson, tall, rangy, sporting a thick dark beard, grinned wryly. "Too late for breakfast, too early for lunch."

Benson nodded. "The others should be here in a few minutes."

Taki Nomura, their medical doctor, was next, with Mikhail Prokhorov, the meteorologist, right behind her. They made an unlikely pair: Taki was short, stocky, her round face almost always smiling pleasantly; Prokhorov was not much taller, but gave the impression of size and strength even though his normal expression was dour, downcast.

"That's all of us," said Gonzalez, "except for Ted."

Benson nodded tightly. "We'll give him another couple of minutes."

"Not like Ted to be late," McPherson noted.

"He'll be here," Benson said, with a certainty that he did not really feel.

Connover's ticked that he wasn't named command pilot, he thought. *Is he going to be a soreheaded prima dona? We can't have that. We just can't.*

At that moment, the door swung open again and Ted Connover stepped in, took a swift look around, then walked jauntily toward them. *He looks unhappy*, Benson thought. *But at least he came.*

"The gang's all here," Connover said as he approached the rest of them, pulled out a chair and swung it around backwards. Then he squatted on it, resting his forearms on the chair's back.

"The gang *is* all here," Benson echoed, gratefully.

Still standing while all the others were seated, he began, "I know this is kind of a strange place to have a meeting—"

"We can shoot some pool afterward," chimed McPherson.

"Put time to good use," Prokhorov suggested. "Study Newton's laws of motion."

Gonzalez giggled, "A body in motion stays in motion . . ."

"Until acted upon by an outside force," said Amanda Lynn. "Basic physics."

"Physics isn't the subject of this meeting," Benson said. He tried to make it light, he didn't want to sound like a taskmaster.

"Then what is?" Connover challenged.

Benson hesitated a moment. Then, "This is going to sound corny, I know, but I thought we ought to get together without anyone looking over our shoulders—"

"Except for them," said Catherine Clermont, pointing a lacquered fingernail at the barflies.

"They're not paying any attention to us," Benson said. But he lowered his voice a notch to say it.

"They could be spies," Prokhorov muttered. "Secret agents."

"Look," said Benson, trying to regain control, "I wanted to have this chance for us to be together so we could talk freely."

"About what?" asked McPherson.

Benson had rehearsed his little speech to himself a dozen times. But now it all seemed so trite, so tacky.

"Look," he started again. "We're going to be living cheek by jowl for the next two years. If any of you have developed any problems with the other, now's the time to bring it out into the open."

There. It was said. Benson looked at the seven of them, arrayed along the double table. Some frowns, some blank looks. No one was smiling.

"Well," said Clermont, "I for one am looking forward to the mission. We have all trained for more than two years, *non*? I think we know each other well enough to make the voyage to Mars and back quite well."

Taki Nomura said, "I'm always available for psychological

counseling." Grinning, she added, "You know, talk to your friendly neighborhood shrink whenever your homicidal instincts start to bother you."

A couple of chuckles.

Amanda Lynn almost glowered at Benson. "This isn't about sex, is it?"

"You tell me, Amanda."

Her dark face looking almost troubled, Amanda said, "Well, like you say, we're gonna be locked together for a lotta months. Four men and four women."

"Like Noah's Ark," said Gonzalez.

"We are all adults," Clermont pointed out.

"That's the problem," said McPherson, his bearded face dead serious.

Amanda looked as if she wanted to make a comment, but she had second thoughts and kept her mouth shut.

Nomura said, "As ship's doctor and psychologist, I'll have a supply of pharmaceuticals to dampen the sex drive, if any of you feel you can't control yourselves."

"Modern medicine at its best," McPherson mock-growled.

"This is a serious matter," said Clermont. "We have all been screened psychologically, have we not? We are all responsible persons, not teenaged maniacs."

"I hope so," Amanda Lynn said, with a sigh.

Ted Connover piped up. "Hey, I've got a loving wife waiting for me. I'm not going to screw around."

"I am married also," said Prokhorov. "But two years . . . that is a long time."

Benson thought of his own wife, who had not bothered to move to Houston with him. They had been separated for more than two years now, ever since he'd started training for the mission.

Pushing such unhappy thoughts from his mind, he told his teammates, "We all know how to behave ourselves. At least, I think we do. And, as Taki said, if you feel the need for it, there are medications that can help."

"I guess," Amanda agreed, weakly.

McPherson got to his feet. In his plaid work shirt and Levis he looked more like a bearded lumberjack than a scientist.

Very seriously, he said, "We've all been training for this mission for more'n two years. Hell, I've been training for it most of my life. I lost two toes to frostbite in Antarctica and damn near broke my neck in that truck wreck in the Atacama desert. I'm not going to do *anything* that'll jeopardize this mission. We're going to explore Mars, for Pete's sake! That's not the most important thing, it's the *only* thing that matters."

Silence settled around the table as McPherson sat down again. Then Amanda Lynn clapped her hands together and in less than a second they all applauded.

"That's how I feel, too," said Virginia Gonzalez.

"Me too," Nomura chimed in.

"I also," Prokhorov agreed.

Still on his feet, Benson allowed himself a satisfied smile. "I think we all feel that way. That's good."

"Has anyone ever asked the Toad to run a sex simulation?" The Toad was the director of preflight simulations who came up with all kinds of disaster scenarios for the crew to deal with: nuclear reactor meltdown, rocket engine exploding, he even had the crew try to deal with a stowaway. But there had never been any sort of sex or mating simulations.

Nods and grins around the table.

"No, and I'm not going to ask."

More grins and a guffaw from Prokhorov.

"Anything else?" Benson asked, looking squarely at Connover.

They all glanced at each other, saying nothing.

"Very well," Benson said. Taking in a breath, he went on, "I want you to know that, as the commander of this mission, you can bring any problem you have to me at any time. I'm not here to judge you or to lecture you. I'm here to help. Is that clear?"

More nods of agreement. All except Connover.

Clermont said, "That is very good of you, Bee."

"Hokay," Prokhorov said. "Are we finished?"

Connover, his chin on his arms, said, "I want you to know, Bee—I want all of you to know—that I resent being passed over for command of the mission."

Before anyone could speak, Connover went on, "But I know it was the politicians who decided that, not you and not any of us, not even the suits upstairs at the Center."

"You're a better pilot than I am, Ted, and that's why you're flying the lander to the surface," Benson admitted. "But I know that's not the same as being the mission commander. For what's worth, I'm sorry they didn't pick you."

With a lopsided grin, Connover said, "Hey, so you get to be the first human being to set foot on Mars. What's the big deal?"

Benson could hear the pain in his voice, see it on Connover's face. Pain. But it wasn't anger. At least, Benson didn't think it was anger.

MARCH 12, 2035
EARTH DEPARTURE MINUS 24 DAYS
09:20 UNIVERSAL TIME
SPACEPORT AMERICA, NEW MEXICO

For the first seven minutes it looked like a routine launch. The same type of commercial rocket booster that had carried all the components of the *Arrow*, its cargo, and the teams of technicians who assembled the spacecraft in orbit. Nine successful launches, without a mishap.

The booster lifted off the desert launch stand on a cloudless New Mexico winter night. Only a few hundred spectators braved the bone-chilling weather, far fewer than the thousands who had watched the earlier launches of *Arrow*'s components.

The blinding orange light of the rocket's plume lit the landscape around the spaceport with an eerie, otherwordly glow. This was the last launch in the sequence before the highly anticipated launch of *Arrow*'s crew, in twenty-one days.

Carrying sixteen thousand pounds of hydrogen propellant for the spacecraft's nuclear propulsion system, the booster left the launch stand majestically and began its eight-minute flight into orbit.

It was in the last few seconds of those critical eight minutes that the booster's engines shut down prematurely, likely placing the rocket, and its cargo, into a useless orbit. The air in the spaceport's compact control center suddenly turned a breathless blue as the mission controllers desperately sought to find out what had gone wrong.

MARCH 17, 2035
EARTH DEPARTURE MINUS 19 DAYS
16:35 UNIVERSAL TIME
MARSHALL SPACE FLIGHT CENTER, ALABAMA

Rain was spattering against the windows of the ninth-floor conference room where the hastily picked board charged with reviewing the possible solutions to the problem presented by the wayward propellant stage was meeting. If they couldn't find a way to get that errant stage into its proper orbit, where it could be mated to the waiting *Arrow* spacecraft, the Mars mission would not be able to start its journey on time.

And if the ship missed its narrow few-days-long launch window, the planets would not line up favorably for two more years. *Arrow* wouldn't remain in its parking orbit for that length of time. Even with remote firings of its engines, the orbit would decay and ultimately the spacecraft would re-enter the atmosphere and plunge to a fiery demise.

And the entire Mars program would die with it.

Dr. Conley Fennell, small, dapper in a gray pinstripe suit, with thinning gray hair and a neat pencil-thin moustache, stood at the head of the long conference table, eyeing the men and women who had been named to find an answer to the problem.

"We can do this," he said, in a reedy nasal voice. "The stage will remain in orbit for another two weeks—"

"In the wrong orbit," said the bald, hard-faced engineer sitting halfway down the conference table. Like most of the men there, he was in rolled-up shirtsleeves.

"Tell me something I don't know," Fennell snapped. He was wearing a vee-necked sweater beneath his suit jacket. A New Englander, Fennell could never accustom himself to the frigid air conditioning of the Huntsville center.

"Bickering isn't going to get us anywhere," said one of the three women at the table.

Fennell was the Marshall Center's chief engineer, and NASA's lead man in the program to remove debris from orbit. Known in the media as "NASA's junk man," Fennell was responsible for clearing orbital space of the dangerous pieces of spent rocket stages, fragments of broken spacecraft, inert equipment and other scraps of metal and plastic that infested orbital space, where they could shred working satellites and even endanger the space stations that housed dozens of men and women.

Pointing to the three-dimensional slide hovering in midair at the front of the room, Fennell said, "Look, the stage's orbit isn't that far from the orbit where the *Arrow* is parked."

"But it's losing altitude," said another engineer. "It'll decay and re-enter the atmosphere in a couple of weeks."

"Which means we've got to grab it before then," said Fennell. "That's what the OTVs are for."

"You don't honestly think one of your OTVs can grapple a stage that size, do you?"

"I do," Fennell said firmly. "One of our orbital transfer vehicles can reach the stage, dock with it, and push it to the orbit where the *Arrow* is waiting. We only need a delta v of a few hundred meters per second."

One of the younger engineers, sitting near the end of the table, spoke up. "Okay, your chart shows the delta v budget and where your OTV is located relative to the stage. But what isn't clear to me is the time factor. The OTV has to rendezvous with the stage, grab it—without damaging it—and move it to the orbit where it's supposed to be. All within the next week to ten days."

"We can do that," Fennell insisted.

An engineer from NASA's Langley Research Center in Virginia asked, "We know where your OTV is now, but what's it doing?"

"Currently," Fennell replied, "it's maneuvering a large debris object—a defunct Air Force satellite, actually—into a trajectory that will spin it down to re-entry. If we reprogram it now, it can release the satellite from its robotic arms into a fairly low-risk orbit and start boosting toward the stage. We're running various trajectory options now."

"You can do that autonomously? No crew involved?"

"Controllers on the ground operate the OTVs," Fennell answered, as he clicked the remote in his hand and a new three-dimensional image appeared, showing an animated drawing of the OTV capturing the rogue stage.

"We can do this," Fennell repeated. "And I don't think we have any other choice."

Lou Spearing, the Center's deputy director, hung his head for a moment, as if in silent prayer. Then he looked at Fennell, smiled weakly, and said, "You're right, Conley. We don't have any other options. I say we go for it."

Spearing looked up and down the table. The men and women seated there looked less than enthusiastic, but no voice was raised in objection. They were a conservative bunch, used to having plans they could review and assess for weeks before passing technical judgment, but in this case there was simply not enough time for that kind of thoughtful deliberation.

"Okay," said Spearing. "Let's get it done."

MARCH 28, 2035
EARTH DEPARTURE MINUS 8 DAYS
18:00 UNIVERSAL TIME
THE WHITE HOUSE

"High noon," muttered Bart Saxby.

As NASA's chief administrator, Saxby had his neatly typed resignation in his jacket pocket. If this attempt to grab the wayward rocket stage didn't work, he was ready to fall on his sword and be the scapegoat for the ruin of the Mars program.

Saxby was a handsome man, a former astronaut who had worked his way through Washington's bureaucratic mazes with the skill of a born leader. He had been delighted when President Harper came out for the Mars program, although now he understood that everything—including his career—depended on the performance of Conley Fennell's robotic OTV orbiting more than four hundred miles overhead.

And Fennell's team of technicians sweating at their consoles in Alabama, he added silently to himself.

The Oval Office was tensely silent. President Harper sat behind his imposing desk, Saxby and red-haired Sarah Fleming, Harper's chief of staff, were in cushioned chairs before the desk, angled to see the three-dimensional hologram above the fireplace on the far wall.

It looked as if the wall was actually an opening to another room, another space. In the middle of it, a grainy telescopic view showed the OTV creeping up on the errant rocket stage, its grappling arms extended. The curving blue-and-white panorama of Earth glided past in the background.

Several other White House aides occupied the pair of ornate little sofas by the darkened fireplace. They craned their necks at the view.

"Looks like a giant squid stalking its victim," muttered Ilona Klein, the president's news media chief. She was a smartly dressed brunette, nervously thin.

"Did you hear what Donaldson said on the Hill this morning?" the president grumbled to nobody in particular.

"Senator Donaldson is an ass," groused Fleming.

"I hope the recorders are off," Klein said, looking alarmed.

Recorders or not, the president continued, "He said I should shut down the whole manned space program, the idiot. Cut it out entirely and use the money on 'infrastructure improvements.' He said the little green men on Mars will just have to wait."

"Spend the money on the concrete contractors in his state," said Fleming, clear disgust in her tone.

"He's going to call for an early vote on the NASA budget."

"He wants the party's nomination for president next year," Klein pointed out.

Fleming said sourly, "Billy Donaldson in the White House? I'll move to Australia."

Pointing to the TV screen, the president said grimly, "This had better work."

Or we'll all be looking for new jobs soon enough, Saxby thought.

Steven Treadway suddenly appeared, seemingly standing in empty space near the spacecraft, earnestly explaining the intricacies of the linkup between the OTV and the rocket stage containing the hydrogen fuel for *Arrow*'s nuclear engine.

"Without those final eight tons of liquified hydrogen," Treadway said, "the *Arrow* spacecraft's nuclear engines won't have enough propellant to reach Mars."

From her seat in front of the president's desk, Ilona Klein complained, "Every time he says 'nuclear,' I wince."

"The anti-nuke lobby will be happy if this mission fails."

"Not once they realize the nuclear engine is going to re-enter the atmosphere and crash somewhere."

"In the ocean, most likely."

"You hope."

"Quiet!" the president snapped. "I can't hear what Treadway's saying."

The Oval Office went still, except for the smoothly professional voice from the hologram.

"This is the moment," Treadway was saying, dropping to a near-whisper.

The hologram showed the OTV's extended arms reaching for the attachment points built into the stage's magnesium alloy skin. Slowly, with seeming tenderness, the OTV clasped the gleaming cylinder.

"It looks good." Treadway's voice rose a notch. "Yes! We have confirmation from the Marshall Space Flight Center! The Orbital Transfer Vehicle has successfully captured the rocket stage. Now it will carry it—"

The rest of his words were drowned out in the roar of triumph and relief that shook the Oval Office. The only place where the ecstatic cheers were louder was in the control room at NASA Marshall, where Conley Fennell nearly collapsed under the congratulatory pummeling his staff inflicted on his frail body.

MARCH 28, 2035
EARTH DEPARTURE MINUS 8 DAYS
12:00 UNIVERSAL TIME
THE OVAL OFFICE

After a long day of working the successful space rendezvous, Steven Treadway was tired, but nothing was going to stop him from accepting the White House's invitation to interview the President of the United States.

His employer, The Twitter & *New York Times* Company, paid for him to fly from New York to Washington, D.C., in one of the new Boeing Airvolt commuter planes. It was his first time flying in one of these hybrid electric and aviation-fueled aircraft since they went into service a few months ago. The propeller-driven airplane was powered by traditional aircraft engines during takeoff but switched to all-electric mode once they were in flight. It was somewhat unnerving to hear the roaring engines suddenly stop midflight as the ultraquiet electric motors kicked in. Treadway admired the smooth and quiet ride while they were at cruising altitude, but in the back of his mind he kept thinking something had gone wrong with the engines. *Airplanes aren't supposed to be this quiet*, he thought.

A White House aide was waiting for him with a limousine at Reagan National Airport. The White House's own camera crew and director were already setting up in the Oval Office, the aide explained as they were whisked through the traffic.

Treadway was greeted at the White House door by Ilona Klein, all smiles as she led him along the West Wing corridor.

"I've never seen you in a suit jacket before," she said.

"I've never interviewed the President of the United States before," Treadway replied. Still, he felt a little awkward in the suit and tie that his bosses had insisted on. "Show the proper respect," they had demanded.

"Our camera crew has already set up," she said. "You'll be sitting on one of the sofas by the fireplace. The president will be on the sofa opposite, facing you."

"Fine," said Treadway. "Fine." Yet he felt somewhat nettled that the White House had insisted on having its own crew record the interview.

Still, he felt a thrill of excitement as he stepped into the Oval Office and saw President Harper at his desk. *I'm interviewing the president!* He said to himself. *Science guy hits the big time.*

As the president got to his feet to greet him, Treadway realized that Harper was much shorter than he'd anticipated. Burly, though: he was built like a college wrestler.

The president came around his desk and extended his hand, all warmth and graciousness. Then Treadway shook hands with the camera crew's producer, allowed the sound man to clip a microphone to his jacket's lapel, smoothed his hair and sat down on the sofa opposite the President of the United States.

"Five seconds," said the producer. "Four . . . three . . . two . . ." Then he pointed his trigger finger at Treadway.

He swallowed hard once, then began the interview, going through the first few lines on autopilot. The president smiled and nodded in the right places. Then Treadway asked:

"Life on Mars. Mr. President, you've staked your political career on this Mars mission. Why is it so important that we confirm the existence of life on another planet? More specifically, why is it so important that the United States do this?"

Harper smiled indulgently. "The discovery of life on another planet. When China announced that their Mars sample return mission had brought back organic chemicals found in the Martian soil, including amino acids, the building blocks of proteins, the world changed. We aren't alone. We must go and confirm the Chinese discovery. Even more, we humans must go ourselves, with people and not machines, to find more samples, perhaps even living organisms, and then bring them back here for study. Once it is confirmed, it will be the most startling discovery of all time, don't you think?"

"But why send people? Why not more robotic probes?"

The president replied, "Because human explorers are much more adaptable, much more flexible than robots. Machines can answer questions you know how to ask. On Mars, we're looking at a new, unprecedented situation. There are going to be surprises—and disappointments, too, I imagine. Humans on the scene can deal with those unpredictable situations much better than machines can."

"Despite the costs? And the risks?"

"One human mission will gather more information, make more discoveries, than a dozen robot probes. People are cost effective when you're exploring a new frontier."

"I know a lot of religious fundamentalists who don't think so," Treadway said.

The president grew serious. "Yes, there are some people who think that this contradicts the Bible. They accuse me of colluding with the Godless Chinese to perpetuate a hoax that will drive people away from the church."

"Which is why they've opposed your Mars program."

"Well, I believe that knowledge is always preferable to ignorance." Before Treadway could frame his next question, the president went on, "And if we do confirm that there is life on Mars—even if it's only some microscopic bacterial type of life—it'll show that God's creation isn't limited to our one little world. It'll show that God's bounty is limitless, won't it?"

Treadway hesitated, then replied, "I think I'll leave it to the theologians to debate that one."

Leaning forward to tap Treadway on the knee, President Harper said, "I know there are plenty of people who think that we shouldn't be spending money to explore Mars. Who think we should spend that money here on Earth. Well, it *is* being spent here on Earth. We don't shoot the money into space! It's spent right here, on scientists and engineers, on technicians and mechanics and schoolteachers and truck drivers and grocery workers. It adds to our economy. And the knowledge we'll eventually earn will bring an enormous bonus to our economy. You wait and see."

Treadway felt puzzled for a heartbeat or two. Then he realized that this was the moment to end the interview.

"Well, I couldn't ask for a better summation of your faith in the Mars program than that, Mr. President. Thank you very much."

"Thanks for this opportunity to speak from my heart to the American people."

And Treadway thought, *Too bad he can't run again. He'd get my vote.*

"These things continue to amaze me. I don't know why; you'd think that after the hospital bioprinted a new kidney for my sister that I'd be accustomed to just about anything coming out the side of one of them." Mikhail Prokhorov frowned at the 3D printer.

Hi McPherson grinned through his beard. "It is sorta like something out of *Star Trek*, isn't it?"

The two men, together with Taki Nomura and Catherine Clermont, were standing in the workshop section of the habitation module mockup. Nomura had poured a beaker of clear powdered plastic into the blocky, gray device. It had chugged away for several minutes, then chimed. When Nomura slid its lid open, there rested a perfectly formed lens.

Clermont asked, "Will it work?"

"Sure it will," Nomura replied. She lifted the lens from the printer, held it up to eye as if she were checking its specifications, and then fitted it into the circular housing they had printed a few minutes ago. They then stepped over to the workbench where the body of the telescope they were making rested.

"The objective lens fits here," Nomura said as she tightened the fitting around the newly attached lens. "Now we're ready to test our new telescope and it only took us two hours to build."

"*Voilá!*" said Clermont happily. "I want to go outside and see the Three Sisters."

"Not Mars?" asked McPherson.

"*Non.* We'll see Mars soon enough. The first constellation I learned as a child was Orion and it is still my favorite. One day we will go there also."

"Let's get to Mars first, okay?" said McPherson.

Prokhorov shook his head as if he'd witnessed some sleight-of-hand trick. He said, "It's no wonder the so-called Chinese economic miracle collapsed almost as quickly as it arose. Who needs megafactories when you can have one of these in your garage?"

"This one is a little more advanced than what most people will have in their garages," said Nomura.

"I gathered that when we printed the motor for the telescope mount," said Prokhorov.

"That's why we're briefing you on it now," Taki said. "Bee checked everybody's dossiers. He wants to make sure none of us has missed anything before we go."

Still looking unconvinced, Prokhorov asked her, "You can make *anything* with this device?"

Suppressing a superior grin, Taki answered, "Anything. As long as you have the proper raw materials to put in and what you're making isn't too big for the printer to hold."

Shaking his head again, Prokhorov said, "It's like magic."

"No," McPherson countered, "just technology. Kids are using 3D printers to make everything from model airplanes to electronic circuit boards. And so can we."

"Magic," Prokhorov insisted.

Clermont pointed out, "Any sufficiently advanced technology is indistinguishable from magic."

"Arthur C. Clarke," said Prokhorov, his brow still furrowed. "I've read his work."

Prokhorov relaxed into a rueful smile. "Perhaps you could use it to build more brains for me."

The night was dark and clear. The Moon was down and stars glittered across the heavens.

Ted Connover held his wife's hand as the two strolled along the edge of the lake. From a distance they looked like a pair of college lovers, which they had been—many years earlier. Now Vicki was Johnson Space Center's head librarian. And he was leaving for Mars in four days.

Vicki murmured, "Five hundred days. And nights."

"What'd you say?"

Smiling up at her husband's face, Vicki said, "You'll be gone five hundred days. And nights."

He nodded. "Long time."

"You'll be busy enough, though."

"What's that supposed to mean?"

"You'll have a lot to do, mission assignments and all that. Then you'll be landing on Mars and exploring."

He stared at her for a long, silent moment. Vicki was almost his own height, but where Ted was a solidly built welterweight, she was slim and delicate, like a china doll.

"Honey, I love you. You know that, don't you?"

Arching a brow at her husband, Vicki teased, "Locked away in a tin can for five hundred days and night with four unattached women."

"You're not serious!"

"That Clermont woman is French. And Virginia Gonzalez is a real looker—"

"Come on, now. Catherine's been making eyes at McPherson all through training, and Jinny's not my type."

"Tall and tan and young and lovely," Vicki sang.

"I like 'em short and tiny and altogether beautiful," Connover insisted.

"For sure?"

"For sure." Then he realized, "Hey! You'll be alone for five hundred days, too."

"Not entirely alone."

"I'll tell Thad to keep an eye on you."

She was laughing openly now. "You'd expect our son to be my chaperone?"

"My watchdog," Connover said, in a mock growl.

Suddenly her laughter cut off. "I'm going to miss you, Ted."

He pulled her toward him. "I already miss you, hon."

They kissed, by the gently lapping water, beneath the silent stars.

"I love you, Vicki."

"I love you, Ted."

They pulled apart slightly. Then Connover looked out across the lake. Rising above the blocky buildings of the space center, an unmistakably red point of light gleamed at them.

Connover pointed. "There he is."

"Mars," Vicki whispered.

"Mars," Connover breathed.

Promptly at a quarter to seven A.M. the eight men and women of the Mars-bound *Arrow* spacecraft left the astronaut center and walked, single file, through a crowd of onlookers toward the van that would take them to the waiting rocket booster.

They were wearing sky-blue coveralls and baseball caps. Prokhorov wore his cap slightly askew, as if it was alien to him. Catherine Clermont had hers perched delicately atop her chestnut-brown hair.

As they strode toward the waiting van, the crowd of NASA workers, government bigwigs and news media reporters broke into spontaneous applause and calls of "Good luck!"

Bee Benson led the little parade, looking slightly self-conscious. Behind him, Ted Connover grinned and waved at his wife and teenaged son, standing in the front row of the cheering crowd. The six scientists also waved, almost shyly.

Steven Treadway brought up the rear of the mini-procession, talking nonstop with the miniaturized microphone pinned above the pocket of his usual long-sleeved white shirt.

"The team isn't wearing spacesuits," he was saying, almost in a confidential undertone, "because they won't need them. The vehicle that will carry them into their orbital rendezvous is exactly the same type that has ferried all the equipment and supplies to the *Arrow*, plus the human technicians who put the various modules of the *Arrow* together in orbit."

He drew a breath, then continued, "Their ferry vehicle will mate with the *Arrow*'s main hatch, and the crew will step into their Mars-bound vessel just as safely and confidently as if they were stepping into their own homes.

"And it will be their home, for the one hundred and seventy-eight days it takes them to reach Mars."

In the VIP stands flanking the control center, Bart Saxby watched the van drive off to the waiting rocket booster, silhouetted against the gray morning sky. The meteorologists had predicted cloudy skies, but enough visibility to go ahead with the launch.

Saxby felt a mixture of pride and resentment as the van approached the launch stand. He had had to fight hard to get this final Mars launch done at NASA's facility at Cape Canaveral, instead of at the commercial operation in New Mexico, where all the other launches had taken place.

"Dammitall," he had exploded more than once, "this is a NASA operation, not some tourist excursion. We're going to launch the crew from the Kennedy Complex."

The objections were many and intense, including those of the governor of New Mexico and both that state's senators. The commercial interests that were building their business on space industry and space tourism were apoplectic at the decision.

But Saxby fought all the way to the White House, and after some hard bargaining, President Harper had finally agreed with his NASA chief. The final launch—the big one—would be from the Cape.

Saxby should have felt triumphant, but as he watched the elevator carry the eight crew members to the top of the booster, he found himself worrying.

Every ground launch has been fine—so far, he thought. *What if this one goes sour? We're using exactly the same booster as all the other launches, but what if this one fails? What if we kill those eight people?*

He felt a burning pain in his chest. *Ignore it*, he told himself. *You can't have a heart attack; not here, not now. Tomorrow you can drop dead if you have to. But today you've got to see those eight people safely into their vessel.*

Treadway felt a pang in his chest, too, as he stood on the launch platform, forlornly watching the elevator cab take the crew up to their module atop the booster.

He took a deep breath, then turned to face the camera standing a few feet away. "This is as far as I go, physically. But I'll be with the Mars crew every inch of the way, in three-dimensional virtual reality."

Craning his neck at the booster's upper stage, he continued, "For now, though, all I can do is the same as what you millions of viewers are doing: wish those eight brave men and women good luck and godspeed on humankind's first mission to Mars."

For the first time since he'd been a child, Treadway felt tears trickling down his cheeks.

APRIL 4, 2035
EARTH DEPARTURE MINUS 1 DAY
18:27 UNIVERSAL TIME
KENNEDY SPACE FLIGHT CENTER

Rocket launches are always emotional experiences. No matter how many launches a person witnesses, those last few seconds of countdown get to you. Your heart seems to beat in synchrony with the ticking of the countdown clock.

Bart Saxby was perspiring in the afternoon heat as he stood in the top row of the VIP stands, sandwiched between Florida's senior senator and the White House's chief of staff, Sarah Fleming. The president had wanted to attend this launch, but a sudden crisis in India forced him to remain in Washington.

Several rows lower, Vicki Connover and her fourteen-year-old son, Thad, were on their feet with everyone else. Thad had his fists clenched, his face set in a grim scowl.

He looks so much like his father, Vicki thought as she struggled to keep from crying.

"THIRTY SECONDS AND COUNTING," announced the loudspeakers.

Everyone seemed to hold their breath. Out on the launch platform the rocket booster stood tall and alone, waiting, waiting.

"FIVE . . . FOUR . . . THREE . . . TWO . . . ONE . . ."

Flame burst from the rocket's base, engulfed in a heartbeat by billows of steam, all in utter silence. The launch stand was more than a mile away and no one in the stands made a sound.

The booster rose in elegant grace, breaking clear of the bonds of Earth, lifting into the cloudy sky.

"LIFTOFF! WE HAVE LIFTOFF!"

And then the roar of the rocket engines washed over the visitors' stands, wave after wave of thunder, shaking the world, rattling bones, gushing the breath out of the watchers' lungs.

Vicki burst into tears, whether of joy or fear or desperate longing she didn't know. Through blurred eyes she saw her son, tall, lean, so very young: he was crying, too.

Bart Saxby kept his eyes dry, barely. The searing pain in his chest eased as he craned his neck to watch the booster tracing an arching line across the sky.

"A picture-perfect liftoff," Steven Treadway said. To those in the physical audience he looked a man standing in front of a green screen wearing a mesh net on his head with multiple fiber optic links trailing behind. To those watching on ordinary television or streaming the event online, he appeared to be standing much closer to the launch—close enough to have his clothing catch on fire had the simulation been reality. For the estimated fifty million people who subscribed to the VR Net, they were there with him, experiencing the launch from his auditory and visual point of view. Other physical senses, like the stomach and bone rattling caused by the low frequency sound of the rocket engines were added to the VR stream by technicians who had long since prepared the necessary special effects.

"The eight men and women of the Mars team are on their way into orbit, where they will link up with the *Arrow* spacecraft that will start them on their thirty-five-million-mile journey, the day after tomorrow."

"Whoo-*eee!*" Ted Connover yelled.

He was strapped into the right-hand seat of the crew compartment, Bee Benson on his left, the six scientists behind them.

The booster was roaring and shuddering, shaking so hard Connover's vision blurred. *It's like riding a dragon*, he thought. It brought out the cowboy in him and the yelp of adventure burst forth.

Benson appeared totally calm, as if he were sitting in his living room.

Yeah, Connover thought, *if your living room bucks like a bronco and thunders like a bull.*

"Stage separation in five seconds." In Connover's earphones, the steady, flat, unemotional voice of Mission Control, back on the ground, sounded mechanical, robotic.

BAM! The explosion sent a shockwave through the crew compartment.

"Stage separation," said Benson, tightly.

"Confirm stage separation," Mission Control answered.

The rocket's second-stage engine burn was slightly less thundering and rattling than the discarded first stage had been, but still the crew compartment shook hard.

Connover wanted to turn around and see how the scientists were doing, but the safety harness confined his shoulders too tightly.

"How's everybody?" he hollered over the rocket engine's roar.

A few grunts and mumbles. Benson shot him a disapproving look.

So what? Connover challenged silently. *You can play it Canadian cool; I get excited every time I ride one of these blasters.*

Suddenly the noise and vibration shut off. Just like that. One moment they were shaking and roaring, the next complete tranquility, totally calm.

Not entirely silent, however. Connover heard a pump winding down, somewhere behind them, in the equipment section of the spacecraft.

His arms floated up off the seat's armrests. Microgravity. Weightlessness.

Then Connover saw that Benson's hands were still gripping his armrests tightly. *Not so cool after all,* he realized.

Before he could say anything, though, Benson announced, "Initiating docking maneuver."

In his earphones Connover heard Mission Control. "Confirm docking maneuver initiation."

Loosening his shoulder straps enough to half-turn in his seat, Connover looked over at the scientists.

"How're you doing, team?"

"Fine," McPherson answered.

Prokhorov started to nod, then held himself back. "Every time I go to zero-gee I get woozy. This is my seventh space flight and I still feel . . ." He waggled one hand.

"I'm okay," said Amanda Lynn.

"Me too," Virginia Gonzalez reported. Pointing to her neck, she added, "I put on two anti-nausea patches before we launched."

Taki Nomura said nothing, but Connover saw she looked grim, uptight.

Taki's been in orbit before, he told himself. *She'll be okay. It's just the first few minutes of weightlessness, when all the fluids in your body start shifting around. She'll be fine.*

But she said nothing as she sat rigidly in her seat and gave a short, slow nod.

Thirty-two hours of weightlessness, Connover thought. *Once we break orbit and start the Mars trajectory we can spin up the* Arrow *and get some feeling of weight. Until then, though, it's zero-g.*

He grinned. He enjoyed weightlessness. He had always wondered what it would be like to make love with Vicki in zero-gee.

APRIL 4, 2035
EARTH DEPARTURE MINUS 32 HOURS
5:07 UNIVERSAL TIME
EARTH ORBIT

As their ferry module approached the *Arrow*, Benson glanced at Connover, sitting beside him. The American astronaut seemed outwardly at ease, his arms floating languidly almost at shoulder height, a relaxed grin on his face.

Leaning forward, holding both armrests firmly, Benson focused on the control panel's central display screen. It showed the *Arrow*'s tubular docking station, a big crosshairs painted across its middle.

"Down the pipe," Benson muttered.

Mission Control picked up his words. "On course. Docking in seventy-five seconds."

"Confirm," said Benson.

The docking maneuver was fully automated, although Benson was ready to grab the controls if anything should go wrong. Mission Control was reading off the distance separating the two spacecraft:

"Fifty . . . forty-five . . ."

Connover said, "Nothing for us to do."

"They also serve who stand and wait," Benson quoted.

"Sit and wait," Connover quipped.

The painted "X" was rushing toward them.

"Fifteen," counted Mission Control. "Ten, five . . ."

The screen went blank and they felt a slight lurch. Green lights sprang up on the control panel.

"Docking complete."

"Confirm docking complete," came the disembodied voice. "Nice work, fellas."

"Trained chimpanzee could've done it," Connover muttered, with a smile.

Benson turned to him, made a little grunting sound and scratched under his armpit. Connover looked stunned with surprise. Humor? From Bee?

"Okay," Benson said to the scientists as he unbuckled his safety harness. "Get up slowly. No sudden moves. Don't turn your head if you can avoid it."

Connover floated up from his seat and edged into the aisle behind. The six scientists were unbuckling and getting up slowly, warily.

Connover swam past them to the hatch set into the compartment's floor, opened it, and pulled himself down into it.

Catherine Clermont moved slowly into the aisle, bumping into McPherson, who flinched back from her.

"*Pardón*," Clermont said.

"My fault. After you."

Amanda Lynn pushed herself up out of her chair too hard and she sailed upward, bumping her head against the ceiling panels. "Damn!" she snapped. Virginia Gonzalez, tall and graceful where Amanda was built more like a fireplug, grabbed the biologist's belt and pulled her gently down to the aisle's matting.

"Thanks," Amanda mumbled, her dark face looking embarrassed.

"*De nada*," said Gonzalez.

One by one they made their way to the floor hatch and pushed themselves through, Benson last. Huddled together in the narrow access tunnel, they watched Connover check the small display panel set into the bulkhead that held the main hatch. On its other side was the hatch of the *Arrow*. Its trio of indicator lights were all green.

"Ready to pop the main hatch," Connover said.

"Open it," Benson called, from the end of the line of crew members.

McPherson realized he was holding his breath.

Don't be such a goofball, he admonished himself. *If there's a leak between the two hatches, we'll all be dead in a few seconds. Holding your breath isn't gonna help.*

Connover pulled the hatch open, then opened the hatch of the

Arrow. McPherson felt his ears pop, but there was no other remarkable sensation.

Connover pushed himself through the hatch, then turned back to face the others. "All clear," he said. "Come on over."

Prokhorov, hovering at the head of the line, called to Benson. "Bee, come up here. You should be the first. You are mission commander."

Benson cracked a mirthless smile. "We won't stand on protocol, Mike. You go right ahead."

Already inside the *Arrow*'s airlock, Connover said, "Well, make up your minds. Who's going to be first?"

Prokhorov shrugged and pushed himself through. "That's one small step for a Russian," he said.

"And one giant wait for the rest of us," Amanda Lynn wisecracked, with mock impatience.

They all laughed. All except Taki Nomura.

Slowly they made their way up from the airlock to the interior of the habitation module, drifting weightlessly, like wraiths or newborns floating in the womb.

"Home sweet home," said Virginia Gonzalez, her voice hushed.

"For one hundred and seventy-eight days," Prokhorov said.

Then we go down to Mars and live in the Fermi *module*, Connover told himself. *And I finally get my chance to fly.*

Although each of them had shipped up to the *Arrow* before, to stock the individual privacy cubicles with their personal belongings, now it was different. Each realized this was the real thing. Tomorrow they started for Mars.

Taki Nomura swam weightlessly to her own cubicle and slid the screen shut. Alone, with no one to see her, she began to shudder uncontrollably. *Stop it!* She commanded herself. *You've worked for years to get here, don't let stupid fears overwhelm you. You represent your family's honor, the honor of Japan. You will not succumb to irrational fear.*

It is illogical for you to feel claustrophobic. All your life you've lived in small chambers, surrounded by others: family, college roommates, coworkers. This is no different. Get a grip on your foolish emotions.

The tiny privacy cubicle seemed to close in on her, like a coffin, like one of those old horror films where the walls crush anyone inside the chamber.

Fists clenched, body doubled over, Taki fought her inner demons. *I am here as part of my family, I will not disgrace them. Of all the Japanese who applied for this mission, your government chose you. Do not fail them. Be brave. Be like a Samurai.*

Suddenly she laughed out loud. It was ludicrous. *A Samurai? I am the team's physician and psychologist. I am here to look after the physical and mental health of my crewmates. And it seems I'm the one who needs a therapist.*

"What's so funny?" Virginia Gonzalez's voice called from the other side of the compartment's screen.

Taki took a deep breath, then slid the screen back. "I am," she said. "I was thinking of my parents, back in Osaka, and how proud they must be of me."

Gonzalez arched a finely sculpted brow at her. "And that made you laugh?"

Bobbing her head hard enough to make her rise off the floor, Taki said, "I have a strange sense of humor, I suppose."

Up in the command center, Benson scanned the indicator lights and display screens of the control panels that stretched in a semicircle around his seat. Connover hovered behind him.

"Everything in the green," Benson said. "We're good to go."

Connover said, "Not until we check out the lander."

"Right."

"No sense going all the way to Mars and finding the thing won't work."

"Right," Benson repeated.

Mission protocol called for Connover, who would pilot the lander to the surface of Mars, to check the craft before they broke orbit and started their Trans-Mars Injection burn. That meant that Connover had to get into a spacesuit and pre-breathe its low-pressure oxygen for two hours before he went EVA and worked his way down to the module where the lander was housed.

Pointing to one corner of the control panel, Benson said, "All the lander's systems are in the green."

Connover nodded. "Yeah, but I've got to do a visual check."

"I know," Benson said. "We'd better get suited up."

Another provision of mission protocol was that no one went EVA without a backup crewmember also suited up and ready to go out, should a problem arise. Each of the scientists was trained for space walks, but neither of the astronauts wanted to rely on what they considered amateur talent of the others.

Six hours later, Ted Connover emerged from the payload module that contained the landing vehicle and carefully sealed its hatch.

He attached his spacesuit's tether to a cleat by the hatch and started back along the gridwork truss that formed the backbone of the *Arrow*.

Gliding out and away from the spacecraft as far as his tether would allow, Connover looked up and down its length. Rocket nozzles at the rear, then the bulk of the nuclear propulsion system and its shielding. Big, bulbous tankage holding the hydrogen propellant. The payload module, a combination warehouse and hangar for the lander to protect it from any stray micrometeors that might ping the ship.

Looking forward, up the central truss, Connover saw the rectangular radiator panels that distributed the ship's excess heat, then the much bigger, square dark solar panels that provided the ship's electrical power. The habitation module was half-hidden by the solar panels. From this distance it looked pitifully small.

"You okay out there?" Benson's voice sounded in his helmet earphones.

"Fine," Connover responded. "Everything's hunky-dory."

He heard Benson chuckle. "Haven't heard that expression since I was a kid at my grandmother's house."

Connover grinned inside his helmet and started working his way up forward. But he stopped halfway there and gaped at the splendor of the Earth, sliding by below him. Deep blue ocean, flecked with purest white clouds. On the curving horizon stretched a thin brown area.

Christ, Connover realized, *that's South America. Those are the Andes Mountains.* They looked like furrowed little wrinkles from this height.

"Are you going to stay out there all day?" Benson said. But his tone was light, almost bantering. He'd done plenty of EVA work and he knew how hypnotic the view could be.

"I'll be home in time for dinner, Daddy," Connover kidded back.

APRIL 5, 2035
EARTH DEPARTURE DAY
12:15 UNIVERSAL TIME
NEW YORK CITY

Steven Treadway stood in the middle of the nearly empty television studio, in front of a blank green wall. In the 3D monitor sitting alongside the camera crew, he saw his image in the command center of the *Arrow*, standing between Bee Benson and Hi McPherson. He had thought about wearing sky-blue coveralls, like the crew, but his producer had insisted on his trademark white shirt and slacks.

"Less than an hour to go," Treadway was saying.

Benson nodded solemnly. Pointing to the digital clock on the control panel, he said, "Fifty-two minutes and six seconds."

"Are you nervous?"

Benson looked surprised. "Nervous? No. I don't think so."

"Did you get a good night's sleep?"

"Certainly."

"I'm excited," McPherson said, grinning through his thick dark beard. "I've been working all my life for this, and now we're really going to Mars!"

"Did you get a good night's sleep?" Treadway asked the geologist.

"Like a kid on Christmas Eve," McPherson replied. "You know, if you don't get to sleep Santa Claus won't come."

Treadway chuckled tolerantly, then turned back to Benson. "How important is the timing for your launch?"

"Actually, we have a two-day window for TMI."

"The Trans-Mars Injection burn," Treadway explained. *More NASA*

67

alphabet soup, he complained silently to himself. "That's when you fire the rocket engines that start you on your trajectory to Mars."

McPherson interjected, "Mars and Earth are optimally positioned in their orbits right now. If we miss this window, the two planets won't line up in this way again for two years."

"So it's now or never," Treadway said.

McPherson corrected, "Now or two years from now."

"Yes. Right."

"We're ready to go," Benson said, quite seriously. "We've checked out the spacecraft and all its systems."

Treadway said, "So, in less than—" he peered at the digital clock— "fifty-one minutes, you'll light off the nuclear rocket and start for Mars."

Benson nodded.

"Does it worry you that you're so close to a nuclear reactor?"

"We're fully protected by the shielding," Benson said, matter-of-factly. "Actually, we'll be exposed to more radiation from the cosmic rays in interplanetary space than we'll get from the reactor."

Treadway thought that trying to provoke an interesting reaction from Benson Benson was like trying to get an elephant to fly.

Looking straight into the camera, Treadway said, "In fifty-some minutes this spacecraft's pumps will start tons of hydrogen propellant flowing through the ship's nuclear reactor. The hydrogen will be heated to several *thousand* degrees and stream through the rocket nozzles with more than twenty-four thousand pounds of thrust, pushing this enormous spacecraft into a trajectory that will take it to Mars."

Benson said, "We'll coast most of the way. The TMI burn will only last forty minutes."

"And that's enough to send you all the way to Mars?" Treadway asked.

McPherson said, "It's like throwing a baseball. You heave it as hard as you can and then it coasts."

"All the way to Mars," Treadway repeated.

"All the way to Mars orbit," Benson corrected.

Looking directly into the camera again, Treadway said, "And I'll be with you every mile of the way—virtually."

Benson broke into a genuine smile. "Glad to have you aboard, Steve—virtually."

※ ※ ※

Ted Connover sat strapped into the pilot's seat in the command center, marveling at how the ship responded—no, how it *felt*—as they went through the final moments before TMI burn. *She's alive*, he said to himself. He could feel the pumps chugging, the hum of electric power flowing through the ship's miles of wiring, her air ducts softly sighing. *She's alive.*

Benson floated into the compartment and strapped himself into the left-hand seat.

"Everything okay back there?" Connover asked.

"They're all strapped down in the galley, watching the TV screen."

"They'd get a better view from the observation blister."

"Can't squeeze all six of them into the blister."

"Yeah. Well, anyway, we get a good view up here," Connover said, pointing to the thick quartz window that curved atop the control panel.

Benson agreed with a nod.

The speaker grill on the control panel squawked, "TMI in two minutes."

"Copy TMI in two," Benson replied.

Looking through the window, Connover saw the blue-and-white curve of Earth and the narrow strip of blue atmosphere hugging it.

So long, Earth, he called silently. *See you in a couple of years.*

And he thought of Vicki and Thad, watching their TV set at home. *Wish they had a 3D set*, he thought. *I should have bought one for them. Are they nervous? Frightened?*

Nah, he told himself. *They know we'll be okay. But two years is a long time. Thad'll be graduating high school by the time I get back.*

"TMI in one minute," Mission Control announced. A row of lights on the control panel flicked from amber to green.

"Reactor powering up," said Benson, his voice flat, emotionless. Connover marveled again at how self-contained Bee could be. It was taking all his self-control to keep from fidgeting like a kid on his first roller-coaster ride.

"Reactor core temperature nominal."

"Copy nominal core temp."

"Pumps starting."

"Copy pumps."

Thirty seconds to go, Connover saw. He licked his lips. Time seemed to stretch like taffy. *Einstein was right*, he thought. *Time is relative.*

"Thirty seconds."

So long, Vicki. So long, Thad. I'll bring you back your own personal Mars rocks.

"Fifteen seconds."

Connover listened to the automated countdown, his pulse thumping in his ears. He glanced over at Benson. Cool as an iceberg. *Maybe that's why they picked him over me; Mr. Cool instead of the cowboy.*

More than six hundred feet down along the ship's gridwork backbone, tons of liquefied hydrogen began to flow through the nuclear reactor and, superheated, out the rocket nozzles.

"TMI burn," said Mission Control.

Connover felt the push in the small of his back, felt the ship vibrating, felt a totally surprising pang of remorse, regret. He barely heard Bee's clipped acknowledgement that TMI burn had started. He knew he was leaving Earth to travel farther than any human being had traveled before. He'd thought he would feel triumphant. Instead he felt a sense of—what? Disappointment? Fear? No, what he felt was loneliness.

"Good luck, *Arrow*," said Mission Control.

The ship was thrumming. Not the bone-rattling roar of a liftoff from Earth, but a gentler, smoother surge of thrust that was starting them off on their long, long journey.

Connover turned to Bee, who looked distracted, almost perplexed. And he understood why. The mission timeline called for the ship's commander to make some pithy, quotable, optimistic statement for the benefit of the media and the history books. If he didn't come up with something soon, the moment would be lost. Connover knew that Bee had been rehearsing whatever the hell it was he wanted to say, but now he seemed tongue-tied with stage fright. He grinned inwardly at Bee's discomfort, and immediately felt guilty at his reaction.

Benson seemed to suck up his gut. Lifting his chin, he said, "Houston, Darmstadt, Moscow, Tsukuba. The *Arrow* is away. Our next stop is Mars, where we will take humanity's first steps on a truly alien world for the benefit of all the people of Earth. Wish us luck."

Then he blew out a long, sighing breath.

"Good luck, you guys," Mission Control repeated.

Connover realized that Bee had touched all the bases by addressing the American operations center first, since the United States was footing most of the bill for the mission, and then other three key partners' operations centers: Darmstadt for the European Space Agency, Moscow for the Russians and Tsukuba for the Japanese.

Clicking the microphone off, Benson turned to Connover and said, "Ted, can you believe it? We're really on our way. I was actually starting to wonder if this day would ever come."

Connover grinned at Bee. *Underneath that layer of ice he's as excited as I am,* he realized.

"I knew it would happen," Connover said. "I just wasn't sure it would come along during my lifetime. It's been more'n sixty years since Apollo. Hell, von Braun thought that we'd go to Mars in the nineteen eighties. He was off by damned near half a century."

"Better late than never," Benson said, with some fervor. "Did you hear that they're going to announce the crew for the next mission later this week? We'll get back about a month before they depart. We might even be out of quarantine in time to shake their hands."

"Maybe. Senator Donaldson wants to cut out the manned space program altogether," Connover said.

"That's crazy."

"You know that and I know that. But there's a lot of people who think the same way he does."

Benson tilted his head slightly. "Well, our going to Mars ought to take the wind out of his sails."

Connover brightened. "Yeah, that's right. 'Specially if we find something really big. Like life-forms."

"Amanda says the best she's hoping for is maybe finding organisms that have survived from when Mars was a lot warmer and wetter than it is now."

"Martians."

"Microscopic things. Bacteria, something like that."

"But they'll be Martian, just the same," Connover insisted. "We'll be big heroes when we get back."

Benson smiled patiently. "We have to get there first."

"Yeah."

"Let's take it one step at a time."

Connover said, "Well, the first step has worked out all right. We're on our way."

"Right. We're on our way."

APRIL 5, 2035
EARTH DEPARTURE
09:30 UNIVERSAL TIME
THE ROCK

Not much happened in the vicinity of the rock as it followed its long, looping path around the Sun. Nothing of particular interest came anywhere near it. Interplanetary space between Earth and Mars was a near-perfect vacuum, averaging no more than five atoms—*atoms*—per cubic centimeter. Even if the rock had been sentient and possessed of the latest scientific instruments, it would never have noticed the occasional hydrogen atom that collided with it during its seemingly endless journey around the Sun.

Newton's laws were at work. A body in motion remains in motion—unless some outside force acts upon it.

The rock hurtled along as it had for fifteen million years, undisturbed in its orbit between Mars and Earth. However, it was moving blindly toward a spot that, although currently empty, would soon be occupied by another object.

Newton's inexorable laws would dictate that these two objects would meet in a violent collision. The second of the two objects was not an inert chunk of rock, but rather it had been purposefully created and powered by the nuclear fires of its engines and the ingenuity of humankind.

In Transit

APRIL 5, 2035
EARTH DEPARTURE
17:03 UNIVERSAL TIME
THE *ARROW*

Catherine Clermont suppressed an urge to giggle at the newsman. Steven Treadway was standing in a TV studio in New York City, of course, but thanks to the virtual reality electronics aboard the *Arrow*, he appeared on the monitor screen in the vessel's small geology lab to be standing in front of her. As carefully instructed before the TV show began, Catherine looked at the monitor screen and Treadway's image.

We make a good-looking couple, she thought. Even in her NASA-issue sky-blue overalls, Clermont had carefully arranged her hair and makeup; her petite figure looked trim and attractive, she knew. And Treadway was dashingly handsome, tall, his smile gleaming.

Yet somehow he looked boyish, slightly disheveled, his customary white shirt a bit askew, as though he had pulled it on at the last moment without checking how it fit. His dark hair, normally perfectly smoothed, was a little disarrayed. He looked . . . excited. That surprised her.

"I'm reporting from the geology laboratory aboard the *Arrow*," he was saying, a little breathlessly, "as it starts out on its six-month flight to Mars."

He is excited, Clermont decided. *Truly. Just as if he were actually here with us.*

"The crew is in good spirits," Treadway continued, "after their departure this morning at 7:45 Central U.S. Time. All the ship's systems are performing as planned and the crew is optimistic and upbeat about their historic voyage."

Focusing on Clermont, Treadway said, "To get a perspective on leaving the Earth for a mission that will take the better part of two years, I'm speaking with one of the crew's two geologists, Catherine Clermont."

Clermont nodded and smiled on cue.

"Dr. Clermont, you won't be able to do any geology until you actually get to Mars. How are you going to spend your time over the next one hundred seventy-eight days?"

"Oh, I have plenty to keep me occupied," she said, keeping her smile in place. "I plan to keep up with the latest work in my field by reading the scientific journals in their digital editions. And I will check all the tools I will use in the field once we arrive on Mars, to make certain they are in proper working order when I need them."

Treadway grinned at her. "Don't you think that will get a little boring after a hundred days or so?"

She made a Gallic shrug. "Well, I do plan to do more than merely read the journals. I am writing a novel—"

"No!"

"Yes. I expect I will have the time to finish the first draft on the outbound leg of our mission. I probably won't have time to work on it during the trip home, though. I will be too busy examining the rocks we collect on Mars."

"A novel," Treadway said. "May I ask what it's about?"

Her smile turning impish, Clermont said, "It is a love story about a field geologist who becomes an astronaut and a handsome news reporter, of course." Arching an eyebrow, she asked, "Any more questions?"

Treadway swallowed visibly, then answered, "No, I think that'll wrap up this session. Good luck with your, er, novel. This is Steven Treadway, reporting virtually from the *Arrow*."

All eight of the crew got together in the galley at the end of the work day. It was a tight squeeze: although the galley had been designed to seat all of them, there was scant room to spare. Lanky Hi McPherson had to pull himself up over the chair's back and slide his long legs under the table.

"We ought to just float," he complained, "while we're still in zero-g. Take advantage of the weightlessness instead of wedging ourselves around the table."

Virginia Gonzalez started to shake her head, but caught herself in time. "I'm having a tough enough time keeping from tossing my cookies, Hi. If you were floating over my head, I think I'd lose it."

McPherson cinched his seat belt. "Sorry, Jinny. I wouldn't want to upset you."

Though the inflated habitat module was less luxurious than the tourist hotels in low Earth orbit, it was still a big improvement over the more Spartan accommodations of the earlier space shuttles and space stations built by governments. The *Arrow*'s habitat had been built by a non-traditional contractor, Harris Space Corporation, which had made its mark by constructing the Earth-orbiting hotel getaways for the uber-rich tourists eager to "go where no one has gone before"— and pay for the privilege.

The orbiting Harris hotels had entertainment options that the *Arrow* did not, such as three-dimensional virtual reality couches and gourmet meals. Plus acrobatic weightless "play" areas that some tourists used to join the 'Zero-G Club.' Harris himself often attributed his corporation's profits to the thirst of millionaires who were quite willing to part with their money for the excitement of sex in orbit.

The space agencies that funded the Mars mission officially frowned on the idea of their crew enjoying sex during their mission to Mars and back. But they knew that eight healthy, intelligent men and women cooped up together for nearly two years were bound to make their own arrangements. "I just hope they're discreet about it," NASA chief Saxby said with a resigned tone.

Benson looked around the table at his seven crewmates. They all looked expectantly at their commander.

"Ginny, your troubles will be over in about an hour," he said, "when we start spinning up the ship. We'll have a one-third-gee the rest of the way to Mars, so we won't be invalids when we get there."

Taki Nomura closed her eyes for a moment. She had seen the results of long-term exposure to microgravity: loss of muscle tone, including the heart muscle. Loss of bone mass, making the bones so brittle a man could not stand on his own feet without danger of snapping a bone. Spinning the ship was necessary, a prudent solution to the problem of long-term weightlessness. Should they for some reason have to make the journey to Mars without artificial gravity, the ship had a pair of treadmills stowed on the ceiling just above the galley—complete with a gyroscope to keep it stabilized and a harness to keep the person using it from simply floating away with each step— as well as a stationary bike and even a bench press that used tensioned cables instead of weights. The whole setup could be used where it was, if they were in zero gravity, or lowered to the deck in the space now occupied by the dining table in artificial-gee. Both were modular and easily repositioned. But spinning the ship to simulate gravity was much the preferable solution. They would arrive at Mars fully conditioned to walk and work on the planet's surface.

"Ted will fire the minithrusters that will spin us up," Benson went on, as if reading from the mission manual. "Before he does that, though, I need for each of you to check that all your equipment and belongings are properly stowed or tied down. We don't want loose stuff flying around and hurting somebody once gravity comes on."

Nods and murmurs around the table.

"Like we rehearsed, the spin-up will take only a few minutes. We'll need to be back in our launch seats and strapped in while Ted gets us moving. I'll go around the comm with each of you and get your 'all clear' before we start the procedure. Okay?"

More nods.

"All right, let's make it happen."

The crew got up at once, taking off in all directions. McPherson slid his long legs out from under the table, bounced off the cushiony ceiling, and bumped into Clermont. His face turned red.

"Sorry," he mumbled.

"*C'est rien*," she replied, with a smile.

Gonzales and Amanda Lynn swam through the hatch together, heading for their privacy cubicles. Benson headed for the control center, almost regretting that within a few minutes gravity would return to their little self-contained world. There'd be a definite up and down. He'd miss the ease and joy of floating weightlessly.

Hi McPherson's normal pleasant grin was gone. He stood staring at the chessboard, scratching at his beard and scowling.

"Something's not right. Your rook wasn't there when I left."

Looking up at him from his chair at the galley table, Mikhail Prokhorov smiled innocently. "Are you saying I cheated?"

McPherson didn't reply. He simply stood there, slightly stooped over the table, staring intently at the board. When he'd left the table for one of the ship's three toilets he had memorized the positions of the pieces on the board. He was certain that Prokhorov's white rook was not where it had been when he'd left.

Sitting down slowly, McPherson said, "I'm not saying you cheated, Mikhail, but something's wrong. I don't claim to have a photographic memory, but I'm reasonably good at keeping up with the pieces during a game and I know your rook wasn't there when I left. I had my next move planned and now it'll be impossible." Looking into Prokhorov's face, McPherson suggested, "Are you sure you didn't accidentally bump the table or something?"

Still smiling, Prokhorov said, "I did not bump the table and I most certainly did not cheat."

"I say you did," McPherson said, more in sorrow than in anger. "I can't believe you'd cheat at a game of chess! What's the point of it?"

Prokhorov pointed a finger at McPherson's chest. "I don't need to cheat, and I certainly don't need to cheat to beat a player as poor as you are. I think you owe me an apology."

Catherine Clermont and Taki Nomura were watching them from the refrigerator/freezer and microwave oven on the other side of the galley. Clermont felt particularly disturbed by the rising heat of their exchange.

"Gentlemen," she said, "there is no need to become angry. I am sure it's just a misunderstanding. And after all, it is only a game."

McPherson got up from the table. "It's only a game, sure. But we've got to be able to trust each other and right now I don't think I feel like trusting or believing anything about this guy."

"It is only a game," Clermont repeated, a little more strongly. "Now get your testosterone in check, Hi. Walk away and get over it."

McPherson's face was reddening, but not from anger. He felt embarrassed. *This isn't the way to impress Catherine,* he told himself. *Gotta cool down. Show her I'm a better man than he is. Cool down.*

He backed away from the table, turned and headed for the hatch. Over his shoulder he said, "I know what I saw, but Catherine's right: it's only a game."

Prokhorov, still grinning, scooped up the chess pieces and put them back into their box. Then he got to his feet, made a little bow to the two women, and sauntered out of the galley.

Clermont turned to Nomura. "Taki, I'm going to talk with Hi. I hate to see him so upset."

Nomura replied absently, "Sure. You do that. Hi could use some TLC right now."

The French geologist hurried out of the galley, leaving Nomura standing by the microwave, alone with her thoughts.

Mikhail did move the rook while Hi was out of the room, she knew. *I saw him. And he saw me watching him. He even winked at me!*

Is this his idea of a joke? Some elaborate Russian prank? Is he sore at Hi for some reason?

As the ship's psychologist I've got to look into this. We're going to be living together for a long time, and we can't afford to have personality clashes. I'll have to talk to Mikhail, see what's motivating him. And Hi, get him to relax more.

Then she wondered, *Should I tell Bee about this? He's the commander, he ought to know if something's afoot that could endanger the crew's morale. But he's got enough to think about. Maybe I ought to keep this to myself until I've talked with Mikhail and Hi. Separately, of course. Those two shouldn't be in the same room for a while.*

❋ ❋ ❋

Two days later, Taki Nomura approached the hatch of the command center, after making certain that Bee Benson would be alone in there.

"Commander Benson, may I have a moment of your time?" Nomura asked, before stepping through the hatch.

Benson was in his chair, looking perfectly at ease among the dials and screens that showed the performance of all the *Arrow*'s systems.

"Sure, Taki, come on in." He jabbed a thumb at the empty seat beside him. "And don't be so formal. We're all team members, shipmates."

Nomura slid into the right-hand seat. "I know. But sometimes it's difficult for me to overcome a lifetime's training."

Benson nodded understandingly. But he said, "Taki, I'm not a samurai. We've known each other for more than two years now and we've got another two to go."

"Yes," she said. "Of course."

"So what's on your mind?"

Feeling more than a little uncomfortable despite Benson's reassurance, Nomura began, "I feel I have to make a report about the crew's psychological condition."

Benson's brows hiked up. "We've got problems? Already?"

"Not problems, really. But there are some troubling indicators that might be pointing to problems in the future."

"Like what?"

"Well, for instance, this morning at breakfast Jinny Gonzalez got very upset when her food was decanted. She actually cursed at it and threw it directly into the recycle slot."

Benson said, "Go on."

"Two days ago McPherson and Prokhorov had an incident over a chess game and—"

"An incident?"

"Prokhorov moved one of the chess pieces while Hi was off in the lavatory. When Hi accused him of it, Mikhail lied to his face. Hi stormed off and Mikhail laughed about it."

"How do you know that Mikhail—"

"I was there. I saw him do it. He cheated, and then denied it all to Hi's face."

"And Hi got ticked off about it."

"Catherine calmed him down afterward. I think she could talk that man into walking out through the airlock without a spacesuit on." Nomura smiled at the thought. "She might even go with him."

Benson's right eyebrow rose. "They're both geologists," Benson said. "They should work closely together. They have a lot in common."

"It's more than geology."

"You think so?"

"I'm a psychologist, Bee, so yes, I think so. Catherine likes Hi, a lot. And I think he likes her, too, but he doesn't know what to do about it."

"Maybe I should talk to him about that."

With a slight shrug, Taki said, "Maybe. But I think Hi would just shut down tighter than a clam. Sometimes men are like little boys."

"So Hi and Catherine are hooking up? That's hard to believe. He's a top-flight geologist, but Catherine's way out of his league, romantically."

"Love is blind."

"Have you asked Mikhail why he cheated at the chess game?" Benson asked, changing the topic.

Forcing herself not to bite her lip, Nomura answered, "Not yet. I wanted to talk to you about it first."

"Okay. You've talked to me. Now talk to Mikhail."

"I will."

"Anything else?"

Nomura closed her eyes and drew in a deep breath.

"Well?" Benson prodded.

"Please forgive me for bringing it up, but yesterday you and Mr. Connover had that shouting match. I don't know what the nature of the disagreement was, but the whole crew knows you and Ted were yelling at each other."

Benson nodded. "It was over nothing, really. I apologized to Ted and we shook hands. Lots of sound and fury, signifying nothing."

Nomura felt far from reassured.

"Frankly, Taki, what you're talking about sounds suspiciously to me like a small group of people locked in an isolation chamber for two years, separated from instant death in vacuum by a few centimeters of aluminum, all trying to keep their cool and get along together until the isolation is over. We were warned this would happen."

"Yes, that is true," Nomura replied, "but I wasn't expecting it to reach this level until we'd been underway for at least two or three months."

Benson rubbed his temple with his right hand, a gesture Nomura knew he did when he was trying to solve a problem or was troubled by something.

Finally he asked, "We aren't heading toward anything like the Mir incident, are we?"

"I don't think so," she said. "I hope not."

Nomura understood Benson's concern. She shared it. The effects of being isolated in space for long durations could be devastating. That's why crews of space stations were rotated regularly: to avoid the mental health issues that inevitably arise when a small group of people are confined together for an extended period of time. It was rumored, but never officially confirmed, that back in the 1980s, personal relations aboard the old Russian space station Mir became so tense that one of the crew members actually stabbed another.

Peering intently at her, Benson asked, "Taki, how are you doing?"

"Me? I'm okay. I don't really mind the physical closeness of the ship. It kind of reminds me of home. But, well, the smells are starting to bother me."

"Smells?" Benson broke into a grin. "Are people not bathing or something?"

"It's not that. It's just the natural smell of people who are closely confined. Not body odor. Not a bad smell. Just a, well, too-close-together smell."

"Huh."

"Please remember that I'm from a culture where people often bathe more than once a day. My father used to come home from his office for lunch and take a quick bath before returning to work for the afternoon. It's just something I notice."

Benson couldn't think of a quip and probably wouldn't have said it to Taki even if he had. She wasn't the type to react happily to his humor. That was one of the reasons he had been picked to command this mission—he could read people fairly well.

"Thanks for giving me a heads-up, Taki," he said. "And please keep me informed. Do you intend to report this all to Mission Control and the crew's personal physicians?"

Each member of the crew had his or her own personal physician back on Earth who knew their medical history in detail. Each personal physician had overseen the crew member's training schedule, conducted regular physical exams, and knew the results of every mental health test they'd been given as they trained for the mission. If anyone on board started showing unusual symptoms, mental or physical, their personal physician would be consulted for advice.

"I should," Nomura answered. "That's what mission protocol calls for."

Benson shook his head. "I wish you wouldn't. What happens among us should stay among us—unless it's really something big."

Nomura frowned, conflicted. She'd known this sort of situation might arise. Now it had, and she had a choice to make.

"We're a family, Taki. We handle our problems among ourselves."

For now, I agree, she thought.

Nodding, "Yes. Of course." But she added silently, *Until the problems become big enough to explode.*

MAY 17, 2035
EARTH DEPARTURE PLUS 42 DAYS
20:05 UNIVERSAL TIME
PRIVACY QUARTERS, THE *ARROW*

Damn, she's good looking, Hi McPherson said to himself, not for the first time since he'd met Catherine Clermont more than two years ago.

He had been taking surreptitious glances at the French geologist all that time. *Not at all voyeuristic,* McPherson told himself. More like a teenager gazing at pictures of a glamorous Hollywood star, distant and unobtainable. Still, here aboard the *Arrow*, his interest in the petite brunette had grown into a full-fledged infatuation.

In the *Arrow*'s tight quarters there wasn't much privacy space. Other than each person's personal cubby, with its closeable screen and Velcro-lined walls for sticking up photographs and charts, there were few places a crew member could go and not be noticed. Each person's sense of privacy had to adapt. Each crew member had to get accustomed to the fact that every move they made could be seen by someone else—even changing one's clothes.

It was at that inopportune time—or very opportune, from McPherson's point of view—that he happened to encounter the object of his infatuation.

Catherine was in the passageway in front of the open screen to her privacy cubicle, her back toward McPherson as she slipped out of her coveralls to put on more casual shorts and tee shirt. McPherson almost walked into the bulkhead as he stared at her bare shoulders, bra strap and shapely bottom.

At just that moment Amanda Lynn happened to come up behind McPherson, who was oblivious to her presence.

"Excuse me, Hiram," she said. "May I get by?"

Startled, McPherson stammered, "Uh, oh, yeah, sure. Sorry about that." He felt like a high schooler who had happened to wander into the girls' bathroom, not-so-accidentally.

"I, uh, I was just going to my cubicle to get my viewer." Even as he said it, it sounded lame it him. Worse than lame: stupid. He could feel his face reddening at being caught in the act of staring at Catherine's nearly bare backside.

"Viewer," Amanda humphed as she squeezed past.

Without missing a beat, Catherine turned around, clad only in her underwear, and smiled at the two of them.

"Am I in the way?" she asked as she smoothly stepped into her shorts and pulled them up to her waist.

"Uh, no, I was just on my way to get something," McPherson mumbled as he made his way past her and rushed to his own cubicle.

"Well," Catherine said as she pulled her shirt over head, "I hope you enjoy the show."

Tonguetied, McPherson ducked into his cubby, grabbed his entertainment viewer, and rushed back through the passageway past the two women, heading toward the galley.

Amanda shook her head as she watched his retreating back. "You shouldn't tease the poor man like that," she said to Clermont. "It's obvious that he's crazy about you."

"Crazy?" Catherine scoffed. "Lustful, more likely. Still, I do like him very much. But I do not think it would be a good idea to let him know."

"Why not?"

Her eyes on the hatch that McPherson had disappeared through, Clermont said, "We are together in this confinement for two years, *non*? If we begin to pair up it will quickly lead to jealousies and anger. And if a pairing should go bad, it could lead to horrible feelings that could jeopardize everything we want to accomplish."

Amanda reluctantly agreed. "Yeah, two years is a long time. But he'd be a truly fine-looking man if he'd just shave off that damned beard."

MAY 20, 2035
EARTH DEPARTURE PLUS 45 DAYS
19:30 UNIVERSAL TIME
THE WHITE HOUSE

Normally, Sarah Fleming seemed as cool as the proverbial cucumber. But at this moment, the red-haired chief of the president's staff looked concerned, even alarmed.

"Mr. President, there's been an accident at the International Moon Base. We don't have many of the details yet, but at least two people have been killed."

President Harper sagged back in his desk chair. "What happened?"

"We're not certain. But the news media claim there was a fire in the main habitat, fed by an oxygen leak."

"My God!"

Harper had just spent a testy half-hour with the Peruvian ambassador, wrangling over that country's drug problems and its impact on mining rare earth metals in the Cordillera Blanca Mountains there. The ambassador wanted the U.S. to give drone aircraft to the Peruvian national police.

One of the successes of Harper's first term had been negotiating a favorable agreement with Peru for American companies to mine ores containing erbium, lanthium and cerium. These rare earth elements were vital ingredients for the electronics industry and China had a monopoly on the world's supply—until Harper's deal with Peru.

Now a drug cartel was waging an undeclared war on the American mining operations, probably bankrolled by China. Harper was willing to send drones to Peru, but only under operational control by the

American military. The ambassador wanted the drones, but not the Americans.

Harper had been elected president on his promise to reverse two decades of American decline in international power and prestige. His re-election in 2032 was based in part on his space program: support for the International Moon Base and—more importantly since the Chinese one-upped the west with their Mars Sample Return Mission— the American-led Mars mission.

And now two killed at the Moon Base. Maybe more.

Sarah Fleming sat tensely in one of the commodious armchairs in front of his desk, unconsciously smoothing her skirt over her knees. He saw that she had a comm bud in her ear.

Glaring at his chief of staff, the president demanded, "How come the goddamned news media knows more about this than we do?"

"The goddamned news media has two reporters at the base, and neither one of them is constrained to know the facts before they shoot their mouths off," Sarah Fleming retorted.

"Two killed," the president muttered.

"We've got calls in to Saxby, at NASA, and the commander of Moon Base. I think it would be a good move for you to personally call the Russians, Europeans and Japanese."

"Do we know if Americans were killed?"

"Not yet. This just happened fifteen-twenty minutes ago." She reached up to touch the comm bud in her right ear. "I'm calling Saxby's deputy administrator, she's the one in charge of the Moon Base operation."

President Harper wanted to jump up and pace the Oval Office. Instead, he sat gripping the armrests of his chair, staring at his chief of staff. Sarah Fleming was exceptionally intelligent and very attractive, a potent combination. Most men found her totally intimidating, but the president had known her for too long to be cowed. They had been colleagues and friends since their first terms in Congress together. She had directed the campaign that got him elected president. When he was re-elected, and most of his cabinet and staff had put in their *pro forma* resignations, the one Harper did not consider even for a moment was Sarah Fleming's.

One hand on the comm bud, she raised a finger of her other hand. "One of those killed was an American. The other was Belgian." She listened some more, then reported, "There was no fire: that's just a news media fabrication. The two killed were working on excavating ice from a newly discovered vein at the bottom of Shackleton Crater when one of the drills failed." Uncharacteristically, Fleming winced. "It shattered and the debris shredded their suits. Explosive decompression. They were dead in seconds."

"Aw, shit," the president said fervently.

"Three others injured," Fleming went on, "but none severely."

She went on with other details, but Harper was already running through the possible scenarios that might play out in Congress and the news media. *Donaldson and his ilk will take up their old yell that space is too dangerous to risk human lives,* he thought. *They'll say that my programs for mining on the Moon and sending people to Mars are too risky. And too expensive.*

How can I counter that? he asked himself. *Tell the people that the dangers and the risks are worth the rewards? That no frontier was ever settled without fallen heroes? Yeah, try that line when the media will be parading the weeping widows.*

"Sarah," he commanded, snapping her attention away from the voice buzzing in her ear. "Get me the names of the people killed and injured. And their bios. I'm going to have to make a statement, probably within the hour. Write one up for me. Fallen heroes. You know the line."

She nodded and rose slowly to her feet.

Harper tapped his intercom key. "What's next?" he asked his appointments secretary.

"The delegation of Four-H clubs," came his secretary's reedy voice. "They're been waiting for ten minutes."

"Give 'em my apologies and send them in. And get me the chairs of the space committees, Senate and House. Squeeze them into the schedule for later this afternoon."

On the screen, it looked as if Treadway were standing in the galley of the *Arrow*.

"Steven Treadway," he said into the camera, "reporting virtually from the *Arrow* spacecraft as it carries its crew toward Mars."

Arrow was already so far from Earth that it took a noticeable several seconds for communications transmissions to cover the distance between the ship and Earth. So this interview was not quite live. Editors had cut out the lags between questions and responses, so that to the TV audience it all appeared as if Treadway were actually aboard the spacecraft, conversing with Ted Connover.

"Today the Mars crew learned about the tragic accident at the International Moon Base," Treadway went on, "in which two lunar technicians were killed—including an American. The crew took the news hard; two on the team here had been to the lunar base during their earlier careers and know several of the people currently living on the Moon, although neither of those killed were personal friends of any of the *Arrow*'s crew. Still, news of the accident struck like a hammer blow here aboard the *Arrow*."

Treadway turned to face Connover, who appeared to be standing immediately in front of him in the confines of the ship. In reality, an unbeknownst to the viewers, Treadway was standing in a replica of the *Arrow* constructed in the basement of the New York City studio. VR mesh on his head, he was busily talking to an empty spot that roughly corresponded to one directly in front of where Connover was looking onboard the real *Arrow*.

Connover, his face deadly serious, said, "Steve, you trained with us. You know the risks involved in space flight as well as any of us. It's a dangerous business, but an important one. Those guys knew the risks and I'm sure they wouldn't want their deaths to jeopardize the work we're doing, any more than I'd want an accident or tragedy aboard our ship to imperil that next flight, that next mission. What they did is important. We need to figure out what went wrong, fix it, and make certain that that particular event never happens again. We need to keep going forward."

Treadway started to ask a question, but Connover wasn't finished.

"Abraham Lincoln said it in his Gettysburg Address," the astronaut continued, "'It is for us, the living, rather to be dedicated to the unfinished work which they who fought here have thus far so nobly advanced.' That's our job. That's our mission."

Treadway shook his head slightly. "No one could have said it better," he said, softly. Turning back to face the camera squarely, he finished, "That was the *Arrow*'s pilot, Ted Connover. I'm Steven Treadway, wishing the men and women of the *Arrow* well from somewhere in space between the orbit of Earth and the planet Mars."

Take it slow and stay calm, Taki Nomura told herself as she waited for Prokhorov to show up. *Be professional. Listen to what he has to say.*

She had chosen the observation cupola, just below the command center, for this one-on-one with the Russian. Just the two of us, nobody else, no recording devices. Try to put him at his ease so he'll open up to you.

Yes, she thought. *Put him at his ease. While you're wound up tighter than a spring.*

She actually flinched when Mikhail Prokhorov yanked the hatch open and ducked through.

"Greetings and salutations," he said, his voice low and grave, his face almost scowling. Nomura realized that Mikhail always appeared to her to be larger than his actual physical stature. Standing next to Bee or Ted Connover, the Russian looked short, dumpy, almost gnomish. But here in the confines of the cupola he seemed sizeable, bulky. The little compartment felt crowded with just the two of them in it.

Prokhorov looked past Taki, through the thick quartz view port.

"It's all empty out there," he murmured. "Empty and far from home."

Taki nodded agreement. "Does that bother you?"

He focused on her. "Is this a psychological exam?"

Suppressing a sudden urge to worm uncomfortably, Taki said, "Sort of."

"On the record?"

"No. Not at all. This is strictly between the two of us. No notes. No reports."

Suspiciously, Prokhorov inquired, "Not even to Bee?"

Realizing this interview was quickly slipping beyond her control, Taki said, "Mikhail, I was there when you and Hi were playing chess."

"That was two weeks ago!"

"Yes, but . . . well, I saw you move your rook."

"What of it?"

"Then you denied it. You lied to Hi's face."

Prokhorov burst into laughter. "Is that what this is all about: that stupid chess game?"

"Why did you do it?" Taki asked.

"To shorten the game, of course. I saw after three moves that Hi is a blundering amateur at chess. I simply wanted to put an end to his misery."

"You cheated."

He stared at her for a moment. "Is that so important?"

"It is if you've destroyed the trust Hi had in you."

"Trust? He's never had any trust in me. He's always regarded me as a needless add-on to the crew. A political appointee, useless."

"That's not so!"

"Isn't it? Ask him."

"I will. But . . . Mikhail, you should talk with him, too. Tell him how you feel."

"How I feel," Prokhorov repeated. "I leave my wife and children for two years—three, if you count the time I spent in training—and what do I get? I get treated like an outsider, a Russian barbarian brought into the team by political pressure."

"I don't feel that way about you," Taki protested.

"Then you're the only one. Hi has Catherine at his side every minute of the day. Bee and Ted work together like brothers. Oh, I know they quarrel sometimes, but brothers do that."

Taki kept silent. *Let him vent*, she told herself. *Let him get it all out.*

"Virginia and Amanda are like sorority sisters. I am alone. Despised and alone."

"I don't despise you," she protested. "And neither do the others. They all respect you, your . . . your competence in your field."

Prokhorov let out a short, sharp bark of laughter. "Competence in my field," he sneered. "There are only a half-dozen people in the world who are specialists in Martian meteorology. Some field."

"But you were picked ahead of all the others."

"Politics. It was all politics."

"Is that what you feel?"

"It is what I know."

Taki pulled in a deep, calming breath as she eyed Prokhorov closely. *He's worked himself up over what we all knew would happen during the trip—separation from family and doubts about his own ability to contribute to humanity's first trip to Mars. If he only knew . . .*

"I'm going to make arrangements for you to have extra time on the comm link to talk with your wife and children," she said.

The Russian shook his head. "That would only make things worse. The others will think I'm getting special privileges."

"But—"

"Besides, it won't do any good. She's left me."

Taki felt it like a physical blow. "Left you?"

Nodding morosely, Prokhorov said, "I asked her to come with me for the training period. She refused. She told me if I went to Mars she would leave me. Then I found that she was already seeing another man, behind my back." Sinking his head into his hands, he moaned, "If I were there, I would . . . I don't know what I would do. But I'm not there. I'm here and seeing you all get along so well just makes me envious."

Without thinking, Taki almost slid her arm around his shoulders, but stopped herself. Instead, she leaned forward to get his attention. "I'm so sorry," she whispered.

"And my boys," Prokhorov almost sobbed.

There's nothing I can do! Taki realized as she resisted every emotion that would allow her to reach out and put her arm around him. Prokhorov would likely not appreciate the gesture and might even misinterpret it, so she kept her hands at her sides. *Even if we were back on Earth, there'd be nothing I could do.*

After a few moments Prokhorov straightened up, his eyes red and puffy. "I'll apologize to Hiram. It was stupid of me to tease him like that."

Taki nodded understandingly.

"But not a word about my personal problem to anyone," he said, sudden steel in his voice. "I can carry my burdens."

"I promise," Taki said. Then she added, "You can talk to me anytime, Mikhail. You don't have to be alone"

He flashed a bleak smile. "Thank you. I appreciate it."

Then he got up and ducked back through the hatch, leaving Taki Nomura sitting by herself in the observation cupola, staring at the distant stars.

Ted Connover saw Prokhorov shamble past the open hatch of the communications center. He leaned forward in his chair and pulled the sliding screen shut. Privacy was at a minimum aboard *Arrow*, and he wanted as much of it as he could get.

The comm center was a tiny compartment jam-packed with the communications gear that kept *Arrow* in constant touch with Mission Control on Earth. Every system aboard the ship was monitored electronically, microsecond by microsecond, and the data radioed to Earth continuously. Located just behind the command center, the "radio shack" was the place Connover went to when he wanted to be alone.

Normally, he would have felt cramped, confined in this narrow compartment. The electronic gear hummed constantly and the booth felt uncomfortably warm. But it was the one place where he could send a message home without any of the others hearing him.

Satisfied that the sliding doors on both ends of the compartment were closed, Connover reached for the headset and slipped it over his ears. Then he tapped the button on the console's keyboard to start a video message.

Keeping his voice low, he began, "Vicki, we're so far out now that the time delay makes it impossible to have a normal conversation, so please forgive me for sending this one-way message to you."

Glancing at the red light that showed the video camera was working, he continued, "First, I want you to know that I love you very much and miss you even more. With each passing day I think about all the time we're still going to be apart and it fills me with mixed feelings. Yeah, I'm excited about being here and making history, but there's a part of me that regrets going on this mission and being away from you and Thad for so long.

"By the time I return he'll be graduating high school and heading off for college. You'll have been dealing with the house and Thad and the whole college search business all on your own and, not that I don't think you can handle it, it's just that I'd like to be there with you and be part of the whole thing and not just a bystander giving armchair quarterback advice from a million miles away.

"Just about the only privacy we get on this tin can is using the toilet or here in the comm shack talking or sending personal messages home. I can deal with the lack of privacy, but I'm seriously wondering how well I'll hold up without you at my side.

"Remember the trip we took to the Giant's Causeway in Northern Ireland? The wonder we felt when we saw those big rock formations that dropped down into the surf and under the sea? That's the feeling I get whenever I look out the cupola window into deep space, but without you beside me it feels kind of empty."

He sighed. "I guess I'm in a melancholy mood. I apologize. I'll try to be more positive. I don't want to leave you feeling depressed after my messages!"

Putting on a smile, Connover continued, "Yesterday Hi learned he was a new uncle. Houston sent an alert message to him and then a couple of hours later he got a video from the hospital. He was on Cloud Nine. They way he pranced around, you'd think he was the father instead of the uncle. Sort of reminded me of how I felt when Thad was born. We don't get a lot of personal news out here; that was a real high point for the whole crew. We all celebrated.

"I've even started feeling some respect for Bee. You know I've never really liked the stuffy little prick. But I've been a good soldier and supported him one hundred percent. Unless he listens to my messages to you, I don't think he has the faintest suspicion that I wished he'd broken his leg a few days before launch. Oh, we had our shoot-outs when we first started off, but it's getting harder and harder to dislike him. He's not really such a bad guy. Really, I think I enjoy badmouthing him more than I actually dislike him. Makes me feel good, for some reason. Go figure that one out.

"Oh, yeah, you asked me to tell you if any of the crew are getting familiar with each other. I haven't seen much of that, but it's obvious that Hi is head over heels about Catherine. All she has to do is ask him for something with that French accent of hers and he practically bounces off the walls to do it. Kind of reminds me of myself when we first met. Funny thing, though; I don't think Hi really understands it. He's all fumbles and fidgets around Catherine, like a kid on his first date, but I don't think he realizes what's going on.

"Come to think about it, it would have been kind of fun to be trapped with you for two years in a tin can between the planets. Whatever would we do to keep ourselves occupied? Better not let myself get too distracted. Too frustrating!

"Tell Thad I'm thinking about him. And remind him to send me a copy of the story he wrote in his creative writing class, like he promised to. You'd think he'd be a little more conscientious with his dad on his way to Mars. But what the hell, he's a teenager."

Connover paused for a heartbeat. Then, "I'd better sign off now. Vicki, just know that I love you and can't wait to see you again. I never realized how much I'd miss your touch. Just thinking about it makes me smile. I love you.

"Bye."

The klaxon's sudden blare jolted Virginia Gonzalez so hard she nearly dropped the cup of coffee in her hand.

It's just a drill, she told herself. Still, the instant raucous blast was louder than anything she had heard in training. Maybe . . .

"This is a solar storm alert drill," announced the silky synthesized voice of the ship's computerized intercom system, flat and unruffled. "Report to the shelter immediately."

Gonzalez was already through the galley's hatch, heading for the sleeping quarters, which also served as the ship's storm shelter.

On Earth, the planet's enveloping magnetic field and thick atmosphere protected life on the surface from all but the most energetic cosmic radiation. Aboard the *Arrow*, the ship's thin skin provided only minimal protection against the constant sleeting of cosmic ray and solar wind particles. But when the Sun burped out a solar flare, interplanetary space was invaded by a wave of deadly high-energy particles. The ship's lightweight alloy skin and the inflated fabric structure of the galley were transparent to such subatomic bullets.

The high-energy protons and heavier atomic nuclei of a solar flare could kill unprotected humans. As the ions burrow through a human body, they could cause cancers and other somatic damage that could be fatal.

To help protect against this lethal danger, the ship's sleeping area was surrounded by thicker fabric walls holding bladders filled with water. The water would absorb all but the most energetic of the incoming particles, protecting the fragile crew inside the shelter. Still, the highest energy particles, though relatively rare, zipped through the water-filled walls and irradiated the human crew, raising their risk of developing cancers later in life.

The ship's electronics and other systems were hardened to survive a solar storm's worst radiation. The human crew would have to huddle in the protected sleeping area for the hours or even days that the storm's radiation cloud enveloped the ship.

Gonzalez saw that all seven of her crewmates were already in the sleeping area by the time she got there. The klaxon was still blazing away, but its noise was muted inside the shelter.

Bee Benson clicked the stopwatch function on his wristwatch and smiled at them. "Ninety seconds. Good job, people."

Amanda Lynn poked a finger in Gonzalez's direction. "You were last, Jinny. One hour on the treadmill."

The others all laughed, while Gonzalez managed a weak smile.

In a real solar storm the crew would undoubtedly slip into their individual cubicles to relax until the radiation level outside dropped back to normal. But this was only a drill.

"Bee, how long do you intend to keep us penned up in here?" McPherson asked. "I don't mind being close to my friends, but I have a video running."

"A movie?" Connover asked.

"A report from the drill team at Lake Vostok," Catherine Clermont replied. "Most interesting."

Amanda said, "Hey, I'd like to see that, too. Have they found any new organisms beneath the ice?"

"We didn't get that far into the video before the horn sounded," McPherson replied.

At that moment the klaxon abruptly turned off, signaling that the threat—or, in this case, the drill—was over.

"Okay," Benson told them. "Back to work."

"That's what an extremophile looks like up close and personal," Amanda Lynn was saying, pointing to the shapeless blobs on the display screen.

Virginia Gonzalez peered at the screen. "Like amoebas," she murmured.

"Sort of."

Arrow's minuscule biology lab was barely large enough for the two of them. Gonzalez, tall and leggy, was wearing gym shorts and an oversized sweatshirt. The shorter, stockier Lynn was in mission-standard sky-blue coveralls. They sat side-by-side on foldable stools that looked flimsy, but were perfectly adequate in the ship's one-third gravity.

Lynn pointed to the screen, "I picked that one out of a lake in Antarctica that's been covered with ice for several million years. It's called a psychrophile."

"Amazing to think it could survive that long and under such cold conditions. Most of the extremophiles I've heard of are near volcanic vents on the ocean floor or someplace really hot."

"This one thrives in the cold. Little bugger's filled with natural antifreeze: temperatures below freezing don't bother it at all."

Her eyes riveted to the screen, Gonzalez asked, "You expect to find something like that on Mars?"

"Hope so," Lynn replied. "The amino acids and other biomarkers the Chinese found were in the ice of the permafrost underground."

Before Gonzalez could ask another question, Lynn pointed to the screen and explained, "This kind of bacterium is a methanogen. It excretes methane as a waste product of its metabolism. The earliest satellites we placed in orbit around Mars detected whiffs of methane, but the latest ones haven't found any trace of the bug farts—"

"Bug farts?"

Lynn's normally dour face broke into a bright smile. "Yep. Bug farts."

She clicked the remote in her hand and the screen went dark.

Gonzalez got to her feet and stretched. "So you'll be working with Catherine and Hi once we get to Mars."

Nodding, Amanda said, "They do the digging, I examine what they've brought up."

"Hi will do the digging," Virginia said, a slight smile on her lips. "He won't let Catherine get her hands dirty."

"I don't care who does the digging as long as they bring me their results."

"It doesn't bother you that Hi's a chauvinist? The way he hovers around Catherine. He thinks she's a little porcelain doll."

Amanda shrugged. "Most men are bigger and stronger than most women. I don't mind letting Hi do the muscle work."

She flashed back to a memory of growing up in Detroit, how her brothers would walk with her, protect her on their way through the bad neighborhoods they had to get through to reach school. *That's what men are built for,* Amanda thought. *Some of them are born rapists, some are born protectors.*

Virginia interrupted her thoughts. "Do you think Catherine and Hi have made it yet?"

Amanda shook her head. "If they have, they've been awfully quiet about it."

Giggling, Virginia said, "Maybe they put gags in their mouths."

"That's kinky!"

"What about Mikhail?" Virginia pursued. "I know he's married, but he looks so lonely."

"You getting the hots, girl?"

Her smile turning sly, Virginia replied, "Just looking over the field."

"If I got excited over any of them, it'd be Ted. He's cute, and I bet he'd be fun."

"He's married, too."

"Yeah. What about Bee?"

"Also married," Virginia said, with a theatrical sigh.

"Yeah, but I hear his marriage is on the rocks."

"Maybe. But he's such an iceberg," Virginia said.

"You try to melt him down a little?"

"No!" But then Virginia's expression turned thoughtful and she said softly, "I wonder if you could, though."

Amanda shook her head. "It wouldn't work."

"You mean you wouldn't try it?"

"Look at me. Short and squat. And black, to boot. Now you, you're tall and slim and good-looking."

"And Hispanic."

"What's that got to do with it?"

Suddenly tired of this subject, Virginia said, "Enough fantasizing. I'm not going after any of these guys. We have a job to do, and screwing around will make everything too complicated."

Amanda nodded agreement. "You're right. We're dedicated scientists, not those female acrobats from the latest porno simulations."

"Acrobats?"

"If you'd seen some of the positions they take, then you'd know why I call them 'acrobats.'"

"You've seen them?"

"A few," Amanda said, almost defensively. "But I didn't bring any of those vids aboard the ship with me."

"I wonder if Mikhail has. Or Hi?" Virginia mused.

"Ted might," Amanda said. "But not Bee."

Virginia laughed. "That's right. Bee will maintain proper discipline, just like it says in the mission manual. And so will we, dammit."

"Yeah, sure. And only four hundred and forty-two days to go."

For Vicki Connover it was a routine day of running errands, except that her son Thad was in the car with her. School was out for the summer, and he had surprised his mother by volunteering to accompany her as she zipped from store to store, buying groceries and household supplies.

The hum of the car's electric motor was barely audible as they drove down Bay Area Boulevard from the Gulf Freeway. She'd taken the car off AutoDrive once she left the freeway and already felt burdened by actually having to steer. There were some roads that hadn't been approved for AutoDrive due to the many stops and starts required, not to mention the frequent side roads and shopping center entrances that made it difficult for the automated systems to have the reliability the insurance companies demanded. It was amazing to Vicki how quickly she'd become accustomed to having the tiresome chore of navigating traffic be assumed by the car. One of these days she wouldn't ever have to drive; she'd just get in the car and tell it where to go.

Vicki was impatient for the new technology to become universal, although she was certain that Thad barely noticed the change. The transition to AutoDrive had occurred during his childhood and he'd grown just as accustomed to it as she had to the electric car revolution of her youth.

But Thad was not entirely in favor of it.

"It's not really a motorcycle, Mom," he was saying as they dove toward the freeway. "It's a motor *bike*. A Honda CBR. It's really neat."

"It has a gasoline engine and isn't equipped to drive for you?"

"You don't 'drive' a motorcycle, Mom. You *ride* a motorcycle. And, yes, it has a gasoline engine: single cylinder, four stroke, liquid cooled, fuel-injected two-hundred-forty-nine-cubic-centimeter engine. It gets about sixty to seventy miles per gallon."

Thad was smart enough not to mention it could go from to zero to sixty miles per hour in six and a half seconds.

Visions of fatal accidents filling her thoughts, Vicki replied, "It's awfully dangerous, though."

"Mom, I'm a good driver! I'm careful!"

"It's not you, honey. It's all those other idiots on the road."

"I can stay off the freeways, if that's what's bothering you."

"I don't know. Let me talk it over with your father."

"Jeez, he's a zillion miles away!"

"I'll ask him about it the next time he calls."

Thad slumped back in his seat, pouting teenagedly. "You asked me what I wanted for my birthday," he grumbled. "I want a motor bike."

"Thad—"

The driver of the truck approaching them on the opposite side of the road was distracted by the submarine sandwich that was sliding out of his hand. Had his truck been able to use AutoDrive, it wouldn't have been an issue. Vicki, still talking with her son, didn't see the rear of the semi-trailer swerve into her lane until it suddenly loomed right in front of her. She did what any driver would do: she mashed on the brakes and turned hard right in a vain attempt to avoid a head-on collision.

The quiet of the drive was shattered by the shriek of tires on the pavement and the sickening crunch of her car's Fiberglas frame impacting against the aluminum and steel truck at a closing velocity of seventy miles per hour. The frame of Vicki Connover's car shattered, as it was designed to do, to absorb as much of the energy of the collision as possible. Airbags deployed to cushion the occupants' impact against the plastic dashboard and steering wheel.

Unfortunately, the laws of physics have no pity. The more massive truck kept coming forward after the impact, tipping over in less than a second and completely flattening the car beneath it.

Vicki Connover and her son Thad scarcely knew what hit them before they were crushed to death by the errant truck.

The truck driver hardly received a scratch.

"So who the hell's going to tell him?"

Nathan Brice, normally as impassive as a Zen guru, nearly shouted the question. The *Arrow*'s flight director, Brice had once been saber-slim, but years of desk work had given him a noticeable belly and thinned his light brown hair. A veteran of three missions to the International Space Station and one to the Moon, he sat at his desk in rolled-up shirtsleeves as he glared at Bart Saxby's image on his office's wall screen.

Saxby, in his own Washington office, looked equally distraught. "What about other family members?" he asked.

"There's no other immediate family," answered Pat Church, sitting in front of Brice's paper-strewn desk. "Vicki and Thad were all he had."

Church was Ted Connover's personal physician; he had known and worked with the Connover family ever since Thad had been an infant. He felt more like an uncle to the boy than simply the family's doctor. Church had been an aspiring astronaut who had failed to make the cut when he'd applied at the end of his residency at Baylor. Nearly six feet tall with buzz-cut black hair that was just starting to show flecks of gray, Church had often been mistaken for the astronaut he'd aspired to become as he strode through the halls of the Johnson Space Center.

Saxby looked at the two of them from the wall screen. "Well," he said, "it will have to be one of you two. Your call, Nate."

Brice grimaced and turned to Church. "You know him better than anybody else, Pat."

Church nodded grimly. "Yeah. I ought to be the one to tell him. Poor guy."

Saxby said, "Tell Benson about it first. He's the commander up there. Let him decide if he wants to do it or if he wants you to do it."

"Good thinking," Brice said.

Church repeated, "Poor guy."

The news hit Bee like a kick in the gut. To him, the *Arrow*'s crew was like family. He remembered the day, just a week or so before they'd left Earth, that Ted had told him his son had passed his driver's test and was soon to be "unleashed" on the unsuspecting drivers of Texas. Ted loved his wife deeply and was very, very proud of his son.

"So you think you should be the one to tell him?" Bee asked Pat Church's image on the comm screen. He was sitting in the command center, and glanced nervously over his shoulder, worried that someone might come in.

In his head he counted *one thousand, two thousand, three thousand, four thousand . . .*

The time-lag in messages to and from Earth was getting longer each day. *Arrow* was hurtling outbound from Earth at more than 25,000 miles per hour; the ship had covered so much distance that communications were plagued by unnatural pauses at the end of each transmission, even though the messages moved with the speed of light. Normally, it was a pain in the butt. Now, with this news, it was torture.

"Absolutely," came Church's reply at last. "Although there's a part of me that would love to chicken out and let somebody else give him the bad news." He let out a sigh. "But it's part of my job, I guess. Anyway, who'd be better to assess its potential impact on Ted's performance?"

"Okay," Benson agreed. "Let's do it like this. I'll tell him that you're going to call in ten minutes for a private consult. In the meantime, I'll let everyone else know what's happened. I want to know how he took it as soon as the two of you are finished talking. And I'll want to know what we should be doing, saying, watching for, on our end."

One thousand, two thousand, three thousand . . .

"Sounds good."

Shaking his head, Bee muttered, "They'll have been buried for damned near two years by the time he gets to visit their graves. That really sucks."

One thousand, two thousand, three thousand . . .

"That's an understatement," Church finally said. "Okay. I'll call back in ten minutes."

Bee clicked off the comm set. *Good Lord,* he thought. *We all knew the risks we were taking. But this . . . this is awful. How's Ted going to take it?*

One look at Pat Church's face and Ted knew the news from home was bad.

Bee had told him Church wanted to talk with him one-on-one. Now Ted sat alone in the comm shack and felt his whole body turn to ice.

"Both dead?" he heard himself ask.

After the interminable delay, Church nodded solemnly. "It was instantaneous. They didn't suffer."

"That's good." But in Ted's mind, he was raging, *Didn't suffer? They're dead, for Christ's sake! Dead!*

"I'm sorry, Ted."

"Yeah. Me too."

One thousand, two thousand . . .

It was as if he were disembodied, floating miles away and watching this poor slob sitting there with his guts ripped out.

"If there's anything I can do," Church said, looking miserable.

Bring them back, Ted replied silently. Aloud, he said only, "Thanks, Pat. I appreciate it."

Church ended the transmission and the comm screen went blank. Ted sat there thinking, *If I'd been with them, if I'd been driving, I could've avoided the accident. I could've reacted faster than Vicki did.*

And then he realized, *Even if I didn't, at least I'd be dead, too. I'd be with them.*

When he finally came out of the comm shack and walked into the galley, the whole crew was standing there, somber, subdued. All of them staring at him, waiting for him to come apart at the seams.

Bee put a hand on his shoulder. "Ted, we're all so sorry about the accident. Thad was a great kid and I know you were very proud of him."

Ted looked into Bee's eyes and saw genuine sorrow there. He looked past Benson to the others, all tense with grief.

"I appreciate your support," he heard himself mouth the words. "I . . . I don't know what to say. It was just a simple, stupid traffic accident and now they're dead." Suddenly the enormity of it hit him. The finality. The utter, implacable finality of it.

"They're dead," he repeated. "Oh my God, Vicki's dead!" He broke into racking sobs and buried his face in his hands.

Instantly, every eye in the room went teary. Amanda and Catherine pushed past Bee and wrapped their arms around Ted, sobbing openly.

Benson pawed at his own eyes and fought down the ache in his gut. *Straighten up, mister,* he growled to himself. *You're the commander here, you can't go to pieces like the rest of them.* Yet he was proud of his crew, his little family, and how they were showing their concern and compassion for one of their own.

And beyond that, he was also considering how this tragedy might affect the success or failure of their mission. Would it bring them all closer together, or would it drive a wedge between Ted and the rest of them?

Should we abort the mission and return home? If Ted becomes dysfunctional, maybe that's what we'll have to do.

Bee blinked his eyes dry and headed for the control center, leaving the others to commiserate with Ted.

We're fifty-nine days into the trip, he was thinking. *A sizeable distance from Earth.* Aborts early in the mission, seven to fifteen days out, were the easiest. But as they moved further out the Earthcontinued on its march around the Sun—and so did Mars. The orbital mechanics would allow an abort up to ninety days out—about a month, plus. I've got thirty days to make the decision, Benson knew.

The return flight won't be very quick. It'll take the better part of a year before we're back on terra firma. But that's faster than going on to Mars and certainly less risky. We need Ted. We need him fully functional. Getting home in a year is a lot better than the mission's planned two-year duration, especially if Ted's in an emotional crisis and cracks up the landing on Mars.

Home in a year, Benson thought as he stepped into the command center. *But that will mean we've failed. The whole mission would be a complete bust.*

He'd have to talk over the options with Nate Brice and the rest of the Mission Control team. But not now. Later. *Now's the time for the crew to help Ted, to be his surrogate family, to see him past this crisis if we can.*

Benson sat there, surrounded by the dials and screens of the control panel, their soft hums and beeps somehow soothing him. He wanted to cry, for once in his life to let it all out and show Ted that he cared.

But he couldn't do it.

Looking properly somber, Steven Treadway stood in front of a computer-generated image of the *Arrow* against a background of stars.

"Today a personal tragedy unfolded aboard the Mars-bound spaceship *Arrow*, now millions of miles from the crew's homes and families.

"The ship's pilot, American astronaut Ted Connover, learned that his wife and only son were killed in an automobile accident near their home in Clear Lake, Texas.

"*Arrow*'s crew is now the most remote group of humans in the history of the human race, and there is absolutely nothing that can be done to help this grieving father to deal with the reality that his wife and son are dead and will have been dead for nearly two years before he returns from Mars.

"Ted Connover's crewmates are supporting him as best they can, of course, and messages of support are pouring in to Johnson Space Center from all around the globe, including personal condolences from President Harper and heads of state as diverse as the prime minister of Japan and the president of the Maldives."

Looking toward the image of the *Arrow*, Treadway pronounced solemnly, "Ted, the world grieves with you. Though you are millions of miles away from home, you are not alone.

"Steven Treadway, reporting."

JUNE 14, 2035
EARTH DEPARTURE PLUS 70 DAYS
17:22 UNIVERSAL TIME
GALLEY, THE *ARROW*

Her eyes wide with disbelief, Amanda Lynn watched the whole thing happening. She and Taki Nomura were sitting at a table in the galley enjoying one of those rare moments when people open up, really *open up*, about their families, their lives, their personal joys and sorrows. Taki was talking about her parents, both deceased, and how their passion for education drove her early life and her decision to become a physician. They were so engaged in the conversation that they might have missed what was going on at the table across the way if Mikhail Prokhorov hadn't raised his voice so brazenly.

The Russian had been sitting with Ted Connover, their heads bent together over a pair of sodas as they talked together quietly.

But then Prokhorov's voice rose. "As you Americans say, shit happens. You're not the only one with troubles. Get over it."

Connover straightened up as if someone had slapped him in the face.

"I knew a man in Magnitogorsk," Prokhorov went on, "who was hit by a train on a country road one night. He'd been out drinking and for some stupid reason he stopped his car on the railroad tracks and passed out. He never knew what hit him. Wham! He was gone. Three weeks later I saw his wife out on a date with a guy she'd met at the funeral."

Through gritted teeth, Ted asked, "What's your point, Mikhail?"

"Shit happens, my friend. I know you loved your wife and it won't be easy for you, but at least we have a few good-looking women here you can match up with."

Connover stood up so suddenly his chair toppled over backwards. "This conversation is over!"

Prokhorov got to his feet, too. "You think you're the only one with troubles? My wife's left me! You don't see me moping about it. Be a man, Ted."

Amanda forgot her conversation with Taki. She felt her pulse thumping in her ears. She'd met insensitive jerks like Prokhorov before, but she never expected the Russian to be so blatant about it. *How'd he ever get selected for this mission? He's a trainwreck himself.*

As Ted stormed out of the galley, leaving Prokhorov standing at the table, she called to him:

"Hey, Mikhail, what rock did you crawl out from under? You think any of the women on this ship would hook up with an asshole like you? Ted's wife's been gone less than a week and you're acting Attila the Hun. Why don't you just shut up and show some sensitivity? If you can't do that, just shut up."

Prokhorov stared at her for a moment, then broke into a smile that showed no trace of guilt. "I love you too, dark lady," he said, with a gracious little bow.

Then he sauntered out of the galley, leaving the two unfinished sodas on the table instead of putting them in the recycler.

Amanda stared after him, then turned back to Nomura. "How in hell did he get through the psychological tests? Somebody that obnoxious must have showed signs of it during the training period."

Nomura hesitated before replying, "He has his own problems, Mandy. He was fine during training, but then his wife left him. I think that's hit him a lot harder than he's willing to admit."

"We ought to stuff him out an airlock," Amanda growled.

"I'll talk to Bee about it. Maybe he needs some advice from a man."

"I'm sure going to stay as far away from him as I can."

With a wry smile, Taki said, "Aboard this ship? That won't be very far, will it?"

"Not far enough," said Amanda.

JUNE 15, 2035
EARTH DEPARTURE PLUS 71 DAYS
03:17 UNIVERSAL TIME
COMMUNICATIONS CENTER, THE *ARROW*

Ted Connover realized he was spending most of his free time in the comm shack, sending messages to his dead wife.

He woke up with the vague memory of a dream that had racked his troubled sleep: he'd been back in college, trying to find the classroom where he was supposed to be taking a final exam. He awoke still looking for it.

Wearing only his shorts and a sleeveless undershirt, Ted tiptoed through the sleeping area, barely aware of the light snores and mumbles of his crewmates. He slipped into the comm shack, sat in its only chair, and turned on the audio recorder.

Keeping his voice low, he began, "Vicki, I miss you. There are so many things I want to tell you about the trip, about how much I love you, how much I miss you, and now I can't. I don't even know why I'm recording this. You'll never hear it and I know I'll never play it back, but for some reason I've got to send you one more message."

He hesitated, thinking, *Maybe this is therapy. Maybe this is how I'm trying to work my way through this.*

Taking in a deep, shuddering breath, he continued.

"Did it hurt? God, I hope you didn't suffer. And Thad. Poor Thad. I so wanted to be there when he graduated from college, when he got married, when he . . . when he . . . gave us a grandchild."

He was on the verge of breaking into tears again, he knew. Sucking in a deep breath, Ted fought for self control. At last he resumed: "Did

119

I ever tell you that one of the reasons I accepted this slot, going to Mars I mean, was not just because I've always dreamed of going to Mars but because it was going to be that start of something big. Something bigger than you and me. Bigger even than our country. It's the start of our species finally growing up and leaving the cradle. And I wanted to be a part of it so I could share it with my wife, my son, dear God, with my grandchildren. And now? What's the point? What's the goddamned point?"

Forcing back the tears that welled in his eyes, Ted went on, "Enough. Enough of my selfishness. I'm starting to cry because I miss you. *I miss you.* You're wherever you are and I'd like to think that a part of you is here with me now. But I don't think I can believe that. But, Vicki, I want to believe it! *I miss you so much!*"

JUNE 24, 2035
EARTH DEPARTURE PLUS 80 DAYS
16:48 UNIVERSAL TIME
THE CAPITOL, WASHINGTON D.C.

"What's this all about, Billy?" asked Senator Martin Yañez.

Hiding a pang of distaste at being addressed so familiarly by such a junior member of the subcommittee, Senator William Donaldson replied, "What else? I want your vote."

The two men were alone in the spacious conference room allotted to the Senate Subcommittee on Space. Part of the Senate's Committee on Science, Commerce and Transportation, the space panel was one of the many subcommittees that included consumer protection, product safety and insurance; communications, technology and the internet; aviation; the Coast Guard; and transportation, merchant marine infrastructure, safety and security.

During President Harper's first term, the Congress had formed a select committee for the Mars mission. But once the mission had been launched, the select committee was dissolved and the Mars mission, as far as the United States Senate was concerned, had to compete for attention and funding against airplanes, ships, consumer protection, scientific research, the internet and a host of other concerns.

"My vote?" Senator Yañez asked innocently. "On what?"

Unconsciously glancing over his shoulder before he spoke, Donaldson said, "It's time to shut down the manned space program."

Yañez and Donaldson were sitting at one end of the long, gleaming table. Aside from the two of them, the plush dark leather swivel chairs along the table were empty. So were the slightly less sumptuous chairs along the marble walls. Yet they kept their voices low.

They were an odd couple. Donaldson was lean and flinty, a caricature of the New England schoolteacher he had once been. What was left of his once-blond hair had long ago turned dead white. He wore a dark three-piece suit, as always, with his trademark "Don't Tread on Me" lapel pin. Yañez was stout, almost corpulent, his suit jacket flapping unbuttoned, the front of his shirt straining across his girth. Instead of a tie he wore a silver and onyx bolo.

"Kill the manned space program?" he hissed. "Are you crazy? My constituents would hang me in effigy! And not by my neck, either!"

Donaldson put on a reassuring smile. "Don't get yourself in an uproar. Killing NASA's manned space operations will mean *more* business for your state's private spaceport, not less."

Yañez's beefy face showed doubt.

Donaldson explained, "If we get NASA out of the manned space business, where are the corporations that're working on the space station and the moon base going to go for launch services? To New Mexico!"

"Or California," Yañez replied guardedly. "Or Texas."

"You'll get your share."

Shaking his head slowly, Yañez objected, "How can you even think of cutting manned space with that crew heading out to Mars?"

Donaldson put on an air of a patient schoolteacher educating a backward Latino.

"They'll abort the Mars mission, bring those people back home."

"Abort it?"

"Their pilot's wife just died in an auto accident. He's in no emotional shape to fly the crew to the surface of Mars. He'll kill them all."

"Ted Connover? He's solid as a rock."

"Not from the psych reports I've seen," Donaldson countered. "He's become moody, keeps to himself. Which is pretty damned hard to do on that floating Winnebago of theirs."

"They've still got more than three months before they reach Mars. Connover will pull out of it by then."

"Will he? What if the psychologists at Johnson determine he's not in shape to fly the lander? Even if they don't, we can find plenty of shrinks here in D.C. who'll decide our way."

Yañez stared at his subcommittee chairman.

"And there's the accident at the moon base," Donaldson went on. "Two people killed, one of them an American. How do you think the public will react if the whole Mars crew gets killed?"

"Jesus."

"You'll be saving lives, Marty. It's the only decent thing to do."

Yañez loathed being called "Marty," but he nodded thoughtfully. "Saving lives, huh?"

"But we've got to act now, right away. The Mars ship reaches its point-of-no-return in ten days. After that, they've got to go on to Mars no matter what."

Again Yañez shook his head ponderously. "I don't know, Billy. The president is a hundred and fifty percent behind manned space."

His smile turning just the slightest bit sly, Donaldson said, "That's another reason to act now. Take the wind out of Harper's sails. Cut his balls off."

And finally Yañez understood. Harper had beaten Donaldson for the party's nomination for president, won the election and then won re-election.

Donaldson's been nursing that grudge all these years, he realized. It's the old political axiom: Don't get mad, get even.

Leaning back in the softly yielding swivel chair, Yañez asked the crucial question.

"What's in it for me?"

Donaldson closed his eyes briefly. "Oh, I suppose that we could get the Department of Transportation to tighten up its regulations on private space launching facilities." Before Yañez could object, he went on, "Tighten them in a manner that New Mexico can meet, and Texas and California can't, without spending a lot of money on improvements."

"That's pretty tricky."

"But it can be done."

Yañez thought it over for all of ten seconds. Then he stuck out his thick-fingered hand. "You've got a deal, Billy."

Donaldson's smile turned genuine. "I appreciate it, Marty. You won't regret it."

JULY 21, 2035
EARTH DEPARTURE PLUS 107 DAYS
17:14 HOURS
INFIRMARY, THE *ARROW*

"So how do you feel?" asked Taki Nomura.

Ted Connover was sitting in the only visitor's chair, at one end of Nomura's minuscule desk. The infirmary was pocket-sized: not even one bed. If anyone got sick or was injured, they'd be placed in their own privacy cubicle.

Ted's eyes flicked to the unblinking red light of the recording camera before answering, "Okay, I guess."

"Sleeping all right?"

A nod.

"Dreams?"

A shrug. "Nothing special. They usually fade away when I wake up."

Taki said nothing. *She's like one of those Buddha sculptures,* Connover thought. *Her lips smile but those almond eyes are trying to x-ray me.*

"You're eating well," she said.

Connover grinned. "Considering the food aboard this bucket, that might be a sign of insanity."

"The food could be better," she conceded.

For a long moment they faced each other, saying nothing. Then Nomura very clearly reached out one hand and clicked the camera off. The red eye closed.

"All right, Ted. The official part of this examination is over. Now it's just you and me."

125

Looking just the slightest bit suspicious, Connover asked, "So what do you want to know that I haven't already told you?"

"How you really feel."

"Like I said, okay."

"You said, 'Okay, I guess.'"

Almost sheepishly, "Yeah, I did, didn't I?"

"So what's the 'I guess' all about?"

Connover bit his lips. Then, "I . . . I feel sort of . . . numb. Like I'm embalmed or frozen in ice, kind of. Like I'm empty inside."

"You're holding your emotions in check."

"Maybe. I don't know." Suddenly he wanted this interview to be over. "I'll tell you one thing, I'm getting damned sick and tired of everybody pussyfooting around me. Ever since Vicki's accident, it's like they're waiting for me to crack up or something. Hell, Mikhail's the only one who's talked to me straight for the past week."

"Mikhail can be insensitive."

"Maybe. But at least he tells you what he really thinks."

"And the rest of us don't?"

"No. Not really." Before Taki could reply, Ted went on, "Oh, you've all been very supportive, really. I shouldn't complain. It's just that . . . that . . ."

"That what?"

"You all look like you're walking on eggshells around me. I'm okay. Vicki and Thad are dead and there's nothing I can do about that. Let's get on with the job and stop treating me like I'm some wounded animal, for God's sake."

"Is that what you really want?"

"Yes!"

Nomura smiled at him. "You know that Houston's been on my back about you. They're worried you might not be up to the job."

"Christ, the job's all I've got left! Let me do what I came here to do."

"That's fine by me, but the Mission Control people are wondering if they shouldn't order an abort."

"Abort!" Connover snapped. "That's fine. That's great. They abort the mission and we go back home and for the rest of my life I'll know that it was my fault we didn't get to Mars. Goddamned paper-pushers. And they think *I'm* crazy!"

Taki burst into a delighted laugh. "You're right, Ted. They're the crazy ones."

"Damned straight."

"No abort," said Taki.

"It's too late to abort, anyway," Connover said, almost to himself. "We're past the ninety-day mark. If they ordered an abort now we'd have to go all the way to Mars anyway, swing around the planet, and come home. Might as well land and carry out the mission."

"Might as well," Taki agreed.

Connover nodded enthusiastically.

More softly, she said, "I'd trust you with my life, Ted. I hope you know that."

His face, his whole body relaxed. "I know it. But thanks for reminding me. I appreciate it."

"The whole crew is with you, Ted."

"I wonder if Bee would obey an abort order," Connover mused. "Probably would. He's too straight-laced to tell 'em to go to hell."

"Would you?"

"If I were in Bee's place? Yep, I'd tell them where to stuff it."

"I don't think I'll put that in my report."

"Put it in. What're they going to do, fire me?"

Nomura smiled at him. "Okay, Ted. I'll make my report to the chief of the psych team. Suitably edited."

"Whichever," Connover said, getting up from the tiny chair. "Thanks, Taki."

"Just doing my job," she said. But once Connover had ducked through the narrow hatchway, Taki started to wonder if the big boys back at Johnson would accept her report or override it.

Suddenly the ship lurched. Taki rocked sideways in her chair and the alarm klaxon began to howl.

Collision

Not unlike the collision between the massive eighteen-wheeler and the lightweight, energy-efficient car that had killed Ted Connover's family, the collision between the tiny rock and the massive *Arrow* was governed by the laws of motion that had been established when the universe began, nearly fourteen billion years ago.

If the rock were stationary, then it wouldn't look all that intimidating. Measuring only a little more than a foot in diameter, on Earth a person could have picked it up and moved it easily. But it wasn't stationary. It was moving at more than thirty miles per second relative to the *Arrow*.

After swinging through the inner solar system for nearly fifteen million years, the rock finally encountered another sizeable body. It struck the *Arrow* along its latticework spine, nearly severing the beam that kept the primary modules of the spacecraft together and functioning. Chunks of debris, mostly aluminum alloy crosspieces that made up that part of the beam, sprayed outward from the point of impact and plowed into the habitat module where the crew lived. Tens of tiny holes perforated the thin skin of the inflated section of the habitat, immediately causing a pressure drop inside. Other shards penetrated the thin aluminum skin of the crew's sleeping area, piercing the walls and allowing the precious water in the radiation shield to spray out into space. Still other fragments impacted the ship's propellant tanks and propulsion system.

There was no explosion visible from the outside. An external observer would have seen the ship suddenly shudder and then expel a spray of fragments that collided with the other, intact portions of the ship. The rock was also fragmented: each of several dozen splinters went whirling into new trajectories around the Sun, likely to orbit peacefully for more millions of years.

Inside the ship it was like an earthquake. In less than a second, the crew went from a pleasant one-third gravity to being thrown around like rag dolls. The full-spectrum lights went out; a heartbeat later the emergency lights penetrated the darkness, but feebly, dimly.

The shirtsleeve environment, with its constant gentle hum of air circulators, abruptly changed into a frenzied rush of air escaping into space through the many holes torn in the habitat module's skin. The boring sameness of day-to-day routine instantly gave way to chaos and near-panic as the little self-contained ecosystem that was the *Arrow* instantly changed into a death trap.

Chaos. There was no other word to describe the scene playing out before Benson's eyes. A moment ago he had been sitting at his post in the command center, talking with Virginia Gonzalez about her research work on laser communications. Now he was trying to figure out what the hell had happened as he struggled to regain his orientation in the near-darkness and chaos enveloping the *Arrow* and her crew.

Through the open hatch he could hear shouts of confusion and fear. And that damned klaxon was beeping away maddeningly.

Thanks to years of training, Benson reflexively reached for the control panel and banged the button that turned off the wailing klaxon. *Everybody knows we're in trouble,* he told himself. *Mission Control knows it, too; or at least they will in another few seconds.*

The first order of business when air is leaking from the ship is to put on the emergency air masks and survive long enough to figure out what's happened and how to deal with it.

Gonzalez was staring at Benson like the proverbial deer caught in the headlights, clutching the edges of the chair she was sitting in, frozen with sudden terror.

Okay, Benson said to himself, *they made you the commander; now command.*

"Get your air mask on! Now! Feel that wind? The air's blowing out of the ship. If you don't move you'll be dead. Go!"

133

Gonzalez blinked and stirred herself. She rushed to the wall panel that held the masks. She wasn't alone. From wherever they had been at the moment of impact, the entire crew reacted as they'd been trained and grabbed for the masks that were stowed in each section of the habitat module.

Benson moved too. He knew that he only had minutes to pull a mask from its locker and slip it over his head. Not designed for EVA in space or on Mars, the emergency masks were simply face-covering protectors with small air bottles designed to be worn during an emergency such as this. They had enough air to keep a person alive for about two hours in a low-pressure environment. Long enough to find and repair all but the most serious of hull breaches. But the masks had none of the self-contained pressurization and heating/cooling systems of the full EVA spacesuits.

As Benson tightened the straps of his mask his mind was racing. What happened? Either they hit something or something blew up. Whichever, it was bad. The ship was losing air and the status board was lit up like a Christmas tree: some green, too much red.

Slapping the intercom button, he called, "Emergency Comm. By the numbers, sound off!"

"Connover, in the galley." Ted's voice sounded strong, firm.

"McPherson, in the geology lab."

Clermont added, "Catherine also."

One by one the entire crew reported that they were alive and wearing the emergency masks. All but Prokhorov.

"Where's Mikhail?" Benson asked, as the crew crowded into the control center. With their air masks on, he couldn't see if they looked shocked or frightened. But they were all wearing their masks. Nobody seemed to know where the Russian was.

"Taki. Catherine. Go find Mikhail. Take a mask and get it on him. I don't know how much atmosphere is left, we need to get him some air, wherever he is. Go."

Nomura and Clermont went through the hatch. Benson was clearly in reaction mode as he directed the crew toward what it would take to survive.

"Ted, you and Hi get the patch kit and find the breach. Given the rate we're losing air, it's not going to be small. And there might be more than one."

Turning to Gonzalez, "Virginia, get on the comm and make sure we can still call home. Double check the telemetry stream and see if the smart guys can tell us what the hell happened out here.

"Amanda, I need you to secure whatever's not buttoned down and to note any and all damage you see while you're doing it. Come back as soon as you can and give me a report."

Clermont appeared at the hatch. "We found Mikhail. He was in the lav and whatever happened knocked him off his feet and he hit his head on the bulkhead. He was unconscious, but he's coming around now. Taki is looking after him."

"Thanks, Catherine," said Benson. "Let me know more once Taki's had a chance to check him out."

With a wisp of a smile, Catherine added, "It was quite a struggle to pull up his pants."

A few giggles. Benson grinned. *They can still laugh. That's good,* he thought.

One by one the crew left the command center to check on damage and report back to Benson. Once alone, he turned to the status board to see what kind of shape the ship was in and what their chances of surviving the next few hours might be.

It didn't look good. Benson already knew that something really bad had happened, but he didn't fully appreciate the extent of the damage until he surveyed the panel lights in front of him. Scarcely a system warning light remained unlit.

Depressurization. He didn't need the status board to tell him that. *How fast are we losing air? How much time do we have before we'll have to get into the EVA suits to survive? And how long can we live in the suits?* Ten hours, twelve at best, he knew.

Water was leaking from the radiation shield that protected the habitat. Not an immediate life-threatening problem, but one that would have to be fixed. Quickly.

Backup communications antenna offline. Again, not an immediate problem, as long as the primary antenna was functioning.

Power generation down by forty-five percent. That means something's damaged the solar panels, Benson realized. The ship needed those solar arrays to power the life-support systems, the lights, the food freezers and the ship's heaters.

Spacecraft stabilization alert. Something was causing the ship to vibrate. He could feel it in his shoes, a slight shuddering, like a man trembling from the cold. Or from fear. If the display screen's graph was accurate, the vibration was slowly increasing as the ship rotated to produce artificial gravity. Left unchecked, the vibrations were going to get worse, Benson figured.

That could put more stress on the main truss than it's designed to handle. We could break apart! Have to deal with that as soon as we can.

With relief, he saw that the nuclear reactor and propulsion system were offline as they were supposed to be. No alerts showing radioactive leakage from the fission reactor. The status lights for the reactor and propulsion system were all green, except one. One of the hydrogen propellant tanks was showing yellow. Either the Integrated Vehicle Health Monitoring systems, IVHM, had detected a disturbance and was running a self-diagnostic, or there was a slow hydrogen leak, too small to warrant a full-blown warning, but enough of a concern to call for continued monitoring. Considering the immediate issues facing them, Benson decided that a yellow alert would just have to wait.

The ship jolted again, hard enough to slam Benson into the forward panel. He heard yelps and curses from down the passageway. As he steadied himself, his heart sank: the light on the propellant management monitor went from yellow to red. *We're leaking propellant. That's bad.*

"Bee, you've got to see this," Connover shouted over the open intercom. "Hi and I found the source of the air leak and we're trying to patch it, but that last bump knocked us around before we could get started."

Connover sounded excited, but in a good, controlled way. To Benson, Ted sounded eager, almost happy to have something vital to do.

"We looked out the aft window at the solar arrays and the boom," the astronaut went on, "or what's left of it. The truss is broken in several places and unless we do something soon it's not going to stay in one piece."

There was no trace of fear in Connover's voice. He'd found a problem, now the job was to solve it.

For a moment, Benson considered going down to the aft window to see the damage for himself. But only for a moment.

Instead he spoke into the intercom microphone, "Virginia, do you have Mission Control on the line? If so, patch me in. I need to talk to them ASAP about the boom."

"Got 'em. Coming right up. You're on."

"Houston, we've had a major event here," Benson said. "Probably a collision; I don't see anything telling me there's been an onboard explosion. I know you're getting telemetry so please tell me if I've got it wrong." Without waiting for a response he went on, "Whatever hit us damaged the truss connecting the hab module to the rest of the ship. It may be about to snap. If that happens we'll go flying off in one direction while the rest of the ship, including the propulsion system, goes off in another. I think we need to stop the rotation to take the stress off the truss and buy us some time so we can go EVA and see about reinforcing the damaged section. What do you think?"

One thousand, two thousand, three thousand, four thousand . . . The interminable time delay irked Benson terribly.

"*Arrow*, we copy." Benson didn't recognize the voice. One of the techs who manned the comm board on what was supposed to have been another boringly routine day. "We're pulling in every support team in the place. They're looking at the telemetry. I'll hand your message to the structures team ASAP and get you an answer. Might take a few minutes, though."

"Houston, we don't have a few minutes. I need to know now whether despinning us or keeping the spin as is will be the least stress on the boom. Right now we still have spin and artificial gravity, but we're wobbling all over the place."

One thousand, two thousand, three thousand, four thousand . . .

A different, deeper and more authoritative voice answered, "Commander Benson, we can't have a definitive answer for you until we've taken the telemetry and run it through the simulations, maybe even building some new finite element models of the damaged boom. Can you take some pictures of it so we can see where it's broken?"

The ship quivered again. The emergency lights flickered and almost went out.

"Houston, we don't have time for models and simulations! I need someone there, someone with the goddamned experience to tell me what their intuition says and I need it now!"

One thousand, two thousand, three thousand,. four thousand . . .

"We hear you, sir, but we don't have that person in the center right now. It's going to take some time."

"We can't wait. I'm going to tell Ted to slow our rotation rate and see if we can't some stress off the truss."

One thousand, two thousand, three thousand, four thousand . . .

"That's your call, Commander. You're there and we aren't. Do you know you've got a propellant leak?"

"I'll worry about that later. Virginia, keep them on the line."

"Will do, Bee."

JULY 21, 2035
EARTH DEPARTURE PLUS 107 DAYS
17:53 UNIVERSAL TIME
JOHNSON SPACE CENTER, HOUSTON, TEXAS

Nathan Brice was having an early lunch in JSC's spacious cafeteria, enjoying a quiet few moments alone, away from the bustle and tension of the control center. Even on a routine, quiet day there were always people clamoring for his attention, decisions to make, emotions to deal with. He was fastidiously tucking his napkin into his shirt collar when a breathless technician from the Mission Control center raced up to his table.

"They've been hit by something!" the young man blurted.

Brice shot to his feet. "*Arrow*?"

"Yessir. Prob'ly a meteoroid."

Rushing toward the exit, napkin fluttering under his chin, Brice asked, "How bad's the damage?"

"It looks pretty bad. Don't know the full extent yet."

His open jacket flapping as he ran for his car, Brice called to the youngster, "Get everybody you can find! Roust them all, wherever they are! The whole team."

"I will!"

The car was like an oven after just half an hour in the Texas sun. Brice revved the engine and punched the air conditioner on full blast, then peeled out of the parking lot and headed for the Mission Control building.

His mind raced. *What could possibly hit them way out there? It had to be a meteor. Of all the mother-loving, good-for-nothing, goddamned shit-faced things that can happen, out in the middle of nowhere, they've hit something.*

Raising his eyes to heaven as he hunched over the steering wheel, Brice muttered, "Thanks again, God. First you nearly let the propellant mission go bad, then you killed Connover's family. What's next, a plague?"

By the time he swept into the Mission Control center, Brice had vented his rage and seemed to the harried engineers and technicians to be cool and very much in command. Each of the lead engineers huddled around him as he slid into the chair of his console. In three minutes he had a good picture of what had happened to the *Arrow*.

"Get Benson onscreen for me," he said into the Bluetooth as he clipped it over his ear.

It took a few seconds, but at last Bee's image took shape on his console's center screen. Even through the clear plastic air mask that Benson was wearing he looked drawn, hard-eyed, his lips pressed into a thin line.

"What's your status, Bee?" asked Brice.

Then he waited for the reply.

At last Benson snapped, "That's what we'd like to know."

"Status?" he repeated calmly.

Again the wait.

Then, "Air leaking. Propellant leaking. Our main problem is that the truss is damaged and our spinning is putting too much stress on it. It could snap."

"Despin," said Brice immediately. No simulations, no model analyses. Just the one word.

When Benson replied, his lips had curved slightly into a tight little smile.

"Thanks, Nate. That's what I thought we should do."

"Good. Take it all the way down to zero. You'll have to put up with microgravity until we get the situation analyzed and come up with a fix."

This time Benson's smile was broader. "Right. By the way, do you know you've got a napkin stuck under your chin?"

Senator William Donaldson was lunching in the Senate dining room on she-crab soup. To his Massachusetts constituents he professed a preference for New England-style clam chowder. But this Carolina dish was his real favorite.

Sitting across the table from him was Professor Oliver Jansen, chief of MIT's robotics laboratory.

"We could design robots to do anything those astronauts can do," Professor Jansen was saying, rather sullenly, Donaldson thought. Jansen was a round-faced man with longish dark hair and the largest hands Donaldson had ever seen.

"Do you mean on the space station or on the Moon?" asked the senator, between spoonfuls.

"Either one. And that includes the people heading for Mars, as well. Robots could do whatever they can do, and at a fraction of the cost."

"You actually have robots that can do whatever a human being can do?"

The professor blinked. Once. Twice. "We'll have them, once we get the funding we need for development."

Donaldson eyed the professor warily. "And how much would it cost to develop such robots?"

Jansen waved one of his large hands. "Less than a billion."

Which would go to MIT, Donaldson thought. *Quite a feather in my cap, steering a billion-dollar program to my state.*

His press secretary appeared at the dining room's entry, brushed past the venerable maitre d' and hurried to Donaldson's table.

The senator saw him approaching. *He looks excited,* Donaldson thought. Then he wondered idly why they were still called "press secretaries." The news media had moved into the digital age with alacrity. Newspapers were anachronisms now.

The young aide leaned over Donaldson's shoulder and announced, "Senator, there's apparently been an accident on the Mars ship!"

"What do you mean, apparently?"

Still standing, the press secretary explained, "I have a friend who works in Mission Control, in Houston. She phoned me just a few minutes ago. Very hush-hush, but they've run into trouble up there."

Senator Donaldson digested the news in a heartbeat. "Get to NASA's public relations chief for confirmation. Find out how serious the problem is."

"Right," said the aide. And he dashed off, past the maitre d', who frowned disapprovingly at the disturbance in his restaurant's normally placid atmosphere.

Professor Jansen was frowning too. "They could all get killed, couldn't they?"

"It's a possibility," Donaldson allowed. "They're a long way from home, a long way from help."

Shaking his head, the professor said, "If we'd sent robots we wouldn't have to worry about it."

Donaldson nodded agreement. But in his mind he was already shaping the speech he would make on the Senate floor, calling for an end to all human space flight, an end to risking the lives of our best and brightest young men and women.

Benson headed down the passageway from the command center toward the aft window where Connover and McPherson were feverishly working to patch a thumb-sized hole in the ship's skin. Fortunately, the ship's computer had detected the leak and already stopped trying to replenish the module with air from the reserve tanks, preventing the waste of precious air while the repairs were underway.

The goal now was to stop the leaks before air pressure got so low in the module that they'd have to don their EVA suits.

Benson nodded to the two men as he peered out the window at the barely illuminated aft section of the ship and the truss connecting them to it. The sunlight cast long shadows, making it difficult to distinguish the individual beams that made up the truss. But just below the solar panels Benson could see that several segments were gone and others were bent at least twenty degrees off their proper alignment.

That's why we're wobbling, he realized at once. *Unless we do something soon the other segments of the truss are going to break and we'll be lost.*

Nomura's voice broke into his thoughts. "Bee, this is Taki," she called over the intercom. "We're at risk of hypoxia from the decreasing pressure. We need to be on the lookout for the symptoms: light-headedness, confusion, fingers and toes tingling. If that starts to happen, I need to know about it."

"Did everybody copy that?" Benson said. "We've trained for this, but our bodies don't always know it. Keep aware of how you feel and let Taki know if you think you're starting to feel any of those symptoms."

Without listening to the crew's responses, Benson turned to Connover. "Ted, I need you to kill the ship's rotation. Get up front and get on it. Now. You'll need to slow us down gradually, don't make it a sudden stop. I'm not sure how much longer we'll stay together if we keep spinning. I'll help Hi finish the patching while you get to it."

"On my way," Connover handed the patch kit to Benson and started forward.

The ship shuddered again. Benson looked up and through the window he saw one of three remaining unbroken segments of truss snap, sending small pieces of debris sailing outward and away from the ship. The sunlight glinted from the debris as the pieces spun away, quickly becoming lost in the starry abyss of deep space.

That's what's going to happen to us, Benson thought, *if I've made the wrong call. If the stress produced by firing the cold gas thrusters to stop the spin snaps the last two of the truss' segments, we're cooked.*

He shook his head. This isn't the time for second-guessing. He glanced over at McPherson, who was busily slapping patches on the holes in the skin and sealing them with epoxy.

"Bee, I've got this just about finished." McPherson said. "If you need to be somewhere else, go to it."

"Right. Thanks." Benson handed McPherson the patch kit he was carrying and headed for the privacy cubicles, where Prokhorov was recovering from his head injury. *Before tackling the next shipboard crisis,* he told himself, *I ought to look after the health of the crew—at least briefly.*

Prokhorov was zippered into his sleep bag, his heavy-lidded eyes half open. His forehead looked as if he'd been hit with a crowbar, red and swollen, with an inflamed brownish spot forming just above his eyebrow. Taki Nomura was crouched over him, gently laying a wet compress across the injury.

"It's not as bad as it looks," Nomura said, looking up at Benson.

"Glad to hear it," he said. "You'd better give the medics back at Mission Control a report on his status as soon as you can leave his side."

"I'm all right," Prokhorov muttered thickly. "Just a little dizzy, that's all."

"You get some sleep now," Taki told the Russian. "You'll be fine."

Benson went with her as she headed along the passageway toward the infirmary. "I gave him a dose of painkillers. He'll sleep for several hours. When he wakes up, he'll have a lump on his head, but nothing worse."

"You x-rayed him?"

"Not yet. When he wakes up. I don't expect an x-ray of his head to show anything."

Benson almost laughed. "You mean his head's empty?"

"No," Taki replied, with a perfectly straight face. "Actually, it appears to be completely solid."

The ship shuddered again. Taki lurched into Benson, who reflexively wrapped his arms around her stubby form.

"That's probably Ted applying the brakes to stop our rotation," he explained to her.

Benson went to the intercom microphone on the passageway bulkhead. "Listen up, people. Ted's despinning the ship. We're going to be in microgravity for a while."

Maybe a long while, he added silently.

Another wobble, and then one heavy, prolonged lurch. Benson leaned against the bulkhead for support. After what seemed like an eternity, he felt himself drifting away from the bulkhead, his arms floating up toward chest level. For the first time since their trans-Mars injection burn, they were effectively weightless.

"Ted's stopped the rotation," he said into the intercom. "We're back in zero gee. Anything that's not tied down or Velcroed in place is going to be floating around."

Microgravity was not a welcome sensation. The crew had become accustomed to a pleasant one-third-gee, Benson included.

Benson felt his stomach rising up into his throat. His sinuses felt stuffy and everything went woozy when he turned his head. He knew that the rest of the crew was experiencing the same disconcerting sensations.

Free fall. The name said it all. Benson felt as if he were dropping from a great height, and there was no bottom to the chasm he was falling through. Like being on a roller coaster as it reached the top of its climb and started racing downslope at a dizzying speed, the feelings produced by free fall were exhilarating and nauseating at the same time. And it never stopped. It was only a matter of time before someone upchucked.

Not me, Benson resolved. *Especially not wearing this damned mask.*

JULY 21, 2035
EARTH DEPARTURE PLUS 107 DAYS
22:15 UNIVERSAL TIME
GALLEY, THE *ARROW*

Once the leaks had been repaired and normal atmospheric pressure restored to the habitation module, the crew used the safety belts of the galley seats to strap themselves down. They no longer needed their air masks.

They were slowly getting acclimatized to weightlessness again; only Hi McPherson had succumbed to space sickness, and that hadn't happened until he'd taken off his mask. Fortunately, Catherine Clermont had been close enough to pull out one of the sickness bags that had been stashed at convenient locations throughout the module and handed it to Hi just in time.

Even Mikhail Prokhorov joined them in the galley, sporting an egg-sized bluish lump on his forehead.

"Good thick Russian head," he joked weakly as he strapped himself down. Then he added, "I wish I had good thick Russian stomach, too. I feel full of butterflies."

Benson had considered standing to talk to them, as usual, but thought better of it. The sight of him hovering off the floor—or, worse still, floating across the galley—might start an unpleasant round of upchucking. The thought of the noise and smell almost made him heave.

So he remained strapped into his chair, all eyes on him, as he sketched out the ship's condition.

"It looks like we were hit by something, probably a meteoroid, not a large one, but big enough to nearly sever the central truss that connects us to the propulsion system and the propellant tankage. The shrapnel produced when the object struck peppered the ship and did a significant amount of damage."

He paused. They were all waiting for better news, he knew, but he had to tell them the truth, the whole truth, and nothing but the truth.

"The air leaks were minor, really, and they've been patched. To keep the ship from flying apart, Ted slowed our rotation to zero."

"And our gravity along with it," quipped Amanda Lynn.

Benson flashed a quick grin at her. "It's either zero gravity or the ship breaks apart. The truss seems to be holding together now, but it's back to zero-gee countermeasures for us from here on out."

"All the way to Mars?" Prokhorov asked.

"And back again," said Benson, mentally adding, *If we get that far.*

A few groans and mutters from the crew. Zero-gee counter-measures meant four hours a day of vigorous exercise on the treadmills and weight machines to keep muscle tone and bone mass from deteriorating.

"We've got a water leak in the main bladder," he went on. "It'll have to be patched before we lose too much. We've also got a propellant leak in one of the TEI tanks. That's going to be a bitch to repair. We're venting hydrogen at a rate that'll leave the tank empty; that means a one-way trip to Mars if we don't fix it soon. I've asked Mission Control for a repair plan; they're looking at the engineering telemetry and working it out. Somebody's going to have to go EVA to fix both leaks."

"At the same time?"

"Hopefully. We don't have much time to spare."

Benson tried to read the expressions on their faces as they stared at him, waiting for him to continue. He saw fear, but not panic. They had problems to solve and they looked to Bee to lead them to the solutions.

Jabbing a finger at Nomura, he said, "Taki, you'll need to get two of us ready to go outside in the next couple of hours. It's going to be Amanda and me. We've all trained for EVA and I need the rest of you at your stations keeping up with what the ship's doing while we're outside."

Connover's brows knit. "Bee, no offense to Amanda, but I'm the best one to go out with you for this."

"I'm sure Amanda won't take offense and you shouldn't either. I need you inside to handle any emergencies that might pop up. We don't know what other systems might have taken a hit and we can't afford to have both of us outside if something comes up."

Before Connover could object, Benson added, "Besides, mission regs say that both astronauts should not go EVA at the same time unless it's absolutely unavoidable."

Amanda Lynn glanced at Connover, then turned back to Benson. "Hey, I'll do my best," she said, in a tone that was half-assurance, half defensive.

"I know you will, Amanda," Benson said. "That's why I want you out there with me." Looking at Gonzalez, he went on, "We've also lost our backup communications antenna. Virginia, I'm leaving that problem to you. I expect some ideas from you once we've fixed these more pressing problems. Any questions?"

Prokhorov raised his hand.

"Mikhail?"

"Once you fix the leaks, are we turning around for home? I'm no hero. It's time to go home."

Benson had expected that question to come up, sooner or later. They all knew the answer, or they should have known it. But it was the mission commander's responsibility to confirm the bad news.

"We can't turn around now. We don't have enough fuel. If this had happened two weeks ago we could have done it, but we're past the point of no return now. We've got to coast on out to Mars and let the planet's gravity turn us."

"You mean we're going ahead with the mission?" McPherson asked. He seemed actually happy at the prospect.

"That, I don't know, Hi. We'll have to dip into Mars' atmosphere and aerobrake into orbit. Whether we go down to the surface or head back to Earth immediately depends on a lot of factors that we just don't have enough information to decide on as yet."

Catherine Clermont murmured, "We just have to stay alive."

Benson nodded. "Right. Our first priority is to stay alive. That's why we need to get moving on those repairs. We also need to make sure there isn't anything else about to go wrong before we have a chance to batten down the hatches. Any more questions?"

The seven of them looked around at each other. No one spoke.

"All right, then. Amanda, you and I get together with Taki for EVA prep. The rest of you get to your stations."

Standing in the mockup of the *Arrow*, Steven Treadway put on his most somber expression as the director pointed his finger at him.

"This is Steven Treadway, reporting to you from our studio in New York. The news from space is grim this evening. The Mars-bound spacecraft *Arrow* has been hit and severely damaged by an errant meteoroid, a tiny piece of rock that has put the lives of the eight men and women aboard that ship in grave peril."

Treadway walked toward the wall of the habitat and, at least as it appeared to the viewers, walked right through it and into deep space. For Treadway, the walk was simply toward an opening in the side of the mockup; the special-effects wizards were taking care of the rest. Viewers now saw Treadway walking beside the *Arrow*'s badly mangled truss, viewing an image enhanced from one originally taken by a hand-held camera pointed through the aft window of the spacecraft's habitation module.

"Normally, as the *Arrow*'s embedded reporter, I would be with the crew through our virtual reality link. But at this moment, I'm keeping my presence low-key, while the spacecraft's valiant crew struggles to repair the damage to their ship."

CGI animation then showed a rock striking the *Arrow*'s central truss, with debris flying everywhere, seeming to fly right through the reporter standing beside the ship. A soundtrack added a crunching noise—a feat of imagination, since sound cannot be propagated in the vacuum of space.

Treadway allowed himself a tight smile. "Fortunately, only one member of the crew was hurt from the collision, and that was a minimal injury. Mikhail Prokhorov, the Russian meteorologist, suffered a blow to his head when the meteoroid struck, but he is mostly recovered now."

The screen went back to the view of the damaged truss.

"The condition of the ship is uncertain," Treadway went on. "The central truss connecting the crew's habitat to the nuclear propulsion system took the brunt of the meteoroid strike, and has been nearly severed. From the reports we've received, if the crew hadn't quickly stopped the ship's rotation, the *Arrow* might have broken apart and the crew would have been stranded halfway between Earth and Mars. We're told the ship is leaking water and fuel, and there might be damage to other systems that has not yet been fully assessed."

The screen showed an old video clip of an astronaut getting into an EVA suit, assisted by a trio of technicians.

"Mission commander Bee Benson and biologist Amanda Lynn are now preparing to go outside in their spacesuits to fully assess the damage and try to repair the water and fuel leaks. This will be the first time humans have performed an EVA so far from home."

The camera tightening on Treadway's dead-serious face, he said, "Even though the *Arrow* is still speeding toward Mars at several thousand miles per hour, Benson and Lynn will appear motionless as they exit the relative safety of the ship, since they are traveling at the same velocity. For safety reasons, they won't be allowed to use the new Space Maneuvering Units, or SMUs, that are so commonly used during spacewalks at several of Earth's orbiting space stations. Mission Control is insisting that they remain tethered to the vehicle at all times, just in case something happens during the EVA and they have to be pulled back inside the ship. Not using the SMUs also gives them an additional four hours they can spend outside the ship. The SMUs themselves are rather large, limiting the size of the astronauts' oxygen tanks to providing them with only a two-hour supply.

"To prepare for this crucial spacewalk, Benson and Lynn are now wearing respirators and pre-breathing pure oxygen. Due to the critical nature of their spacewalk, they are not going through the customary twenty-four-hour preparation for EVA that has been standard astronaut protocol since the days of the Apollo program.

"Instead, Benson and Lynn are going through an abbreviated protocol that will allow them to go outside the ship in less than three hours."

The screen showed a clip of two astronauts working in spacesuits outside a space station in Earth orbit.

Treadway continued, "Going from the pressurized cabin of the *Arrow* to the vacuum of space is not as simple as putting on a spacesuit and opening a hatch. Without pre-breathing low-pressure oxygen and taking the proper precautions, the astronauts could succumb to the bends and even die. First observed in deep-sea divers, the bends is caused when the human body goes from normal air pressure to the much lower pressure of a diving suit or a spacesuit. Nitrogen bubbles form in the bloodstream, causing severe pain, debilitation and even death. Fortunately the crew is trained in how to prevent this, and they're taking those steps now."

Turning partway toward the big wall screen, so that he stood in profile against the image of the battered *Arrow*, Treadway said fervently, "Good luck, Commander Benson and Amanda Lynn. Good luck to all of the crippled *Arrow*'s gallant crew."

He turned back to face the TV camera for a closeup. "Steven Treadway reporting."

JULY 22, 2035
EARTH DEPARTURE PLUS 108 DAYS
03:40 UNIVERSAL TIME
EXTRAVEHICULAR ACTIVITY, THE *ARROW*

Like most space missions, the *Arrow* ran on Universal Time, so it was already past three A.M. on July 22 when Benson and Lynn emerged from the main airlock, trailing long flexible tethers.

Bee yawned inside his bubble helmet, thinking, *Maybe we should have waited and got a night's sleep before doing this.* Then he immediately answered himself, *Right. Like you could sleep.*

As he moved carefully hand-over-hand across the grips that studded *Arrow*'s exterior, Benson surveyed the damage the ship had suffered. The ship's exterior lights illuminated its massive frame and modules clearly.

Benson could see a fine mist of water leaking from the bladder just under the habitat's outer skin. He had no way of knowing how much water had already been lost, but losing any of the precious stuff was losing too much.

Hydrogen propellant was leaking from the Trans-Earth Injection tanks, propellant they would need when the time came to break free of Mars' orbit and start the journey back to Earth. The TEI tanks were nearly three hundred feet from where he hovered, tethered to one of the handgrips, on the other side of the propellant tanks they would use to enter Mars orbit. Between Benson and the TEI tanks was the mangled section of the main truss.

"What a mess," he muttered.

Amanda, hovering on her own tether a dozen feet from him,

said in an awed voice, "The impact shattered the truss almost completely."

"And some of the debris must've arced over and hit the water bladder and TEI tanks."

"So what do you want me to do?" she asked.

"First things first," he said. "Follow me."

Carefully keeping his tether from snagging on any of the damaged truss sections, Benson crept hand-over-hand toward the water leak. Lynn followed close behind him. He could hear her breathing hard from the exertion.

He was already sweating inside the EVA suit.

"How're you doing, Amanda?"

"Okay. Fine. I guess."

He knew that although Amanda was a biologist and not an astronaut, she had been cross-trained for EVA work, just like the rest of the crew. She had done several spacewalks on the International Space Station.

She'll be fine, he told himself. Still, he kept one eye on her. *Don't want to lose her, or get her hurt.*

At last he reached the spot where the water was leaking. The hole wasn't particularly large, but the water was spraying out like a fountain. The plume rose into the blackness of space, rather than the blue sky of Earth, water droplets immediately condensing into ice pellets and forming a contrail the swept outward as far as his eyes could see. Not good.

"Amanda, we need to stop the leak without letting the ice crystals cover our suits or, more importantly, our helmets. The last thing we can afford is to go blind out here."

"How much water do you think we've already lost, Bee?"

"Hard to say. Too much, whatever it is. We'll probably have to ration water for the rest of the trip, even if we can stop the leak now. So let's get to it."

Patching the water leak was surprisingly easy. Benson was able to position himself on the side opposite from the spray of spewing ice crystals. Gripping the patch carefully in his gloves, he pushed it directly into the stream. For a moment he was afraid that he'd misjudged and deflected the plume onto Amanda, but he got the hole covered and she smeared epoxy generously around the edges of the patch.

Smiling to himself, Benson remembered that the epoxy set much better in the vacuum of space than in air.

"That does it," he said.

"Less than an hour," Ted Connover's voice sounded in his helmet earphones. "Good work, Bee."

"Thanks. Taki—we're going aft to take a look at the propellant leak. How're our vitals?"

Nomura, inside the infirmary studying the readouts from their suit sensors, replied, "Vital signs all in the normal range, except for overheating a bit. Turn up your suit fans, Bee. You too, Amanda."

Benson tapped the key on his wristpad and heard the fans whine a little higher.

"You've got a little more than five hours of oxygen supply," Nomura went on. "You're good to go."

"Okay," said Benson. "Amanda, you ready?"

"Ready."

He looked aft along the handholds that ran down the truss toward the massive propellant tanks. The TMI tanks looked intact. No apparent damage. *We'll have the propellant we need to go into orbit around Mars*, Benson knew. *Good.*

But the TEI tanks were leaking, too, even though he could not see an obvious plume spouting from them. The ship's sensors reported they were losing propellant. *Could the sensors be wrong?* Benson wondered. *Maybe the impact of the collision knocked them off.*

Too good to be true, he thought. *We'll have to go down there and see what's what. If we've lost as much as the sensors say, we might not have enough for the Trans-Earth Injection burn. We'll be stranded at Mars.*

Pushing those fears to the back of his mind, Benson looked at the mangled mess of broken crosspieces and twisted aluminum struts where the collision had occurred. Of the twelve crosspieces, only two remained undamaged. Furthermore, only two were holding the ship together.

"Ted," he called, "we'll have to do something to strengthen the damaged section of the truss. Otherwise, the stress when we ignite the nuclear rocket for the Mars capture burn will probably make them buckle and break."

"Don't want that," said Connover.

"Amen."

"I'll ask the bright boys back home to give us some ideas," Connover said. "Uh, Bee, I just got a batch of bad news. Mission Control has studied the telemetry and they say we've lost a lot of propellant. A lot. Their calculations say that if the leak isn't patched in the next seven to eight hours we won't have enough H_2 to get home. The LAD isn't working well and they say we might already have passed that point. They're also worried about the water leak. It was huge."

Benson frowned. The Liquid Acquisition Device—LAD in NASA's infinite jungle of acronyms—was the sensor in the propellant tankage that monitored the amount of liquid hydrogen remaining in the tank. Benson knew LAD readings could be off by as much as ten percent in zero-gee, but from the sound of Connover's voice, the situation was even more serious.

"We'd better get down there, then, and patch the leak," he said.

"Bee, should Hi and I get ready to come out in case you can't fix it in time? It'll take us three hours to pre-breathe pure oxy."

"Right. Get started. We might need some extra hands out here."

JULY 22, 2035
04:14 UNIVERSAL TIME
EARTH DEPARTURE PLUS 108 DAYS
THE WHITE HOUSE

"Ladies and gentlemen, the President of the United States."

For this special briefing to the news media, the reporters and commentators had been assembled in the classically decorated East Room, which was large enough to hold them all, plus the dozens of photographers, bloggers, and camera crews. Though a few of the participants were wearing VR equipment, they still hadn't been able to convince the White House to allow them to physically interact with the president during one of these events, an engagement that would undoubtedly raise viewership by orders of magnitude for the organization that was able to pull it off.

They all got to their feet as President Harper strode in, wearing a dark blue business suit and carefully knotted gold tie, which complemented the gold and white decór of the venerable room.

His podium had been set up beneath Gilbert Stuart's full-length portrait of George Washington, which had been saved from destruction by Dolley Madison when the British army burned the Executive Mansion during the War of 1812.

Harper felt bone weary, physically and emotionally exhausted by this long day's news from the Mars mission. But he glanced up at the painting and reminded himself that this house had seen its share of excruciatingly difficult times.

Turning a weary smile to the newspeople, he motioned for them to be seated.

"First, I want to thank you all for coming out so late in the evening. I had considered holding this briefing tomorrow morning, but the American public—and the world—shouldn't have to wait all night to learn what's happened to the *Arrow* and her crew."

Harper went through a succinct description of the accident that had struck the Mars-bound spacecraft: the collision, the damage to the ship, the crew's reaction.

"I've got to say," he concluded, "that Commander Benson and all his crew have come through this very difficult and demanding experience with flying colors. There was only one injury, a slight bump on the head, to the ship's meteorologist, Mikhail Prokhorov."

Several dozen hands shot into the air and the room filled with urgent cries of "Mr. President! Mr. President!"

Harper hesitated as he noticed his wife standing at the rear of the room with Ilona Klein, his news media chief. He nodded to his wife as he called on the reporter from *Space Live!*, hoping that it would be a softball. It wasn't.

From his seat in the front row, *Space Live!* reporter Adrienne Anderson asked the most important question of them all. "Will the crew survive this accident?"

"They've survived so far," Harper replied. "Their life-support equipment is undamaged and their morale is excellent."

"But it's been reported that one or more of their fuel tanks has been punctured. Will they be able to continue the mission?"

Harper said tightly, "We intend to."

Without waiting to be called on, Fox News' Gloria Miller—bright, blonde and brassy—asked, "Will they have sufficient propellant to go all the way to Mars and back?"

"They're coasting to Mars right now, so they won't use any propellant until they have to go into orbit around the planet."

The next dozen questions all harped on the propellant issue. President Harper temporized by telling them that the top experts at NASA were working on the problems raised by the propellant leakage.

At last a lean, lanky, potbellied younger man got to his feet. "Len Eames, the *Science Daily Show*. I'm sure you're aware that Senator Donaldson has called for an end to all manned space missions. Doesn't this accident prove his point, that it's too risky to send humans into space?"

Harper had been waiting for that one. His jaw set and his eyes focused on the nearest TV camera, he answered, "It was risky to cross the Mississippi and settle the west. It was risky to first fly airplanes. It was risky to go to the Moon. But brave men and women took those risks and we're all better off for it."

"Yes," Eames said, "but Senator Donaldson intends to bring his proposition before the Senate Subcommittee on Space. What's your reaction to that, sir?"

Bristling, President Harper replied, "There will be no cutting of the manned space program while I'm President of the United States."

But he knew that he was already a lame duck, with little more than eighteen months to remain in office.

JULY 22, 2035
EARTH DEPARTURE PLUS 108 DAYS
04:20 UNIVERSAL TIME
EXTRAVEHICULAR ACTIVITY, THE *ARROW*

As Benson and Lynn worked their way cautiously across the damaged section of truss and headed toward the leaking propellant tank, Virginia Gonzalez's voice sounded in their headphones.

"Bee, the video feed from your helmet is crystal clear, but the feed from Amanda's has a lot of static. Her audio is fine, so whatever's causing the problem seems to be limited to video only."

Benson puffed out a breath. He knew that if this were an ordinary spacewalk—as if any spacewalk was ordinary—then the flight rules would require that Amanda return to the airlock and end her EVA as quickly as possible. The camera feed was considered mission critical, for safety reasons. The rules were quite clear.

But this wasn't an ordinary spacewalk.

"Noted," he said to Gonzalez. "Amanda will stay with me unless something else goes off nominal. I need her help."

"Copy that."

"How're Ted and Hi doing?"

He could sense Virginia's shrug. "They're down at the main airlock, pre-breathing oxygen and getting into their EVA suits."

"Right," said Benson.

Only then did he look across toward Amanda to see if his decision was okay with her. He felt grimly pleased when she gave him a silent "thumbs up."

"Okay, kid," he said to her. "We've got a propellant leak to fix."

"Let's do it," Amanda said.

"Right." He turned back to face the mangled truss. "Now we have to figure out how to get across the damaged area and down to the aft tank so we can figure out how to patch the damned thing."

"Okay."

"We've got to cross over the damage using what's left of the handholds, and without snagging our suits on the broken spars. Then we have to make sure our tethers reach across without getting caught or cut. Sharp edges and spacesuits just don't get along."

"Bee, I'm with you. Let's get closer and figure out how to get across."

Benson nodded, straightened himself out as best he could, then turned himself to face the damaged truss.

Make certain nothing has changed, he said to himself as he looked hard at the broken and twisted spars.

Satisfied that it hadn't, he began to pull himself hand-over-hand toward the aft section of the ship—and the mangled area of the truss. Amanda followed closely behind him, mimicking his slow, careful moves.

It took about ten minutes to reach the damaged section. It looked much worse close up than it had from the habitation module's aft window. Part of the truss was simply missing, blasted out into deep space along with the fragments of whatever had hit them. About six feet of the truss was damaged, including two feet that was just empty space and two intact spars. They were all that was holding the ship's modules and tankage together.

The top and bottom edges of the broken truss segment were a tangled mess of fractured and bent spars, their broken ends razor sharp. To Benson they looked like twisted, angry claws; any one of them could rip a pressure suit open and kill the person wearing it.

"We've got to get across this mess," he told Amanda.

She said nothing.

Turning weightlessly to face her, Benson said, "I'll go across first. You watch me. Once I'm across, you follow me."

"Okay." Amanda's voice sounded shaky to him.

"If I don't make it," he said, "you go back inside. Let Ted and Hi come out. Don't you try this on your own."

"Don't worry, I won't."

"Right."

Feeling like a beached whale struggling to get back in the water, Benson pulled himself slowly across the shattered section of truss, splaying his legs outward from his torso so he could move above those reaching sharp claws, imagining himself to be a tightrope walker working upside-down, crossing the rope hand-over-hand. He wasn't aware that he was holding his breath until he'd crossed to the other side and allowed himself to exhale a long, relieved sigh.

To Amanda he called, "If you can keep your legs outstretched and go hand-over-hand like I did, you should be fine."

"Sure," she said.

It didn't look to him that Amanda needed any advice. He watched as she swung into a handstand and began making her way, carefully but smoothly, across the damaged area toward him. She looked much more graceful than he thought it was possible to be inside the stiffly cumbersome suit. *Like a ballet dancer in zero gravity.*

Once she'd made it across, he could see her bright smile of satisfaction through the faceplate of her helmet.

"You were saying?" she quipped.

With a grin of his own, Benson replied, "I was saying that we'll have that leak patched in no time."

"That's what I thought you said."

Ahead of them, the truss stretched past the presumably undamaged tanks that held the propellant they'd need to enter Mars orbit, the big oblong radiators that bled off the excessive heat generated by the nuclear reactor, the ungainly cargo module that contained the Mars lander, and then the leaking Trans-Earth Injection tanks.

"The tanks are farther away than our tethers can reach," Benson told Amanda. "They're not long enough to reach the TEI tanks. None of the designers thought we'd have to go on a tethered EVA farther than the lander. They didn't think we'd have to do this at all and, if we did, that we'd use the SMUs to get here and back quickly."

"We'll have to get to the tanks untethered?" she asked.

Benson said, "It's just a few meters." But he was clearly unhappy at the prospect of giving up the safety tethers.

Amanda nodded, her movement barely noticeable inside her helmet. Simple gestures were lost to astronauts in spacesuits. The bulky suits hid small body movements.

Benson and Lynn made their way slowly along the truss, stopping finally at the huge storage module that housed the lander. Benson was still awed by its size. The lander inside it was designed to leave the *Arrow* once it had attained a stable orbit around Mars, then fly through the planet's thin atmosphere and land on the surface. After spending thirty days on the surface, it would boost them back to the *Arrow*, waiting for them in orbit.

"It's a shame we came all this way and we probably won't get to land on the surface," Amanda said, wistfully.

"It'll be more of a shame if we come all this way and don't get to go home," Benson said. "We'll take time to mourn for what might have been after we make sure we fix what has to be."

He jabbed a gloved finger at the last handhold on the skin of the cargo container, at the side of the module's hatch. The designers had not bothered to place handholds any farther aft.

Their destination was less than thirty feet away, but without being tethered, and without handholds, it looked more like thirty miles.

Benson hesitated, knowing what he had to do but wondering if he and Amanda could do it.

How long have we been outside? he asked himself. He thought of asking Gonzalez, at the comm console, about their timeline, but decided against it. *Don't want them to think I'm worried*, he said to himself.

He knew Ted and Hi would be able to come out in another hour or so, if needed. Benson resolved that he and Amanda would finish the repair task. He hoped. The backup team won't be needed. He hoped.

Benson blinked sweat out of his eyes as he and Amanda inched along aftward until the looming shapes of the TEI tanks filled their horizon.

No warnings from Taki, he told himself. *I guess our vital signs are all okay.*

Still, he asked Lynn, "How're you doing, Amanda?"

She puffed out a breath before answering, "Okay. Just following you on down the yellow brick road."

If she can make a joke she must be all right.

The leak was clearly visible, just as the leak from the water bladder had been, but in a different way. There was no spray of ice grains to betray its position. The liquid hydrogen in the tank expanded into gas as it spurted from the tear in the tank's skin, and hydrogen is colorless.

But Benson could see that a piece of the forward truss structure was embedded in the smooth skin of the tank, sticking into it like a murderer's stiletto.

When the object struck the ship and shattered the truss, this one small segment had been propelled aft, most likely flying alongside the ship almost parallel with the truss itself, until it rammed into the big tank that blocked its path.

Pointing, he said for the benefit of those listening in the ship, "That must be the source of the leak."

Gonzalez's voice from the comm center confirmed, "Sure looks that way."

Ted Connover spoke up. "That's got to be the source, Bee."

"How're you guys doing?" Benson asked.

"Pre-breathe almost complete," Connover replied. "Now if we can get Hi's beard jammed into his helmet we'll be good to go in a half-hour or less."

"Right." Benson turned his attention back to the leaking tank.

Amanda asked, "How do we get up there?"

Benson looked at the smooth surface of the tank, unmarred except for the truss segment sticking out of it some fifteen feet above where they were.

Amanda piped up again. "We're at the end of our tethers, Bee."

If that was supposed to be funny, Benson saw no humor in it.

"We're going to have to detach our tethers," he said.

"And then what?"

He tried to shrug inside the suit, failed. "If the tethers reached that far, I could jump toward the spot where the leak is and grab onto the broken piece of the truss. Assuming I made it, I could remove the shard, cover the hole with a patch and then you could reel me back in."

"But if you miss?"

"My next stop would be Alpha Centauri, I guess."

Neither NASA nor any other space agency approved untethered spacewalks. The danger of an astronaut floating away from the ship was too great. Unlike swimming, where someone who fell out of the boat had a chance of getting back by reacting against the water, in the vacuum of space there is nothing to react against. If an astronaut floats away from the ship there is no way for him to get back, not unless he is carrying a propulsion rocket on his backpack.

Benson shook his head inside his helmet. "I'm not sure we can take the risk, Amanda."

"But the leak . . ."

"I know. I know. We've got to do *something*, but jumping into the wild black yonder without a tether isn't a viable solution."

"Bee, we do have a tether," Amanda said, her voice eager, excited. "We just disconnected ourselves from it back at the lander."

He immediately grasped her suggestion. "We'll have to go back and cut a piece long enough to reach from here to the leak. We'll tie the loose end to the handhold here."

"That'll work! Won't it?"

"It's better than floating off to infinity."

"Or beyond."

"Let's get started."

It took forty-five minutes to get back to the cargo module, cut a fifty-foot length of the tether, and return to the leaking TEI tank. Benson tied one end of the tether to the last of the handholds. Looking up, he was surprised to see Amanda reattaching its other end to the belt of her suit.

"What're you doing?"

"I'll make the jump, Bee. You stay anchored here and pull me back."

"The other way around, you mean."

"No, Bee. Let me do it. I can patch the hole. I don't want to be the anchor man. I'm afraid of messing it up, and that'll mean I've killed you."

"Bullshit."

"Really, Bee. Let me make the jump. Please. I'll feel a lot better that way. I can do it."

"All right," he heard himself say. "You jump, I'll be your anchor."

"I'm ready," she said.

Trying to hide his unease, Benson said, "Right. Let's do it."

Ted Connover called from inside the ship. "Bee, we're ready to come out."

"Hang loose," Benson said. "We'll call if we run into trouble."

"Why don't you wait and let Hi and me come out and help you?"

Shaking his head, Benson replied, "Don't want to risk both our astronauts if we don't have to. Besides, every minute we wait is another couple hundred pounds of hydrogen squirting out into space."

"But—"

"Sorry, Ted. You and McPherson stand by. Amanda's going to try to reach the leak."

"Amanda?" Connover practically squeaked with surprise.

"Yes, Amanda. We're ready to go now."

Amanda nodded inside her helmet. But she had a sudden flash of memory of her miserable attempts at ballet lessons in school. The teacher was as kind as she could be, but she made it clear that a chunky, heavy-legged ballerina just wasn't going to make the grade.

I can do this, she told herself as she stared at the leaking TEI tank. *I've got to do it!*

"You ready?" Benson's voice in her helmet earphones sounded tense.

"Yeah," she responded. "Ready."

"Go."

Amanda bent her knees as best as her suit would allow, and launched herself toward the damaged area of the tank. *I'm flying!* she marveled. *Being weightless helps.*

She hit the tank with a thud that only she could hear, the sound carrying from the tank through her suit by conduction. But she had landed too far from the broken truss spar to reach it. She bounced off the tank and started drifting away from the ship. Before she could panic she felt the tug of her tether. Bee was pulling her back to safety. For the first time since she'd been a child, Amanda offered up a swift prayer of thanks.

"Not so bad," Benson was telling her. "You almost made it."

She grabbed the truss beside him, saying, "Let me try again."

"Right."

This time her leap was right on the mark. She thumped against the tank and wrapped both her gloved hands around the undamaged truss segment before the momentum of her impact pushed her away again.

"Gotcha!" she exclaimed.

"Good girl!" Benson called.

A moment's exultation was all she got. Benson quickly demanded, "What do you see, Amanda? Remember, your video isn't working, so all we've got is your voice report."

"I see the damage," she answered. "It's a pretty big tear." She put her gloved hand over the leak. "I can feel the gas escaping. Pushes against my fingertips."

"You'll have to pull the spar out of the hole," Benson said.

"Yeah, I know," she said. To herself, she added, *Without jerking myself off the tank altogether.*

Slowly, deliberately, she wormed the broken piece of truss out of the hole it had dug into the tank's skin.

Blinking sweat out of her eyes she cried, "Got it!" and held the twisted length of metal up in one hand like a victorious warrior.

"Roll over on your back before you throw it away," Benson told her. "That way the recoil from your throw won't push you off the tank."

"Good thinking, Bee."

Amanda tried to lie flat, but her bulky backpack made her feel as if she were laying on a pile of rocks. Gripping the truss segment with both hands, she tried to recall how she made two-handed free throws when she played basketball in school.

She lifted the segment over her head and heaved. It disappeared into the blackness of space. *Bet that's a record for free throws*, she thought. *A zillion miles.*

"Great toss!" Benson called.

Rolling slowly, cautiously onto her belly, she pulled out the patch kit and got to work. *Be extra careful*, she told herself. *Hydrogen is sneaky stuff.*

Standing at the base of the big, curving tank, Benson was thinking the same thing. Hydrogen leaked through almost everything. The lightest element, its atoms were the smallest of them all. Even in its diatomic form, H_2, the stuff leaked through seals that held everything else.

Amanda took no chances. She covered the leak with a patch and smeared it with gobs of epoxy. Then she slapped more patches around the edges of the first one and sealed them firmly, too.

At last she got up on her knees and said to Benson, "It's covered."

"You're sure?" he asked.

"This sucker's covered," Amanda insisted. "Nothing's going to get out now."

Benson felt a wave of relief wash over him. Amanda sounded totally sure that the leak was fixed. But just to make certain, he called to Gonzalez, "Virginia, ask Catherine or Mikhail to check the LAD reading."

"Copy LAD reading," Gonzalez replied.

"Bee, this is Ted," Connover's voice came through his helmet earphones. "Hi and I are ready to come out."

"I don't think you'll have to. Amanda's got the leak covered."

"You're sure?"

Looking up towards Amanda, Benson saw her give a thumbs up.

"I'm sure," he said.

Gonzalez put the icing on the cake. "Bee, Mikhail says the LAD shows the leak has stopped. Propellant level in the tank has stabilized."

"Best news I've had all day," Benson said.

"Two days," came Connover's voice. He sounded happy, relieved.

"Two days. Right." As he started pulling Amanda's tether in, he thought, *I'm going to sleep for at least a week*. The thought pleased him.

JULY 23, 2035
EARTH DEPARTURE PLUS 109 DAYS
12:17 UNIVERSAL TIME
PRIVACY QUARTERS, THE *ARROW*

Strangely, Benson slept less than six hours. He awoke in his privacy cubicle feeling refreshed but grungy, after his sweaty EVA work.

Nobody else seemed to be in their quarters. *They must all be working. Even Amanda. Good,* he thought. Time on the job is time spent not moping or worrying about our situation.

Briefly he considered skipping the shower he so dearly wanted. Don't know how much water we've lost. It gets recycled from the shower, he knew, but he worried about being profligate.

His nostrils decided the matter. If I show myself to the others smelling like this, they'll throw me in the shower whether I like it or not.

Fifteen minutes later, showered, shaved, and wearing a fresh set of coveralls, Benson headed toward the galley.

The entire crew was there, most of them strapped into chairs. Hi McPherson and Catherine Clermont were hovering by the refrigerator/freezer, choosing selections.

It's lunchtime, Benson realized. He saw Amanda sitting beside Virginia Gonzalez, both of them wolfing down slices of soymeat. Prokhorov, sitting across the table from them, picked listlessly at his lunch.

"Good morning, sleepyhead," Taki Nomura called to him.

"You mean good afternoon," Ted Connover corrected.

"What's the matter, Mikhail? You don't like frozen fruit tarts?"

173

"My stomach is protesting," the Russian said bleakly. "If only we had some borscht."

Looking around the table, Benson asked, "Who's watching the store?"

"I'll get back to the bridge in a couple of minutes," Connover said. "We've been jabbering with Mission Control all morning. They've been analyzing our telemetry."

"And?"

Hiking his eyebrows, Connover said, "We're going to have to do something about the truss. The structural guys say it'll never take the gee forces we'll face during Mars orbit insertion."

Benson nodded. "We'll have to patch it somehow."

"Yeah, but the bright boys back home haven't come up with a 'somehow.'"

"They will," McPherson said, as he let his lunch tray hover in midair while he helped Clermont slide into her chair.

"We've got more than two months before we reach Mars," Amanda said. Benson thought she might have crossed her fingers under the table.

"All systems in the green?" Benson asked Connover as he glided away from the microwave.

Ted nodded. "We lost a lot of water, though. Mission Control thinks we'll have to start rationing."

"Propellant?"

"They're still working on that. But from the looks on their faces, it's going to be bad news."

Benson took in a breath and forced himself onto the only unoccupied chair. His tray floated a few inches above the table while he strapped himself down.

"Well," he said, "we're all alive and healthy. The ship is functioning. Things could be worse."

Mikhail Prokhorov made a sound that was halfway between a laugh and a dismissive snort. "Bee, you remind me of the man who fell out of the window on the fortieth floor of the building. As he passed the twentieth floor he said, 'So far, so good.'"

Everyone chuckled. Except Benson. He thought that the Russian was right. So far, so good. But they were going to hit the sidewalk soon enough, he knew.

❊ ❊ ❊

Television screens and 3D sets around the world showed Steven Treadway standing in the *Arrow*'s passageway, between the command center and the galley. Beside him stood Taki Nomura, no taller than his shoulder. What the audience did not see was the subtile editing done to cut out the time delay.

"This is Steven Treadway reporting from the damaged Mars spacecraft, *Arrow*."

Treadway wore his crisp white shirt, but his usual smile was gone. He looked deadly serious, concerned, almost mournful.

Turning to Taki, he said, "This is Dr. Nomura, the crew's physician and psychological counselor." Nomura nodded and tried to smile.

"Taki," Treadway asked, "How is the crew handling this grave emergency?"

Nomura's face revealed nothing as she said, "We're all concerned, of course. But we've trained for years to face emergency situations. Each of our team members is in good spirits, psychologically. No one was really injured and all the ship's systems are functioning."

"But the damage to the ship—"

"It's being analyzed and steps to correct the damage are being assessed."

Treadway nodded minimally. "I've got to say that watching the video feed from the ship was emotionally shocking. I can only imagine how you all felt."

"It was a jolt to us all, no doubt about that."

"But you've recovered magnificently."

With the ghost of a smile, Taki replied, "That's what we're trained to do."

"And the damage has been repaired?" Treadway asked.

"Most of it. Commander Benson and Amanda Lynn, our biologist, went EVA and plugged the leaks in the water bladder and TEI tank."

"That's the tank that holds the fuel needed to return to Earth."

"The propellant, yes."

"What about the damage to the central truss?"

"Mission Control is working out a repair plan."

Treadway nodded, more deeply. "I've got to say, this accident really stunned me. And as I watched the video feed, I realized that I was seeing what had happened several minutes ago. It was so frustrating!"

"We're so far from Earth," Nomura said calmly, "that it takes a few minutes for our video feed to reach you."

"I wanted to do something to help," Treadway went on, "but all I could do was watch the video, knowing that I was looking into the past and there was nothing I could do about it."

"You're very considerate, Mr. Treadway," Taki said, soothingly. "We all appreciate that."

Looking somber, Treadway turned to face the hovering camera and concluded, "This is Steven Treadway, reporting virtually from the damaged *Arrow*, as it limps toward Mars."

"What the hell?" Bart Saxby snapped.

He was sitting in his office on the ninth floor of NASA headquarters, staring at the headline in the *SpaceBlog* news feed on the TV screen built into the wall opposite his desk. Saxby could feel his blood pressure rising as he read the article beneath the headline.

"'Confidential NASA briefs give the crew of the *Arrow* less than a fifty-percent chance of returning home alive,'" he read aloud.

Turning to Robin Harkness, NASA's director of human spaceflight, Saxby's voice rose. "Dammit, they're quoting verbatim from the text of the report you handed me less than two hours ago! How in God's name did they get that information out of here and onto the net so fast? Worst of all, who the hell's leaking it to them?"

Harkness, a career bureaucrat, was trim and taut from years of playing tennis and squash at every opportunity. He frowned as he replied to Saxby, "There aren't too many people who've seen that report, and I know all of them personally. I can't believe that any of them would sneak something this explosive to the news media."

Saxby was red-faced with anger. He and Harkness were both political appointees. He knew that both their heads would roll if it turned out that someone highly placed in NASA was leaking sensitive information to the media even before they'd had a chance to brief the president.

"Damn, damn, damn!" Saxby grumbled, running a hand through

his thinning gray hair. "I'm supposed to brief the president this afternoon and it's already out on the news. How do we do damage control? Never mind the leak, for now anyway. I've got to get a story together."

Harkness pressed his hands together as if praying. After a moment, he said, "Bart, the best damage control might be to go public. If we try to cover up their chances and they don't make it back safely, then you, me, and the president will look bad. The public hates coverups and that's what we'd be doing."

Saxby glared at him, but said nothing.

"If we get lucky and the crew makes it home," Harkness went on, "then it'd still look like we tried to cover something up. I think we—you—should go public with the assessment and all the details right after you meet with the president. Today, if possible. The more time goes by, the more likely it'll blow up in our faces."

Grudgingly, Saxby said, "I'll need the story that goes with this. It's got to describe the situation honestly, yet hold out the possibility of salvation. The crew will see all the crap the media puts out and we can't afford to have them lose whatever hope they have."

Harkness was about to reply when the intercom on Saxby's desk said, "Sir, Senator Donaldson is on line one."

"Oh shit," said Saxby, sinking his face into his hands.

"The president will see you now."

Bart Saxby thought that, under normal circumstances—if you can ever call having an audience with the President of the United States normal—those words would have been just about what any aspiring bureaucrat or politician would be eager to hear. But these were not normal circumstances, and the NASA administrator was not particularly eager to have this conversation.

President Harper was seated at the middle of the conference room table flanked by Sarah Fleming, his chief of staff, the National Security Advisor, and several aides. One of the White House official photographers was tiptoeing around the table, taking pictures, while a videographer captured the entire meeting.

No one rose when Saxby entered the conference room, nor did he expect any of them to. He was accompanied by Robin Harkness and the agency's chief scientist, Marion Dupree. No one was smiling.

Harper was busy scribbling a note on the bottom of an official-looking sheet of paper. All the paper in the White House looked official to Saxby. President Harper glanced up and motioned for Saxby and the others to take seats on the other side of the table, facing the president and his staff.

The president finished his writing, looked up and scanned the room with troubled eyes, then settled his gaze on Saxby.

"Bart, what's the status of the *Arrow*? Sarah told me you had important news and it couldn't wait."

"Mr. President, I'm afraid the news isn't good."

Fleming's green eyes narrowed. "Then the news media reports are true?"

"Pretty much, I'm afraid."

The security advisor shook his heavy-jowled head. "How in hell did the media get this information before the president?"

With a glance at Harkness, Saxby replied, "We're looking into that."

"This is a serious leak," the NSA man said.

Raising one meaty hand, President Harper said, "Let's not get fixated on that. Not yet. What's the status of the *Arrow*? That's what I want to know."

"We've looked at how much propellant they've lost, how much water leaked away, and the structural condition of the spacecraft. At best, it's a fifty-fifty chance that the ship will break apart when they try to enter Mars orbit."

"Then don't go into Mars orbit," said one of the president's aides, a youngish man with thick blond hair and owlish eyeglasses.

"They've got to go into orbit around Mars. Otherwise they can't get back to Earth."

"They can't turn around?"

"Not without help from Mars' gravity field."

"My God in heaven," Harper muttered.

With a sigh, Saxby added, "And they'll have to stay at Mars for thirty days, whether they go down to the surface or not. That's how long it will take for Earth and Mars to line up properly so that the ship can make the journey back home."

Before anyone could reply to that, Saxby went on, "That's what is needed for an undamaged ship to return. But the *Arrow* is damaged, heavily damaged. And we don't know if they have enough propellant left to make it back home."

"You don't know!" the National Security Advisor snapped, like a prosecuting attorney confronting a defendant.

"We're grinding through the numbers. Comments about so-called exact rocket science aside, we always carry some reserve propellant and we often have to use it, for one emergency or another. But here we're talking about a trip of hundreds of millions of miles.. There's a lot of uncertainties involved."

"So . . . ?" President Harper asked.

"So, at this point, we don't know for sure whether we can get them back home or not."

Obviously holding his temper in check, the president demanded, "When will you know?"

"Sometime shortly before they arrive back here at Earth. If they don't have to perform any major course corrections, if they don't have to use extra propellant . . ."

"What if they do have to use extra propellant?" The NSA man asked.

Saxby hesitated a heartbeat before answering, "Then they'll sail past the Earth and we'll never see them again."

"That's unacceptable," said President Harper.

"Yes, sir, we know. But there's another problem, as well. A more pressing problem."

"More pressing than losing the whole damned crew?"

With a reluctant nod, Saxby explained, "Yes, sir. They also took a hit in their water reservoir and they lost a lot of water. Even with recycling there simply isn't enough water to keep them alive for the trip home. They'd run out before they got halfway back. And that assumes minimum rations of water from today onward."

Saxby felt as if he wanted to crawl into a hole and come out on the other side working in a no-stress job where human lives were not hanging in the balance.

The president looked grim. "So you're saying that even if they survive getting to Mars and leaving again, and if they have enough fuel to get home, they'll come home dead due to a lack of drinking water?"

"Dead or very sick. Yes, sir. That's what I'm saying. I wish to God that I weren't, but that's what we're up against."

The National Security Advisor fixed Saxby with an accusatory stare. "You mean there's no other option? Didn't we already send supplies to Mars to keep the crew alive while they're on the planet's surface? Why can't they pick up those supplies, bring them back to the ship, and use them for the trip home?"

"We've looked into that," Saxby said. "Even if we bring all the water back from the surface habitat to the ship, it won't be enough. There are also the risks of sending a team down to the surface under these circumstances."

Sarah Fleming spoke up. "Weren't we ready to take those risks? This was supposed to be a Mars landing expedition, wasn't it?"

"Yes, but again, that was for an undamaged ship. The crew will have been without artificial gravity for many weeks by the time they arrive at Mars. Their bodies will be weakened by cardiovascular deconditioning, general body muscle loss, and increased bone brittleness. If we send someone down to the surface to offload supplies from the habitat onto the lander, there's a high probability that they'll fail."

"Fail? Why? Was the habitat damaged?"

"No, Ms. Fleming. It appears to be in good shape. But without the artificial gravity produced by spinning the *Arrow*, the crew will have atrophied muscles and brittle bones. Not a good situation. If somebody goes to the surface and falls due to muscle weakness, there's a really good chance of breaking a bone because of the embrittlement. Not a pretty picture."

"So what do we do about it? Do they know?" The president asked.

"No, we haven't told them yet. The propellant problem leaked to the news media this morning but the water crisis is still under wraps. That's one reason why I'm here. I need to be the one to break the news, before it leaks to the media and the crew finds out from the internet news feeds." Saxby looked Harper straight in the eye. "And before I do that, I had to let you know the situation."

The president looked like he wanted to erupt, throw a tantrum, break things with his bare hands. With an obvious effort, he took a deep breath and calmed himself.

"All right, Bart, you've checked the box. Now call a news conference and tell all the facts. I hold you responsible for finding a solution that doesn't end up in complete failure and the loss of the crew."

Saxby nodded wearily. "For what it's worth, we've got all of our best and brightest people working on this."

"You'd damned well better," said the president. "The entire future of human spaceflight is hanging on this. If we lose this crew, Donaldson and his ilk will have the ammunition they need to stop all human missions."

"And sweep the elections next year," said Sarah Fleming.

"We're doing our best," Saxby told them. It sounded like whining, even in his own ears.

JULY 24, 2035
EARTH DEPARTURE PLUS 110 DAYS
17:30 UNIVERSAL TIME
GALLEY, THE *ARROW*

Ted Connover was smiling when he said it, but he still expressed the crew's prevailing opinion, "How far up shit's creek are we, Bee?"

All seven of them had assembled in the galley, looking to Benson for reassurance, for some shred of news that was favorable. Instead he gave them a straightforward, honest assessment of their predicament. Not one to mince words, Benson laid it all out on the table, hoping that someone would come up with *the* bright idea that could save the day—and their lives.

"The propellant leak was a disaster averted," he told them. "The chunk of debris that punctured the tank also acted as a sort of partway plug to keep the leakage rate low, so we only lost reserve propellant. There should be enough propellant to get us home, just barely."

He saw Connover's brows rise, but Ted kept his mouth shut. For once.

"The water leak, well, that's another story altogether. The engineers back home haven't come up with a solution yet, but they're working on it."

An expression of alarm broke out on Taki Nomura's normally stolid face. "We're going to run out of water? All of it? Including the radiation shielding?"

"Including the radiation shielding," Benson replied evenly. "The leak was apparently a gusher before we got out there to patch it. By the time we're about halfway home there won't be any water left. Not for drinking, not for radiation shielding. And that's if we go on minimal water rations beginning today—which, by the way, we are."

"Up shit's creek without any water," Connover muttered.

Prokhorov said dourly, "We might just as well kill ourselves now and save all the misery." Then his face brightened. "I know! We can have an ongoing lottery and space the losers, one by one."

"We're not spacing anybody," Benson snapped. "Cut the crap, Mikhail."

Almost reluctantly, Hi McPherson asked, "Taki, how much water do we consume in a day?" he seemed embarrassed that he didn't already know the answer.

"Two to three liters per day, depending on your body mass," Nomura answered.

Benson explained, "The bright guys at Mission Control took that into account in their analysis, including how much we can recycle and what's left in the tanks. We could probably get by with less for a while, but not for more than the year we'll need to get home."

"These are all preliminary figures, right?" asked Amanda Lynn.

Benson nodded, but he said, "Don't expect them to change much. And if they do change, it'll probably be for the worse, not the better."

Virginia Gonzalez shook her head. "You're a real ray of sunshine, Bee."

Benson held back the angry retort that immediately flashed through his mind. "Don't shoot the messenger, Virginia. I'm just laying out the facts, as best as we know them. I want you all to understand the situation we're in."

"Of course," Catherine Clermont murmured.

Connover was unwilling to accept the news without trying to find a way out. "Bee, you said they're looking at us going down to the *Fermi* habitat and bringing up water from there?"

"They looked at it. We were supposed to live there, all eight of us, for thirty days. They supplied the habitat with enough water for four months—"

"Gotta love those bean counters and their margins," McPherson said.

"If we were to go down to the surface, and we could find a way to store it on the lander, it would weigh six to seven hundred pounds. The lander can't handle that load with all eight of us aboard."

"Then we can send down a skeleton crew," Connover suggested, brightening. "You and me, Bee. Or me and Hi."

"But that would be extremely risky," said Nomura. "We'll have been in zero-gee for more than two months. One trip and fall could result in a broken bone."

"Inside the spacesuits?" Connover asked.

Taki hesitated, but then answered, "It's a risk, Ted. A big risk."

McPherson said, "It's not a bigger risk than dying of thirst."

"Agreed," Benson said firmly. "So that's what we'll do. We just need to decide who goes to the habitat and how they transfer the water to the lander."

"And we've got more than two months to figure it out," Connover added.

Benson looked around the galley to see if they all agreed. Several heads nodded. Clermont looked thoughtful, perhaps doubtful.

Prokhorov grumbled, "You make my stomach hurt, Bee."

"Sorry, Mikhail, can't be helped," Benson said. "All right, that's it for now. Let's get back to work and see if we can come up with any more good ideas."

As the group broke up and headed for their various work stations, Benson thought that Connover showed a marked improvement in his attitude. Since the deaths of his wife and son, Ted had been uncharacteristically quiet, almost withdrawn. Now he seemed fully engaged again, even eager. *Dark clouds and silver linings*, he thought.

Then he remembered that if they didn't find a way to repair the fractured truss, they'd never get to the surface of Mars. The *Arrow* would break up when they tried to enter Mars orbit. They'd all die more than thirty million miles from home.

Hi McPherson saw that the galley was empty. *Everybody else has already eaten,* he thought. He himself had spent the nearly two hours since Bee's discussion of their situation in the geology lab with Catherine. All his life, McPherson had preferred getting his hands dirty with good, solid work to sitting around and stewing about one problem or another.

Okay, we're in a bad fix, he thought. *But it's not hopeless. Never hopeless, not as long as your heart beats and your brain works.*

Working with Catherine was fun, but distracting. Hard to concentrate on analyzing spectrograms of soil samples scooped up by the automated rovers trundling across the frozen sands of Mars when this utterly lovely French woman was close enough to touch, to caress, to kiss.

He shook himself, trying to force such thoughts out of his mind.

Catherine had finished their analysis and sent the results back to Mission Control, then excused herself with, "Time for dinner, Hi."

He had nodded and replied, "Guess so," still bent over the rainbow of colors that revealed what the Martian soil was made of. He'd been looking for traces of water, knowing it was most likely impossible for liquid water to exist on Mars' cold, barren surface, but peering hopefully at their last spectrogram nonetheless.

When he'd finally gone down the passageway to the galley, he felt disappointed that Catherine wasn't there.

There was a big piece of note paper pasted to the water tap. **ONE CUP PER DAY.** Signed by Taki Nomura. *She's put us on the honor system,* McPherson thought as he filled his drinking bottle. *Maybe that's the wrong way to do it. Maybe we should guzzle all the water we can, have a regular old-style Roman orgy of water drinking. Use it all up and put an end to our misery as quickly as we can.*

Shaking his head, he knew that he was thinking nonsense. *We can't give up. We've got to do our best, no matter how hard it is. We've got to figure out a way to get through this.*

"You look a thousand miles away."

Surprised, he turned so quickly he nearly upset the tray he was carrying. Catherine Clermont was hovering beside him, looking slightly amused, cool and warm at the same time, totally beautiful. He saw that she was wearing a fresh set of coveralls.

"I . . . I was just thinking."

"*Tres bien,*" said Catherine. "Thought makes man wise. Wisdom makes life endurable."

He sucked in a deep breath. "Life's going to get very tough on this ship, Catherine."

With a slight nod, Clermont said, "Yes. But endurable, *non*?"

"I hope so."

They filled their trays and coasted weightlessly to the nearest table. Hiram let his tray hang in midair as he helped Catherine into a chair. While she buckled herself in, he pushed himself down onto the chair next to her, buckled the safety belt around his lap, then reached for his tray to pull it down to the table top.

Half-distracted by Catherine's presence, McPherson's hand bumped the edge of the tray, and his water bottle wobbled off it. Hi grabbed for the bottle, accidentally squeezing some of the precious water out of it. The water broke into little globules and floated away on the current of the air blowers

Catherine laughed lightly. "You should chase down the globules, Hi. They're getting away from you."

"It's too much trouble," he answered, smiling to hide his embarrassment. "I'll just take half a cup."

"You can share some of mine," she said.

A genuine smile lit his bearded face. "That's awfully kind of you."

"*C'est rien.*"

They started in on their meals, but after a few swallows Catherine said, "Hi, have you thought about the fact that we might not get home? I'm not thinking only of the water problem. Ted has told me about the broken truss."

McPherson's head snapped up from his forkful of freeze-dried chicken. "Ted? When did you talk with him?"

"When I was changing for dinner."

"In your privacy cubicle?" McPherson's voice rose half an octave.

Looking halfway between puzzled and amused, Clermont answered, "In the passageway. It was all very innocent, I assure you."

Trying to bring his voice back to normal, McPherson asked, "So what did Ted have to say?"

"When we try to enter Mars orbit the ship might break apart, unless we come up with some way to repair the truss."

"Oh. Yeah, I know that."

"It is very serious."

"The brain trust back at Mission Control is working on a way to repair the truss. Once they've got it figured out, they'll shoot the instructions to us and Bee or somebody will go EVA and make the fix."

"Yes, of course," Catherine murmured.

"And once we get to Mars," McPherson went on, with a confidence he didn't really feel, "we'll go down to the surface and get all the water we need from the *Fermi* habitat."

"And nothing else will go wrong before we get back home. I wish I could believe that. I don't want to die out here."

"Well, none of us does."

She sighed. "It makes me think of the things I want to do and did not have the courage to think of doing until now. Looking death in the face makes one think about such things."

"Like what?"

Catherine leaned closer to him, close enough that he could smell her hair. At that moment he thought it was the sweetest smell he could imagine.

"Hiram, I want you," she whispered. "Now. I've wanted to be with you since we were in training, and I can't help but think you feel the same way."

McPherson nearly choked on his chicken. He could feel his face turning red.

He managed to stutter, "I . . . have I been that obvious?"

"Terribly."

McPherson sat in silence for several heartbeats, staring into Catherine's soft brown eyes. He wanted to reach out and take her into his arms, but the rational part of his mind made him hesitate. Besides, he told himself, these damned seat belts will hold us down to our chairs.

"Catherine," he said slowly, carefully, "I've thought about damned little else ever since we first met in training. But . . . but here, on this cramped little bucket, I just didn't think it would be appropriate. I mean . . . hell, you sat through the same lectures I did when we were in training. When they were telling us we shouldn't fraternize, all I could think about was fraternizing with you."

With a knowing dip of her chin, Catherine said, "I honestly believed I could put away my human feelings for the duration of the trip and be the egghead scientist. But I can't. Especially now that there's a chance we might not live to see home again."

McPherson leaned back in his chair and stared at the luke-warm chunks of chicken on his plate.

Feeling elated and miserable at the same time, he told her, "Catherine, I can't. I just can't. Not because I don't want to. You're a very beautiful woman. You're also a very beautiful person, someone I'd like to know better and, well, I'd like to think that if we have something between us it would be more than physical, more than just a desperate attempt to get away from the fact that we might not have a tomorrow."

Clermont looked at him, pursed her lips, then smiled sadly.

"Hi, you are going to be a great catch for some lucky woman. Old-fashioned morality is very rare."

"I'm not—"

She patted his hand. "I'm not so ruled by my hormones that I can't control them when I need to. And I do want to, now."

McPherson felt his face reddening again. At last he said, "Well, let's finish eating and help get this ship back together so we have more to look forward to than dying out here in the middle of nowhere. I've got some very important business to attend to when we get back to Earth."

Catherine smiled. "So do I."

Ted Connover stood next to the latest generation 3D printer that sat in the rear of the habitat's third level, behind the exercise equipment. It was an unassuming-looking device: essentially just a box with a flat panel display that was used to show a Computer-Assisted-Device file of whatever was programmed to be printed.

Ted was fully trained on the 3D printer and knew that as long as it functioned properly there were only a few things aboard the *Arrow* that couldn't be repaired or replaced by it.

"I saw my first 3D printer at the local community college," Ted was saying. "The instructor called it a 'first generation *Star Trek* replicator.'"

Virginia Gonzalez was staring at the device. To her, it looked like the one she had at home in her garage, except that perhaps it was a little more sleek and streamlined.

"To be honest," Connover went on, "I had no idea what he was talking about. I hadn't seen any *Star Trek* shows at the time, but I knew it must be something fantastic because of the excitement in his eyes."

"*Star Trek* was a good show," said Hi McPherson. "When I was a kid I bought every episode and streamed them wherever I went."

Connover ignored Hi's comment. "Then the instructor showed me how it worked. He poured in some plastic powder, at least I think it was plastic. He uploaded *to the printer* the specs of the chair we'd designed using some cheap CAD software. And, voila! A few minutes later we smelled that burning plastic smell and before our very eyes a

191

chair was being formed, layer by layer, until we had a piece of furniture that Barbie could have used in her pink doll house."

"You printed a Barbie chair in a university mechanical engineering department?" Gonzalez asked, amused incredulity clear in her tone.

"It was a community college, not a university," Connover corrected, "and yes, we built a Barbie chair. The instructor wanted to start small, I think, probably because he had a limited budget. But I also think he wanted something practical."

"Or he had a daughter who was into Barbie," said Virginia.

"Maybe," Connover conceded. "In any event, I was mesmerized. To me, that 3D printer was like magic. That semester, we printed gears, tools, even a toy car with wheels that actually moved. All that with a hobbyist 3D printer and design software we found on the Internet. That was twenty-some years ago, at the beginning of 3D printing and now I understand why he said it would change everything."

"It sure as hell has," McPherson said. "I don't know what I'd do without mine. Just before we left I printed a replacement rotor for my 1984 Mazda RX-7. God, I love that car."

Virginia agreed. "I have an electro-optical 3D that I use to make replacement boards for my antique radio collection. I've got radios that go back to the 1920s and I have to improvise. The newest printers can make circuit boards, old-style transistors, just about any other radio part you can imagine."

"Vacuum tubes?" Connover asked.

Crestfallen, Gonzalez shook her head. "No."

"Not yet," said McPherson.

"I don't think I've made a trip to a hardware store in the past three years," Connover said. "Can't say I cried a river when the printers started driving hardware stores out of business."

"And toy stores," McPherson added. "And box retail stores, even the companies that ran sweatshops in Asia and Africa."

More thoughtfully, Gonzalez pointed out, "I guess we ought to remember that 3D printers changed everything about the global economy and supply chain. Printers like this one here," she pointed, "got cheap enough for the masses, and lots and lots of people were put out of work."

Looking annoyed, McPherson asked, "Now that we've had our global economics lesson and decided what we all want for Christmas,

JULY 28, 2035
EARTH DEPARTURE PLUS 114 DAYS
13:15 UNIVERSAL TIME
EXTRAVEHICULAR ACTIVITY, THE *ARROW*

Inside his EVA spacesuit, tethered to the truss near the spot where the rock had done its damage, Ted Connover looked into the darkness of deep space. He stared at the stars, gleaming steadily like unblinking eyes watching him.

Makes you feel pretty small, he said to himself. *Small and lonely.*

His thoughts drifted to Vicki and Thad, as they always did when he had time to think, to remember.

I wonder if they're out there, looking back at me. Are they sad? Are they with God, whatever that means? I'm the one who should have died. I'm the one who decided to go to Mars, to leave them millions of miles away. He squeezed his eyes shut. *I'm the one who should have died, not them!*

"Ted, are you with me?" Virginia Gonzalez's voice sounded sharply in his helmet earphones.

He snapped back to the here and now. Turning to look at Virginia's spacesuited figure, he replied, "Yeah, Jinny, I'm here. I was just . . . thinking."

"I hope you were thinking about the repair. I was starting to wonder."

"No, I was just . . . thinking. But now it's time to get to work. Let's get this job done so we can go home."

"Copy that!"

With deliberate, careful motion, Connover reached into the toolbag that contained the makeshift spars and clamps that the engineers back on Earth had designed and uploaded to the *Arrow*'s 3D printer. He'd run through the process for attaching them to the truss at least fifty times in the past day and a half, using the simulated truss that they'd also printed out for the same purpose.

But those simulation exercises had been performed in the ship's pressurized habitat, first using his bare hands and then the gloves of his EVA suit. Now he was outside, in the vacuum of space, in the bulky, cumbersome suit. Once the suit was pressurized, the gloves had ballooned as they always did, making it a real effort to flex his fingers or grasp anything.

"Steven Treadway, reporting from the damaged *Arrow*."

Treadway appeared to be hovering weightlessly beside Bee Benson just inside the ship's main airlock, where Prokhorov and Amanda Lynn were helping Ted and Virginia out of their EVA suits, all of them in zero-g.

Although this news report appeared to be live, from the *Arrow*, the spacecraft's distance from Earth made a truly live interview impossibly awkward. So Treadway had asked his questions from the 3D virtual reality studio in New York and Benson had answered them from the ship. The long pauses in-between, while their messages crossed the gulf of space, were edited out at the studio. Then the patched-together interview was aired and gave the impression that it was all happening in real time.

"Astronauts Ted Connover and Virginia Gonzalez," Treadway intoned, "have just reentered the ship after three hours outside, working to repair the badly damaged main truss that connects the crew's living and working habitat to the propulsion system they will need to bring them home."

Gonzalez looked drawn, tired. Connover was grinning, though, and made a "thumbs up" signal with his still-gloved hand.

"It appears their repair effort has been successful," Treadway said. Turning to Benson, standing beside him, he asked, "Commander Benson, is that right? Was the repair made successfully?"

"Yes it was, Steve," Bee replied. "Mission Control has confirmed that the truss is now strong enough for us to enter the Martian atmosphere and use its drag to slow us into an orbit around Mars."

"That's very good news," said Treadway, smiling.

Benson's grin was much wider. "It sure as hell . . . it certainly is."

Putting on a more concerned expression, Treadway said, "Many viewers have been asking why you have to continue to Mars and stay there a month before you can begin the trip home. Why can't you start home sooner?"

On tens of millions of television screens around the world, the image of the *Arrow*'s airlock area gave way to a computerized 3D animation showing the orbits of Earth and Mars, with the position of the *Arrow* marked between the two.

Benson's voice explained, "We've got to wait until the Earth moves along its orbit to the place where we can reach it. If we leave Mars too soon, Earth won't be where we need it to be."

Treadway's voice said, "Even with the nuclear rockets that power the *Arrow*, the ship can't move wherever it wants to. The ship is still subject to Newton's laws of motion and orbital mechanics."

"Right," said Benson.

"Unless the ship arrives at Mars and departs on schedule, it won't have enough fuel to return to Earth."

The animation gave way to the "live" scene at the *Arrow*'s airlock. Connover and Gonzalez were almost completely out of their EVA suits, only their leggings and boots still had to be removed. Their undergarments, lined with water tubes for cooling, made them look a bit like thinned-down versions of the Michelin Tire man.

Still standing beside Treadway's virtual image, Benson said, "We have to follow the path we started out on. No detours allowed. Even if we decide not to go down to Mars' surface, we'll have to stay in Mars orbit for thirty days before we can start for home."

Treadway nodded understandingly. "But the good news is that the truss has been repaired."

Benson smiled again. "Yes, that is good news. Very good news."

Standing in the airlock area, looking at a monitor screen that showed Treadway, millions of miles away, Benson resisted the urge to cross his fingers.

The truss is repaired, he said to himself. *But will the patch hold up when we enter Mars' atmosphere?*

)))) IV ((((
Mars Approach

AUGUST 1, 2035
MARS ARRIVAL MINUS 86 DAYS
14:12 UNIVERSAL TIME
NASA HEADQUARTERS, WASHINGTON D.C.

Bart Saxby, Robin Harkness and Nathan Brice, flight director for the Mars mission, sat behind a table on the stage in the NASA press center, facing a room full of reporters, photographers and camera crews. Seated along the table with them were representatives of the Japanese, French, Russian and Canadian space agencies, plus a pert-looking brunette NASA public affairs officer.

Saxby wondered if he looked as tired as he felt. That sullen pain in his chest had returned. Nerves, he told himself. He always gotten chest pains when he was anxious or edgy.

He hadn't been sleeping well since the accident, and had been awake this day since four A.M. He'd been in his office by five-thirty and had his daily teleconference with the mission team in Houston at six, where he was updated on what had happened in the *Arrow* while he'd been trying to sleep. At eight-thirty he had a ten-minute discussion with Sarah Fleming, the president's chief of staff, and now here he was—baggy-eyed and strung tight—ready to answer questions from an aggressive gang of news hounds.

Be positive, he told himself. *Be upbeat*. If they get the impression that the crew's in trouble it'll be like sharks sensing blood in the water: feeding frenzy.

Saxby wished he could be on the *Arrow*, with the crew, on his way to Mars. As a former astronaut, he preferred the problems and perils of space flight to the daggers and land mines of a hostile news conference.

The order of the questions had been determined by lottery, with the first going to a reporter from one of the twenty-four-hour news channels and the remaining bouncing between online outlets, television and web broadcasting stations, newspapers, blogs, and just about anyone with a presence on the net lucky or tenacious enough to get into the pool.

The first half-dozen questions were about the health of the crew, their families' reactions, and the overall condition of the spacecraft. Saxby was content to let Harkness, the agency's director of human spaceflight, handle most of the answers.

The questions were coming faster now, and they were getting tougher.

"You mentioned that the damaged solar arrays have been partially repaired," asked the science reporter from the *Washington Post*. "Why bother with solar panels when the spacecraft's nuclear reactor is undamaged? It is undamaged, isn't it?"

Saxby glanced at Brice, who grasped the microphone in front of him with both hands, like a stranglehold.

"The reactor is in perfect condition," Brice said, forcing a smile, "but it isn't bimodal. It's designed for propulsion, not generating electrical power."

"Wasn't that a mistake?"

"No. Our design team considered making it bimodal, but it quickly became obvious that it would be too complicated. It would add a lot of weight to the spacecraft and drive up the cost. We just didn't have the budget—"

"So cost factors prevented you from making the reactor deliver electrical power," the reporter said. It wasn't a question.

"Cost was part of the equation," Brice said, his smile gone. "But only part. The deciding factor was complexity. That's why we decided to use solar panels for the ship's electrical power."

The next questioner was one participating virtually, a woman who ran a spaceflight blog in Quebec, with her youngish face peering intensely and in 3D from the one of the monitors set up for that purpose.

"So what about the solar arrays?" she asked. "Can you tell us about the fix?"

Glad to be in positive territory, Brice replied, "The solar arrays were damaged by the meteoroid strike and we initially thought the crew would have to make do with less than half-power for the rest of the mission. Fortunately, the damage was limited to only one section of the panels."

"So—"

Brice refused to be interrupted. "When the onboard computer detected the initial damage it shut down two entire sections of the solar array as a precaution. Once we isolated the problem and restarted the system, the spacecraft regained most of that lost power. They're now operating at about eighty-five percent of normal power."

"Will that hold up all the way to Mars?"

"Yes," Brice said firmly.

Saxby leaned into his microphone and amended, "We see no reason why it shouldn't. We know the solar flux all the way to Mars, the amount of sunlight that will hit the panels. We see no problems with electrical power aboard the *Arrow*."

The lean and lanky chief of the *PhiladelphiaInquirer.com*'s Washington bureau, got to his feet like a carpenter's ruler unfolding.

"We've seen reports that the water recycling system isn't working at full capacity and the crew doesn't have enough water, even with whatever they might be able to bring back to the ship from the habitat on Mars' surface. I've consulted with some medical professionals and they tell me that the crew simply can't survive with less than half water rations for the return trip. Do you have some sort of contingency plan or are those eight men and women going to die of thirst on their way home?"

There it is, thought Saxby. *The land mine.* The pain in his chest flared.

The nine men and two women sitting along the table looked back and forth at each other. Saxby realized it was his responsibility to handle this hot potato.

"We're still working on the water problem," he began. "The crew immediately reduced water consumption by twenty-five percent, which we know is enough to allow them to survive for a long time. But it just isn't good enough to get them home."

"Then what can we expect?"

"We currently estimate that they will run out of water within just a few months of their departure from Mars."

The reaction from the audience was palpable. The reporters stirred, muttered, began to shout questions.

"Please!" Saxby shouted at them. "Mr. Goldstein has the floor."

"Does that mean they're going to die before they can get back to Earth?"

"It means," Saxby said, raising his voice again to quiet the buzzing chatter among the reporters. "It means that we haven't worked out a solution to the problem. We're still looking at all the possibilities."

A reporter from the European Union jumped to his feet. "Cannot the water recycling system be repaired? Can they use parts from the habitat on Mars to fix the recycling system?"

Saxby felt grateful for the question. Nodding to the European, he explained, "The *Fermi* habitat does have a water recycling system, but it isn't designed to work without gravity. Recall that Mars has a gravity roughly one-third of Earth's, but the *Arrow* spacecraft is effectively in zero gravity."

He paused and realized that every eye was on him. Even the others along the table were focused on him.

"The recycling system on the *Arrow* was designed to work with or without gravity, since we knew that the ship would be in zero gee for a portion of its flight, but we intended to rotate the ship to give it a Martian gravity level for most of the mission. The ship's recycling system and the system on the *Fermi* simply are not compatible. We saw no reason to add to the *Fermi* habitat's complexity by making it capable of operating under weightless conditions. That would be like designing an automobile to operate under water. It just doesn't make engineering sense."

Saxby was tempted to hide the real reason, but could not. "Don't forget the cost. We could have made all the *Arrow*'s systems fully redundant and cross-compatible with the *Fermi* habitat if we'd had the money. The engineers would have enjoyed the challenge and the safety people would have loved the inherent redundancy. But there was never enough money."

Saxby sagged back in his chair and half-listened to the rest of the questions. The propellant leak. The increased risk of radiation exposure from the ship's water loss. How will the repairs to the truss hold up?

Saxby had asked himself those questions thousands of times

since the accident. And the answer was always, *I don't know. I just do not know.*

The woman from Quebec roused him by asking directly, "Mr. Saxby, what about the crew's mental health? I know that many psychology experts were worried about the crew's ability to maintain their sanity for such a long trip under the stressful conditions of deep space flight. But with this accident and the rather bleak prospects for their safe return home, how are they holding up?"

Saxby knew the official answer. And the crew had put on good faces during their ongoing interviews with Steven Treadway. But he also knew what the realities were.

"Ms. Marquez," he replied, "that's a question that hits home with me personally. I know these people. They've all had dinners in my home, and of course we've been working together professionally for years. I personally recruited Amanda Lynn to join the agency."

He hesitated, then plunged ahead. "I've been in space. I have some idea of the stress they're under. We have a team of experts watching them all very closely, and the ship's medical officer, Dr. Nomura, is also a licensed psychologist. To answer your question—they are responding *very* well to the pressure. In fact, they're holding up as well or better than the experts have predicted. They're doing their jobs, day by day, and we're providing them with all the support we can. I would like to ask each of you in the media to do the same and report what's going on in that spacecraft fairly and honestly. Please remember that they have access to the news nets out there and they can hear, watch and read whatever you report. So please make it accurate and be sensitive to who will be receiving your words."

Then Saxby pushed his chair from the table and got wearily to his feet. "Thank you all very much. That's all for today."

As he walked slowly away, he heard the reporters behind him getting to their feet. No applause, but no calls for more answers, either.

Okay, Saxby thought, rubbing his chest. *That's over and done with. Time to get back to work.*

Amanda Lynn glided through the access tube, avoiding using the handrails as much as she could because she liked the sensation of flying that weightlessness provided. Using the handrails seemed like cheating to her.

When her head popped through the hatch at the end of the tube she saw Bee, Virginia and Taki gathered at one of the galley tables, engaged in animated conversation. She launched herself toward them.

"Hey guys, may I join you?"

"It's the human torpedo!" Virginia laughed and held up her hands as if trying to protect herself.

Amanda stopped herself by grabbing one of the unoccupied chairs. "Whassup?"

Virginia grasped her bottle of rehydrated smoothie as Amanda pulled herself down onto the chair and reached for the ends of the safety belt.

"We were just talking about how bored we are," Gonzalez said. "You know things are bad when some of the smartest people in the world traveling to Mars on a crippled spaceship start complaining that they don't have enough to do."

Taki Nomura said, "We knew that boredom was a risk, but we didn't expect it after the accident. Boredom combined with a sense of helplessness can be a serious issue."

"Helplessness?" Amanda asked. "I don't feel helpless. Do you?"

"Come on now, Mandy," Virginia countered. "Be honest. Don't you feel . . . well, trapped?"

Amanda looked at them for several heartbeats, trying to sort out just what it was that she did feel, deep down in her soul. At last she replied, "Not trapped, exactly. Worried, certainly. I mean, I wish we hadn't hit that damned chunk of rock, but we seem to be limping along okay. So far."

"So far," Benson agreed.

"It's Ted I'm worried about," Nomura said. "We all run the risk of depression, but Ted's lost his family. I know it's hit him hard, but he's going about his business as if nothing's happened."

"You want him to break down and cry?" Benson snapped.

"Maybe it would be better if he didn't hold his feelings in."

Virginia said, "What worries me is the water problem."

"Says the lady with the smoothie in front of her," Amanda teased.

"I'm staying within my water ration," Virginia answered.

Benson said, "The brain trust back home is looking at workarounds for our water problem."

"But so far they haven't come up with anything," Virginia pointed out.

"Not yet," Bee conceded.

Taki said, "The psychologists back home tell me that worrying that we're going to die, combined with all this time on our hands with nothing to do, nothing productive to accomplish, is just ripe for negative thinking. And in Ted's case, with the extra emotional load he must be carrying, they're getting pretty worried."

"I'm not worried about Ted," Bee told them. "He's strong. He'll be okay."

"Or he'll crack up and walk out an airlock," Taki said.

Virginia took another sip of her smoothie. "So, Mandy, with all this talk of suicidal depression and death, do you still want to join us?"

Amanda looked at the three of them and saw a mixture of emotions on their faces. Taki looked worried, but then she always looked worried. Maybe it was the bone structure of her face. Or her personality. *Doesn't matter,* she thought. *She has a damned good reason to be worried.*

Bee looked stolid, impassive, like a statue carved out of granite. He wouldn't show any fear at the edge of hell. The "captain's burden" is what she'd heard it called. Like the skippers of those old-time vessels who went down with their ships.

And finally there was Virginia, with her striking good looks and her superior attitude. She was the only one of the three of them that might crack, Amanda reckoned. She wondered if Virginia's smoothie might be spiked.

"I'll join you, but you'll have to change the topic of conversation. I hate depressing talk. When I was growing up in Detroit I heard a lot of 'you can't do that' or 'it'll never work' or 'they'll never let a black woman do that.' I just decided to ignore such talk and get on with what I wanted to do."

"And you succeeded so well," Virginia sneered, "that here you are, on a crippled spacecraft heading for Mars."

"Beats Detroit," Amanda countered.

They all laughed.

"Seriously," Amanda told them. "I mean it. No more negative talk! Please!"

"Okay," said Benson. "We'll put aside the negative talk and deal with the boredom. What would you like to do today?"

Taki suggested, "How about taking your weekly physicals a couple of days early?"

That elicited a chorus of boos.

"I know," Amanda said. "Why don't we download one of those murder mystery games? You know, where each of us playacts as one of the characters, and we try to figure out which one is really the killer."

No one objected. Amanda felt good: she'd found a way to get them focused on the positive. For her, this made it a good and productive day.

Benson was strapped into his seat at the galley table, finishing the last scraps of his late lunch, when Dr. Nomura glided into the galley and bent over him.

"May I speak with you privately?" she whispered.

There was no one else in the galley, and Benson could see from the troubled expression on the physician's face that something was bothering her.

"Sure, Taki," he said, trying to put her at her ease. "Have a seat, or a float, whichever you prefer."

Nomura pulled herself down onto the chair closest to Benson and strapped herself in, glancing around the empty galley like a conspirator afraid that someone was eavesdropping.

"Mikhail is very sick," she said, her voice low.

"Mikhail?"

"I'm certain that he has gastric cancer."

"Cancer?" Benson yelped.

Nomura nodded, her expression miserable.

"Are you sure? I know he's been troubled with persistent nausea, but I thought he was just having trouble adapting to weightlessness."

"That's what I thought, too, but it's been months and space adaptation syndrome just doesn't last that long. He's lost weight, which isn't surprising because he's not eating much. But his abdomen is swollen."

"Appendicitis maybe?"

Taki shook her head. "After I realized it wasn't SAS, I checked that out. He presented some of the symptoms of appendicitis so I drew some blood to see if he had an elevated white cell count. Nada. But he showed anemia. Then I checked his stool. He's passing blood and the DNA sampling confirms he has cancer."

"Lord almighty," Benson groaned.

"It's worse. He knew it before we left."

That bit of news made Benson sit up straighter and look squarely into Taki's earth-brown eyes. "Explain."

"The stool sampler is supposed to catch things like this. Every time we have a bowel movement it automatically screens for over a thousand metabolic disorders, cancers, markers for inflammation that could indicate heart disease, etc. I'm supposed to be alerted if anything turns up. He found a way to turn it off. He said he found out about the cancer a few months before we left and decided to hide it."

"Did he tell you this?"

"Yes. And he said that dying out here was infinitely preferable to dying back on Earth—alone in a hospital bed. His personal life is a mess. His wife even left him."

"Poor bastard. What can you do to help him?"

"Out here there's nothing I can do except try to make him comfortable."

"He doesn't have any vital duties until we get a lot closer to Mars," Benson mused. "I thought he was just moping because he didn't have much to do."

"If we were back on Earth he'd be under the care of a specialist, have a complete CT scan, then surgery followed by chemotherapy."

"Will he survive until we get home?"

"I've spoken with Mikhail's personal physician back in St. Petersburg and he's pulling together some specialists who can make a better prognosis than I can."

"Best guess."

Taki hesitated before answering, "Doubtful."

"What about the stool sampler? Have you fixed it? And what about everyone else? If it's been turned off, then none of us have been screened lately."

"He told me how he turned it off and yes, I turned it back on.

Instead of waiting on the passive scans to notify me of a problem, I set the system to send me a complete diagnostic on everyone for the next week. I'll look at them closely and make sure nothing else is happening."

Benson grimaced and cursed inwardly. "I'm not superstitious," he muttered, "but it looks like we're God's dartboard. First Ted's family gets wiped out, then the damned meteoroid hits us. Now this. Is this ship jinxed?"

Taki Nomura had no answer for him.

The Labor Day weekend had just ended, and Congress' summer recess was over. Washington was still hot and muggy, though, as Senator William Donaldson stepped briskly from his air-conditioned limousine to the ground-level door of the Capitol building.

The first meeting of his subcommittee on Space, Aeronautics and Related Sciences was due to convene in twelve minutes. Plenty of time to ride the elevator up to his office, check with his personal assistant for any urgent business that might have come up overnight, take a quick leak in his private lavatory, and then get to the subcommittee meeting room.

Donaldson mentally counted the votes he could rely on. With Yañez in his pocket he had a solid majority. A bipartisan majority, at that. A rarity these days. Good material for next year, he thought. Show the voters that Bill Donaldson can get the opposing party to cooperate with his initiatives.

He chuckled to himself as he left his office suite, followed by a half-dozen aides, and strode down the corridor toward the conference room. Donaldson exuded an air of competence and cordiality; he was a smiling, handsome, vigorous man, lean and fit, his white hair swept back off his forehead, his dark pinstripe suit proclaiming a man of conservative tastes who nonetheless had a sense of style.

Yes, Donaldson said to himself, *this is going to be a good day. Let Bob Harper choke on it.*

The subcommittee's conference room was actually filled. Every member was present, a surprising turnout for the first day of Congress' return from its summer recess. Donaldson was pleased. He had made certain every member of the subcommittee knew in advance what the day's agenda would be. They had all responded as he'd hoped they would.

He gladhanded his way around the table, smiling broadly at his fellow members, working his way along the opposition's side of the table before moving to his own party's side. Everyone was cordial, warm and friendly, while the cameras clicked away.

As soon as the photographers left the room, however, the smiles vanished. All except Donaldson's.

"I'm delighted that each and every one of you is here," he began. Tapping the agenda laid out on the tablet screen before him, he went on, "We have a very important decision to make this morning, a very important decision."

Every lawyer knows never to ask a question in court that he doesn't already know the answer to. Donaldson went one step farther: he never asked his subcommittee for a decision that he didn't know they had already decided.

But one of the women on the other side of the table, a middle-aged, sour-faced African American from Texas—where the Johnson Space Center directed NASA's human spaceflight program—looked decidedly unhappy.

"William," she said in a tone that was almost combative, "we can't recommend to the full committee that we stop all crewed space missions."

"Why not?" Donaldson asked, knowing what the answer would be.

"It would put an end to an American dream," she said.

"That's not so, Judine. Americans are flying into space on private rockets. Americans are working in the International Space Station and on the Moon."

"But what about Mars? What about going farther, pushing the envelope, exploring new worlds?"

"What about the risks of human lives?" Donaldson countered. "What about those eight men and women who are never going to return from Mars alive?"

A senator from Donaldson's own side of the table shook his head. "That's a terribly negative way of looking at it."

"No, it's the accurate way of looking at it," Donaldson insisted. "We've spent billions of the taxpayers' dollars on this Mars fiasco and all it's going to get us is eight corpses."

Dead silence fell on the room.

Then the Texan said, softly, "There's still a chance that they'll make it."

Donaldson held up his thumb and forefinger a hair's breadth apart. "That much of a chance."

The woman sat there stolidly. "I still can't vote to cut out NASA's entire human spaceflight program."

"Because?"

"Because it'll mean closing down the Johnson Center. We'll lose thousands of jobs! I'd get booted out on my butt next November."

They'd finally arrived at the real reason, Donaldson knew, smiling inwardly.

"The Johnson Space Center could turn its talents to supporting all those private companies that are doing human space flights," he said, a trifle smugly.

"That won't add up to a fraction of the Center's present budget."

Shrugging, Donaldson said, "But it would reduce NASA's overall budget, save the taxpayers billions per year."

"And lose thousands of jobs in Texas."

Donaldson looked up and down the table. *Pretty much as I expected,* he told himself. *States with NASA facilities don't want to lose their federal funding. States without NASA facilities couldn't care less.*

He folded his hands on the table top and looked his Texan adversary in the eye. *Time to be magnanimous,* he told himself. Time to make a gesture.

"I see your problem, Judine," he said. "I understand the difficulties you face. Maybe we can work out a compromise."

The senator from Texas looked surprised, then hopeful. "A compromise?"

Over the next hour the subcommittee wrangled over several different possibilities. In the end, they decided not to recommend cutting NASA's entire human spaceflight program. But they did agree—decisively—to cut all funding for the planned follow-on mission to Mars.

"All right," Donaldson told them at last. "I think we've come to a good decision. There will be no more human missions to Mars. One disaster is enough."

Nods of agreement up and down the table. Some were reluctant, others wholehearted. Donaldson sank back in his chair and put on a look of weary acceptance. He had gotten what he'd come for. *There won't be any more human flights to Mars,* he said to himself. *That'll gut NASA's human spaceflight program. Once I'm in the White House we can cancel the whole program. Screw Texas!*

This was as close to heaven as Hiram McPherson could imagine. He was huddled in the *Arrow*'s observation blister looking out at Mars in all its ruddy glory, his arms wrapped around Catherine, holding her close.

His senses were on overload as he simultaneously saw what no other human being had ever seen so close, the planet Mars, and held the woman he'd come to hold so dear over the past two and a half years.

"It's beautiful," Catherine murmured, her head leaning back on his shoulder as she stared out at the red planet.

Hi nuzzled her neck with his beard. "Not as beautiful as you."

"No," she agreed lightly. "Perhaps not. Now, if there were canals, that would be different, *non*?"

"There could be cities and palaces," he said, "but they still wouldn't compare to you."

"You're very sweet, Hi."

He looked out at the world they were rapidly approaching. "Is this how Adam and Eve felt, do you think?"

She glanced up at him. "I don't know. I'm not particularly religious."

"I don't consider myself to be overly religious, but that doesn't mean I don't believe in God," McPherson admitted. "To me, that planet out there is proof that God exists. And what I feel for you is proof positive."

Catherine thought that over for a moment. "I suppose I would call myself a deist. I believe that there is a God, but I doubt very seriously that a God who could create something as vast and majestic as the universe could possibly take an interest in you or me, or anyone, for that matter. Even Jesus."

"You don't understand the concept of infinity. An infinite God can handle all that, and more."

"Perhaps," she conceded.

"I mean, I've had too many things happen in my life that I've attributed to God—good things and bad. I just can't believe that we're here on our own. Love, music, art, even science stare us in the face every day; I can't believe that God didn't have a hand in their existence. Let alone our self-awareness, our ability to do good and to do evil."

"But what about the evil in the world, Hi? What about the evil out there? What happened to Ted, the loss of his wife and son, was that an act of your God? Was the rock that nearly killed us all part of some grand plan? How could an all-knowing, all-loving God possibly have allowed such things to happen?"

He shrugged, almost like a Frenchman. "You know, people have been debating those ideas since there have been people. We aren't going to resolve them now and I'm not going to let this get between you and me while we've got Mars to look at."

Catherine snuggled closer to him. "I agree. God or no God, this is a time to relish."

"Look." McPherson pointed. "That's Olympus Mons. The biggest mountain in the Solar System."

For long moments the two of them watched silently staring at the huge volcano and the trio of smaller ones lined up near it. Each one of them was taller than Everest.

"Look at Olympus' base," McPherson murmured, his geologist's instincts aroused. "It's bigger than the state of Idaho!"

But Catherine asked, "Hi, do you think we'll make it home?"

Her sudden change of the subject caught him by surprise. *But it shouldn't have,* he told himself. *That question is staring us in the face, just like Mars is.*

"I honestly don't know, Catherine. I'd like to think so. Mission Control seems to think the truss repair will hold up when we go into orbit. We'll find out tomorrow when we make our MOI burn."

"Aren't you frightened?"

McPherson blinked at the question. "Frightened? No. I don't think I am. Concerned, sure. I don't want to die. I don't want any of us to die. But if it happens, I'm glad I'll be with you when it does."

She reached up and kissed him gently on the lips. McPherson held her close enough to feel the beat of her heart.

"I don't want to die," she whispered. "I don't want you to die."

"It all depends on the water and propellant problems," he said. "If we can bring up enough water from the surface. If we can fix the recycling system."

"Who's going down to the surface? Has Bee told anyone yet?"

"He hasn't told me. I suspect he'll tell us all together, after we've established ourselves in Mars orbit."

"We should both go," Catherine said, more firmly. "We are the geologists, *non*? What good would it be to return to Earth without any samples? We are the obvious choice."

"Adam and Eve on their new world," he said.

But he was thinking, *the first thing we've got to do down on the surface is figure out how to get the water in the habitat up here for the return flight. Rock samples are important, but survival comes first.*

"Here we go." Ted Connover spoke the words quietly, almost as if talking to himself, as he touched the keyboard buttons that unlocked the ship's nuclear thermal system.

Sitting beside him in the command center, Benson nodded. This was Connover's task. *I'm strictly a bystander,* he told himself. *Unless something goes wrong.*

The *Arrow*'s computer was now in control of the Mars Orbital Insertion burn: Connover's touch of a finger had removed any human override by turning off the inhibitor. The timing required to put the ship in orbit around Mars was complicated, the necessary maneuver was so precise that only the computer could make it happen with a minimum expenditure of precious propellant.

Scanning the status screens on the display board in front of him, Connover saw that they were all in the green. They'd start to feel the tug of acceleration in a few seconds, he knew. Benson had made certain that the rest of the crew was firmly strapped to their chairs in the galley.

"Houston, *Arrow* here. MOI burn initiated."

It will be thirteen minutes before Houston gets the message or sees our telemetry stream, Benson thought. *By then we'll either in orbit around Mars or dead.*

Connover looked intent, all business. But he was smiling, grinning actually. *Like a kid running his favorite computer game,* Benson thought.

Down at the other end of the ship, thousands of pounds of liquid hydrogen were being pumped through the activated nuclear reactor, where they were heated into gas and fired out the rocket thruster cones.

"This is it," Connover said as the acceleration pressed them back in their seats.

The ship shuddered and began to vibrate.

"What the hell is that?" Connover blurted.

Benson heard a low-frequency hum. It grew louder and the vibration got worse. Benson felt as if somebody had attached a tuning fork to his bones, making them quiver and tickle at the same time. And it continued to grow in intensity.

"What's going on?"

"I don't know," Connover replied, his eyes flicking across the status board, looking for the cause of the vibration.

It kept getting worse, a full-blown tooth-rattling tremor.

"Ted, amber lights!" Benson pointed a shaking finger at the status board. "The radiators are close to their transient acceleration limits."

Connover's lips were pressed into a thin line. "Amber alerts in the sensor attachments, too," he muttered. He began to use his right index finger to pull all the various sensor readings and camera views of the ship's exterior onto the central screen from which he could control virtually every aspect of the propulsion and other critical systems. Tap, drag, double tap, finger-flex, reduce—all almost too fast for Benson to follow.

"Damn! I think I understand what's going on, and there's absolutely nothing we can do about it."

"Fill me in!" said Benson. The shaking was so bad now that his vision was blurring.

"It's the replacement spars we printed. They're not as good a fit as the original spars. We had to attach them well beyond the point where the originals were bonded to the truss structure."

"I know that."

"They changed the natural frequency of the truss," Connover said, his voice rising slightly, "and now we're getting harmonics induced by the thruster burn. It'll keep on building to some equilibrium point as long as we're firing the engines."

"How long before we're at equilibrium?"

"Better be damned soon. Otherwise we'll shake ourselves apart—probably at the seam itself. That's the most vulnerable part of the ship right now."

The intercom squawked. "Hey, what's happening?" Hi McPherson's voice, loud and impatient.

Benson tried to keep his own voice even as he responded, "Some vibration from the repaired section of the truss. Should be ending soon."

Connover nodded grimly.

Red lights began popping up on the board. "Ted, the radiators are well beyond their design acceleration loads."

"Nothing we can do. We have to brake into orbit, if we don't we're dead. If the ship breaks into two pieces during the burn, we're dead. I may be ready to join Vicki, but I don't want you guys coming with me."

Benson stared at him. "After we're out of this mess, you'll have to explain that one to me."

Connover tapped on the screen. "Never mind. Nobody's going to die today. Look."

Benson felt the vibration easing away.

Connover grinned. "Bingo. We're past the danger zone."

"God, I hope so."

"Me too!"

OCTOBER 26, 2035
MARS ORBITAL INSERTION
13:42 UNIVERSAL TIME
JOHNSON SPACE CENTER, HOUSTON, TEXAS

The screen at the front of the room dominated the wall on which it was mounted. On the screen was the time-delayed broadcast from the *Arrow* as it entered Mars orbit.

Commander Benson was smiling as he sat in the command center and announced to his crew, "Ladies and gentlemen, we are in orbit around Mars."

The whoop that erupted from the *Arrow*'s galley was swallowed in the much bigger roar from the Mission Control team and the invited guests seated behind the team's rows of consoles.

The Mission Control engineers and technicians were hopping up and down, pounding each other's backs, laughing with wild relief. The flight director, the trajectory lead, the newly constituted accident recovery team all erupted in their own outpouring of delight.

No matter that what they were seeing on the screen had actually happened thirteen minutes earlier. No one seemed to notice that Benson was perspiring visibly.

Administrator Saxby let out a relieved sigh as he rose from his seat and walked carefully to the podium that had been placed in the only open corner of the huge room. He tapped on the microphone to make certain it was on and waited for the celebration to die down.

News cameras turned to him as he cleared his throat and the celebratory uproar quieted.

"Clearly," he said, "this is a momentous day in human history. A multinational team of Earth's finest men and women are now in orbit around our sister planet, Mars, after a harrowing trip that nearly ended in disaster. Thanks to the efforts of the crew and many of you right here in this room, the *Arrow* has arrived safely at Mars and its crew can now go about exploring the planet and preparing for a safe trip home."

Saxby closed his eyes and resisted the urge to massage his chest. He had memorized that little speech. And another one that he would have used if the MOI burn had failed.

Then he added, "While we continue watching our friends and colleagues do their jobs and begin preparations for sending a skeleton crew to the planet's surface to replace their lost water and other consumables, let's not forget how far we've come. Let's thank our international partners, without whom this mission might never have happened."

Everyone in the room applauded heartily. Saxby basked in their approval. Just a few weeks ago it looked like the mission was ruined and the *Arrow*'s crew was doomed. Now they had a chance, a slim chance but a chance nonetheless.

He knew that Prokhorov had been stricken by cancer, but that information had been carefully hidden from the news media and the public. *Benson and his people have enough on their hands without a bunch of bloody vultures doing a death watch.*

Saxby pressed the keyboard button that activated the communications link with the *Arrow*.

"Commander Benson and the crew of the *Arrow*, this is Administrator Saxby. On behalf of the nations that have joined us in this mission, on behalf of all the grateful people of planet Earth, I would like to thank you for your sacrifice and your heroism in making the momentous journey to our sister planet. We are with you. And we'll see that you get safely home, so help us God."

Words are tools, Saxby said to himself. *Words are weapons.* He remembered from his history books how, at one time, Winston Churchill's words were practically all that Britain had to stand against Nazi Germany. That and the English Channel.

Right now, all we can do for those eight people at Mars is send them words that might help them. They have a much wider gulf to cross than the Channel. I hope our words can help them make it.

❈ ❈ ❈

Steven Treadway was sitting in the barber's chair while a trio of makeup artists hid the wrinkles in the corners of his eyes and carefully brushed his dark brown hair. His open shirt collar was covered by a recyclable paper bib.

"So they made it to Mars?" asked the chief of the makeup team, a middle-aged Italian American with a heavy Bronx accent.

"Less than half an hour ago," Treadway said. "That's why we're going on the air at this time of the morning."

"Something special, eh?"

"Something very special."

The door banged open and a trio of three-piece suits marched in, led by Elmer Quinn, the network's chief of programming.

"Out," snapped Quinn and the three makeup people disappeared as if by magic.

Treadway frowned, despite his botoxed brow. "Hey, I'm on the air in—"

Quinn silenced him with an upraised finger. The network executive looked like a pugnacious leprechaun: short, wiry, thinning reddish hair and an expression that could curdle milk at twenty paces.

"Steven, how do you plan to play this broadcast?" he asked, his voice sharp and nasal.

"Play it?" Treadway felt suddenly alarmed.

"What's your approach going to be?"

Behind Quinn, his two flunkies looked as bleakly dismal as their boss.

Shifting uncomfortably in the barber's chair, Treadway said, "They've made it to Mars, for chrissakes! It's a hell of an accomplishment."

"So you're going to do the rah-rah bit?"

That was a trap, Treadway knew. "I'm going to play it straight. They've made it to Mars, despite the damage to the ship. They deserve some congratulations."

Quinn folded his arms across his chest. "You know they'll never get back to Earth alive."

"That's not for certain. If they can bring up the water that's—"

"I don't want this network to be a cheerleader for NASA," Quinn snapped.

"But those poor saps on board the *Arrow* can hear and see everything we broadcast. We owe them—"

"We owe them fair and impartial reporting. The fact that they made it to Mars doesn't mean shit compared to the problems they're still facing. I've had experts from three different universities looking into this, and they all agree that the chances of those people getting home alive are practically nil!"

"But if they can bring up the water from the surface—" Treadway tried to argue.

"If they can do that, it's a step in the right direction," Quinn granted. "But I don't want you to build up the public's expectations too high. I won't have this network take part in a NASA coverup."

"There's no coverup," Treadway said.

"See to it that you give the public the full story. No cheerleading. Got it?"

"Got it."

Quinn nodded once, apparently satisfied despite the scowl on his pinched face. He turned and left the makeup room, his two flunkies at his heels.

Treadway watched them sullenly. *If Quinn stops suddenly, the two of them will go right up his ass,* he thought.

The makeup crew came back in and Treadway tried to make himself relax in the chair. *Bad enough we have to hack and splice our way around the damned thirteen-minute delay between here and Mars,* he grumbled to himself. *Now this.*

He closed his eyes and sucked in a deep breath. *Fair and impartial,* he told himself. He remembered that old-time newspaper publisher Joseph Pulitzer once famously said that the three most important things in reporting the news were accuracy, accuracy and accuracy.

Okay, Treadway sighed inwardly. *I'll be accurate.*

OCTOBER 26, 2035
MARS ORBITAL INSERTION
14:12 UNIVERSAL TIME
NEW YORK CITY

Although he was actually located in front of a wall-sized green screen in the TV studio, on millions of TV and 3D sets around the world, a smiling Steven Treadway appeared to be standing in profile in the observation cupola of the *Arrow*, looking out on the ruddy, pockmarked planet Mars.

"There's nothing this reporter can say to add to the historic events that played out today onboard the *Arrow* here in orbit around Mars. The crew of eight, in a crippled ship and facing an uncertain future, successfully navigated to Mars and established themselves in orbit around the red planet right on schedule. The makeshift repairs required to keep the ship in one piece held, despite some worrisome moments in the last part of the maneuver that allowed them to capture into orbit."

Turning full-face to the camera, with the image of Mars behind him, Treadway continued, "I spoke with the ship's commander, Bee Benson, about their immediate plans and whether or not they would carry through with their scheduled landing and exploration of the Martian surface."

The image of Treadway was replaced by a close-up of Benson.

Treadway's voice asked, "Bee, do you intend to carry out the landing and exploration portion of the mission now that you're here at Mars?"

His face the picture of earnestness, Benson replied, "Steve, we don't

231

know yet. We plan to send someone down to get water. As for the exploration program, that decision will have to be made in consultation with the people in Mission Control, back home. My personal feeling is that it would be a colossal waste to come all this way, to have gone through all we've gone through, without doing some exploration."

"Now that you've had such a successful milestone, how's the mood of the crew?"

"Well, we're certainly very glad that we made it. As you know, it was an open question until just a few hours ago. There's nothing like success to breed optimism about the future. So despite the challenges we still face, I'd say the crew is pretty upbeat. Once we get the water up here, I'm sure the mood will improve even more."

"Thank you, Commander Benson."

Benson's image winked out, replaced once again with Treadway's face and the brilliant red sphere of Mars hanging over his shoulder.

"Despite Bee's can-do attitude," Treadway said, his face and tone suddenly full of grave concern, "I would be remiss if I didn't remind our viewers that the prospects for the *Arrow*'s crew still look grim. Without a solution to their water problem it's highly unlikely that they'll ever make it home alive.

"I've been allowed unprecedented access not only to the crew, but to the dedicated team of engineers and scientists supporting them here at home. NASA's best and brightest are working hard to find a solution, but so far without success. This reporter would like to be optimistic, but my obligation to objective reporting demands that I be realistic, as well.

"Will they make it home? We just don't know."

Treadway turned away from the camera to look out at Mars again and the camera focused on the red planet, close enough to touch. Almost.

At Mars

President Harper and Susan Fleming sat alone in the Oval Office, watching the events at Mars and in Houston on the 3D viewer above the fireplace. Harper wasn't scheduled to speak directly with the Mars crew until sometime the next day, well after they'd done all the work associated with settling into Mars orbit.

Time enough for me to get some spotlight, Harper thought.

He knew, though, that he'd have more to talk about than the usual congratulations and praise for their courage and ingenuity. He was planning to break the news to them that theirs might be the last mission to Mars for some time to come.

On the very day they nurse that damaged ship into Mars orbit, Harper thought, seething, *Donaldson gets the damned committee to ax the next mission. He's out to kill manned spaceflight altogether, even if he has to do it by inches.*

Drumming his fingers impatiently on his desktop as Steven Treadway droned on from the 3D screen, Harper blurted, "Susan, I'm not going to let this budget cut go unchallenged."

Fleming turned toward him. "They still have to get the House of Representatives to agree to the cut."

"The House will go along with it. Especially if the *Arrow*'s crew doesn't come home alive."

Fleming was wearing a forest-green skirted suit that complemented her brick red hair very nicely. *Where's your passion, Susie?* Harper asked silently. *Redheads are supposed to be fiery.*

"Mr. President," she said slowly, carefully, "I know you're committed to space exploration, but the feeling on the Hill is that it's not only very expensive, but dangerous as well. With the accident at the Moon base and now the *Arrow* nearly crippled, it's no wonder that the committee voted to cut the next Mars flight. It was nearly a unanimous vote."

Harper stared at her. "Are you saying that I should go along with them? Undo everything we've accomplished in space?"

She held up a hand, palm outward, like a stop signal. "Let the private companies operate the space station and the Moon base. We can keep on exploring Mars and the rest of the solar system with unmanned missions."

"No!" Harper exploded. "The American public will not stand by and watch us dismantle human space exploration—especially not now, with so much at stake."

"You'll have to explain that one to me. What's changed that makes human spaceflight more important now than it has, or hasn't, been over the last thirty years?"

"Life! Life on Mars. That's what's changed. Set aside the philosophical and theological considerations that everyone seems so preoccupied with and think about the financial implications."

"Now you'll really have to explain," she said.

"Shortly after the Chinese published the chemical signatures of the prebiotic samples they brought back from Mars, I got a call from Evgenia Gunnarsson from NexGenPro Pharmaceuticals. She said that their researchers think the chemistry is too similar to Earth life to have evolved totally independently. In other words, Earth life and Mars life appear to share a common origin. What's more, they think the Martian chemicals might actually hold promise for a whole host of new drugs to treat everything from heart disease and diabetes to cancer. I asked Petra to pull together an independent science peer review panel on their findings, all totally in the black, and report back to me. They did. And they confirmed what NexGenPro claimed. Not only are we about to rewrite the biology textbooks, we may be on the edge of a revolution in medical treatments."

"Why in God's name have you and Petra kept this bottled up? It seems like this would have pushed support for the mission over the top."

"And make the whole Mars mission effort look like one big subsidy for big pharma? No, we had to keep the mission about science and exploration. You know as well as I do that pharmaceutical companies are barely above pond scum in popularity, especially after that genetic profiling scandal back in 2026. Having the mission tied to them would have been the kiss of death."

"Bob, unless you do something, we just don't have the votes."

"I'll make an issue of it, but without mentioning NexGenPro. I'm not going to let this go down without a fight."

Fleming made a face like a schoolteacher trying to pound some sense into a stubborn little boy. "You're a lame duck. You don't have the clout anymore. And there are other issues where you should be putting your energy and your interest. Panama, the Middle East—"

"God himself can't bring peace to the Middle East," Harper grumbled.

"Going to the mat over human spaceflight is the wrong move. You don't want your presidency to end with a black eye. Maybe you should go public with the genetic angle."

Harper was fuming. "This is personal, too. You didn't see what happened when the space shuttle program got killed and we didn't have another vehicle to replace it. The layoffs, the demoralized workforce, the whole damned country wondering why we had to buy tickets into space from Russia."

"That's not the same thing."

"A lot of those laid-off workers came from my congressional district. I swore then and there that I would never let that happen again. If Congress kills the Mars follow-ons, then the money will just vanish from the NASA budget and into some entitlement programs or the defense department black hole and we miss a chance at having U.S. companies lead the world in new drugs and medical treatments derived from good old-fashioned Yankee ingenuity and rockets."

"Robert," Fleming said sternly, "it's a different world today—in large part because of you and your administration. We have a real chance for world peace, even in the Middle East. We're making progress on new energy technologies and climate change. Unless you do something, like go public with the new drug treatment stuff, Congress will win the argument to spend our limited resources on programs with more clearly defined near-term payoffs."

"Susan, you sound like you agree with them."

"Just because I understand their argument doesn't mean that I agree with them. But you've got to know when to stand firm, when to bend with the wind, and when to change the rules of the game. That's politics. We don't have the votes to force Congress to continue the Mars program. We can grandstand, but we'll lose and you'll leave the White House as a loser. I don't want to see that. So you need to change the game."

"I can't. At least not yet," Harper admitted.

"Then the best thing you can hope for now," Fleming said, "is to get those eight people back home alive. This is going to be our last human mission to Mars for some time to come."

Still unconvinced, President Harper said, "Didn't Saxby tell us that the lander for the next launch is just about complete?"

"Yes. And the next habitat launch is set for a little over a year from now. Right in the middle of next year's presidential campaign."

Shaking his head, Harper said, "In the short term it'll be more expensive to cancel the contracts for the next mission than it will be to finish the hardware."

"That's for the short term," Fleming replied. "The long-term reality is that Mars is going to be explored by robotic vehicles, not human beings."

Ted Connover couldn't believe it. "Cancelled the follow-on mission?"

Virginia Gonzalez stood between Connover's chair and Benson's, her sculpted model's face tight, grim.

"I just picked it up on the *Worldnet* feed," she said. "I thought you'd want to know right away."

"Cancelled it?" Connover repeated.

"Cut the funding for it," said Gonzalez.

Benson was frowning, too. "No funding means no mission."

"They can't do that," Connover insisted.

"It's done," Gonzalez said. "At least, the Senate's voted that way. The House of Representatives hasn't voted on it yet."

"They'll go the same way," Benson reasoned. "The House is more likely to make a rash decision than the Senate."

Connover felt it like a blow to the heart, almost as painful as the death of his wife and son.

Benson was saying, "Virginia, you'd better get everybody together in the galley. They'll all want to know about this."

"We're supposed to get a message from the president in half an hour," Gonzalez said.

"Right. But get them together now. I'll break the news to them and then we can listen to the president."

The whole crew gathered in the galley, all except Prokhorov. They all looked glum, subdued.

"Where's Mikhail?" Benson asked Nomura as he floated through the galley hatch and saw them strapped down on their chairs. All except McPherson, who had perched himself halfway up the bulkhead—directly over Catherine Clermont.

Taki replied, "He's sleeping in his bunk."

He must be pretty sick, Benson realized. With a resigned sigh, he thought it was just as well. He wished he were asleep in his bunk, too, instead of facing this spirit-crushing news.

The rest of the crew was quiet, hushed, all eyes on the wall screen that showed nothing but the emblem of the President of the United States.

Benson's eye was caught by the expression on Connover's face. *Ted looks lost in thought, like he's trying to find a way to undo what those yo-yos in the Senate have done. Good luck, Ted. All the luck in the world. In two worlds, come to think of it.*

President Harper's message came exactly on time, a canned bundle of congratulations and platitudes about their success in achieving orbit around Mars. The whole thing was probably prerecorded. Thanks to the communications lag, there was no way the crew could respond to the president's little speech, not with almost a quarter of an hour separating them.

But then Harper shot a look to somebody off-camera, and his pasted-on smile vanished.

"Alright," said the president, "the official part of this message is over. Now I'm talking to you off the record."

He looks like he's ready to shoot somebody, Benson thought.

The president said, "You've heard about the vote in the Senate to defund the follow-on mission. I want you to know that I'm against it, and I'm going to fight it with everything I've got. My staff tells me I'm making a mistake, that Congress is determined to end the human exploration of Mars. But I'm going to fight this stupid decision anyway, even though it may cost me."

Benson saw that the president was dead serious.

Rubbing the bridge of his nose, President Harper said, "You may think you're all alone out there, but you've got at least one friend in a high place." And the President of the United States smiled, like a man facing a Bengal tiger with nothing but his bare hands.

The wall screen went blank.

The crew stirred.

Amanda Lynn wisecracked, "We've got one friend, and a hundred enemies."

"Five hundred and some, if you add the House of Representatives," McPherson chimed in.

"So what does this mean?" Amanda asked, totally serious now. "Is there going to be a follow-on mission or not?"

"Probably not," said Benson. "Even with the president supporting us, Congress holds the purse strings."

"So we limp home and then watch everything we've worked for over the year get put into mothballs?" Gonzalez asked.

"Put into the garbage can," McPherson grumbled.

"If we can get home," Amanda reminded them.

"There must be something we can do," said Clermont. "After all, we, our accident—it appears to be one of the reasons the vote went the way it did."

"Yeah, but what can we do about it?" McPherson asked.

Benson unclicked his seatbelt and floated up out of his chair. "What we can do," he said, as firmly as he could manage, "is the job we came out here to do. We have no control over how the politicians vote, but we can at least do our jobs as best as we can."

Ted Connover nodded slowly. And smiled. Benson thought that Ted looked . . . happy.

For the first time since Vicki and Thad's deaths, Ted Connover felt vibrantly alive. Human exploration of Mars was important, it was being threatened, and he was in a position where he could do something about it. He was more than thirty million miles from the dorks running Washington and he had come up with a plan that would force them to continue exploring Mars. They would never see it coming until it was too late. Or so he hoped.

He was strapped into his chair in the galley, sitting alone, nursing a not-too-bland nutri-shake drink, running the numbers through his head again while he still had the solitude he needed for thinking. The rest of the crew would be filtering in for lunch pretty soon, he knew.

Sure enough, Bee Benson glided through the hatch and hovered in front of the refrigerator.

Over his shoulder, Benson asked, "Mind if I join you?"

Connover looked over at him. "Groucho Marx would answer, 'Why? Am I falling apart?'"

Benson frowned in puzzlement as he pulled out a prepackaged meal and slid it into the microwave oven.

"Groucho Marx?"

"Old-time funnyman. The Marx Brothers. You must have seen some of their movies."

Shaking his head slowly, Benson said, "I don't think so."

Connover shrugged. He noticed that Bee looked serious,

concerned. *For all his stiff-upper-lip pose,* Connover thought, *our noble commander is just as worried about things as the rest of us.*

Bringing his meal tray to the table and strapping himself into the chair next to Connover, Benson said, "Ted, you know we've got to go down to the surface and get the supplies from the habitat. We especially need the water."

Connover nodded.

"I've gone over the numbers again and again," Benson went on. "Even with the water from the habitat, we'll run out long before we get home. The ECLSS was designed to recycle ninety percent of what we use, but with it running at reduced capacity there's simply no way for our water to last long enough."

"And you're telling me this because . . . ?"

Benson clasped his hands together on the tabletop, as if in prayer. "I know you think you should've been picked to run this mission. I've seen that look on your face so many times since we launched that it's almost become my mental image of you."

"Bee, I'm not—"

"Let me finish. You know, you probably should have been put in command. You're capable and you know how to work with people. But what happened to your family . . . well, it was probably a good thing that you weren't in command. And you know it."

"That's not what I expected you to say, Bee."

"To tell you the truth, I didn't expect to say it. But the fact is that I need your help. I'm not used to being dealt hands that I can't use to my advantage, one way or the other. And the hand this crew has been dealt is a losing hand. I don't see any way around it."

Connover pursed his lips, then said, "The objective evidence says you're right."

"I know I'm right. But I wish to God I were wrong. I spoke with Taki. She filled me in on what to expect as we go home with only about half the water we need. It's bad."

"How bad?"

"Very. With only half of our normal water ration, in a few weeks we'll start to lose our ability to think clearly; concentration will become all but impossible. Next will be confusion and some of us will likely have seizures. Then kidney failure—complete shutdown of the kidneys. From there, death is only a few days away."

"That's pretty damned bad," Connover agreed. "Are you sure we'll be that low on water?"

"The numbers don't lie, Ted. Even if you land on Mars by yourself and load the ascent stage with all the water stored in the habitat, that will postpone the kidney failure and death part by about a month or so, but it'll still happen. This will be a ghost ship by the time it reaches Earth."

Connover took a deep breath. "So you want me to take the lander down by myself, load up the water, and then come back here and die?"

"I don't much like the dying part, but yes, that's the situation."

Leaning a little closer to Benson, Connover asked, "What if I told you I had a better idea?"

"I'd say I wouldn't be surprised. That's why I'm here. I'm all out of ideas and the bright boys back in Houston are just as stumped as I am."

Connover broke into a boyish grin. "Bee, I'll be glad to take the lander down to the surface and load up the water. But I want to take some people with me."

"People? As in more than one?"

"As in more than one."

His brows knitting slightly, Benson said, "I can see you wanting to bring somebody with you to help with the loading work. I was thinking of Hi, if we could separate him from Catherine for a couple of days."

Connover started to shake his head, but Benson continued, "But do the math, Ted. I'd rather not have an extra person on the ascent stage taking up valuable weight that could be used for water."

"You don't understand, Bee. I'd like to take as many people to the surface with me as I can. I'm staying there, and I hope some of the crew will stay with me."

"Stay? On the surface?" Benson looked alarmed at the thought. "You want to die on Mars?"

"I don't want to die at all, either on this ship or on Mars."

Benson's expression morphed from disbelief to suspicion. "You want to be a martyr."

Very seriously, Connover replied, "Just after Vicki and Thad died, yeah, I wanted to die too. But not now. Now I've got a mission to do and I don't intend to die doing it. And nobody who comes down to the surface with me is going to die, either."

"So what you're saying . . ."

"What I'm saying is that some of us go to Mars and live in the habitat while the rest of you go back home with enough water to see you through."

Benson blinked several times, trying to digest the idea.

"But if you send the habitat's water up to us, what will you do for water?"

Connover actually chuckled. "Are you kidding? We've known since the old Viking landers that Mars has water, and lots of it. It's frozen below the surface. Permafrost. We'll just go out and get it. The ECLSS system in the habitat can recycle water with the same efficiency that the undamaged system here in the *Arrow* could. We'll have plenty of water."

"Huh. Maybe. But what about food?"

"None of our food here in the ship was damaged by the accident. We'll take down whatever food we would have consumed on the trip home and add that to the stockpile that's already in the habitat. We can also start up the experimental hydroponics garden and grow some vegetables to supplement our supplies. And we can reduce our caloric intake to extend the food supply."

"What about air?"

"Come on, Bee. You know that's not a problem. We recycle the air up here with close to one hundred percent efficiency. Same thing down in the habitat. We can even electrolyze some of the Martian water to get all the oxygen we need."

Benson rubbed his jaw. "But, Ted, even with all that, you'll run out of food sooner or later. You'll die down there! There aren't going to be any more missions to Mars."

Connover's grin widened. "Aren't there? You think the public will stand for those fart-brains in Washington letting us die on Mars when they could send the follow-on mission to rescue us? Bee, they'll *have* to let the follow-on mission go ahead! Either that, or be accused of murder."

Benson sagged back in his chair. "Ted, you're either suicidal or brilliant. Maybe both."

"I'm not either one. I'm just a guy in a tough situation looking for a way out of it. I think this plan will save our lives and just might be the right thing for the human race in the bargain."

"You know Mission Control won't stand for it."

"Fuck Mission Control," Connover snapped. "If *you* decide to do it, what can they do to stop us?"

"There's a dozen different ways you could get killed on Mars."

"Any of them as bad as dementia and kidney failure?"

Benson had no answer for that.

Benson watched as the rest of the crew came into the galley and began loading their trays with lunch. He noticed that they were all very careful about filling their bottles with water. Several of them added nutri-shake powder to their drinks. Benson found himself wishing for a smoothie.

As soon Nomura entered, he glided over to her.

"Taki," he said, keeping his voice low, "is Mikhail well enough to come to the galley?"

Nomura nodded somberly. "Well enough physically, but he's in a real Russian funk. He prefers to be alone."

"Would you ask him to join us here? It's important."

She looked puzzled, but turned in midair and pulled herself through the hatch.

Everyone else was seated by the time Nomura came back with Prokhorov. *Mikhail doesn't look so bad,* Benson thought. *Maybe he's lost a little weight.* But the expression on his face was bleak. *I guess I'd look the same way if I were in his place.*

Prokhorov saw that Benson was eyeing him. He drew himself into a parody of a soldier's stiff posture and raised his right hand to his brow.

"I am present, my commander, as you ordered."

Benson couldn't help smiling. "How are you feeling, Mikhail?"

"Terrible, thank you."

Nomura took him by the elbow and steered him weightlessly to the fridge and microwave.

Most of the others were already eating by the time Taki and Prokhorov had strapped themselves into their chairs.

Gripping the back of his chair to keep himself from drifting away, Benson said, "Ted and I have been talking about a plan he's cooked up that might save our necks."

That got their attention. Even Prokhorov's head snapped up to look intently at Benson.

"Ted, it's your show." Benson pulled out his chair and forced himself down onto it.

Without getting up from his own chair, Ted said simply, "Several of us go down to the surface and live in the habitat while the rest of you go back home, with enough water to take care of you for the whole trip."

For a few heartbeats no one said anything. They all looked wordlessly at Connover, digesting the idea.

At last McPherson spoke up. "And what happens to the people who volunteer to stay on Mars? Do we build a memorial to ourselves?"

"We live on Mars," Connover replied, "until the follow-on mission comes to pick us up and bring us home."

"But the follow-on's been cancelled," Virginia Gonzalez said.

"They'll un-cancel it."

Amanda Lynn broke into a bright smile. "You mean you'll shame them into sending the follow-on."

"That's extortion," said McPherson.

"It's either that, or they'll be responsible for our deaths," Connover said, grinning crookedly.

Their questions came thick and fast after that. Water. Food. Air. Much the same as the questions Benson had asked earlier, and Connover gave them the same answers.

"We can do this," he insisted. "And we might even get a little exploration work done while we're down on the surface."

Prokhorov quieted them all by spreading his arms in a gesture for silence. "Ted, if your plan works, it could mean that I return to Earth alive and able to undergo medical treatment."

Connover nodded. "I guess it does, Mikhail."

Benson floated up from his chair again and resumed command of the discussion. "I have a question for all of you to consider. Should we ask Mission Control's opinion of this plan or should we just go ahead with it on our own?"

"On our own," Connover immediately replied.

"We can't do that," Gonzalez objected. "Houston's got to know."

"Not ahead of time," Connover insisted. "If we tell them about it now, they'll want to clear it with NASA Headquarters, the White House, Jesus Christ and all twelve of the apostles."

Amanda giggled.

"No," Connover said, "we present them with a *fait accompli*." Turning to Clermont, he asked, "That's the way it's pronounced, isn't it, Catherine?"

She smiled. "Close enough, Ted."

Benson said, "We've all got to agree about this. Do you want to go ahead with this or not?"

Prokhorov shrugged his shoulders. "Ted's plan gives us a glimmer of hope, at least. Otherwise we all die somewhere between here and home."

Taki said, "Mikhail, I can't guarantee that you'll make it all the way home. I don't have the facilities, the training . . ."

The Russian smiled benignly. "Not to worry, little doctor. If I die, I want to die fighting."

"Is anybody opposed to Ted's plan?" Benson asked.

"I want to go down to the surface with you, Ted," McPherson said.

"Me too," said Catherine.

"One more?" Connover asked.

Amanda raised her hand. "I'll have a chance to confirm what the Chinese found. Maybe even find actual Martian microbes," she said.

"Anybody opposed?" Benson asked again.

No one stirred.

"Right," said Benson. "Ted, you work out the details. We don't say a word about this to Houston until the four of you are on the surface."

"Then all hell breaks loose," Gonzalez muttered.

"Let 'em boil in their own juices," Connover said. "It's about time somebody made those assholes do the right thing."

Benson said nothing, but in his mind he pictured himself standing blindfolded before a wall, facing a firing squad.

What the hell, he said to himself. *Even that would be better than dying of thirst halfway between Mars and Earth.*

Connover was working on the treadmill, puffing and sweating for the three hours Taki had demanded from each person who intended to go down to the surface.

Build up your muscle tone, he told himself. *Strengthen your bones. No good going down to the surface if you can't stand up to Mars' gravity. It's only one-third-gee. Three hours a day isn't that much.*

It wasn't easy work. He had to hold on to the handlebars every minute of his workout. Even at that, if he let his mind wander his feet might drift up off the treadmill's surface and he'd be floating weightlessly instead of improving his muscle tone.

Benson glided through the gym's hatch and hovered before him.

Without breaking stride, Connover asked, "What's up, Bee?"

"We're in the home stretch, Ted. I just want to check out a few details with you."

"Go right ahead," Connover puffed, glad that he'd been prescient enough to wear a headband. Otherwise sweat would sting his eyes and he'd have to stop his workout to wipe his brow and that would send him floating up off the treadmill altogether.

"Hi and Catherine are set to go with you, right?"

Connover nodded. "And Amanda."

Benson's expression tightened. "Is she . . . all right with this?"

"With what?"

Obviously distressed, Benson said, "Well, Amanda's going to be living in a tin can with you for months on end and—"

"Hey, what've we been doing in *this* tin can for months on end?"

"I know, but down on the surface it'll be different: just the two of you, really. I mean, Catherine and Hi are paired up and that means you and Amanda . . . well, you know."

The bell on the treadmill chimed and Connover stopped running. "Bee, Mandy's a grown woman. She knows what she's doing."

Benson looked unconvinced.

"I'm not going to attack her, for God's sake."

"Do you think I should talk to her?"

"About the birds and the bees?" Connover snapped. "I think she already knows about that."

"I worry about what Houston's going to think about it. And the news media."

"Who cares?"

"I guess I'm too straightlaced," Benson admitted. "But, well, you're going to be the first human being to set foot on Mars, Ted. I don't want some preacher to dirty the moment."

Connover laughed as he reached for the towel that he'd left in midair. "You want me to take a vow of chastity? Or maybe we could rig a chastity belt for Amanda."

"Be serious, Ted! The first person to step on Mars. We don't want a sex scandal ruining everything."

Connover felt a jolt of emotion. "Hey, that's right. I'll be the first guy on Mars! I hadn't thought of that."

"Well, you're no Neil Armstrong, Ted. You're doing something that's either incredibly brave or incredibly stupid. Maybe both. But you're going to be the first human being to set foot on Mars."

His voice lower, Connover said, "It was supposed to be you, Bee."

Benson tried to shrug nonchalantly. "I'm okay with it. No worries on that score."

Connover searched Benson's face for a sign of regret, or jealousy, or perhaps even anger. Nothing. Whatever was going on in Bee's head, his face wasn't showing it.

"For what it's worth, I'm sorry," he said.

"It's okay," Benson repeated.

Connover was certain that Bee had prepared a statement to make when he first set foot on Mars, something appropriately historic.

"Hey!" he suddenly thought. "What about Catherine and Hi.

They're actually going to be shacking up once we get down to the surface, I bet."

A pang of alarm flashed across Benson's face. "That's right. They've been together for so long that I think of them as a married couple."

Connover couldn't resist poking, "Maybe you ought to give *them* the morality lecture, instead of Amanda and me."

Clermont and McPherson were huddled again in the observation cupola, staring at Mars.

"Tomorrow we go down there," Hi said to her, softly.

Catherine arched a brow at him. "Adam and Eve on their new world?"

"It's hardly the Garden of Eden," he said.

"It will have to do."

Suddenly feeling awkward, McPherson stammered, "Catherine . . . before we go . . . I think we ought to get married."

Her eyes widened. "Hi, are you proposing to me?"

"Yes. Will you marry me?"

Her smile warmed the Solar System. "Yes. With all my heart and soul, yes."

He wrapped his arms around her and they kissed passionately.

But then Catherine pushed away, slightly. "How can we be married? There is no priest here, no minister, not even a justice of the peace."

McPherson grinned at her. "We have a captain, don't we?"

"Bee? He can marry us?"

"The captain of a ship can. Why can't the captain of this vessel do it for us?"

Catherine broke into a delighted laugh. "Tonight! Before dinner!"

"Let's find Bee!"

They squeezed through the cupola's hatch, only to see Ted Connover coming at them through the narrow passageway. For an instant, Hi's senses told him that Ted was dropping down the tube toward them. He blinked and registered that he and Catherine were above Ted, and he was rising to meet them.

"Ted, where's Bee?" Hi asked, a huge grin splitting his beard.

"I just left him, back in the galley. He wants to talk to the two of you."

Catherine said, "Hiram has just asked me to marry him. And I accepted."

Ted burst out laughing. "I think Bee wants to talk to you about that."

"Let's find him," McPherson said.

All three of them laughed as Connover started backing weightlessly along the tunnel, with McPherson and Clermont using the handgrips to propel themselves in the same direction. Ted was humming "Here Comes the Bride" loud enough for them both to hear him.

They found Benson in the command center and broke the news to him.

"Me? You want me to marry you?"

"Yes!" they replied in unison.

"I don't think that's legal."

Connover groused, "Come on, Bee, there isn't a lawyer within thirty-five million miles."

"But—"

Very seriously, McPherson said, "Bee, legalities aside, we want to be married. It's the morality of the situation that we're talking about. We can always do it again when we get back." Turning to Catherine, he added, "You want to get married in the Vatican?"

Her laughter was delightful. "The mayor of my home town in Normandy will do just as well. And it will be less expensive."

Benson was just as serious. "You're certain about this? Both of you?"

"Yes," said Catherine.

McPherson said, "Even if we die on Mars, I want Catherine to be my wife."

Breaking into a smile, Benson said, "Right. I'll be proud to do the honors."

Connover added, "And you can honeymoon on Mars."

McPherson was trying to stand straight and tall. In zero gravity the human body tends to curl slightly and the arms float up to chest level, like a person doing a dead man's float in a swimming pool. He forced his arms down by his sides and tried to look reasonably dignified.

The geologist had rummaged through his personal clothing and found a gray turtleneck pullover that he hadn't worn before.

Not a tux, he thought, *but it'll have to do.*

Now, standing in the galley between Benson and Connover, he stared at the open hatch and tried not to fidget as he waited for his bride.

Prokhorov hovered by the hatch with one of the surface-imaging cameras in his hands, ready to act as the official photographer by taking pictures with a camera designed to perform surface science, not take portraits. Mikhail looked pale, drawn, but he broke into a grin as Virginia Gonzalez floated through the hatch, looking quite solemn, followed by Amanda Lynn and then Taki Nomura. At last Catherine glided through, wearing a white short-sleeved blouse and sharply creased white slacks.

Benson had searched the net for a wedding ceremony and finally found one from an Anglican liturgy. Connover and Prokhorov had used the 3D printer to fashion a pair of plastic rings that looked somewhat silvery.

Catherine floated to McPherson's side. She had to put out her hand

257

and grasp his arm to stop herself. She was smiling gracefully; Hi was grinning from ear to ear.

Looking down at his printout, Benson began, "We are gathered here in this company and in the eyes of God . . ."

The ceremony was brief and simple. At its end, before Benson could say, "You may kiss the bride," Hi wrapped Catherine in his arms and kissed her so hard that Connover whistled and shouted, "Okay, break it up!"

Dinner was raucus, edging toward the racy, with jokes about honeymooning on Mars. To everyone's surprise, Benson produced a small bottle of cognac.

"I was saving this for when we returned to Earth, but this is an even happier occasion," he told the crew.

He left unsaid the fear that none of them might make it back to Earth.

There was barely enough for each of them to have one small drink, but somehow the occasion got even noisier after it. Even Prokhorov joined in the cheer as he told outrageously smutty jokes about wedding nights.

Catherine took it all with smiling grace, while McPherson blushed through his beard.

At last Benson announced, "Time to retire. Big day tomorrow."

"Big night tonight," said Virginia. Turning to Catherine, she revealed, "Taki and Amanda and I have moved your sleeping bags to the cupola. That's your wedding night suite, Catherine."

Unexpectedly bold, Nomura said, "It's far enough from our privacy quarters so that you won't disturb us."

Prokhorov brightened. "I can bring the camera!"

McPherson pushed himself up from his chair and reached for Catherine's hand. "No thanks, Mikhail. To all of you, thanks for everything. This has all been . . . well, kind of overwhelming."

Catherine stood up and smiled a soft, "*Tres merci.*"

Benson watched them slip through the hatch on their way to the cupola. Once they were gone, he turned to the rest of the crew.

"Big day tomorrow," he said tightly.

Connover nodded. "We tell Houston what we're doing."

"Right," said Benson.

Prokhorov fished his phone from his breast pocket and, waving it

over his head, proclaimed, "Not before I send the wedding pictures to
our friend Treadway."

Benson said, "Send it to Mission Control, Mikhail. Let them decide
if they want to break it to the news media."

Prokhorov grinned crookedly. "Mission Control first. Then to
Treadway. He is one of us, is he not? Our virtual crew member. He
would want to be part of our happiness."

Benson thought it over for a second or two. "Okay, Houston first,
then Treadway."

He realized that Houston—and Washington—were going to go
apeshit once they realized what Connover was doing.In comparison
the wedding would be a non-issue as far as the NASA brass was
concerned.

In the command center all by himself, Benson put in a call to
Nathan Brice, the mission flight director. After a nearly fifteen-minute
wait, Brice's lean, sharp-eyed image appeared on the communication's
system display screen.

Nathan's lost weight, Benson thought as Brice impatiently asked,
"What is it, Bee? You said it was urgent."

Benson glanced at the digital clock that showed the time in Houston.
Half-past noon. I must have dragged him away from his lunch.

Thankful for the time-lag between messages, Benson said, all in a
rush, "Ted's going down to the surface with McPherson, Clermont and
Lynn. They're going to ship the habitat's water up here to the *Arrow*
and then remain on Mars while we start back to Earth."

But Brice was already saying sourly, "This isn't about that wedding
you performed, is it? You ought to know better than that, Bee. You're
not empowered to marry people. Our legal people are up in arms
about it."

Benson almost smiled as he thought of their messages passing each
other in opposite directions, zooming through interplanetary space at
the speed of light.

Light travels faster than sound, he remembered the old adage.
That's why some people appear to be bright, until you hear them speak.

"Connover is *what*?" Brice erupted. "Who the hell authorized that?
What are you doing, Bee? Have you gone nuts? You can't let them go
down to the surface, they'll die down there!"

Very patiently, Benson explained the entire plan while Brice fumed and fulminated.

"I absolutely forbid it!" Brice was shouting. "You don't have the authority to change the mission plan! You can't do this!"

All the while, Benson calmly ticked off all the details of their plan. He ended with, "They'll live on Mars until the follow-on mission gets there to pick them up and return them home."

"Follow-on mission?" Brice demanded. "What follow-on mission? There isn't going to be—"

Benson clicked off the transmission. *I won't need the comm link,* Benson told himself. *Once Nate tells Washington, I'll be able to hear the explosion all the way from Earth.*

The "Mars wedding" was the lead-off story for the network's evening news. Steven Treadway appeared to be standing with the crew as Catherine Clermont and Hiram McPherson exchanged their vows aboard the *Arrow*.

"Even in adversity," Treadway intoned, over their muted voices, "love blooms and endures. Today, from the *Arrow* spacecraft in orbit around Mars, came the surprise news that the crew's two geologists, Hiram McPherson and Catherine Clermont, were married. The ceremony was conducted by the spacecraft's captain, Commander Bee Benson, with the entire crew in attendance."

The camera tightened to a close-up of Treadway's smiling face. "I must admit that I should have seen this coming. Hiram and Catherine have become very close in the months of their voyage to Mars. No other wedding ceremony in human history has been performed in such an environment and in such circumstances. I daresay it will likely be many years before there's another like it.

"Many of you are probably wondering about why they would bother getting married at all. To many, the idea seems rather quaint and old-fashioned. It turns out that Hiram *is* quite old-fashioned. In fact, he's a practicing Christian from a rather conservative church and told me that he not only wanted to marry Ms. Clermont, but quote, 'spend the rest of my life and eternity after that with her.' A nineteenth-century man with a twenty-first-century problem, so, of course, they were married virtually."

Treadway's face grew more somber. "But what about the legality of such a marriage? I spoke with several legal experts and got, as you might expect, a variety of views. Professor Maxine Chiemeka of Georgetown University had this to say."

The image of a graying, round-faced African American woman appeared on the screen, with her name and affiliation spelled out beneath it.

"Strictly speaking," she began, in a softly pleasant voice, "ship's captains cannot perform marriages at sea, on dry land, or by extension, in deep space simply by their virtue of being the captain of a ship. And no state in the Union has enacted a statute explicitly authorizing ships' captains to officiate at marriages. If Commander Benson happens also to be a member of the clergy or has some state license that otherwise gives him the authority to perform a marriage, then they are good to go. Otherwise, I would recommend the couple renew their wedding vows in a more traditional setting when they get back home."

Treadway reappeared onscreen, sitting behind a news anchor's desk. "Thank you, Professor. So while their marriage may not be legally recognized here on Earth, I suspect the happy couple doesn't much care. After all, what laws really apply at Mars? The more important question is, will they be able to get back to Earth alive and well?

"In the meantime, we wish Catherine Clermont and Hiram McPherson all the best.

"Steven Treadway, reporting."

can somebody please tell me how this 3D toy is going to help us?"

"We're going to print replacement spars for the truss," said Connover.

"Replacement spars?" McPherson looked skeptical.

"The engineers back at Mission Control will have a design ready to upload to us later today or early tomorrow," Connover said. "Once we have the file, we can feed it to the printer, put in the raw materials, and build ourselves the spars we need."

Gonzalez asked, "Why don't we use this gizmo to replace the water and propellant we've lost?"

Connover shook his head. "It can only make things from the raw material we put into it. We don't have any spare hydrogen. Or oxygen, for that matter."

"But we have raw materials for the truss?" McPherson asked.

Nodding vigorously, Connover said, "Yep. Down in the storage bays. Iron filings, carbon dust—"

"You mean soot?" Gonzalez interrupted.

Connover chuckled. "That's right: soot and lots of other materials."

McPherson scratched his beard as he said, "You think we really can repair the truss?"

"I do," said Connover. "I really do."

And he thought, *We'll get through this. You guys will get back home safe and sound, back to your families. But I don't have a family to come home to. I don't have anybody back home.*

Ted Connover figured the geology lab would be the one place where he could have some privacy. Hi and Catherine weren't going to barge in on him; they were tucked into the cupola. The rest of the crew were in their privacy cubbyholes, which provided about as much privacy as an airport's men's room.

Nobody would bother him here, he figured. He felt tired and nervous after the long day and the evening's festivities. He also felt a mounting excitement: tomorrow morning we leave the *Arrow.* Tomorrow we land on Mars.

He propped his compupad on the lab's one desk and touched the video recording feature.

"Hi, Vicki," he said, very softly. "Yeah, it's me again recording another message for you that I know you'll never receive. But if ever there was a time when I needed you and your advice, this is it. Am I doing the right thing? Should I just take the lander to the surface myself and not bring the others along?"

He tapped the pause button.

Despite his outward show of self-assurance, Connover had deep-seated doubts about his plan.

Connover shrugged. What was that line from Shakespeare, something about the idea that we owe God a death, if you give it this year you're quits for the next.

Well, he thought, *if I've got to die, I'd rather die on Mars. Better to be a lion than a lamb.*

He resumed recording.

"Catherine married Hi today. Bee performed the ceremony. The flatlanders back on Earth say it isn't really legal, but it was official enough for Hi. He's a Christian, he claims, and he didn't want to consummate his relationship with Catherine unless they were married. Just an old-fashioned guy, on his way to Mars. Catherine seems quite content with it. She must be Catholic, but I don't think she's a fanatic about it. Well, I hope their feelings for each other are as deep as the feelings you and I shared. I'd hate to think they rushed through a jury-rigged ceremony just because we're in a crisis situation. But from the looks on their faces it was more than that."

He hesitated, then said firmly, "Vicki, staying on Mars is the right thing to do. I'm certain of it. We'll survive and we'll keep Mars exploration alive while we do it. After your death, well, I almost gave up. But now my life has meaning again, a purpose. I'll make you and Thad proud of me. But, Christ, how I miss you!"

Connover felt tears coming. He forced them away and ended his message. "One day I'll join you, honey. But not this day."

He shut down the compupad thinking, *Not this day. Unless those idiot politicians refuse to send the follow-on.*

Nathan Brice stood behind the last row of consoles in the Mission Control center, gnawing on a fingernail. He hadn't told anyone about his conversation with Benson the afternoon before; he had marked the communication **PRIVATE** to keep it out of the comm log that anyone could see.

If Bee goes through with this crack-brain scheme, Brice was saying to himself, *the shit's going to hit the fan big time. And I'll be the first one to get spattered.*

The Mission Control engineers were at their consoles, monitoring everything going on in the *Arrow*, from the environmental control system's air pressure to the stores of food remaining in the freezers, from the latest medical files beamed down to them by Taki Nomura to Commander Benson's morning report, which was due in a few minutes.

On the *Arrow* it was a little past two in the afternoon.

The engineers at their consoles were not known as the most socially astute people in the world, but they were among the brightest. They had watched McPherson and Clermont's wedding with detached amusement, cracking a few obscene jokes until Brice had reminded them that the newlyweds might never get home.

That had been yesterday. Then Benson had dropped his bombshell in Brice's lap and the flight director had tossed sleeplessly all night, wondering if he should buck the news up the chain of command.

He had decided not to. If Bee has second thoughts, if one of the crew balks at this crazy-assed idea of Connover's, nobody had to know what they had planned. But if they went through with it . . . Brice shook his head and tried to ignore the consequences.

A few of the controllers had mentioned the fact that the crew hadn't been following mission protocol for the past few days, but they attributed that to the impromptu wedding. The crew psychologist had mentioned to Brice that the crew seemed strangely focused on some goal that she couldn't fathom. She had put it down to their predicament, their preparation for sending Connover down to the surface to bring back the water that they would live on during their return trip to Earth.

A supply of water that would run out long before they got to within a million miles of home, Brice knew.

And then Benson had told him about Connover's plan, and the crew's agreement to it.

Now Brice stood, a bundle of aggravated nerves with a pot belly and ragged fingernails, and waited for the inevitable.

Several of the mission controllers sat up straighter in their chairs, all at the same time.

"My God," the deputy flight controller yelped, "it isn't just the two of them going down to the surface. It's half the crew!"

Brice squeezed his eyes shut, knowing that what his controllers were seeing on their screens had happened more than thirteen minutes ago. He found himself whispering, "Good luck, you guys."

During his sleepless night, he had played over in his mind every scenario he could think of that might get the team home safely. And for all his deliberations, he had to agree that Connover's scheme was the only one with half a chance of succeeding.

Half a chance, he said to himself. *Better than none.*

Most of the controllers were turning around in their chairs, looking at him, expecting him to do something, to change what had happened thirteen-some minutes ago.

Fingering the microphone clipped to the collar of his short-sleeve shirt, Brice asked crisply, "Commander Benson, what's going on? Why are half the crew going down to the surface? That's not in the mission plan."

That should cover my ass, he thought. *Unless some bozo digs into my private communications.*

The mission psychologist tore her Bluetooth off her ear and ran up to Brice. "They're doing the Lifeboat Scenario! Those four going down to the surface have decided to sacrifice their lives so that the other four might live!"

Brice suppressed an urge to laugh in the woman's face. Instead, he said very calmly, "I don't think so. Connover's not the martyr type."

"But they'll die down there!"

Raising one bony finger, Brice said, "Let's hear what Benson has to say about this before we jump to any conclusions."

"Connover's suicidal!" the psychologist insisted. "He's been depressed since his wife and son died."

Brice snapped, "So what do you want me to do about it? Whatever they're up to, they've already done it. We can't stop them."

Then he pulled off his microphone so his words would not be recorded.

Crooking a finger at the deputy flight controller, he ordered, "Mack, get the logistics team together right now. I need to know how long those four can survive in the Mars habitat. If they're going to try to live on Mars we need to give them the best advice we possibly can from day one."

The deputy flight controller said, "You're thinking what I'm thinking, Nate. But why? We both know there won't be another mission. It's been cancelled!"

For the first time in more than twelve hours, Brice smiled. "Mack, those people are type Alphas. The kind of people who sign on for a two-year trip to Mars. But they're not suicidal. They're going down to the surface of Mars, not out the airlock. They think they can survive. And that Washington won't cancel the follow-on and let them die. It's brilliant!"

"Yeah, brilliant," the deputy flight commander said shakily. "Let's just hope they don't end up dead heroes."

"That's why I need the logistics data. *Now!*"

Mack said, "Yeah," and scurried away. The psychologist looked worried, perplexed.

Picking up his microphone and repinning it to his collar, Brice called for the communications director. "Sandra, put me through to Saxby in Washington. He needs to know what's going on here."

"What *is* going on here?" Sandra asked.

"A stupendous act of bravery and stupidity, rolled into one."

Sitting at the controls of the crew transfer vehicle, Ted Connover turned as far as he could inside his bulky EVA suit to look at the three people squeezed into the narrow little compartment behind him, the people he would be spending the next few years with in the cramped habitat waiting for them on the Martian surface.

The crew transfer vehicle was not pressurized. Connover thought of it more as a flying broomstick than a real spacecraft. It had room for four spacesuited astronauts, lined up along its skinny spine like riders on a tandem bike, a few bottles of nitrogen gas, and minuscule thrusters. That's all. The CTV was designed to move people back and forth among the various modules of the *Arrow*, nothing more. It would have been useless, for example, for Benson and Lynn's repair EVA.

In their white fabric pressure suits and bulbous helmets, Connover's teammates looked like three imitations of Frosty the Snowman. They were about to ride from the *Arrow*'s habitation module down along the truss to where the lander was stored, close to the nuclear reactor.

Even inside her EVA suit, Catherine looked as lovely as ever, smiling gently as she went through their departure checkout list. Behind her sat Hiram, who was going to be the envy of every fantasizing male back on Earth for being stranded on another planet with such a good-looking wife; he looked equally happy to be departing for the surface. He was alternately looking at his own

269

checklist and at his bride, as if to make certain she hadn't changed her mind and decided not to go with him after all. Ted didn't think that would be possible.

He paid particular attention to Amanda, last in the row. He had been very polite and professional with her, and had tried to make it clear that he had no physical designs on her. As far as he was concerned, he was still a married man and he intended to remain true to his wedding vows. Ted understood that two to three years of isolation was a long time to go without some sort of physical release, but he had no intention of allowing himself to go down that path.

Checklists complete, Ted received word from Benson that he was clear to undock and depart. But before doing so, he wanted to give everyone one last chance to change their minds.

"Anyone having second thoughts about this?" he asked.

"Are you kidding?" McPherson said. "We're about to become the first residents of another planet! Whoo-ha!"

Connover winced: Hi's boisterous shout almost melted his helmet's earphones.

"And the first married couple," Catherine added, more softly.

"Let's go," said Amanda, her face set in sheer determination.

"Okay," Connover said, grinning as he turned his attention to the CTV's controls. "Here we go."

He started the unlocking procedure that would allow them to fly down the length of the ship to the lander.

They all felt the thud of the docking mechanism's release and the transfer vehicle floated free. Connover tapped the forward cold-gas thrusters to give the little ship a small kick up and away from the habitat, then slowly turned the ship to point it aft and gave the rear thrusters a squirt to give them the velocity they needed to reach the rear of the *Arrow*, where the lander was housed.

They could see the damage to the truss and the makeshift repair. The payload module that housed the lander loomed large and bulbous as they approached it.

All onboard the CTV were awestruck at the sight of Mars almost completely filling their field of vision as they cleared the broken truss and moved away from the habitat. The orange desertlike terrain stretched as far as their eyes could see, ending on a hint of white that was a polar ice cap. Like Earth, there was a thin atmospheric envelope visible, but instead of being a softer shade of blue, it, too was orange/brown in color. It was truly an alien world and they knew it would soon be their home.

"Look at Mars," Amanda breathed. "It's so beautiful."

Benson's voice suddenly boomed in their earphones. "Ted, do you copy?"

"Bee, we can hear you fine. Not a good time for a chat, though: I've just cleared the break and we're about to dock at the payload module."

But Benson continued, "They've just put two and two together down in Houston and the shit is about to hit the fan. For now I think we can talk freely, since our cross-talk isn't automatically forwarded back home. But once we get home and they review everything, the brass will know that I didn't try to stop you."

"Yeah, well, that's a long time from now, Bee. And besides, the logs will show that you really didn't have a choice. If we didn't do this, the *Arrow* would become a ghost ship for sure."

As he spoke, Connover touched the forward thruster control to slow their speed as they approached the payload module.

After a moment's pause, Benson said, "Then let the log also show, for the record, that I think you guys are heroes and that I look forward to hearing all about your stint on Mars, firsthand, when you return home. I plan to be there to greet you."

"I'm looking forward to it," said Connover. "And, Bee, one more thing."

"Name it."

"Make arrangements for there to be flowers on Vicki's and Thad's graves at the first of every month until I get back. Okay?"

"Deal. And good luck on Mars."

NOVEMBER 5, 2035
MARS ARRIVAL PLUS 10 DAYS
16:24 UNIVERSAL TIME
MARS LANDER *HERCULES*

"Why'd they name this bucket *Hercules*?" Amanda Lynn asked, her voice dripping with sarcasm. "Looks more like a ninety-eight pound weakling to me."

The four of them were hovering just inside the payload module's airlock hatch, still in their EVA suits, even though the module was pressurized. A row of overhead lights lit the cavernous area dimly.

It's like being inside the belly of a whale, Connover thought. And in its middle sat the *Hercules*. The lander looked spindly, like a child's toy.

The bird was simple and functional, not designed for long-duration flight, but for the quick missions from orbit to the ground and back again. Its forward end was a blunt heat shield, from its rear hung a rocket nozzle. Not much in between: a tubular windowless fuselage with bulges forward that contained the parachute packs.

The Martian atmosphere was thinner than Earth's high stratosphere, but it was still dense enough to burn the ship like a meteor if they came in at the wrong angle.

Weightlessly they glided to the lander. Ted undogged its airlock hatch and one by one they entered the *Hercules*. Its interior was simple, Spartan, functional. Cockpit and seven seats behind the pilot. Big empty cargo hold, which they would fill with water from the *Fermi* habitat, waiting for them on the surface. And storage lockers for the rocks and soil samples the explorers would want to bring back with them.

273

No bunks, no privacy quarters, only one minimal lavatory. Once on the surface they would live inside the habitat.

Ted had thoroughly checked out the lander over the past two days, while Hi and Catherine carried in the food rations they would need during their extended stay on the surface and stored them in the cargo bay's lockers. To his enormous relief he had found that the *Hercules* had not been damaged at all by the meteoroid hit; it was ready for flight.

As the four of them settled themselves in the cockpit, Ted powered up the ship's electrical system, then pressurized the interior with air from the tanks resting beneath the floorboards.

"You can take off your helmets now," he told his teammates. Then he added, "But keep them within arm's reach, just in case."

As he unfastened his own helmet, Ted looked over his shoulder and saw that Amanda was cradling her helmet in her lap. He grinned at her. "Taking no chances, huh, Mandy?"

"None that I don't have to take," she replied.

Placing his own helmet between his booted feet, Ted started the preflight checkout. "We'll be departing the *Arrow* in two hours," he told them. "We'll be in a powered descent, and the ride will get a little rough when we bite into the atmosphere. But it's only a short ride. Once we undock and get clear of the *Arrow*, we should be on the ground in seven minutes."

"Just get us down in one piece," McPherson said, with some fervor.

Ted nodded and suppressed an urge to admit to them that the flight was known among the engineers who had planned it out as "seven minutes of terror."

Instead, he called Bee, in the *Arrow*'s command center.

"I'm ready to unlatch the CTV."

"Copy CTV unlatch," Benson's voice replied.

"Unlatched," said Connover. "She's all yours now, Bee."

"Right. I have control of the CTV. Autopilot is engaged."

They heard a small thud. Ted called up the view from the *Arrow*'s external cameras and saw, on his control panel's screen, the crew transfer vehicle slowly moving away from the payload module.

"You've got her, Bee."

"No, the computer has her. I'm just here as a backup, in case the computer has a problem."

"Feeling redundant, are we?" Ted joked.

"Sort of. But that too shall pass. I've got to get this crew home safely. I'll have time to worry about being redundant later."

Ted looked up and saw through the overhead window that the payload module was splitting in two, as if some gargantuan surgeon were cutting open the belly of the whale. Uncounted stars stared down at him, hard and unblinking. *Where's Mars?* he wondered, forcing down a sudden wave of fear.

As they felt the bumps and thumps of their disconnect from the payload module restraints, Ted rehearsed in his mind the steps that the ship would have to go through. Seven minutes of terror.

Once they floated free of the *Arrow*, the lander's chemical rockets would have to fire to reduce their orbital speed and let them descend into the Martian atmosphere and not drop like a rock toward the surface of the planet. Friction from the thin air would slow them quickly; then they would deploy the high-altitude parachutes to slow their descent further.

That's where the greatest uncertainty lay. If the upper atmospheric winds were too strong they might find themselves coming down much farther from the habitat than they had planned. Same thing if the winds were weaker than predicted. It would be up to him, Ted knew, to make last-minute corrections in the ship's course before they jettisoned the chutes and started the final descent, using the rocket engines. It was his responsibility to use the main rocket engine to hover momentarily and correct for any trajectory errors.

"Starting retroburn," he announced. Then he added to the three behind him, "Hold onto your hats."

They felt a brief surge of acceleration pushing gently against them.

"Retroburn complete," Connover reported.

"Copy retroburn complete," came Benson's voice. "Have a pleasant flight."

"Thanks."

The lander began to buck and shudder. "All normal," Ted shouted to his companions, over the growing wail of the wind.

The wind outside was screeching like a wailing banshee. The lander's vibrations peaked, then began to ease away.

A thump as the parachutes popped out of their containers and then a big lurch when they filled. Ted heard grunts and groans behind him.

"We're not slowing much!" McPherson said.

"Enough," Ted replied, his eyes on the trajectory trace displayed on his main screen.

Then he looked up and saw, through the overhead window, the three big, beautiful parachutes billowing brilliant white against the auburn Martian sky. *Good chutes*, he said to himself. *Gorgeous chutes.*

But one of the parachutes started fluttering and folding up on itself.

Ted immediately took the ship off autopilot and grabbed the tiny control yoke. He thumbed the buttons on the yoke that would fire the attitude control thrusters. The lander tilted awkwardly and began swaying like a pendulum.

Bang—Bang—Bang. Ted fired the thrusters to get the ship in the upright attitude they needed to land properly. Otherwise the lander would hit the ground at an angle and the landing gear would collapse under them.

Ted's eyes were riveted on the navigation screen, next to the countdown clock. The pendulum swing was slowing noticeably and the nav graph was showing green again. The clock was counting down the time to estimated touchdown.

"Gonna be a hard landing," Ted told his teammates. "Hang on."

The primary rocket engine ignited again and they were pushed into their seats.

"Touchdown in twenty seconds!" he yelled. "Brace for impact!"

WHAM! The *Hercules* slammed into the surface. The shock of the impact caused Ted to bite his tongue, drawing blood. The ship creaked like an old man settling into a chair. Then all sound, all sense of motion, stopped.

"We're down," Ted said, wiping sweat from his brow. "Welcome to Mars."

VI

On Mars

NOVEMBER 5, 2035
MARS LANDING
20:22 UNIVERSAL TIME
NASA HEADQUARTERS, WASHINGTON D.C.

Bart Saxby sat behind his desk with growing anxiety as he and a handful of aides watched the four crew members suit up and head for the lander.

"Get Brice on the horn," he growled, rubbing at the smoldering pain in his chest. "Now!"

"But they're in the middle—"

"Now!" Saxby shouted.

Robin Harkness, the director of human spaceflight, reached for the telephone on Saxby's desk.

"Won't he be busy monitoring the lander's launch?" asked Saxby's deputy director, a comely middle-aged woman who knew the intricacies of Washington politics better than the engineering of space missions.

"I don't care if he's building the Great Wall of China," Saxby growled. "They've torn up the mission protocol and I want to know why."

Harkness, lean and narrow-eyed with suspicion, reported, "Comm director says Brice can't be disturbed for another five-ten minutes."

Saxby fought down the urge to explode. Instead, he sat at his desk, his chest burning, and watched the *Hercules* lander's departure from the *Arrow* and its plunge into the Martian atmosphere.

One of the TV screens on Saxby's office wall was blank, but the voice of Commander Benson was coming from it.

"Copy retroburn complete. Have a pleasant flight."

The deputy director said, "Have a pleasant flight? He sounds like an airline steward, for God's sake."

Grimly, Saxby said, "That's Benson's sense of humor."

"Trajectory looks good," Benson was saying. "Hey! One of your chutes spilled!"

Saxby squeezed his eyes shut and held his breath.

"Good stuff, Ted. Correction is on the nose."

He breathed again.

Then Connover's voice announced, "We're down. We're on Mars."

"Good stuff, Ted," Benson repeated.

Saxby seethed.

"It looks like four of them went down to the surface," Harkness said.

"Looks like," said Saxby.

"That's not in the mission protocol. They have to clear any protocol changes with Brice."

"That's why I'm waiting—"

His desktop phone console buzzed. Saxby snatched up the handset. "Nate! What the hell is going on?"

He punched the speaker button and replaced the handset. Everyone in the office heard Brice's slightly nasal voice, calm and flat.

". . . four of them will stay on Mars, Bart. It's the only way the rest of the crew can get back to Earth alive."

"Alive!" Saxby snapped. "And what about the four of them on Mars? How long can they last there?"

A heartbeat's pause. Then, "Until we send the follow-on mission to pick them up."

As Harkness and the others barked and shouted at Brice, Saxby remembered the letter of resignation he had written when the final propellant stage for the *Arrow* had limped into the wrong orbit, eight days before the crew left Earth orbit and started for Mars.

I'll have to get it out of the recycle bin before I see the president, he realized.

It was almost 6:30 P.M. in Washington, cocktail hour, as Bart Saxby's limousine pulled up at the White House's entrance. A pair of stone-faced Marine guards in their olive drab uniforms stood at attention as Sarah Fleming watched Saxby climb out of the limo.

He looks like he's aged ten years, Fleming thought as she studied Saxby's ashen, drawn face.

"Hello, Bart," she said, extending her hand to him. "The President is waiting to see you."

"I bet he is," Saxby said.

She led him down the corridor to the Oval Office in the west wing, past two more security checkpoints. Fleming was in her usual skirted business suit, sky blue; Saxby wore a typical bureaucrat's dark gray suit—with his resignation letter in its inside jacket pocket.

President Harper was alone in the Oval Office as Saxby and Fleming entered. He got up from behind his desk and gestured the two of them to the little round table in the far corner of the room.

"What happened up there, Bart? First a wedding and now this. The news media is in a feeding frenzy."

Saxby sat down and admitted, "Mr. President, we have a sort of revolution on our hands."

Harper's dark, suspicious eyes focused on him like a pair of lasers. "A revolution?"

Saxby explained Connover's plan to the president.

"And Benson let him do it?"

Nodding unhappily, Saxby replied, "Both of them have come to the conclusion that the only way to save their lives is keep half the crew on Mars, living in the *Fermi* habitat, while the other half comes back home."

"The four returning home, they'll have enough water to make it?"

"Yes sir, if Connover and the others can ship it to them on the lander's ascent stage."

Frowning slightly, the president asked, "Your flight monitor, what's his name?"

"Brice. Nathan Brice."

"He let them get away with this?"

The pain in Saxby's chest flared again. "I don't think he knew about it beforehand."

"Didn't know?"

"Benson and Connover presented him with a *fait accompli*, apparently."

"Apparently?"

Saxby broke into a rueful grin. "If Nate knew about it beforehand, he's too smart to admit to it."

The president did not smile back. "So let me get this straight. You've got four people stranded on Mars and four on their way home."

"They will be on their way home in a few days."

"And that includes the Russian, the one who has cancer."

"Yes sir. They're hoping to get him home soon enough for him to get proper treatment."

"And the four people on Mars?"

"Both geologists and the biologist, in addition to astronaut Connover. They're eager to start exploring the planet."

"They have food, water, supplies?"

"Enough food for a couple of years, if they're careful. And they plan to mine water from the permafrost beneath the ground."

"How long can they last?"

"Two years, maybe a little longer. My logistics people are working on the details."

"And when they run out of food?"

Saxby hesitated. *Speak truth to power*, he heard in his head. "Before they run out of food, the follow-on mission will arrive at Mars."

"Follow-on mission?" the president snapped. "There isn't any follow-on mission. It's been scratched from your budget."

Sitting up straighter in his chair, Saxby said, "It'll have to be reinstated, Mr. President. Otherwise, those four people will die on Mars."

President Robert Harper stared at Saxby for what seemed like an hour. Then his stern face eased into a smile.

"Yes," said the President of the United States, "we'll have to get Congress to reinstate the funding for the follow-on mission."

"That won't be easy," Sarah Fleming objected.

"Neither is exploring Mars," said the president.

And the pain in Saxby's chest dwindled and disappeared.

NOVEMBER 5, 2035
MARS LANDING
16:59 UNIVERSAL TIME
THE *HERCULES*

"We're down. Welcome to Mars," said Ted Connover, wiping sweat from his brow. "Everybody okay?"

"I am good," Catherine replied.

"Shaken, but not stirred," quipped McPherson.

"My butt hurts but otherwise I'm okay," Amanda said. "What about the ship?"

"I'm running the diagnostics now." Connover scanned his control panel. Three of the four landing legs showed amber, the fourth red. Yet the ship was standing erect and everything else was in the green. He smiled tightly. *This bird might look fragile, but those guys in Huntsville built her right.*

Still strapped into their seats, the four of them were resting on their backs, legs in the air. For the first time in months they felt the force of gravity, but it was gentle, easy.

Glancing through the window over his head Connover could see reddish dust billowing. *We hit hard enough to raise a plume,* he thought. But already the dust was wafting away.

Ted's piloting had put them down less than a hundred meters from where the *Fermi* habitat stood waiting.

"Listen," said Catherine Clermont.

Connover heard creaks and groans from the base of the ship, where the rocket nozzle was cooling off. Somewhere a pump was gurgling softly.

But there was something else. Something strange. A soft sighing sound, almost like a moan.

"The wind," Catherine whispered.

"Yeah," said McPherson.

"The wind of Mars," Amanda Lynn said, with awe in her voice.

Benson's voice, from the speaker grill on the control panel, broke their spell. "What's your status, Ted?"

"Looks like the landing legs are beat up, but everything else looks good. The ascent stage is in good shape and we're all fine."

"We were holding our breaths up here," Benson said. "I imagine some of the engineers in Houston passed out when the chute failed. You did a great job recovering."

"Hey, that was one of the failure modes we simulated, remember? I think I did a better job landing this bird for real than I did in the simulation. In the sim, the lander was damaged and venting atmosphere, wasn't it?"

"The Toad will be proud of you," said Benson.

Ted broke into a fleeting smile. Thank God for the Toad and all the disasters he'd thrown at them during training.

"I'll buy him a beer when we get back," Ted said.

Benson reverted to the business at hand. "Before too much time passes we need to get you on the PR feed with a status. You know, the whole 'the Eagle has landed' thing."

"Okay, I'm ready."

"Right. Three, two, one, go."

Connover looked at the red camera eye on his control board and put on a serious face. "*Hercules* Base here. Humanity's first visitors to Mars have landed safely on the red planet. We four are going to make our home here on Mars until we can be rescued and returned to Earth. It is our sincere hope and prayer that our friends aboard the *Arrow* return safely to Earth and that this is just the first step in our exploration and settlement of Mars. We're now going to prepare for our short walk across the Martian plain to the habitat where we'll be living for many months—our home away from home. Thank you for your support and your good wishes."

The camera eye winked out.

"Nice job," said Amanda.

"They'll be hard pressed to cancel the follow-on after they hear that," McPherson said.

Maybe, Connover thought as he unbuckled his safety harness. *But never underestimate the short-sightedness of politicians.*

"How soon do leave for the habitat?" Amanda asked.

"We've got to complete the post-flight checklist and then start the prebreathing. We need to get there before sunset, so that gives us a few hours."

Three hours later, wearing their white surface suits and helmets, they were ready to leave the lander. The habitat was clearly visible in the distance, looking strangely out of place, a gleaming artifact of aluminum in the middle of the empty reddish rock-strewn sands.

Instead of a ladder, the crew descended to the surface in an open-cage elevator that had been built into the side of their ship. Designed to carry no more than two astronauts at a time, the elevator was meant to prevent any falls that might occur while climbing down a ten-meter ladder from the ship's airlock to the planet's surface.

Connover was to be the first person to actually set foot on the red Martian sand, followed by Catherine.

Ted stepped out of the airlock and onto the elevator platform. He stopped and looked out at the scene. *This is totally different from being on the Moon,* he realized. On the Moon the sky was infinitely black and the ground a glaringly bright barren desert. "Magnificent desolation," Buzz Aldrin had called it. And the Moon's airless surface was completely quiet. The only sound Connover had heard on the Moon's surface was his own breathing inside his spacesuit.

Here on Mars, the sky was a soft beige color with a few wispy cirrus clouds high overhead. The ground was a burnt orange, deepening to rust red in the distance. They had landed in a flat, undulating plain, but there were mountains in the distance, or hills, at least. And while his own breathing was the loudest sound Ted heard, there was also a faint sighing whisper outside, the feathery sound of the Martian breeze brushing past his helmet.

The elevator reached bottom and stopped. Ted unlatched the protective gate and stepped off onto the surface of Mars.

"I'm on Mars!" he said aloud. *I'm the first person to walk out onto the surface of Mars.*

"Turn around!" Catherine called, sounding excited.

He turned and saw that she held her camera up to eye level. He knew that this was part of the mission protocol but still he felt surprised, almost annoyed that he had to pose and make another speech at this incredibly intense moment.

But he knew that a billion or more people back home would be watching this and hanging on his every word. Unfortunately, his mind went blank and at first all he could do was grin.

Hoping that Catherine's camera could pick up his smile even through his helmet visor, Ted Connover said:

"The crew of the spacecraft *Arrow*, representing all the peoples of Earth, comes to Mars in peace and in the name of science and exploration." Then he went farther than the script. "We are explorers turned refugees by circumstances beyond our control. May this, our temporary new home, keep us safe until we can return to Earth."

Catherine put the camera down and Ted switched to their private audio channel. "How'd I do?"

"A *prix d'or* performance," she said. "Your family would be proud of you. I am honored to be here with you."

Feeling a tear welling up, Ted replied in a lowered voice, "Thank you, Catherine. That means a lot to me. I just hope you and Hi can be as happy as we were. If you are, you'll be among the most content, happiest people on Earth . . . er, Mars, that is."

He started walking around the upright lander, bending as far as he could in the stiff spacesuit to look at the landing legs. One of them was crumpled from the impact of hitting the ground, the other three were bent but holding firm. *Good enough,* he thought. *She should stay erect on three legs, even when we load the ascent stage with the water.*

McPherson's voice grated in his earphones. "How about sending the elevator back up here so we can get in on the fun?"

Ted stepped back to the elevator and pressed the button that started it upward.

"Come on down, you two," he called. "Catherine and I can't stand around here all day waiting for you."

"We're ready to join our fellow Martians," Amanda said.

Catherine said, "Martians? I hadn't thought of it that way before, but I suppose we are Martians now, at least for a while. If that is the case, I want my Martian husband down here with me right away."

Ted heard Hi's reply. "Even on Mars, the women are impatient for the men to get things done."

Millions of men around the world will guffaw when they hear that remark, Ted thought. *And quite a few women will undoubtedly send e-mails of reproof to NASA for Hi's insensitivity.* Ted thought it was funny, but he didn't want to appear sexist by laughing at it. He was, he told himself, the first human being on Mars and the person responsible for keeping his fellow crew members safe on this exotic, alien world.

But, as the elevator brought Amanda and Hi down to the ground, Ted couldn't help thinking, *I'm really here on Mars! Yahoo!*

NOVEMBER 5, 2035
MARS LANDING
21:28 UNIVERSAL TIME
FERMI HABITAT

It all seems surreal, Catherine Clermont thought as she trudged across the sandy surface of Mars from the lander to the habitat. Hi walked beside her, Ted and Amanda were slightly ahead of them. In their surface suits, Catherine thought of them as four white, helmeted strangers on a new world.

The suits would not remain white for long, she knew. They were kicking up reddish orange dust as they walked. Already their boots and leggings were turning pink.

The Sun looked strangely small, but it was shining brightly out of a nearly cloudless butterscotch sky. *Unreal,* Catherine repeated to herself. *Like a dream.*

"It sure is different from walking on the Moon," said Ted, his voice crackling in their helmet earphones.

"Only you would compare it to the Moon, Ted," McPherson said. "The rest of us are comparing it to that planet we came from: you know, it's called Earth."

"You're just jealous that you can't compare it to more than one world," Ted shot back.

"Might be some truth in that," Hi conceded.

They could see their new home just ahead, its shining aluminum exterior looking odd compared to the rough orange landscape surrounding it. A big cylindrical shape, with a pair of inflated wings on either side of it. Catherine shook her head inside her helmet. *It does not look as if it belongs here,* she thought. *It looks alien.* Then she realized, *We are the aliens here!*

Ted spoke up again. "Before we go inside we need to hook up the reactor."

He pointed off to their right. The reactor module was sitting about a hundred feet from the habitat, about the size of a minivan standing on its rear end, with four legs holding it upright. Atop it rose four large black square panels that looked like solar arrays; they were the radiators that would bleed away most of the waste heat generated by the nuclear reactor when it started operating at full power.

"Ted, are you sure that the Russians provided the right cables to connect their reactor to our habitat?" McPherson asked.

"Helluva time to think of that," Amanda quipped.

Ted replied, "I'm confident they got it right. Remember, they also made the reactor for the *Arrow*'s propulsion system and it worked right, didn't it?"

"How long will it take to power up?" asked Catherine.

"A few hours. In the meantime we'll go inside the habitat and start checking it out. She's been running on standby mode: low power from her solar arrays since she landed here. Houston says everything is working, but I'll believe it when we've checked it all out personally and we bring her up to full power."

It took the better part of an hour for them to power up the reactor and carry the power line to the connector plug on the base of *Fermi*. It wasn't as awkward to work in the surface suits as the EVA suits they'd used aboard the *Arrow*. They didn't balloon as much, weren't as stiff.

Hi and Amanda were monitoring the performance of the reactor as it powered up, while Ted and Catherine lugged the power cable across the orange sand toward the habitat.

Suddenly, Ted started laughing.

"Ted, are you all right?" Catherine asked, alarmed. "What's so funny?"

"Catherine, did you know that Vicki and I were campers? We'd take our pop-up camper out several times a year and spend weekends among nature. Well, as close to nature as you can get in a state park campground, anyway."

"Thad, too?" she asked.

"Thad, too. He got his first cactus stab before he was four years old,"

Ted remembered. "Anyway, one of the setup routines with those campers is connecting the camper's power cord to the outlets at the camp site. What we're carrying here doesn't look so different from what we carried back in those days, and the *Fermi* sort of looks like a big-assed camper to me. We're camping on Mars!"

She couldn't help herself and Catherine began laughing too. It felt good, a relief from the tension.

They reached the habitat and Ted connected the cable, then carefully toggled the switch just above the connection that transferred the habitat from internal to external power.

"Let's go check out our camper," Catherine said, still chuckling.

NOVEMBER 6, 2035
MARS LANDING PLUS 1 DAY
01:00 UNIVERSAL TIME
NEW YORK CITY

It was eight P.M. in Manhattan and a time when millions of viewers would be watching television, streaming their favorite 3D movie, or catching up with friends online.

But like all the other media and content providers, Steven Treadway's corporation was pre-empting their regular programming (a reality series set on the Moon) for a news special about the Mars landing.

Treadway sat in a comfortable armchair on the set, flanked by Ilona Klein, the White House public affairs director, NASA's Bart Saxby, and Senator William Donaldson.

The floor-to-ceiling green screens surrounding them on three sides showed views of the *Arrow* in orbit around Mars, the *Hercules* lander on the surface, and the *Fermi* habitat.

Treadway looked properly serious, Klein was visibly nervous, Saxby taut. Senator Donaldson resembled a thundercloud about to spit lightning.

Treadway heard the traditional, "Four . . . three . . . two . . ." in his ear button, then the floor director pointed his forefinger like a pistol.

"Good evening," he began. "I'm Steven Treadway, reporting from our studios in New York and, thanks to the wonders of virtual reality, from the *Fermi* habitat on the surface of Mars, where four human explorers landed earlier today."

The first segment of the show was boringly predictable, Treadway thought as he solicited statements from the White House PR chief, then Saxby and finally Senator Donaldson. They all—even Donaldson—offered congratulations to the four men and women on Mars.

Things became more interesting once they cut to the interviews that had been recorded earlier from the Mars habitat. The interview had already been spliced together by technicians so that it appeared that Treadway and the Mars landing team were conversing in real time.

He appeared to be standing in the airlock section of the *Fermi* habitat, with the four explorers crowding around him in the cramped space.

Catherine Clermont and Hi McPherson talked about how eager they were to go out and start studying Martian geology firsthand.

"There are signs here that water once flowed across this plain," Clermont said, while McPherson nodded vigorously behind her.

"Water means life, doesn't it?" Treadway prompted.

"It might," said Hi. "We know that on Earth all forms of life require water. That's why it's so important to study the water ice just under the Martian surface."

Turning to Amanda Lynn, Treadway asked, "You're the team biologist. Do you expect to find life on Mars?"

Her dark face splitting into a gleaming smile, Amanda replied, "There *is* life on Mars. Us. We're here now."

Treadway quickly covered his surprise. "Yes, of course. But I mean Martian life. Life-forms that are native to Mars."

Amanda's smile dimmed noticeably. "We don't know. Not yet. The Chinese robotic mission found traces of chemicals in the soil that might be prebiotic." Before Treadway could ask, she explained, "The kind of chemicals that led to the development of life on Earth."

Treadway prompted, "And you believe those chemicals mean that life once existed here on Mars?"

"That's what we're here to find out. Maybe there are still the Martian equivalent of bacteria surviving underground, living off the water from the permafrost."

"Well, good luck searching for Martians," Treadway cut Amanda off.

Then he turned to Connover. "And here," he beamed his broadest smile, "is the first human being to set foot on the planet Mars, astronaut Ted Connover. A big day for you, Ted. A really big day."

Grinning back at the reporter, Ted countered, "A big day for the human race, Steve. It wasn't just me that set foot on Mars. It wasn't even just the four of us. It was the thousands of people who built our spacecraft and all that went into that endeavor. It was the whole crew of engineers and scientists from half a dozen countries who guided us and monitored our mission. It was the entire human race, reaching across thirty-five million miles to extend the human frontier to another planet."

Treadway actually swallowed visibly, looking impressed by Ted's eloquence. "A great day," he replied weakly.

"Damned right," Connover said.

The wall screen that showed the interview went dark and the cameras on the floor of the studio lit up, showing Treadway sitting with his three guests.

Treadway put on his serious face and said, "A big day, indeed. But the question is, will those four brave men and women ever be able to return home again?"

Turning to Saxby, he asked, "What are their prospects, Mr. Saxby? You're the head of NASA. What lies ahead for those four men and women on Mars?"

With a quick glance at Senator Donaldson, Saxby answered, "They have food and supplies enough to last them two years, maybe a little more."

"Water?" Treadway asked.

"They're going to send the water that the *Fermi* habitat has stored up to the *Arrow*, so that Commander Benson and the rest of the crew will have enough water to get back to Earth."

"And what happens to Connover and the others on Mars?"

"*Fermi* has equipment to mine water from the permafrost beneath the ground's surface."

Ilona Klein interjected, "They should have plenty of water."

"But their food will only last for two years?"

She nodded tightly. "That's right."

"And then what happens?"

Saxby said, "We had planned to send a follow-on mission to Mars next year. The hardware is almost complete. We can send a skeleton crew on that flight and bring our people home."

Klein said, "But funding for the mission has been eliminated." And she cast a stern eye at Donaldson.

The senator stirred himself and said, "Congress has voted to cut the funding for the follow-on mission, that's right."

"But why?" Treadway asked.

Donaldson unconsciously ran a hand through his dead-white hair. His face was pinched, hard-eyed as he leaned toward Treadway.

"Human spaceflight is not only incredibly expensive, Steve, it's incredibly dangerous. We're risking the lives of those astronauts. Haven't we killed enough people in space? When do we admit that it's just too risky for people to go flying off into such danger?"

Looking plainly exasperated, Saxby asked, "So you want to leave those four people stranded on Mars? Let them die there?"

"The scientists tell me that the four of them will probably get so much radiation on Mars that it'll kill them. You send a rescue mission and you'll find four corpses when it gets to Mars."

"That's not so!" Saxby snapped.

"That's what the scientists tell me," said Donaldson. "I'm sure they've told you the same thing."

"They have *not*! The *Fermi* habitat protects them from harmful levels of radiation."

"And what protects them when they're outside the habitat, working on the surface? What protects them if there's a major solar flare?"

Saxby was getting red in the face. "The radiation they're exposed to will do nothing more than raise their chances for cancer by five percent or so."

"So they'll die of cancer."

"Maybe. When they're in their eighties or nineties."

"If they live that long."

"They won't live that long if we don't send the follow-on mission to rescue them."

"More billions down the rathole."

Ilona Klein raised both of her hands and made a shushing gesture with them. "Let's not lose our tempers, gentlemen."

Treadway was delighted to see the two men losing their tempers on his show. But he nodded agreement with Klein.

"I see that we're running out of time, people. Maybe we should just wrap up this discussion with a final statement from each of you. Senator? Your thoughts?"

Donaldson closed his eyes briefly, then said, "We're witnessing a tragedy in the making. Those four people on Mars decided for themselves to go down to the planet's surface. Mr. Saxby, here, and the rest of the NASA hierarchy didn't even know about it until they were on their way down to the surface."

Saxby started to object, but Treadway silenced him with a murmured, "You'll have your turn next, sir."

Donaldson went on, "Sending humans into space is expensive and very, very dangerous. We shouldn't do it. Those four people on Mars are very brave, of course, but they're also very foolish. The overwhelming chances are that they'll never get back to Earth alive. Sending a rescue mission will simply endanger the lives of another group of fine, brave, but misdirected young men and women."

Treadway waited half a second to make certain that Donaldson was finished, then turned to Saxby.

His face gray, grimacing with pain, Saxby said, "We can't sit by and let those four men and women die on Mars. That's all there is to it. We've got to save them. Period."

Treadway saw that the floor director was frantically slicing his forefinger across his throat, the signal that their time was up.

He looked into the camera and said, "Should we try to save the explorers on Mars or would we be endangering more lives? That's up to you, the people, to decide.

"Steven Treadway reporting."

"It is much smaller than I thought it would be," said Catherine as she stepped from the airlock section of the habitat into the living quarters that would be their home for the next year or more.

The four Mars explorers had just finished their brief interview with Steven Treadway, an awkward session made tedious by the quarter-hour lapse between questions and answers.

Now they were going into their new home.

Connover said, "Don't forget that this is only the basic part of what's been designed to be a modular, expandable camp. This is only the habitation module. The science modules are supposed to come on the follow-on."

"It's still pretty small," Amanda said. She looked down, doubtful, the adrenaline from their landing and interview gone, spent.

They had all removed their helmets and gloves for the interview with Treadway. Now they forgot about mission protocol and moved into the living quarters still in their dust-spattered surface suits, tracking a fine layer of red grit wherever they stepped.

This central part of the habitat resembled one of the modules of the International Space Station. It was a hard-walled cylinder that contained their sleeping quarters, the galley, and the computer and communications hardware. Like the *Arrow*, this section of the habitat would serve as their radiation shelter; it, too, was lined with water to absorb incoming cosmic rays.

The inflatable wings outside the central module deployed once the habitat signaled that it had landed intact. The wings, made from an amorphous material kept warm until it was deployed, hardened in the cold atmosphere of Mars, self-rigidizing so that they would not need air pressure to maintain their shape.

Catherine asked, "Ted, where do we start?"

"You three start unlatching the boxes and moving them into the wings. I'll check out the life support, power and communications systems. I want to make sure everything's working the way it should before we give Bee the 'all clear' for departure."

McPherson nodded. "Yeah. I'd hate to find out we had a plumbing break after Bee's left orbit."

Amanda complained, "Ted, it's cold in here. Can you turn up the heat?"

Remembering that Amanda had spent a good part of her career studying extremophile life-forms in Antarctica, Ted grinned as he replied, "Don't want our South Pole explorer to feel cold. The habitat's been running on minimum power for two years. The heat will come up soon, now that the reactor's been activated."

Pointing to their boots, he added, "First of all, though, let's get these boots off and stored in the airlock. See the dirt we've already tracked in? Somebody's going to have to vacuum that up."

"Not me," Catherine and Amanda said in unison.

McPherson laughed. "A man may work from sun to sun," he quoted the old adage, "but a woman's work is never done." Then he added, "Because they wait for a man to do it for them."

Catherine gave him a fierce scowl, but she could only hold it for a second. "I'll do the vacuuming," she said. "This time. Then we take turns."

Ted nodded. *Home sweet home,* he thought. *One big happy family.*

But he heard the wind of Mars sighing past outside, and he knew that once the Sun went down the temperature out there would begin plummeting toward one hundred degrees below zero. *I'd better check out the heating system first of all.*

NOVEMBER 7, 2035
MARS LANDING PLUS 2 DAYS
16:15 UNIVERSAL TIME
COMMAND CENTER, THE *ARROW*

Sitting alone in the command center, Benson watched the surface of Mars sliding beneath his orbiting ship, waiting to see the thin blue layer of atmosphere become visible just before the Sun dipped below the horizon. *Thin as an onionskin*, he thought, remembering that Earth's atmosphere didn't look much thicker from orbit.

The sight reminded him of how fragile their existence was. On Earth that thin film of atmosphere was a protective sheet that nurtured and sustained life. But here on Mars it was another part of an alien environment that could kill an unprotected human, too thin to breathe even if it was pure oxygen, which it was not. Mars' atmosphere—what there was of it—was almost entirely carbon dioxide. Unbreathable. And too thin to protect the surface from incoming meteoroids.

Benson sighed inwardly. There was no sense denying that he was jealous of Ted for taking what was supposed to be *his* role. But on the other hand, he knew that it had to be this way.

In just a few days, if all went according to plan, Ted would send up a collection of rocks gathered by Hi and Catherine aboard the lander's ascent stage, flying on autopilot. And the vital water from the *Fermi* habitat.

A stray thought wandered into his mind. *Will Amanda find anything she'll want to send back to Earth? Some evidence that life once existed down there?*

Whatever, he said to himself, *once we pump the water into our tanks and remove whatever rocks they've sent up, we crash the* Hercules *on the other side of the planet from the habitat so the seismologists back on Earth get a sampling of data about Mars' internal structure. If the seismometers in the habitat register any data.*

And then it's time to go home. It's going to be a long trip, in more ways than just the number of days we'll be in flight. I hope Mikhail makes it all they way. Taki says his chances are only fifty-fifty. But at least we'll have enough water to make it.

The Arrow *is too far from the habitat to see it from orbit. I'd need a telescope anyway, it's too small to see with the unaided eye.*

"Thanks, Ted," Benson murmured. "I just hope your sacrifice won't be in vain."

And the *Arrow* slipped into the darkness of the night side of Mars.

Standing in the airlock, McPherson called through the open hatch, "Come on, Catherine. It's time to get out and collect those samples."

He was smiling inside his suit helmet, knowing full well that he sounded like a stereotypical husband waiting for his wife to get ready for a trip outdoors. *Some things remain the same,* Hi thought, *even on another planet.* Fortunately for him, Catherine had no problem with his stereotypical behavior. She had her own stereotype.

"Be patient, *mon tresor,*" she replied.

McPherson's grin threatened to split his beard. *Mon tresor,* he thought. She calls me her treasure.

He looked through the open hatch at the module that served as their "all purpose" room. It was here that they had spent their first two days on Mars, storing their supplies, eating, talking, and, when the cold Martian night set in, sleeping. Hi frowned when he thought about sleeping in those damned hammocks. It was one thing to put up with the hammocks for thirty days, as the mission plan originally called for. But two years? And there was no privacy at all; the four of them slept within arm's reach of one another.

When are we going to make love? Then an idea occurred to him. *Maybe here in the airlock. Close the inner hatch and it's totally private in here. Not even a window. Or better yet, the auxiliary airlock, on the other side of the habitat. Nobody will be using that one; it's just for emergencies.*

Well, he told himself, *this is an emergency if there ever was one.*

Catherine rounded the corner from the right inflated wing of the habitat, in suit and helmet, with Amanda close behind her, in her coveralls. The right wing was where they had stored their food and general supplies. For some reason it seemed colder in the right wing than the left, though McPherson hadn't felt really warm since they had landed.

Connover approached from the left wing, coffee mug in hand. Hiram had quickly learned that Ted wasn't quite human in the morning until he'd had at least one cup of coffee. Hi hoped the supply of the stuff they had brought with them would last the whole time they were on Mars. He didn't know if their medical supplies included caffeine pills.

"Okay," Ted said, jovially, "now's the time for you geologists to earn your keep. You're scheduled for a three-hour EVA this morning. You stay within walking distance of the habitat. Then an extra hour for you to transfer the samples you've collected to the *Hercules* ascent stage."

Standing in the airlock, McPherson thought, *Tell me something I don't know, Ted.*

Connover plowed ahead. "Tomorrow you've got another EVA with a similar timeline. After that, Amanda and I will go out to the *Hercules* and prep her for launch back to the *Arrow*. Are you good with that?"

"So a total of six hours is all we get to collect samples?" McPherson complained. "And how much did this trip cost the taxpayers?"

"You'll have plenty of time to go rock hunting after Bee starts the *Arrow* back to Earth," Connover replied.

McPherson understood what Ted left unsaid. *The rocks that go back with the* Arrow *have a decent chance of getting into the hands of geologists on Earth. The rocks we pick up afterward might never leave Mars.*

Amanda broke into his thoughts. "Remember, you two have to wait inside the airlock while the UV lamps decontaminate you. We don't want Earth microbes polluting the Mars environment."

"As if they could survive out there," McPherson grumbled. "It's below freezing, there's no oxygen in the air, no water."

"*Practically* no oxygen or water vapor," Amanda corrected. "We can't take chances."

"We understand," said Catherine, as she stepped over the lip of the inner airlock hatch.

"Remember those bacteria that survived more than two years on the Moon, stowing away on board one of the Surveyor probes," Amanda reminded them. "No air at all, no water, yet they stayed alive."

"Stubborn little buggers," McPherson admitted.

Waggling a stubby finger at his tall, lanky form, Amanda insisted, "Well, we don't want any of those stubborn little bugs infecting Mars."

"Yes, ma'am," said McPherson, with the proper degree of contrition in his voice.

Amanda was smiling as the airlock's inner hatch swung closed. The panel next to the outer hatch showed a green light, indicating that the airlock was filled with air at normal pressure, and a blue light which signaled that the ultraviolet lamps were on.

McPherson fidgeted impatiently.

Standing beside him in the narrow compartment, Catherine murmured, "*Patience, mon amour.*"

She had been trying to teach Hi some conversational French, but he was not a fast learner. He had decided, though, that taking time to learn his wife's language was a good way to keep his mind diverted from the struggle for survival they were facing.

"*Oui,*" he replied.

Catherine laughed, a delightful sound in his ears. "Conversation in French. *Merveilleux.*"

He grinned back at her.

Then the blue light winked off and they heard the clatter of the pump sucking the air out of the chamber. The green light turned amber. The sound of the pump grew fainter and higher-pitched. Then it quit altogether and the panel's red light showed that the airlock was now in vacuum.

Clicking off his suit radio, Hi leaned close enough to Catherine so that their helmets touched. "I was thinking," he whispered, his voice carried to her ears by conduction, "that we could turn the auxiliary airlock into a honeymoon suite."

She looked surprised, but then she smiled and nodded. "Tonight."

"*Ce soir,*" he agreed.

Then he pressed a gloved finger on the control button and the hatch swung open. They stepped out onto the surface of Mars.

NOVEMBER 8, 2035
MARS LANDING PLUS 3 DAYS
12:24 UNIVERSAL TIME
ELYSIUM PLANITIA

I've seen this before, somewhere, McPherson thought as he and Catherine stood outside the airlock. The hint of familiarity tugged at his memory.

The plain that humans had named Elysium stretched out to the horizon and beyond. Although McPherson knew it was well below freezing outside his suit, the area looked warm, almost inviting, with the Sun shining bountifully out of the cloudless sky.

All around them was rusty desert in shades of orange and red. The ground undulated, dipping here and there in little gullies, rising in sinuous mounds. Rocks and pebbles were sprinkled everywhere, some of them as big as a compact automobile. Very few craters, although he noticed some pockmarks, as if fingertips had been poked into the sand. Off by the horizon was a row of reddish bare hills, their flanks creased with furrows.

Pointing to the hills, Catherine said, "Water flowed there once, long ago."

"Water, or some other kind of liquid," he replied.

"Water." She had made up her mind.

Absolutely barren, McPherson saw. Not a tree or a bush or even a blade of grass.

"Well, there's no water here now."

"Below the ground," said Catherine. "Permafrost. The satellite sensors showed it."

Nodding inside his helmet, McPherson thought that the earlier satellite readings *indicated* the presence of permafrost below the surface. They didn't prove it. And they didn't show how deep underground the ice might be.

"I've been here before," he murmured.

"*Quoi?*" What?

Searching his memory, McPherson realized, "Arizona. Up in the Navaho territory. It looks like this."

"Truly?"

Chuckling, he explained, "Oh, the badlands out there look like a Garden of Eden compared to this. But the feeling is the same. Not desolation, but . . . well, a stark kind of beauty."

"I prefer Tahiti," said Catherine. "Even with the tourists."

McPherson laughed. "No tourists here."

"Not yet."

She started toward the *Hercules*, standing against the butterscotch sky, but McPherson touched her arm and pointed off toward their right.

"Let's go this way," he said. "We've seen the area between here and the lander. Let's go someplace different."

Catherine couldn't shrug inside her surface suit, but he heard it in her voice. "If you wish."

A little over an hour later, Catherine and Hi were making good progress eastward. They had no roving vehicle, so their exploration was limited to how far their feet could take them. Both carried sample collection bags slung over their shoulders, high-resolution cameras tucked into their leg pouches and spindly looking ExtendArms clipped to their right wrists. Their prime objective was to locate and mark any sites that looked promising for finding water ice.

Catherine suddenly gasped. "Look! A stream bed!"

It certainly looked like the bed of a stream that had dried up long ago, McPherson thought. Like an arroyo in the Arizona desert, waiting for the next cloudburst to fill it with rushing water. *There hasn't been a cloudburst here for a billion years or more*, he knew. *But here it is, like it's been waiting for us to discover it.*

Catherine began picking up rocks with her ExtendArm implement. Electronically slaved to the movements of her right hand, it allowed her to pick up rocks without bending over or kneeling on the Martian sand, potentially damaging her suit.

She held up one of the smooth, rounded pebbles in her gloved left hand. "Eroded by water flow," she pronounced, holding it up for McPherson to examine.

"We'll have to check their chemical composition," he said, "see if there's phosphates or other indicators of water."

"Indeed," Catherine said, stuffing the samples into the collection bag she carried slung over her shoulder. "Indeed."

Looking beyond her, McPherson saw a curved ridge of rock that rose a few centimeters above the sand. *Ancient crater rim?* he asked himself. Leaving Catherine in the arroyo, he went to the rim and started chipping out samples of its rock.

"Two hours," Connover's voice sounded in their helmets.

"Already?" cried Catherine.

"Stow what you've picked up in the ascent stage," Ted commanded, "then come back in."

"Too soon!" Catherine pleaded. "Another hour, please. Thirty minutes, at least."

McPherson couldn't see her face, her back was to him. But he heard the plaintive supplication in her voice, like a child begging her father to be allowed to stay up just a few minutes more.

Connover replied, "Thirty minutes, Catherine, and that's *it*. No arguments."

"No arguments," she said gratefully. "*Merci.*"

They rode the elevator up to the *Hercules* airlock and, after spending nearly an hour carefully labeling each sample case with the precise location and date of its collection, they sealed their finds in the spacecraft's lockers. Both Catherine and Hi kept about half the samples they had picked up. They intended to study them in the habitat's miniature geology lab.

As they trudged back to the habitat, McPherson looked back at the plain of Elysium. Their footprints looked new and bright in the reddish sand. But not strange, not intrusive. *It's like we belong here,* he thought. *It's like Mars has been waiting for us to show up.*

He smiled at the thought.

Senator William Donaldson sat sourly behind his imposing desk, absently swirling a heavy crystal glass of single-malt scotch in one hand as he scowled at the big flat panel TV screen set into the wall above his office's fireplace.

The fireplace was strictly for show, it had never been lit, as far as Donaldson knew. And what was playing on the TV screen was strictly for show, too, he knew. A big, stupid public relations show promoting those idiots on Mars.

Two of them were out in the open, wearing their white suits and helmets. But the suits weren't lily-white anymore. Five days out on the sands of Mars and the suits were turning pink, especially their boots and leggings, and their gloves.

"The atmosphere here on Mars is so thin," the male astronaut was saying from inside his helmet, "that water boils away immediately, even though the temperature is well below freezing."

"Having that damned news reporter with them makes it all look completely ridiculous," Donaldson grumbled to the trio of aides who were watching the broadcast with him.

They nodded in unison.

On the TV screen, Steven Treadway appeared to be standing between the two spacesuited astronauts. Unlike them, he was wearing his usual white shirt and slacks. *Virtual reality*, Donaldson snorted to himself. *Just plain stupid.*

The male astronaut—identified on the bottom of the screen as geologist Hiram McPherson—was holding a small bottle of water in his gloved hand.

Treadway was saying, "Do you mean that if you uncapped that bottle you're holding, the water would boil away? Just like that?"

"That's right, Steve. Look."

The TV camera moved in closer as McPherson unscrewed the bottle's cap. As soon as he removed it the water in the bottle began to froth furiously. In seconds it was all gone.

"Wow!" said Treadway. *An intellectual giant,* Donaldson thought. *And wasn't there a delay? This had to be scripted.*

"And the temperature right now is . . . ?"

McPherson raised his left hand and peered at the instrument cuff on his wrist. "It's twenty-three degrees below zero, Steve. An average summer afternoon on Mars."

"But the air pressure is so low that the water boils, even at such a low temperature."

"That's right, Steve."

"Turn it off," Donaldson snapped. "I've seen enough."

The pert young woman who headed the senator's public relations staff picked up the remote from a corner of the senator's desk and clicked the TV screen to darkness.

"Publicity stunt," Donaldson grumbled.

"Yeah," said his chief of staff, a pudgy, short, balding New Englander with a pouchy-eyed face that masked a keen analytical mind. He had successfully guided Donaldson through many political campaigns. "But that trick of writing your name in the sand with a magnet, that's pretty neat."

"Tomfoolery," Donaldson groused.

"The sand's loaded with iron," said his third aide, his techie guru.

"A striking image," said the PR woman.

Donaldson looked at them the way Julius Caesar must have looked at Brutus, at that last instant.

"Whose side are you people on?" he demanded.

"Yours, of course," said his chief of staff. His normally cheerful round face was quite serious. As he sat up straighter in his chair his unbuttoned suit jacket flapped open around his corpulent middle.

"But this stuff coming from Mars is a real problem," said the PR person. "Audience response has been tremendous, even with the religious groups that want the mission cancelled."

"A lot of kids, though," the chief of staff said. "They don't vote."

The PR person was a light-skinned Hispanic woman. "Great publicity for the Mars people. The numbers show overwhelming support for sending the next mission out there to save their lives."

Donaldson remembered the three laws of politics enunciated by the man for whom this Senate Office Building had been named, Ohio Senator Everett Dirksen: Get elected. Get reelected. Don't get mad, get even.

"All right," he said, putting his drink down on the green Vermont marble coaster atop his desk. "What do we do about this?"

His chief of staff said, "Harper's going to ask you to reinstate funding for the follow-on mission."

"I know that. What do we do about it?"

"You can't oppose it," the PR director said. "You'd look like an insensitive know-nothing."

"Or a murderer," said the tech guru.

Donaldson glared at him.

His chief of staff hauled himself out of the chair and headed for the bar, hidden behind a row of false book spines.

"You've got to give the appearance of going along with the follow-on mission," he told the senator, over his shoulder.

"Give the appearance of caving in to Harper? Never!"

Bending over to pick a bottle of ginger ale from the bar's refrigerator, the chief of staff said, "You want the party's nomination next year? You go along with the follow-on. QED."

"Never," Donaldson repeated, but more softly.

With an amiable smile on his moon face, the staff chief said, "It's politics, William. You've got to give something to get something."

Donaldson frowned as his longtime friend and advisor settled himself back in his chair.

"After all," the man went on, "you at least have to give the impression that you're willing to bend in order to try to save those four nitwits on Mars."

"Give the impression," Donaldson muttered.

"You ask your subcommittee to study the possibility of replacing the funding for the follow-on. You tell the NASA people to appear before the subcommittee and lay out their plans for the mission, together with their best estimate for its chance of success."

Donaldson nodded slowly.

"These things take time, of course. Drag it out until the party's convention next July. Then, once you've got the nomination in your pocket, you just let the follow-on die a natural death. Who knows, by then those people on Mars might be dead anyway and most people will have forgotten all about the chemicals that the Chinese claim to have found."

Donaldson glanced at his PR director, who gave the idea a tentative smile. "It could work," she said.

The tech guru looked less happy.

"As president," the chief of staff said, "you can see to it that we build a monument to the four dead heroes."

Donaldson added, "As president, I'll make sure we don't waste any more money on sending people to Mars."

Sitting in the command center, Benson held one of the Mars rocks in his hands. It had been sitting in an airtight plastic pouch in one of the ascent stage's lockers, together with a scribbled note signed by Catherine and Hi:

> *Bee—Thanks for everything.*
> *Here's a remembrance for you. Bon voyage.*

After thanking them, Benson got detailed instructions from Amanda Lynn on how to handle the rock. To prevent any possible contamination of the *Arrow*, she explained, the rock had to be heated to more than two hundred seventy-five degrees Fahrenheit for more than thirty minutes, long enough to kill any known bacteria, viruses or prions. Only then would it be safe to handle in the ship's open air. As the mission's resident biologist, Amanda took an almost proprietary interest in the rock's "care and feeding."

Now Benson held the rock in his bare hands. It fit into his palm easily, a smooth oblong rust-red stone with flecks of pale gray spotting it. He couldn't help marveling at it.

He held it up to the light for the umpteenth time, trying in vain to see something different about it, something exotic or alien.

It just looks like a rock, he concluded. It would take trained geologists with their specialized instruments to see if there was anything extraordinary about it.

Swiveling his command chair slightly, he called, "Taki, would you come over here, please?"

The ship's doctor was, by default, their chief biologist now that Amanda was down on the surface. She looked up from the console where she'd been checking the *Arrow*'s life-support system and pushed over to Benson.

"What's up, Bee?" she asked as she grasped the back of his chair to stop herself.

"Have you found any signs of life in the samples you've cultured so far?"

She grinned at him. "If I had you would have known it by now. My whoop would probably be heard all the way back to Earth."

Benson nodded. "Yes, I imagine so."

More seriously, Nomura said, "No, so far all the cultures are negative. If there's anything alive in these samples it's not responding to any of the tests I know how to do. If there were any Earthlike bacteria, even just a few, the tests would have shown it in a matter of minutes. No viruses, either, as far as I can tell. I'm running a test for prions back in the bio lab right now, but I don't expect any positive results."

"Well, keep me posted, will you? I can hardly bring myself to put this one down. I keep expecting to see some little green creature wriggling out of it."

With a laugh, Nomura replied, "If you see one, you let me know."

"Right," said Benson. Then, his tone darkening, "I hate to change the subject, but how's Mikhail doing?"

"Today is a better day. He ate a full breakfast and he's talking about resuming some of his shipboard duties. He wants to help with our departure for Earth. I think you should let him."

"Good idea. I can task him with some of the checklists. He's cross-trained for that, and it shouldn't strain him too much. Besides, it won't mess things up too much if he gets distracted."

"Just make sure it's meaningful, Bee," said Nomura. "He's no dummy. If it's just a makework task he'll know you're humoring him and he'll feel hurt."

"Encourage him, not discourage him," Benson said.

"That's the ticket." Nomura floated away from the chair and started for the hatch. "I'll help him get dressed for duty. I'll have him back here in about half an hour."

"Right." Benson watched Taki glide through the hatch, then turned and rested the rock atop the control panel, where he could see it as he worked. They were planning to break out of Mars orbit in two days and there was a lot to take care of before then.

Twenty-some minutes later, he head Prokhorov's raspy voice. "Reporting for duty, Commander."

Turning, Benson smiled to see the Russian standing as stiffly as he could in zero gravity, his right hand raised to his brow, a crooked smile on his lips. Prokhorov looked almost painfully thin: his coveralls hung on his gaunt frame like an oversized sheet. His face was pale and his cheekbones more prominent than they had been a few weeks earlier.

Benson returned the salute and said, "At ease, Mikhail," going along with Prokhorov's parody of military etiquette.

The Russian relaxed, floating weightlessly off the deck a few centimeters.

"How do you feel?"

"Not quite ready for the Olympics," Prokhorov answered. "But I can work."

"Fine. We're leaving in two days and I can use all the help I can get. We're shorthanded for the return trip, you know, with Ted and the others down on the surface."

"What do you want me to do?"

Benson handed him a thick sheaf of checklists. "I need you to check out every item on these lists before we break orbit and start for home. It's dog work but it needs to be done. Can you do that?"

Prokhorov glanced at the lists. "Aye-aye, sir!"

Benson grinned at him. "Right. Then get to work, sailor."

NOVEMBER 16, 2035
MARS LANDING PLUS 11 DAYS
10:56 UNIVERSAL TIME
ELYSIUM PLANITIA

Amanda Lynn slowly turned three hundred and sixty degrees, surveying the terrain with eager eyes.

"Pirouetting?" asked Connover.

"Yeah," she teased. "Want to dance?"

This was Amanda's third excursion outside the habitat, but the first she'd done with Connover. Mission protocol prohibited anyone going outside alone. Even so, one of the two people remaining inside had to suit up and pre-breathe low-pressure oxygen, in case there was an emergency that required an extra pair of hands.

"I'm no Fred Astaire," he wisecracked back at her, "but I bet I could do pretty well in this low gravity."

"Or on the Moon, even better."

Connover got a sudden flash of himself dancing with Vicki in the Moon's one-sixth gravity. *Fred and Ginger*, he said to himself.

Amanda started walking toward the desiccated stream bed that Catherine and Hi had discovered. Connover trudged along behind her, carrying the core sampler over one shoulder.

"We should have placed the habitat farther north, up by the edge of the ice cap," she complained. "Better chance of finding something there."

"Something alive, you mean?" Ted asked, trudging along beside her.

"Or like the chemicals the Chinese found. Amino acids, PAHs, stuff like that. But what I'd really like to find are fossils. That would be a clear sign that more complex life once existed here."

He felt his brows knitting. "How could you tell something's a fossil when you don't know what Martian life-forms might look like?"

Amanda went silent for a few steps. "Well," she said at last, "if it's got legs, that's a pretty good clue."

"But what about microbes? Bacteria, single-cells organisms? They don't have legs."

"They leave chemical traces, like an elevated level of carbon twelve, or PAHs."

"PAHs?"

"Polycyclic aromatic hydrocarbons. They're precursor compounds, tarry, sticky stuff that helps to glue bigger molecules together. It'd be hard to build up really big molecules, like amino acids or proteins, without them."

"And carbon twelve?"

"The lightest isotope of carbon. Living organisms take up carbon twelve, in preference to the heavier forms of carbon. Find rocks or soil samples with a higher level of carbon twelve than normal, you've probably found the remnants of life."

"Yeah, but how do we know what's normal here on Mars?"

Even through her helmet visor, Ted could see the flash of Amanda's grin. "That's what we're here to find out."

Connover shook his head inside his helmet. "Well, anyway, I'll settle for finding water."

"Ice," Amanda corrected.

"Yeah, right."

"This is the fossil stream bed Catherine marked out," she said.

"The arroyo, yeah," said Ted, as he began to unlimber the core sampler. "Time to get to work."

The sampler was a piece of specialized, Mars-unique engineering. Unlike a bulky, heavy traditional drill that would grind its way through the surface layers of sand and rock, the sampler was more like a mole. Only about a foot long, it looked like a mechanical bean bag.

Ted set it upright on its built-in mount and worked its head about six inches into the sand. Motioning Amanda to stand back, he thumbed the button that activated the tool.

Bam bam bam! Bam bam bam! The sampler began to alternately shorten and lengthen itself as it burrowed into the ground. In less than a minute it disappeared from their view.

"So this is one of the toys our geologists play with?" Amanda asked.

"Once it's gone down a couple of meters it'll take samples and wriggle its way back up to the surface so we can pack 'em away."

"Just warn me before it comes back so I don't jump out of my skin."

"It's worked fine for Hi and Catherine," he said.

"Except that it hasn't found any ice."

Connover stared at the hole in the ground. *Water,* he thought. The maps generated from satellite sensors claimed they were sitting on a veritable ocean of permafrost. But their core samples hadn't turned up any ice yet. *If we don't find ice in the next month or so, we'll run out of drinking water.*

And die, here on Mars.

Briefly he thought about their odds of survival. *Too late to worry about that now,* he knew.

"So it's going six feet down?" Amanda asked.

"Two meters," Connover said. *Six feet deep,* he thought. *Deep enough for a grave.*

"You think this is a likely spot to find the ice?" he asked as he waited for the mechanical mole to reappear.

"Maybe. Some of the unmanned landers squatted down right on top of permafrost. Their landing rockets blew off the top few inches of dust and there was the ice, right underneath."

"It's not right underneath here," Connover complained.

"That's why I said we should have put the *Hercules* down farther north. For all we know, this area is a total desert."

"But the satellite sensors—"

"Ground truth, Ted," said Amanda, almost wistfully. "The sensors detect emissions that the geologists interpret as due to buried permafrost. But until you actually dig up ice, the sensor readings have to be taken with a grain of salt."

"Ground truth," he muttered.

At last the mole returned. Connover removed the chips of rock from its mechanical teeth and handed them to Amanda.

"Doesn't look like ice," he said.

"No, they don't."

"You think there might be ice inside them?"

"Don't know until I get them under the microscope and do some chemical tests."

As they started back toward the habitat, Connover asked, "So what's on your schedule tomorrow?"

"Pretty much the same as today: dig in the morning, then spend the afternoon analyzing what we've dug up."

"With a shower in between."

"Dream on."

Connover thought about the shower. It would feel good to get the sweat off. They were recycling over ninety percent of the water they used—not good enough to permit showering too frequently.

Maybe we could conserve water by showering together, he thought. And immediately rejected the idea. Don't be a jerk, he told himself. *Besides, Amanda would probably sock me in the nose if I suggested it to her.*

Benson watched the digital clock on the control panel counting down the final seconds to ignition.

He was alone in the command center. The three others were in the galley, strapped into their chairs. One of the display screens before him showed an animation of Mars and Earth swinging in their orbits to the precise spot where the *Arrow* would light up its nuclear engine and launch itself out of orbit around Mars to start its year-long flight back home.

As the clocked ticked toward zero, Benson tapped his communications console. Ted Connover's face appeared on the screen.

"Thirty seconds and counting," Benson said tersely.

Connover nodded. "Good luck, pal. Safe journey."

"We'll be back for you, Ted. We'll be back if I have to walk the whole way."

Grinning tightly, Connover replied, "Just get yourself home, Bee. We'll be okay here."

"So long."

"Bon voyage."

The clock showed zero and Benson heard the muted growl of the rocket engines lighting up. He felt a gentle push on his back, nowhere near the kind of acceleration he was accustomed to launching from Earth.

Tapping the intercom icon, he announced, "We're on our way, people."

In the galley, Virginia Gonzalez smiled at Taki Nomura and Mikhail Prokhorov. "Next stop, Earth," she said.

Taki smiled back at her, but quickly turned to look at the Russian. He was perspiring visibly, and grimacing.

"Mikhail, are you in pain?" she asked, alarmed.

He made a weak smile. "Only when I breathe."

"Bee," she called, "I've got to get up."

"Wait a few minutes," came Benson's voice from the overhead speakers. "Once the thrust cuts off you can move around again."

"No," Taki said, as she started unbuckling her safety harness. "Now."

It actually felt easier to move, she found, with the slight acceleration giving a feel of some gravity instead of weightlessness.

"You sit there," she said to Prokhorov. "I'll get some painkillers from the pharmaceutical stores."

Prokhorov nodded. Virginia asked, "Is there something I can do?"

"Stay with Mikhail. I'll be back in a minute."

It felt unusual, after all the weeks in zero g, to have some weight again. But it was also disorienting. Down seemed to be in the direction of the compartment's rear bulkhead, not the floor.

Nonetheless, Taki made her way to the ship's tiny infirmary and pulled a bottle of pills from its storage rack. More than half-gone, she saw. She popped the lid and the bottle slipped from her hands, pills spilling out languidly and peppering the infirmary's rear wall.

"Damn!" Taki snapped.

She scooped up a handful and "climbed" uphill back toward the galley. Virginia and Mikhail were still in their chairs. He looked pale and sweaty; she was worried.

"Are you all right?" Virginia asked her.

Taki nodded tightly, grabbed a bottle and went to the water tap. She was in such a hurry, she didn't check the seal the bottle's lip made around the tap before she turned on the water. The damned water went everywhere, splashing off the bottle and spattering toward the rear of the galley.

"Damn!" she said again.

"What's going on back there?" Benson's voice demanded.

"Everything's under control, Bee," Virginia half-lied. Taki had managed to get some water into the mug and brought it and the pills to Mikhail.

"Thank you," Prokhorov said, weakly.

"Acceleration cutting off in ten seconds," Benson announced.

Sure enough, the feeling of weight disappeared and Taki felt herself floating in midair. She welcomed the sensation.

Benson's voice told them, "We're through the keyhole, on course for home."

Good, Taki said to herself. *Now if only we can keep Mikhail alive long enough to get him there.*

Benson awoke with a start. Something had disturbed him from a deep sleep and he wasn't sure what it had been. Enmeshed in his sleep cocoon, he listened to the gentle hum of the air fans, thankful that they were working. That meant the ship still had electrical power. No alarm klaxons. Everything seemed to be normal.

There it was again! A gurgling sound, coming from outside his privacy compartment. *Somebody's strangling,* he realized.

Moving faster than he thought possible, Benson wriggled out of his cocoon and pushed through his cubicle's flimsy privacy screen.

The noise was coming from Prokhorov's cubbyhole, and it didn't sound good.

Launching himself into the Russian's cubicle, Benson flicked on the overhead light. Mikhail's eyes were rolled back in his head and a mixture of vomit and blood was spraying from his mouth. Benson fought back a surge of nausea.

"Taki!" he yelled. "Mikhail's in trouble! Wake up!"

Ignoring the grotesque spherules of blood and vomit floating in the air, Benson reached for Prokhorov's mouth and pried it open, hoping to see if something was blocking his airway that might be cleared to prevent him from choking to death.

Taki appeared at his side, blinking sleepily, as Benson's fingers found Prokhorov's tongue twisted and lodged at the very back of his throat. He quickly curled his finger around it and pulled it forward. Prokhorov made another sick gurgling sound and spewed out more blood.

"Bee, move aside," said Taki, wide awake now. "I'm here. Let me check him out."

Benson edged away and Taki hovered over the sick man. Bee saw that his hands were covered with blood and, looking down, so were the skivvies he'd been sleeping in.

Virginia was holding the compartment's privacy screen to one side, her face tense, wide-eyed. "Is he going to be all right?"

"Doesn't look good to me," Benson said. "But we'll have to wait for Taki to tell us, once she's finished checking him out."

He drifted into the narrow central area of the crew quarters and saw that somebody—probably Virginia—had turned on all the lights.

Gesturing toward the obscene blobs floating through the area, he said to Virginia, "Let's get this mess cleaned up before it spreads all over the ship."

She nodded and went to the storage compartment between her bunk and Taki's to pull out a handful of cleaning wipes. Wipes and barf bags had been stored in every section of the ship to deal with the possibility of nausea that can come from space sickness.

Benson realized that the gag reflex that comes from smelling someone's vomit still existed in zero gravity. But he fought it down as he and Virginia cleaned up the mess. *We could have used one of the hand-held vacuum cleaners,* he thought. But then he wondered if so much vomit and blood would have fouled up the hand-held.

Taki floated out of Prokhorov's compartment, looking grim.

"Bee, we need to tell Mission Control that Mikhail's condition is getting worse and there's nothing I can do. I don't know why they didn't detect the cancer before we left home, but it must have been in its earliest stage and the medics back in Russia just missed it."

"Don't beat yourself up, Taki. It isn't your fault. I bet the team is scouring his records to see how his condition slipped past them."

"I know, but still . . ." Taki shook her head. "I was expecting space sickness and maybe a broken bone once we landed on Mars, but nothing like this. Bee, I'll be surprised if he lives another week!"

"A week?" Benson asked, alarmed. "But he seemed so much better just a couple of days ago. How could he decline so quickly?"

"It happens. Sometimes even the sickest people rebound near the end. Just ask hospice workers. Patients who seem to be at death's door suddenly perk up and get better—for a few days. Then they sink away and die."

Virginia asked, "Can we do anything for him?"

Taki bit her lip before answering, obviously trying to come up with something positive. "I think the pain medication I gave him made the seizure he just experienced worse, so I don't dare increase the dosage. I need to stay with him and one of you will have to relieve me when I'm sleeping. Otherwise he might seize again and choke himself to death."

"Right," said Benson, grimly.

"I'll do whatever you need me to," Virginia promised.

As he headed back for his own cubbyhole, Benson started to think about conducting a funeral in space. *I'll have to talk it over with the experts back home,* he said to himself. *Once Mikhail dies we'll have to do something with the body and we don't have many options. We don't have a morgue on the ship, or even a freezer big enough to take his body. We can't just put him in a sample bag and leave him here in the cabin, for sanitation reasons if nothing else. And there'd be plenty "else." I don't want a dead body hanging around the place.*

As he pulled off his blood-soaked skivvies and reached into his storage locker for a fresh set, Benson thought, *We'll probably have to send him out the airlock and bury him in space. He'd probably like that. If he regains consciousness, I'll ask him.*

He didn't want to make that decision by himself.

A day later, Mikhail slipped away peacefully in his sleep.

NOVEMBER 20, 2035
MARS LANDING PLUS 15 DAYS
19:48 UNIVERSAL TIME
WASHINGTON D.C.

"So he died of cancer," said Senator Donaldson. It was not a question.

His chief of staff nodded somberly. "Poor bastard."

The two men were sitting in the Senate dining room, lunching on she-crab soup and scotch. It was nearly three P.M. in Washington, the dining room was quiet, almost empty. Donaldson preferred to have his meals in near-privacy. *Nothing was worse,* he thought, *than interrupting a fine lunch by being forced to get up and gladhand some supporter—or rival.*

"And he got the cancer from space radiation?" This time it was a question, but there was hope in Donaldson's voice as he asked it.

His chief shook his head. "Nobody knows. The Russians claim their medical records don't show any cancer, otherwise they wouldn't have cleared the man to go on the mission. But you know how the Russians can be . . . well, slipshod, sometimes."

Donaldson put down the spoonful of soup he had brought halfway to mouth.

"They weren't slipshod this time," he said firmly. "The man did not have cancer when he left the Earth."

"You can't know that for sure, Bill."

"I'm sure enough. He got cancer from all the radiation in space that they've been exposed to."

His chief of staff eyed him critically. "Then why haven't any of the others in the crew come down with cancer? For God's sake, NASA and

329

the Russians will bring out seventeen dozen medical experts to shoot
you down on that one."

"Coverup."

"Be serious, Bill!"

"I am serious. The space environment is dangerous, too dangerous
for human beings. I've been saying that all along, and this Russian's
death proves it. Plus, if it is too dangerous for people, then how could
bacteria on Mars survive?"

The chief ran a hand across his bald pate, a gesture that Donaldson
knew meant he was perplexed, conflicted.

"It'll work," the senator insisted. "It proves I've been right all along.
And if we let them send that follow-on mission to Mars, we'll just be
sending another shipload of fine young men and women to their
deaths."

His old friend and advisor was clearly unhappy. But he murmured,
"That might work. That just might work."

Benson had been shocked, at first, by Mission Control's decision.
But Nathan Brice himself got on the horn to spell it out for him. With
the quarter-hour time-lag in communications, they didn't have a
conversation or a discussion. Brice told him what the NASA brass had
decided and Benson listened, unhappily.

"It'll be like a burial at sea," said the NASA flight director, "except
that you don't let go of the body. You put him in an EVA suit, take him
outside and put him in the cargo module, where the lander used to be.
There's plenty of room and he'll be shielded from sunlight. The
cryogenic cold in there will preserve the body so that our medical
people can examine him when you bring him back."

Benson didn't like it, but he knew it made sense. Once the *Arrow*
had established itself in orbit around the Earth, transfer vehicles could
bring the crew back to the ground—both the living and the dead.

So now Benson and Virginia Gonzalez wrestled Mikhail
Prokhorov's dead body out of the *Arrow*'s main airlock, while Taki
Nomura stood by in the control center.

"I feel like a damned ghoul," Benson complained as they began
towing the spacesuited body toward the empty cargo module.

"No," said Virginia, "this is the right thing to do. Now we can return
him to his family and they can give him a proper funeral and burial."

"After a couple of dozen pathologists get finished tinkering with him."

"Still, it's better than letting him drift off into space, alone forever," Virginia insisted.

"Maybe."

"He should be put to rest with his family. That's what I would want."

"Mikhail was divorced and I don't think he had any children."

"Are his parents still living?" Virginia asked.

"I don't know."

Virginia said, "He'll probably get a hero's funeral when he's returned to Russia."

"Right. Well, he's got one main qualification for being a one-hundred-percent hero, that's for sure. He's dead."

NOVEMBER 21, 2035
MARS LANDING PLUS 16 DAYS
04:00 UNIVERSAL TIME
NEW YORK CITY

Contrary to the sneers of her many critics and detractors, Deirdre Wilcox was not a flake, nor was she a close-minded mouthpiece for the lunatic fringe. She had won a university degree in moral philosophy and she was bright, intelligent, and vivacious on camera: a dark-haired, green-eyed beauty who had been smart enough to augment her natural figure judiciously and to dress well enough to show it off without being blamed for exhibitionism.

Steven Treadway loathed her. While he had laboriously worked his way to the top of the network's news staff by hard-edged reporting and unbiased interviews, Deirdre Wilcox was just a rung below him, always reaching to scramble higher. If she had slept her way up the ladder, as was rumored, Treadway was unable to find with whom, despite considerable digging.

The two of them were sitting side-by-side in a pair of comfortable leather armchairs in the TV studio, flanked by a pair of guests. Sitting next to Treadway was chief of the NASA Johnson Space Center's medical division, Dr. Lencio Ochoa. Next to Wilcox was Ulan Quinn, the author of a moderately successful book claiming that astronauts had discovered the remains of an alien spacecraft on the Moon, but NASA's bureaucracy had hushed up the find.

"This is a sad day," Treadway began the double interview. "Two weeks ago Commander Benson, aboard the *Arrow* Mars spacecraft, performed a wedding. Today, he interred the remains of Russian

333

meteorologist Mikhail Prokhorov outside their spacecraft. The *Arrow* has become a sort of interplanetary hearse, bearing the dead body of one of the ship's crew back home."

Flashing a considerable amount of leg, Deirdre Wilcox jumped in with, "It's truly unfortunate." She smiled sadly and asked Dr. Ochoa, "I understand he died of cancer. Is that right?"

Ochoa was short and blocky, with slicked-back dark hair and a pencil-thin moustache. He nodded somberly. "Cancer of the stomach."

"And it was caused by the radiation he's been exposed to in space?"

The physician's deep brown eyes went wide. "No! That doesn't seem to be the case. Of course, we won't know for certain until we've examined the body."

"You'll perform an autopsy," Deirdre said.

"Yes. Certainly."

"But he didn't have cancer when he started the trip to Mars, did he?"

Ochoa squirmed uncomfortably in his chair. "That's not certain. His physicians in Russia passed him for the mission, but he might have been carrying the first stage of a tumor that they didn't detect."

"And that tumor was made worse by the radiation in space."

"That's . . . a possibility," Ochoa said weakly.

Treadway tried to regain control. "The team that's been monitoring the *Arrow*'s flight from the very beginning reports that radiation levels have been well within what they expected, not dangerously high."

"Coverup," snapped Quinn. He was middle-aged, his shoulder-length light brown hair just starting to show streaks of gray. His face was lean, sallow, with narrow suspicious eyes. He wore a suede jacket over unpressed Levis and clasped a slim notebook computer on his knees with both hands.

Treadway bristled. "You can't accuse—"

But Deirdre leaned forward enough to block the camera's view of Treadway and turned to Quinn. "This wouldn't be the first time NASA's covered up news they didn't want the public to know, is it?"

Tapping on his notebook, Quinn said, "I have documented evidence here of seventeen NASA coverups, including the *Challenger* disaster of January 28, 1986."

"Now wait—"

"And of course there's the coverup of finding that alien spaceship on the Moon."

And so it went, until the break for the first commercial.

Treadway jumped up from his chair and shouted to the program's director, "I am *not* going to allow this man to turn the show into a UFO nuthouse!"

The show's producer, in the booth above the set, spoke coolly into Treadway's ear bud. "Steve, calm down. The switchboard's swamped with calls."

Furious, Treadway yanked the communications bud out of his ear and leaned over Quinn. "This show is about the death of Mikhail Prokhorov. Period. Confine yourself to that subject or get the hell off the set!"

Quinn looked up at him like a child wrongly accused of stealing cookies. "If that's what you want," he said softly.

Turning to Deirdre Wilcox, Treadway added, "And stop upstaging me."

She merely smiled and crossed her long legs.

The interview resumed with Treadway asking Dr. Ochoa, "Is the radiation in space really dangerous, Doctor?"

Ochoa nodded somberly. "Of course it is. Interplanetary space is drenched with high-energy particles of the solar wind, plus cosmic rays from beyond the solar system."

"But the Mars crew is protected, isn't it?"

"We wouldn't have sent them to Mars if we felt they were in serious danger." Ochoa glanced at Quinn as he continued, "We've had experts studying this problem for years. We know the levels of radiation to be expected and we've seen to it that the spacecraft is adequately shielded. There is no danger of its crew being exposed to lethal levels of radiation. None whatsoever."

"Even in that shelter on the surface of Mars?" Wilcox asked. "It was designed to be occupied for only thirty days, wasn't it? And now those four men and women will have to stay in it for a year or even more."

"The *Fermi* habitat is adequately shielded," Ochoa insisted. "As is the *Arrow* spacecraft."

"But those people on Mars will be working outside the habitat, in the open, protected by nothing but their spacesuits," Wilcox prodded. "Won't that be a problem?"

Beside her, Quinn was nodding vigorously. Treadway glared at him.

Dr. Ochoa replied, "The crew on the surface of Mars may incur a slightly higher dose of radiation when they work outside the habitat, but not enough to endanger them."

"Is that true?" Wilcox insisted. "Surely that much radiation must have an effect?"

Frowning slightly, Ochoa replied, "Oh, their risk of eventually contracting cancer in their later years might be increased by a few percent. Nothing more."

Looking somewhere between shocked and angered, Wilcox said, "They'll be killed by cancer?"

"I said their chances of contracting cancer might be a few percent higher. In their later years. When they're seventy or eighty."

"Not before then?"

"Even if it happens sooner, most cancers can be handled if they're caught in their earliest stages."

"Most," Wilcox murmured. "If."

Quinn couldn't contain himself any longer. "How many former astronauts have already died of cancer?"

Ochoa looked surprised. "Why, I don't know."

"I've got the figures right here." Quinn began tapping on his notebook.

"Hold it," Treadway said firmly. "I've seen those figures: former astronauts have come down with cancer at just about the same rate as the rest of the population. And, as Dr. Ochoa just said, most cancers are treatable if you catch them early enough."

"That's right," Ochoa agreed.

Wilcox looked unconvinced.

Before she could say anything, Treadway said to Ochoa, "So the reality is that the spacecraft and the *Fermi* habitat on the surface of Mars give adequate levels of protection against radiation."

Ochoa nodded vigorously. "Yes. That's true."

"Even against solar flares?" Wilcox asked.

Ochoa sighed before replying, "Both the *Arrow* and the *Fermi* have special storm cellars to protect their crews against the elevated levels of radiation during a CME event."

"CME?" Treadway prompted.

"Coronal mass ejection. What's popularly called a solar flare."

"Radiation levels get very high then, don't they?" Wilcox asked.

Nodding again, Ochoa said, "For a day or two. The crews will have to stay inside their storm cellars until the radiation level goes down to normal."

"No going outside on the surface," Treadway said.

"Goodness no!"

Wilcox asked, "What if someone is caught out on the surface when a flare strikes?"

Ochoa actually chuckled. "That won't happen. We have satellites and telescopes on Earth monitoring the Sun constantly. When a CME occurs we have many hours, sometimes even days, before its radiation cloud reaches Earth—and even longer before it gets to Mars."

"If the flare is detected in time," Quinn said.

"We detect them whenever they occur," insisted Ochoa. "No problem. The astronauts get plenty of warning time."

Quinn looked doubtful. "So you say."

DECEMBER 5, 2035
MARS LANDING PLUS 30 DAYS
14:56 UNIVERSAL TIME
FERMI **HABITAT**

Amanda Lynn stared at the jumble of curves glowing on her display screen. The biology laboratory in the *Fermi* was even smaller than the one aboard the *Arrow*, but its equipment was first-rate.

The tip of her tongue peeking out from between her lips, she traced one of the lines with a trembling finger.

"Gotcha!" she whispered.

She had spent the morning digging in the arroyo out on the plain of Elysium, as usual, and as usual took samples of the soil to the bio lab for analysis.

The latest samples had been placed in a small, specially designed containment cell with nutrients that any Earth-based bacteria would immediately begin to eat. If the sample contained anything remotely resembling Earth life, then she would know it.

An LED above the sample container turned yellow and then green.

Amanda's fingers player across the keyboard in rapid fire, telling the computer to bring to the screen plots of various sample parameters, including the measurement of methane gas within the container. One of the plots, showing the concentration of methane and carbon dioxide in the atmosphere above the sample, showed a marked increase in both. On Earth, this would be an early indicator that something in the sample was eating and producing waste gas.

"The little bugger is eating lunch," she said to herself, her eyes still riveted on the display screen. *"No doubt about it."*

This was not conclusive proof that the sample contained life, she knew, but she considered it strong evidence that they had found what they were looking for.

Amanda sat there grinning for several minutes. She could see the reflection of her face in the display screen: round and chocolate dark, with a gleaming bright smile, like a little girl opening her Christmas presents.

Abruptly, she snapped out of her happy daze and began tapping furiously on her laptop computer, composing a report to be sent back to her fellow biologists at NASA's Ames Research Center.

Half an hour later she stepped out of the closet-sized laboratory, into the habitat's central area. Nobody in sight.

She walked past the rolled-up hammocks pinned to the walls and into the control center. Catherine Clermont was sitting there in a slightly pink and brown excursion suit, helmet on the floor at her feet. Her face was half-covered with a breathing mask.

Amanda immediately knew what was going on. *Ted and Hi must be outside; Catherine's prebreathing low-pressure oxy in case they need her out there.*

Clermont sensed Amanda's presence and turned from the screen that showed the two men in their suits and helmets working outside.

"Amanda," Clermont said, through the breathing mask.

"What's going on?"

With a Gallic shrug, Clermont replied, "Hi and Ted are moving the core sampler."

"Again?"

"They are hoping they will hit ice a little farther from the habitat."

"They've already sunk four dry holes."

"Yes."

The elation of her discovery leached out of Amanda. She plopped herself down on the chair next to Catherine's, muttering, "Fifth time's the charm . . . I hope."

"As my Jewish mentor often said, 'From your mouth to God's ear.'"

"Y'know what I think," Amanda said. Without waiting for a reply, she said, "I think they ought to be drilling in the arroyo."

"That's the first site they tried."

"They should try a couple more sites in the arroyo."

"But we agreed not to disturb that area, so you could study it."

Amanda flashed her brightest smile. "I found what I was looking for."

"A fossil?"

"No, not that. I think I'm about to confirm the Chinese discovery."

"You found biomarkers?"

Amanda, nodded, barely able to contain her excitement. "I just sent the data back to Ames for them to cross-check. In about an hour I'll be able to go back and run more tests, but I think we found what we came to find."

"That's great, and I am sure the news will elate everyone back home, but quite frankly, I think I'd rather we'd found water."

Outside, Connover and McPherson had spent the past three hours toting the core sampler to a new location, farther from the habitat.

Ted looked back and saw their bootprints in the rusty colored sand. Each hole they had drilled was farther away from the habitat. *If we don't strike water soon, we'll get so far from the* Fermi *that we won't have enough piping to carry the water back to the habitat.*

"So what do you think, Ted?" McPherson asked. "Is there really any water around here?" His voice sounded tired, dispirited, in Connover's helmet earphones.

Ted lowered himself to the ground. "Take a break, Hi. Don't get yourself overheated."

The geologist sat down beside him. Both their excursion suits were spattered with pinkish dust: the boots and leggings, their gloves and sleeves, their backsides. Connover knew that if the gritty dust worked its way into their backpacks, their life-support pumps might be damaged. That's why he insisted on a thorough vacuuming whenever they returned to the habitat. *Time to open up the backpacks and inspect the equipment inside them, he thought.*

"Do you think there's really any water here?" McPherson repeated.

"You're the geologist, Hi. You tell me."

Reflexively, McPherson went to scratch his beard. His hand bumped his helmet visor instead.

"All the observations show permafrost belowground," he said.

"But how deep? That's the question."

"Deeper than our core sampler's been able to reach."

Connover nodded wearily. "It doesn't do us a damned bit of good if there's an ocean of frozen water beneath us, if it's too deep for the mole to reach."

"We could die of thirst while we're sitting on top of a frozen ocean."

"Poetic."

McPherson took a deep breath, then clambered to his feet. "Well, we're not going to find any permafrost by sitting on our butts."

"You're right," Connover agreed. As he got to his feet, he giggled softly.

"What's so funny?"

"I never thought that being an astronaut would mean drilling goddamned holes in the ground."

McPherson grinned back at him. "We'll make a geologist out of you yet, Ted my boy."

DECEMBER 7, 2035
MARS LANDING PLUS 32 DAYS
02:07 UNIVERSAL TIME
THE *ARROW*

The klaxon jolted the three people on the *Arrow* out of sleep. Benson snapped awake and immediately scrambled to unstrap himself from his sleeping bag.

"SOLAR STORM ALERT," the loudspeakers blared. "REPORT TO THE SHELTER IMMEDIATELY. THIS IS NOT A DRILL."

Fortunately, the shelter was their sleeping area, so there was no need for them to go anywhere. Still, Virginia and Taki tumbled out of their cubbyholes in nothing more than their shapeless tank tops and panties, wide-eyed with sudden fear.

"It's all right," Benson immediately reassured them, shouting over the klaxon's wail. "We're safe in here."

He went to the communications panel on the bulkhead and shut off the klaxon. The sudden silence was palpable.

But Taki said, "Bee, we lost a lot of water. Is there enough in the skin to protect us?"

"Should be," he replied tightly. "Mission Control ran the numbers just before we broke Mars orbit and started home. With the water Ted sent up from *Fermi*, we ought to be okay."

"Ought to be?" Virginia asked. She looked frightened, floating almost a foot above the deck, drifting toward the hatch.

Benson put out a hand to steady her. "Just after the accident, once we patched the leak, it didn't look good," he said. "They thought that a major solar storm would give us a significant radiation dose. Not lethal, but enough to raise our chances of getting cancer by ten percent or so."

Taki said, "But that was when they thought there'd be eight of us aboard using up the water. And no replenishment from the *Fermi*."

"Right," said Benson. "The numbers they ran just before we left Mars orbit looked a lot better."

"And that was for four people," Taki added. "Now we're only three."

"We'll be okay," Benson repeated.

Virginia still looked unconvinced. She glanced around the narrow confines of the area, as if trying to see the invisible subatomic particles that were bulleting through her body.

"It'll be all right," Taki said.

"How high is the radiation level now?" Virginia asked.

"Pretty close to normal, I would guess," Benson replied. "The cloud hasn't reached us yet. I'll have the readings from the command center piped into the comm panels in our cubbies. We'll get minute-by-minute reports."

"Unless the sensors fail."

"They're hardened against radiation, Virginia."

"But we're not."

Taki pushed herself up off the deck and rapped her knuckles against the overhead. "We're shielded, Jin. We'll be fine."

Virginia nodded. "I'm sorry I'm such a worrier. It's just . . . kind of scary."

Rubbing his chin in thought, Benson said, "You know, we could take the emergency box shields from the CTV and bring them in here. They're high-density polyethylene; should give us a good layer of extra protection."

"But we'd have to go out and take it from the crew transfer vehicle," Virginia countered. "We'd have to leave the protection of the shielding here."

"That's all right," said Benson. "The radiation cloud won't reach us for several hours. I'll check with Houston and see if we have time enough to get the box shields from the CTV."

Taki smiled at him. "Yeah, but if you do we're going to be cooped up in something the size of a phonebooth for a couple of days, at least."

"With nothing much to do, except watch the radiation readings," said Benson.

Virginia's worried frown eased into a tentative smile. "Bee, you'll be stuck in here with the two of us."

Taking up on Gonzalez's smile, Taki suggested, "I suppose we could play computer games. Or something."

Feeling his cheeks warming, Benson pushed himself toward the hatch. "I'm going to the command center and check in with Mission Control."

When Houston's CME warning reached Mars, it automatically triggered the alert klaxon, just as it had aboard the *Arrow*.

Catherine and Hi were in the auxiliary airlock, where they had been spending their nights. It was a cramped little space, between the inner and outer hatches, its floor area not quite big enough for Hiram to stretch out to his full length. He had to sleep curled around Catherine's body. Somehow he didn't mind that. Neither did she, apparently.

Catherine snapped to a sitting position. "What's that?"

"Emergency," Hi answered, and immediately felt stupid.

He fumbled in the darkness for the flashlight he always kept beside him, grasped it and flicked it on with his thumb. Then he reached for his coveralls and began tugging them on. Catherine was doing the same.

Through the thick inner hatch they heard the automated warning: "SOLAR STORM ALERT. REPORT TO THE SHELTER IMMEDIATELY. THIS IS NOT A DRILL."

Getting to his bare feet, McPherson cracked the inner hatch open. "We'd better get to the sleeping area."

"Yes. Quickly," Catherine said, zipping up the front of her coveralls.

The lights were on throughout the habitat, and Ted Connover was sitting at the communications console in the command center, looking grim.

"How long do we have before it hits?" he was asking the display screen, which showed a Mission Control technician.

Amanda Lynn came out of their sleeping area, wearing a rumpled pullover shirt that reached her knees.

"Solar flare," Ted told Catherine and Hi before they could say anything. "Looks like a big one."

Glancing around at the hard walls of this section of the habitat, Amanda said, "We should be okay in here."

With all four of them squeezed into the command center, the compartment felt crowded, steamy.

Connover was studying the spiky lines of graphs on the console's display screens.

"No rise in radiation levels, so far," he said. "The cloud's still several hours away."

The network of satellites that had been put in orbit around Mars by NASA and the European and the Japanese space agencies monitored radiation levels above the planet's atmosphere, and performed dozens of other duties, such as relaying communications around the planet and retransmitting messages to and from Earth.

Looking up from the displays, Connover broke into a tentative smile. "We'll be fine in here. In fact, we could probably keep on working as usual, as long as we don't go outside."

Catherine said, "The atmosphere protects us, *non*?"

"Not as much as Earth's atmosphere shields against radiation storms," said McPherson, "but even the thinner air of Mars gives us a decent layer of protection."

Connover nodded agreement. "You know, the safety guys back in Houston were pretty damned conservative when they drew up the mission guidelines. They were using old data, back from the days when they thought that a CME storm could kill you outright if you weren't protected. It turns out that the atmosphere of Mars shields us from most cosmic rays, even though it's a hundred times thinner than Earth's atmosphere.

"If we were outside and exposed to a CME flux, we'd get a bigger radiation dose than we would on Earth, but it'd be about the same as we'd get in an orbiting space station. In here, under the water shield, we'll be fine."

"No worries," Amanda said. She looked far from relaxed, though.

"Not here," said Connover. "It's the guys in the *Arrow* that I'm worried about. They're facing a helluva bigger flux than we'll catch, and they're much more vulnerable."

"Don't they have that portable shelter from the crew transfer vehicle?" McPherson asked. "They could use it to give them an extra layer of protection."

Connover said, "Yeah, they could, couldn't they?"

"Perhaps you should call Bee and suggest it," said Catherine.

Connover hesitated. *Bee's probably already thought of the portable shelter,* he thought. *He doesn't need any suggestions from me. He'll think I'm interfering.*

"Call him," Amanda urged.

With a single curt nod, Connover reached for the communications panel. "Right," he told them, while he thought, *I'll have to chance Bee getting sore at me. There are lives at stake. Including his.*

The teenage boys were, of course, much more interested in their online gaming than with their school homework. All three were juniors in high school, and possessed the latest-greatest computers, notepads, and virtual reality systems. None of them paid much attention to what was going on in the world, except for the Mars mission. They were the demographic that President Harper was trying to inspire by the exploration of Mars, and he'd succeeded. They were hooked.

To an outside observer, the three of them were standing in the jumbled, gadget-crammed bedroom with its unmade bed and telescope standing by the only window, wearing metal-mesh sockhats on their heads as they flailed at unseen enemies like a trio of youngsters being attacked by a swarm of invisible bees.

From their own perspective, however, thanks to the images flooding their minds from the sensor webs affixed to their heads, they were battling hordes of shape-changing Martian monsters hell-bent on taking over their high school. Never mind why the aliens wanted their high school; the game had them totally engrossed.

Manuel, the unofficial alpha male of the pack, was as usual kicking the other two boys' butts by killing upwards of fifty of the wily green monsters in this latest virtual reality simulation to hit the Internet, inspired by the country's renewed interest in space exploration. For high school boys, killing dreaded Martians was the next best thing to lusting after high school girls.

351

Manuel pulled off his sensor web first. He had won this encounter and eliminated the Martian threat, for now. Level three would be next.

"Man, that was great!" he enthused as the other boys peeled off their sensor webs. "I can't wait to try that in the porno mode."

"Your mind is always in the gutter, Manny," Jim complained.

"Best place to be, man."

Billy, the youngest of the three asked, "Hey, did you hear about the *Arrow*? One of the spacewatch feeds is saying that the guy who died was infected with something he picked up on Mars. They've got a video of him showing a Martian creature busting out his gut."

"No way! Are you kidding me?" Jim said. "I thought he had cancer. That's what the science feeds say."

"Yes, way," Billy insisted. "It's all over the news feeds. That video's gross, dude. I sure hope they don't bring that shit back here."

"I don't believe it. You can make anything look real these days. Just look at this game. I can't tell if I'm in your room or at school fighting Martian zombies. Anyway, I haven't read anything like that on the science feeds. You see too many conspiracy theories on those alternative sites."

Both boys turned to Manuel, who was a good six months older than either of them.

With a totally serious expression, Manuel proclaimed, "The space agency won't allow us to get infected. If it's real, the government will send the ship off into the Sun or something and that'll be the last time we go to Mars for a long, long time."

"Geez, I hope not," Billy said. "I was looking forward to meeting those guys when they get back. They're real heroes. And besides, I'd like to go to Mars myself, someday."

"Me too," said Jim.

"Yeah," Manuel agreed. "That'd be great." Then he slipped his sensor net back on his head. "But are you guys ready to kick some more Martian butt?"

"Let me at 'em," said Jim and Billy, as one.

It's like being in jail, Ted Connover thought. The four of us crowded into this tiny space, like prisoners locked in a damned jail cell.

Connover was sitting disconsolately at the command panel, where the jiggling curves of the display screen showed that the radiation level outside their shelter was still murderously high. Catherine and Amanda were bent over some computer game they were playing, hardly more than an arm's reach away. Hi was pacing methodically back and forth: four paces one way, then turn around and four paces back.

He'd rather be back in the auxiliary airlock with Catherine, Connover told himself. *Can't blame him. I'd rather be* anywhere *except this effing Black Hole of Calcutta.*

McPherson stopped his pacing and came to Connover's side. "How's it going?" he asked.

Pointing to the jagged curves, Ted replied, "Still hot enough outside to fry your *cojones* in half a minute."

"No letup?"

"Not yet."

"What's Houston say?"

"Another six hours, at least."

McPherson straightened up and looked across to the two women, still busy with their game. "We're okay in here, though." It was a flat statement of hope.

Connover nodded tiredly. "Yep. Radiation level inside our little igloo is just about normal."

"That's good. We're in—"

"*Fermi,* Houston here."

Both men jerked with surprise. Amanda and Catherine looked over to them, their faces worried.

Nathan Brice's face appeared on the communications screen. He looked tired, pouchy-eyed.

This can't be good, Connover thought.

"*Fermi* here," he said, knowing that his words wouldn't reach Brice's ears for a quarter of an hour. "Go ahead, Houston."

Brice hadn't waited for his reply. "We've been working on this nonstop ever since Amanda's report on the biomarkers. The bio team confirms that everything checks out: complex prebiotic molecules, PAHs, even amino acids. Tell Amanda she's verified the Chinese findings and then some. Good work, guys."

Amanda shot out of her chair and raced to the comm screen, a gleaming smile splitting her dark face. Catherine got up too, more slowly. McPherson pumped both his fists in the air.

"You did it, girl!" He grabbed Amanda in a bear hug that lifted her off her feet.

Connover grinned happily at Brice's image on the screen.

"Thanks for the good news, Nathan."

But Brice was still talking. He concluded with, "By the way, you should be clear of the CME in another four-five hours."

Who cares? Connover thought, as he watched Amanda, Catherine and Hi dancing across the cramped room.

"Satellites show that the radiation level's been normal for six hours now," Connover reported into the intercom. "Storm's over."

In the sleeping area, where she'd been going over the results of their previous excursions on her laptop, Catherine smiled tentatively and asked, "We can go outside again?"

"Don't see why not," Connover replied, still eyeing the displays on his control panel. "But let me check with Houston first, just to make sure."

McPherson called, "Find out how they did on the *Arrow*, Ted, while you're at it."

"Will do."

Benson smiled as he pulled the comm bud from his ear. "Houston confirms it. We're in the clear."

Virginia and Taki, sitting against opposite walls of the box shelter, looked up from the chess game they were playing on their tablets.

"We can get out of this coffin?" Taki asked. She hadn't used that term for the confining shelter before, while they were still in the radiation cloud.

"Back to normal," Benson said, his smile widening.

Taki floated to her feet and started lifting up one section of the shelter. "First thing I'm going to do," she announced, "is take a shower."

Benson raised a cautionary finger. "We're still rationing the water, you know."

"I know. I'll make it quick. Well within the limits we agreed to. But I feel so *grungy*."

Once they had taken the shelter down and stored it, Benson headed for the command center. "I'd better check out the ship's systems," he said.

Virginia followed right behind him. "Bee, when we were cooped up like that I had a lot of time to think about everything."

"So did we all," he said, ducking through the hatch into the command center.

He sat in the command chair. Virginia hovered behind him, grasping the back of the chair to keep from floating away.

"I mean," she said, her voice soft, almost wistful, "we've been gone from Earth a long time now, and it'll be another eleven months before we get home. We almost died when the ship was hit, we've left our friends on Mars where they very well might die, and we've lost one of our team."

He glanced up, over his shoulder, at her.

Virginia went on, "I've read just about every book I ever wanted to read and watched all the videos I can stomach. We've played games with each other and the computer, messed around with the VR simulator and even got some science work done."

Benson turned around in his seat to looked squarely at her. "Where's this leading, Jinny?"

"Bee, I'm scared. The accident, this solar storm, doesn't it frighten you?"

"Yes," he admitted. "A little. But we've come through it all okay."

"There's something else, too."

Benson started to reply, but checked himself.

Without waiting for him to ask, Virginia confessed, "Bee, I'm lonely. I want to be held. I know it's wrong, but I want to be close to you."

"Virginia, there's nothing wrong with wanting to be held." He reached out to her and pulled her down onto his lap. She twined her arms around his neck.

"Bee," she whispered, "make love to me."

"I'm still a married man," he whispered back.

"I know. But you never speak of your wife, and as far as I know, you haven't even sent her a message. Aren't you lonely too? Wouldn't she understand?"

Benson looked at the beautiful woman in his arms and thought about his loveless marriage back home. He and Maggie hadn't been intimate since halfway through his training for the mission; that had been more than six months before he'd taken off for Mars. He had no idea if he had anything more awaiting him when he returned than divorce papers.

He was already reacting physically to Virginia's presence in his arms. He took a deep breath and made up his mind.

"Jinny, I don't give a damn whether Maggie would understand or not. My marriage was over before we ever left for Mars. We're here together and who knows what tomorrow might bring?" Benson barely got those last words out before Virginia's lips met his.

But then she pulled away slightly. "What about Taki?"

"You want her to join us?" Benson grinned.

"No! But I don't want her watching, either."

He sighed. "Well, there's only a few places on this ship where we can get some privacy, and she just might wander in on us, unless we tell her blatantly not to."

Virginia straightened up and pushed her hair back away from her face. It floated weightlessly around her head, like a dark halo.

"I'll tell Taki to stay away from the cupola for the next hour or so," Virginia said. "That is, I assume you'll want me to tell her."

Benson said, "Right."

She gave him a peck on the cheek and then pushed herself off toward the hatch. Benson sat there alone, wondering how all this had happened, astounded at his good fortune. *The most beautiful woman on the team and she wants me!* He broke into an ear-to-ear smile.

Then he realized that he was the only male left aboard the *Arrow*.

Taki Nomura was in the *Arrow's* minuscule infirmary, scanning readouts of the last physicals they had all taken. *I'll have to do complete workups on each of us,* she was thinking, *to see if the radiation storm did any somatic damage.*

Virginia glided through the hatch and hovered before her, smiling contentedly.

Looking up at her, Taki said, "Wipe the canary feathers off your chin."

"It's that obvious?"

"I've been wondering how long it would take you two to get together. You know his marriage is a mess, don't you?"

"I had heard . . . something."

"So he finally broke through his inhibitions?"

Almost giggling, Virginia admitted, "I helped him a little."

"Good for you."

"We're going to be in the cupola, and—"

"And you'd appreciate some privacy. I know. Don't worry, I'm not a voyeur."

"I . . . thank you, Taki."

"Nothing to it."

Virginia started to leave the infirmary, but hesitated. "Taki . . . I'm sorry that . . . well, that there's no one for you."

Nomura made a smile that hardly looked forced at all. "Don't worry about it. I'm from Japanese stock, remember? Stoic." Her grin widening, she added, "Besides, I've got some VR simulations that would make a sailor blush."

Hi and Catherine were glad to be out of the habitat, doing what they had come to Mars to do. This was their eleventh walkabout since they had landed; they'd collected several hundred pounds of rocks and dirt that definitely included biomarker chemicals but, so far, they'd found nothing that Amanda could identify unequivocally as a living organism, or even a fossil.

Nor any trace of water ice.

Their water situation wasn't critical yet. The recycler was working at close to ninety-percent efficiency, and Ted had calculated that at their present rate of usage they had enough water to last for another month, maybe a little more. But with each passing day they were losing a bit more of their water supply.

Both the geologists knew the vital importance of finding water, and had shifted the focus of their explorations from geology "for the sake of science" to geology "for the sake of survival." They no longer bothered to collect samples unless they thought that particular location might be one that could yield water. But each of the sites they had sampled turned up dry—

Mission protocol required that they stay within sight of the *Fermi*, but they had bent that rule slightly and Connover, in his growing worry about the water situation, had let them get away with it. Now, as they headed back and caught sight of the *Fermi*'s dust-stained structure standing against the dull orange sky, they both felt weary and defeated.

Catherine said disconsolately, "I know there's ice out here somewhere. There has to be!"

McPherson tried to shrug inside his excursion suit and, as usual, failed. "If we were at the poles, we'd be swimming in the stuff. The gamma ray spectrometers on the satellites showed frozen lakes just below the surface, enough to fill Lake Michigan twice."

"We should have landed there," said Catherine.

Shaking his head inside his helmet, McPherson said, "The mission planners thought it'd be safer down here, closer to the equator."

"Not if we don't find water."

"The satellite data showed there are pockets of hydrogen all around this area," he said, "but they're isolated and it's impossible to say for sure if the hydrogen is in the form of water ice or bound to some other chemical in the soil."

Catherine clasped Hi's gloved hand as they walked.

"We'll find water here," she said firmly, as if trying to convince herself. "This area was once full of streams and rivers."

"A couple billion years ago."

"I cannot believe they all evaporated without leaving some reservoir underground, some pockets of ice. We simply have to keep looking. We have time."

Less time every day, McPherson thought. But he kept silent.

They trudged back toward the habitat. Catherine remembered the sense of wonder and excitement they had both felt when they'd started exploring this new world. That was almost gone now. Now their walkabouts were more like drudgery—with the fear of failure behind it.

"Hey, you guys, quit being so depressed out there."

Amanda's cheerful voice startled them. They hadn't had much contact with the habitat during their walkabouts, and had unconsciously acted as if their conversations were private—which they were not.

"Amanda," Catherine blurted. "You surprised me."

"Sorry about that. I wasn't trying to scare anyone. But your doom and gloom isn't doing any of us any good, you know."

McPherson replied sourly, "So, you've got something to be chipper about?"

"You betcha! Ted and I finished the prototype garden this

"You're going to put this outside?"

Nodding, Connover went on, "Daytime power will come from the solar arrays on the tips of the booms. We printed those, too, same way that dirt farmers in Africa are printing their own solar panels."

"The spheres will generate enough power to keep the chamber warm during the day," Amanda said. "Plus, they'll charge up the batteries that'll run the heaters overnight."

"Once we fill it with water we'll plant the potato sprouts for our first crop," Connover said.

"Potatoes?" Catherine asked.

Amanda said, "They don't need seeds to reproduce. We just plant the sprouts. We'll let the first harvest sit around for a week or so, until they start developing 'eyes' and sprouting their own roots. Then we'll cut 'em up and grow more potatoes."

"And you're going to move this rig outside?" McPherson asked again.

"Yep," Amanda replied. "Then we'll plant bamboo. It's a root runner, spreads in the water and shoots up new bamboo plants. Houston's sending me some bamboo recipes."

"And we'll grow mint, too," said Connover. "Amanda wants to flavor her tea."

"Later on we'll plant tomatoes, beans, peas and the other vegetables we were going to grow in the hydroponics rig. With any luck, we can get them to self-pollinate so we can keep the lines going."

"We should have brought some bees along," Catherine murmured.

McPherson asked, "But why outdoors? Why are you going to so much trouble to put in heaters? Can't we just use the artificial lighting in here to grow food? Wouldn't that be easier?"

"If we were only planning on one or two hydroponics units," Amanda answered. "But we need enough to feed ourselves, and this place is too small for that. We need the great outdoors."

Connover said, "I'm going to put a camera in the box so we can monitor their growth from here in the habitat."

Amanda pointed out, "One of the reasons we picked potatoes to start with is that they have all the nutrients the human body needs. We can live on potatoes alone, if we have to."

"Like the Irish," said McPherson.

"Potato soup," Catherine said. "Perhaps even *bouillabaisse*."

morning and we're eager to show it off to you. Come on back in.
grab some grub first, and then we'll give you a tour of the first ga
on Mars."

Breaking into a grin, McPherson said, "We're on our way, Ama
"Cheerfully," Catherine added.

Two hours later all four of them were gathered in the left wi
the habitat gazing at a four-foot-by-four-foot rectangular box w
clear lid. Inside the box was a long tray punctured by holes reg
spaced along its bottom. Below each hole was a short, hollow tub
each end of the box was a telescoping boom that extended to a |
of about four feet above the plastic flooring. On top of each boo
a shiny, reflective ball with wires running from their bases into a
electronics pad that was attached to the big rectangular box.

Connover, standing beside Amanda, was smiling with satisf

"While you two guys have been out taking leisurely walks, A
and I have been busy with the 3D printer and some spare parts |
this together."

"This is a garden?" McPherson asked, his voice heav
skepticism.

"Damned right it is," Connover said. "We made the box, th
and the growth chamber out of the same plastic we used to ma
wedding bands. It's strong and resistant to the environment
and we layered it so as to provide some additional thermal pro

Amanda took over. "In the growth chamber you can see t
that we'll fill with water. We'll plant the seeds we brought alon
hydroponics experiments that we were going to do."

She pointed to the two-by-two-foot experimental hydr
chamber that was part of the *Fermi*'s built-in equipment.

"It was too damned small for growing enough food to
Ted resumed, "so we copied its design and used parts of i
garden chamber. Of course, we had some help from the e
back home."

Amanda said, "Hey, they're not here, so we can take all th

Pointing, Connover explained, "We put some resistiv
along the walls and on the bottom. The clear lid gives us a
seal. We can't have our summer harvest freezing in the bal
below out there."

"Okay," said McPherson. "Looks to me like you've thought everything out. When can we expect our first harvest?"

"About four months," Amanda said.

"God willing and the creek don't rise," Connover added.

DECEMBER 17, 2035
MARS LANDING PLUS 42 DAYS
16:08 UNIVERSAL TIME
NASA HEADQUARTERS, WASHINGTON D.C.

Bart Saxby got to his feet and came around his desk as Robin Harkness led Sarah Fleming into his office. Saxby noted with some surprise that the president's red-headed staff chief was a centimeter or two taller than his director of human spaceflight. Then he saw the spiked heels she was wearing.

Gesturing to the small round conference table by his office windows, Saxby said graciously, "Welcome, Sarah. It's good to see you."

As they settled themselves on the chairs, Saxby's administrative assistant carried in a tray bearing a silver coffee pot and three delicate china cups and saucers.

"First of all," Fleming said, "the president sends his congratulations. Your team got through the solar storm with flying colors."

Harkness' lean face broke into a smile. "They've been well trained."

"And I understand the group on Mars is starting a vegetable garden?"

Saxby nodded. "They're settling in for the long haul."

"They confirmed the Chinese discovery, but they haven't managed to find any water yet."

"No," Saxby admitted. "Not yet. And please quit calling it the 'Chinese discovery.'"

Fleming folded her hands on the tabletop as Harkness reached for the coffee pot. "Sugar?" he asked her. "Milk?"

"Do you have any cream?"

Glancing at the tray, "Looks like milk."

"I'll call for cream," Saxby said, pushing his chair back from the table.

"Don't bother," Fleming said. "Milk will be fine."

Once their cups were filled, Saxby said, "I presume this visit is about the follow-on mission?"

"Yes, of course," she replied. "We have a tricky political situation on our hands."

Harkness glanced at his boss, but said nothing.

"On the one hand," Fleming began to explain, "you have four people who will die on Mars unless we send the follow-on to bring them home."

Saxby said, "I don't think there's another hand. We've got to save them."

Shaking her head slightly, Fleming said, "There is another side to this. And it's loaded with dynamite."

Both men fell silent.

Looking stern, almost grim, Fleming continued, "Senator Donaldson is already yapping that this whole situation has been engineered by you NASA people to blackmail the government into sending the follow-on to Mars."

"That's not true!" Saxby snapped.

"It doesn't have to be true," Fleming said. "It just has to be believable."

"We didn't set this up! We didn't steer the *Arrow* into the path of that meteoroid! We didn't tell Connover and the others to stay on Mars!"

"Of course you didn't. But Donaldson is going to sing that song to the public. And isn't it convenient that the rocks that contain biomarkers are among those that remained on Mars and not in one of the rocks on the ship headed for Earth?"

"He's a prick," Harkness said, with some heat.

"But Congress has cut the funding for the follow-on," Fleming pointed out. "Do you have any idea how hard it will be for the president to get it put back into the NASA budget?"

"The hardware is all but finished," said Harkness. "It's going to cost more money to terminate the contracts than to go ahead and finish the job."

"It gets worse," said Fleming. "Suppose you send the follow-on and your people on Mars die while it's on its way. Senator Donaldson and his followers will claim you knew there was no chance of them surviving, but you used them to get the funding back for the follow-on."

"That's a goddamned lie!" Harkness burst.

"But it will play well with the news media." Before either of the men could say anything, she added, "And suppose the follow-on mission runs into trouble. What then?"

"Wait a minute," Saxby said, fighting down the sullen pain in his chest. "The polls show the public is solidly behind sending the follow-on: nearly sixty percent in favor."

"Yes, but if they get to Mars and find your team dead, or if they, themselves, get killed, the public may swing a hundred and eighty degrees against you. Future Mars missions will be just as dead as those four people."

"So what's the president want to do? Let them die on Mars?"

Fleming shook her head once more. "You have to understand that the president is a lame duck. His term ends in thirteen months. He has very little leverage with Congress."

"And Donaldson wants his job," Harkness muttered.

"He certainly does. And if Donaldson gets into the White House, human spaceflight beyond the Moon will be a dead issue."

Saxby leaned back in his chair and wished the pain in his chest would go away. *Heartburn,* he told himself. *You always get heartburn when you get excited. Calm down. Calm yourself, dammit.*

Harkness was asking, "So what is the president going to do?"

"He hasn't made up his mind yet. Viscerally, deep in his guts, he wants to authorize the follow-on. Politically, he's worried that it will turn into a fiasco and hand next year's nomination to Donaldson."

"Why doesn't he just come out and tell the people that Donaldson's wrong about this?"

"Because Donaldson belongs to the president's party, and the president doesn't want to tear the party apart and hand the White House to the Democrats."

Saxby squeezed his eyes shut for a moment, then said, "So what you're telling us is that the next election is more important to President Harper than those four people struggling to survive on Mars."

Fleming glared at him. "What I'm saying is that the president has to look at all sides of this. It's not as simple a matter as you think."

"Seems simple enough to me," said Harkness. "Life or death."

"The president wants to save your people on Mars," Fleming insisted. "But he's got to find a way to do it that won't play into Donaldson's hands."

Saxby stared at her for a moment, then turned to Harkness. "You'd better tell Connover and his team to stay alive."

Fleming smiled tightly. "It would help if they found some water for themselves."

Saxby had to agree. "That it would, Sarah. That it would."

Ted Connover turned away from the window and surveyed the habitat's central compartment. Hammocks hung on the walls. Chairs were scattered haphazardly.

Looks like an encampment more than a temporary shelter, he thought. *All we need is a fire for toasting s'mores.*

After weeks of daily excursions, the ground outside was churned with bootprints. And despite all the vacuuming they did every day, the floor inside the habitat was smudged with the pink ridges of their boot tracks.

He turned back to the window and looked at the five hydroponic gardens they'd built. The plants were doing well in their stout oblong boxes. They didn't seem to mind that the Sun was farther away than on Earth, or that they were growing in a water solution instead of dirt. They wouldn't like Martian dirt: it was loaded with perchlorates and other chemicals, more like bleach than farming soil.

Water, Connover thought. They'd still not found water and they were nearing the point where the problem would be critical. They might even have to raid one of the hydroponics gardens. He hoped it wouldn't come to that.

He and McPherson had spent the morning on another fruitless water search, this time to a rock formation about three kilometers to the west. After studying and restudying the data from the satellites, and with the help of data-processing algorithms developed just for this purpose by some of the brightest scientists back on Earth, they had decided this site was a likely spot for having subsurface ice.

So Ted and Hi had gone out there this morning and found . . . nothing. The core samples were nothing but rock and dirt. No trace of ice.

And when they'd returned to the habitat, Ted found a message from Houston that a dust storm was heading their way. The Mars meteorologists said it would be a big one, perhaps global.

"Just what we need," he muttered.

"What is just what we need?" Catherine asked.

Startled, Connover spun around to see the French geologist eyeing him with a curious smile on her face.

"Hi, Catherine. I didn't hear you come in."

"I was in the biology lab, talking with Amanda."

With a sigh, Ted jabbed a finger toward the communications console. "Latest weather forecast predicts a dust storm. A big one."

"But that is not terribly dangerous, is it?"

"No, not really." Despite his mood, he produced a little grin. "It won't be like the big dust storms in the American Midwest, with a wall of opaque dust obliterating the horizon and gale-force winds."

"Mars is much more gentle, *non*?"

"*Oui*," he said, exhausting his French vocabulary. "We won't see Dorothy and Toto lifted off to Oz."

More seriously, Catherine asked, "How bad will it be, Ted?"

"A drop in barometric pressure," he replied. "Some haze. If you go outside, you might notice a stronger breeze than usual. Nothing scary."

"Nothing to worry about, then."

"We'll have to clean the dust off the gardens and the all the solar panels," Connover said. "After the storm's over."

"The reactor?" she asked. "The dust shouldn't affect it, right?"

McPherson ducked through the hatch. Ted thought that he'd just set a record for being separated from his wife. The two of them always seemed to be within arm's reach of one another.

"Dust? You mean a dust storm? The reactor could be damaged?" Hi asked, his brow furrowing.

"It should be okay," Ted answered. "It's been designed to operate autonomously in just about any weather the planet can throw at us."

McPherson nodded, satisfied.

But Connover worried about that *just about*. Dust storms blow very fine particles of iron-rich sand. With dust covering all of the solar panels, the reactor would be the only source of electrical power for several hours, maybe a day or more. Ted hoped they hadn't gone with the lowest bidder when they built the reactor.

The four of them had dinner together while the usual soft whisper of the Martian wind outside the habitat rose to a low moaning wail. Connover kept glancing at the window. The Sun was getting low on the horizon, but it was still visible through the thickening haze. *It's going to be a noisy night,* he told himself.

But he remembered tornados back home, and a hurricane he'd been through while training in Florida. *This is kid's stuff, compared to that,* he told himself.

Then the lights dimmed and the hum of the air circulation fans dropped a notch. Before anyone could say a word, the power system alarm began to ring.

"Shit!" Ted snapped.

"Something's wrong with the power system!" Amanda blurted the obvious.

Ted bolted from the table and dashed to the command center, McPherson a step behind him, Amanda and Catherine not far back.

"What's going on?" Hi asked.

Connover slipped into the command chair and focused on the power readouts as he banged the button that turned off the screeching alarm.

The lights brightened momentarily and then dimmed again. The pitch of the air circulation fans changed as well, as if they were being strained by the variation in power feeding them.

"What is it?" Catherine asked.

"I don't know yet," Connover said. "Give me a minute to check the status readouts."

"It makes me think of the way the power goes off and then back on during a Houston thunderstorm," Amanda said, her voice just the tiniest bit shaky.

Connover quickly went through the checklists that had been pounded into his head during the months of mission rehearsals they'd gone through prior to launch. Like the drills that had saved their lives when the meteoroid struck the *Arrow*, training now took over Ted's reaction to this crisis. He scanned the status board, followed a few data trails, brought up screen after screen of readouts, almost faster than they eye could follow.

He finally stopped and stared at the schematic diagram showing the primary power connection in the habitat with the nuclear reactor outside. The lower right sector of the reactor was highlighted in a very scary red.

"That's where the problem is," he said, pointing.

"What is it?" Amanda asked.

"I don't know, exactly, but whatever the problem is, that's where it's located."

McPherson leaned over Ted's shoulder. "How serious is it?"

With a shake of his head, Connover replied, "There's an anomaly in the reactor's cooling system, so the reactor automatically reduced its power output to a safe level. That's what's causing our brownout."

"An anomaly?" Catherine asked. "What does that mean?"

"Something's caused less coolant to be pumping through the reactor core than normal. To avoid having the core run hot, maybe dangerously hot, the computer reduced its power output to a level where the coolant flowing through it can remove the waste heat and not melt down the core."

"Are we in danger of losing power entirely?" Catherine asked.

"Maybe," Connover said tightly. "Right now there's no way of telling what the root cause of the problem might be. There's a chance that we could lose the reactor completely."

"Lose all our power?" Amanda yelped. "We wouldn't last a day without power! We'll freeze to death!"

"If we don't suffocate first," McPherson added.

Raising his hands placatingly, Ted said, "It won't come to that . . . most likely. The data is on its way back to Houston, automatically. Once they've had a chance to review it they'll let us know what we can do to fix the problem."

"*Peut-être*," Catherine murmured.

"In the meantime," Ted went on, "I'm going to power down all but the most essential systems to reduce the load on the reactor. Hopefully that will drop its power output below the level that set off the anomaly. That should buy us some time."

"What do we need to do?" asked Amanda.

Connover shot her a grateful glance, glad that she had so quickly turned from gloom to productive problem-solving.

"Let's drop the thermal curtains over the entrances to the two wings so I can reduce the heat in them. Move anything temperature-sensitive into the central section, here. We'll keep it warm with us."

Amanda and Catherine headed for the left wing.

"I'm going to turn down the heat here in the core by a few degrees. Put on your thermals, this is going to be a night to wear them."

McPherson scratched at his beard. "Guess Catherine and I sleep in here with you tonight."

Nodding, Connover said, "Body heat. It's going to be a four-dog night."

The team reacted quickly, moving several items from each wing into the central module. Then they released the drawstrings holding the insulating curtains above the two hatches to allow them to drop into place and be zipped shut. The whole process took less than an hour, which was about the same time it took for data about their problem to reach Earth, then for Houston to summon whatever experts they had on hand to study the situation and send a reply back to Mars.

In that hour Ted could already feel the temperature in the habitat's central area dropping. It was not a happy sensation.

The beep denoting receipt of an incoming message sent a spasm of energy through Ted's tense nervous system. He hit the receiver button and Nathan Brice's face appeared on the central display screen.

"Ted, we've started looking at the data you sent, and we've called in the entire power team to make recommendations. It'll take some time, though, for us to go through the information and come up with possible courses of action."

"Okay, thanks," Connover replied, knowing it would be almost half an hour before his words reached Houston. Silently he added, *Thanks for nothing, Nate.*

Turning to his three teammates, who were standing anxiously behind his chair, Connover said, "Well, there's not much we can do until they have a chance to evaluate the data and give us our options. Better sling up the hammocks and get some rest."

They nodded glumly, looking apprehensive, almost frightened. He wished there was something more he could tell them to ease their fears, but there wasn't.

Hi and Catherine unhooked two hammocks and spread their sleeping bags on them before crawling in. Ted got into his hammock and reached out to switch off the lights. Amanda went to the dining table and tapped away on her tablet in the dim light from its screen.

"You going to stay up all night?" Ted asked her.

"For a while," she said. "I . . . I'm not really sleepy."

"Go to bed," he ordered. "We all need some rest."

With a sigh that was nearly a huff, Amanda got up from the table and, using her tablet as a flashlight, went to her hammock and curled up in it. Once she closed the tablet, the compartment was totally dark.

In spite of his own advice, Ted was too keyed up to sleep. He hung in his hammock, which swayed back and forth each time he shifted position. He could hear the keening of the wind outside, and the room temperature seemed to be getting lower by the minute.

It's not that bad, he insisted silently. *Back home you'd call this good camping weather.* He remembered camping with Vicki and Thad in one of their favorite national parks, he and his wife in their double sleeping bag, looking up at the stars and watching for satellites or shooting stars.

Then there was the night when teen-aged Thad wandered off from the campfire and disappeared for two hours. They'd searched frantically for him and were just about to report the boy missing to the park ranger when he came through the trees, grinning, arm-in-arm with the Camp Host's daughter, as if nothing was wrong at all.

The memories brought tears to his eyes. Whispering so low he barely heard his own words, Ted said, "Vicki, if you can hear me, please know that I love you—and Thad—and that one day I'll join you. But I can't let that happen just yet. These people are here because of me and I've got to help them survive until a rescue ship can get here and take us all home.

"I miss you, honey, and I'll be with you sooner or later. But not now. Not this night."

Then he closed his eyes and finally fell asleep.

Ted awakened with a start. The air was *cold*, far colder than the temperature to which he'd set the thermometer when they went to bed. He exhaled and could see his breath. That meant it was at least forty-five degrees Fahrenheit, about ten degrees colder than he'd planned.

Not good, he thought as he swung his legs out of the hammock. The damned thing swung around and nearly tipped him onto the floor. Steadying himself, Ted saw that Hi was also awake and on his feet.

"It's too damned cold," McPherson complained.

Nodding tightly, Ted replied, "We must have lost more power during the night. I wonder why the alarm didn't go off?"

Catherine sat up in her hammock and clutched her arms around herself. "C'est froid."

Amanda swung easily to the floor. "Not that bad," she said cheerily. "You ought to try overnighting in a tent in Antarctica. Now that's cold!"

Ted padded in his stocking feet to the control panel and checked out the status boards. Sure enough, the reactor had reduced its power output to less than fifty percent overnight. Whatever was wrong was getting worse.

As he scanned the panel he saw that he'd inadvertently set the alarm to "silent" mode when he was powering down systems the night before.

Stupid mistake, he berated himself. That's the kind of mistake that could kill us all.

He'd also turned off the "new message" signal and saw that they had several new messages from Earth waiting. Angry with himself, he reset the system to make sure that any changes in the habitat's systems would not be silent but, instead, would wail out a standard, very audible alarm.

Hiram, Catherine and Amanda finished dressing as Ted went carefully through all the system's readouts. He activated the outdoor camera and saw that the dust storm had ended. It was a sunny morning on Elysium Planitia: the temperature outside had already climbed above fifty below.

He angled the camera to look at their vegetable gardens. They were covered with a thin sheen of dust. Above them, the solar panels looked dusty, but apparently they were turning out some power. The water inside the garden boxes was still liquid. Thank God, Ted thought.

"Can't we make it any warmer in here?" McPherson asked.

Ted shook his head. "The reactor started running hot again

overnight and the system powered it down to compensate. It's now running on less than half-power and the decline is likely to continue unless we can find out what's wrong and fix it."

Amanda looked askance. "Does anyone here know anything about nuclear engineering? I'm a biologist and Catherine and Hi are geologists. Ted, you're a chemist, right? In addition to being a pilot. Did you study reactors in chemistry?"

"Just enough to know that I don't have a clue as to what's wrong with the reactor, other than what the system's already told us about the problem with the cooling system. I know that the reactor uses a liquid coolant, a liquid mixture of sodium and potassium."

"NaK," said McPherson. "You don't want to mess around with that stuff. It explodes if it's put in contact with water."

Ted nodded. "And catches fire if it's in contact with air."

"Sweet," Amanda said.

For a moment, the four of them stood wordlessly, staring at each other.

"At least the storm has ended," Catherine said.

"We'll have to go outside and clean off the dust," said McPherson.

Ted told them, "After breakfast. But before breakfast, let's see what Houston has to tell us."

He tapped the communications console's keyboard and Nathan Brice's face appeared on the central screen, his thinning hair in harried disarray, his normally unruffled expression decidedly ruffled.

"*Fermi*, your lack of response is very troubling. We see from the telemetry that the reactor has powered down to less than fifty percent. Why haven't you answered our previous messages?"

"We slept through them," McPherson murmured.

Two more messages asking why they hadn't replied, then finally the display showed Houston's original message: the power specialists' analysis of their reactor problem.

Holding up one finger, Connover said, "Let me send them a message telling them we're alive."

Into the comm microphone he said, "Houston: *Fermi* here. We've received your messages and are going through the analysis. Will call again once we've digested it. Thanks."

Grinning up at his three teammates, Ted said, "That ought to bring Brice's blood pressure back to normal."

During breakfast, the message alarm beeped and they all scrambled from their dining table to the command center. Ted slipped into the chair and tapped the comm console while the other three clustered behind him.

Nathan Brice's face appeared on the central screen, looking more composed than he had earlier.

"Good morning, *Fermi*," he said, trying to smile and almost making it. "I hope you had a good night's rest."

Connover winced inwardly.

Without waiting for a response that would take most of an hour to reach him, Brice continued, "You've got some work to do before we can figure out exactly how we can fix your power problem. The telemetry from the reactor doesn't look good. Something happened yesterday to the coolant flow, the reactor started to run hot and the automatic feedback loop powered the system down to seventy percent of normal, which it calculated would keep the heat levels to something the cooling system could handle. That's when you had the brownout."

McPherson muttered, "Tell us something we don't already know."

The flight director held up a schematic of the reactor and its cooling system.

"The coolant is liquid metal, sodium-potassium. It's a standard reactor coolant and very safe to use. Unless, of course, you expose it to air or water, then it catches fire or explodes. But there's very little air or water where you are."

"Especially water," Amanda grumbled.

"We think the problem is in the pumping system, but it might also be a problem with the radiators. The engineers here think the radiators are okay: the telemetry from them looks good."

Pointing to the cooling system's pump, he went on, "The pump keeps the coolant moving through the reactor and out to the radiators, where it gets rid of the heat. Very standard layout. The coolant doesn't pick up much radioactivity: it doesn't go inside the reactor, it just flows around it. That's the good news."

Connover nodded, waiting for the other shoe to drop.

"But somebody's going to have to go out there and provide us with some visuals on the physical integrity of the system. Whoever it is will get a small dose of radiation; that can't be helped. The medical people tell us that the dose should be minimal, no worries."

"Great. Just great," McPherson muttered.

Brice continued, "From the telemetry it looks like the pump is malfunctioning. We think one of its blades might have cracked. If that's the case the system's performance will continue to erode until the blade fails entirely and the reactor automatically shuts down."

Dropping the schematic, Brice told them, "Now, the system is modular, and it's designed to be repairable. That means you can get the pump and bring it inside your habitat to check it out. But before you do that you're going to have to power down the reactor, and that will cut off the electricity it supplies to your habitat."

Ted's mind raced. *We'll have to do this in daylight. Clean off the solar panels before we shut down the reactor so we'll have electricity to get through the day. Take out the pump, check it out and repair the bad blade. Get it all done before the sun goes down again.*

Brice was going on, "We've uploaded the full schematics for the pump and the CAD files you'll need to make spare parts with your 3D printer." He took a breath. "We had planned to send backup parts for the nuke system on the follow-on flight. We didn't expect a failure so early in the reactor's life cycle. Bad decision on our part."

"Yeah," Ted whispered.

"The time delay between us," Brice resumed, "means we won't be able to coach you through this in real time. But we'll definitely watch on the monitors and answer whatever questions you have as fast as the speed of light allows."

With that, Brice looked around at the people surrounding him and finished with, "Good luck, guys."

Connover hit the transmit button and said tersely. "Message received. Thanks. We'll do our best."

He clicked off the communicator and got up from his chair, stiffly, as if he'd aged ten years overnight.

As he looked at the faces of his three comrades, he said to himself, *All right, you're supposed to be the leader around here. So start leading.*

"All three of you start prebreathing, right now. Hi, you and Amanda read and memorize how to remove that pump and get it in here so we can repair it. Catherine, you'll have to clean off the solar panels and the tops of the gardens. And the radiator panels, too. I'll download the CAD files they've sent and start the 3D printer going."

"But we don't know if the pump blade is really the problem," Amanda objected.

"Yeah, but we don't have time to do things in sequence. We've got to do 'em in parallel, without wasting a minute. We can't afford to have the reactor totally shut down when the Sun goes down."

"How much time will we have without the reactor?" McPherson asked.

"If we can get the solar panels operating at full capacity, we should be good during the daylight hours. The batteries will give us another six hours, maximum."

"Not enough to get through another night," said Catherine.

"That's why we've got to get moving. Now!"

DECEMBER 19, 2035
MARS LANDING PLUS 44 DAYS
10:21 HOURS UNIVERSAL TIME
ELYSIUM PLANITIA

In their excursion suits and helmets, Hiram and Amanda approached the nuclear reactor module. It stood twelve feet tall on the red Martian sands, looking like any other aerospace "cylinder," except that it rested on three sturdy legs and had massive black panels protruding from its top—the radiators that got rid of the heat the reactor produced.

"Radiation levels increasing," Amanda said, her eyes on the scintillation meter strapped to the wrist of her suit. "Just a tad over Mars background, but it's getting higher as we get closer to the reactor."

"That's to be expected," McPherson said.

"Nothing to worry about."

"Why do people keep saying that?"

They trudged to the big cylinder, then stepped around it to find the hatch that covered its pump.

"Let's do this right the first time," McPherson said. "Quick and smart."

Amanda nodded. "No unnecessary exposure to radiation."

"Exactly."

They checked the heads-up displays in their helmets, then McPherson took the power screwdriver from his belt and started unbolting the panel.

"Ted's purged the pump with nitrogen," Amanda said as she watched him working, swiftly, methodically, "so there won't be any NaK leaking from it when we take it out."

"Good thing," said McPherson as he lifted the panel off and let it drop languidly to the ground. "Don't want any NaK droplets on my suit when we go back into real air."

"Spontaneously bursting into flames could ruin your whole day."

"Right you are. Let's get this puppy out of here."

As they undid the connectors holding the pump in place, Amanda thought she could almost feel the nuclear radiation penetrating her suit and attacking her body. *Like Marie Curie*, she remembered. *She and her husband discovered radium and characterized the properties of the radiation it emitted—and she got a lethal dose over the years and died slowly of radiation poisoning.*

McPherson's voice snapped her attention back to the here and now. "Amanda, did Mission Control say anything about how they're keeping the reactor core from melting down without the coolant flowing?"

"The moderator rods slide into the core automatically when the reactor's shut down. They absorb the neutrons that cause the chain reactions. No neutrons banging around, no fission reactions, no heat."

"And Ted's checked to see that the rods are in place?"

"Sure. You can ask him if you're worried."

"I was just curious, that's all."

But he felt relieved.

Even in Mars' relatively low gravity the pump was almost too heavy for McPherson to remove. He quickly realized that it would take the two of them to carry it back to the habitat and that it would be slow going.

Like Jack and Jill carrying their pail of water, Hi and Amanda toted the pump back to the habitat's airlock.

"I wonder if my children are going to have two heads," he half-joked.

"Or leukemia," Amanda said.

"You're a lot of fun!"

"They can cure leukemia."

"And a kid with two heads can make a good living in the circus," McPherson quipped, half-heartedly.

It was a few minutes past noon by the time they reached the airlock. McPherson noticed that the solar panels and the gardens looked clean.

Then he thought, *We'll have to clean off the reactor's radiators, too; or maybe the wind will do that for us.*

Connover was waiting for them inside the airlock. He took over for Amanda and, together with Hi, toted the ungainly looking pump to the workbench in the habitat's right wing. It was noticeably colder in there; Ted was wearing a heavy pullover sweatshirt.

They placed the pump upright on the workbench. McPherson straightened up and flexed his arms to ease the cramp in his back, then unlatched his suit helmet and pulled it off his head.

The workbench was covered with tools, he saw, and Ted was slipping a pair of protective goggles over his eyes.

"Worried about some residual NaK being inside there?" he asked.

"Not worried. Cautious," Ted replied. "Just in case the purge didn't clean it out entirely. The last thing we need is for a—"

A flash of light made McPherson stagger backwards. Smoke poured from the pump and Ted crashed to the floor, curled up in a fetal ball, wringing his hands.

"Dammit! Dammit!" he moaned.

Stunned, McPherson gaped at Ted writhing on the floor. His face and right hand looked charred, black. Hi was glad Ted had worn the safety goggles.

Abruptly, Hi stirred into action, calling loudly, "Somebody grab a first-aid kit and tend to Ted while I make sure we don't catch fire!"

Smoke was still pouring from the pump, resting upright on the workbench. McPherson yanked the fire extinguisher off the wall. A fire in the confined space of the habitat was the worst nightmare he could imagine. He had to make certain that the NaK hadn't ignited anything else when it reacted with the air.

As he doused the pump and workbench with fire retardant, he saw that nothing else appeared to be burning and the smoke was thinning. He hoped there was no more NaK clinging to the pump's innards.

Amanda and Catherine burst in and knelt beside Ted, spraying anti-burn lotion over his face and right hand. Tenderly, they slipped off his goggles and began to place burn treatment gauze on his face, covering his eyes even though they'd been protected from the flash burn by his goggles.

Amanda said something to Catherine that McPherson couldn't hear, then got up and ducked out of the hatch. Hi saw that there was no fire, and the smoke had dissipated. Amanda came back in, tapping on her tablet. *Looking up how to treat flash burns*, Hi thought.

"Catherine, help me move Ted out to his hammock," he said,

reaching under Connover's shoulders to gently raise him to a sitting position.

"I can walk," Ted said, weakly. "I think."

With Amanda behind them, tapping away on the notebook, Catherine and Hi half-dragged Ted into the central compartment. McPherson held Ted upright while Catherine unpinned his hammock and hung it in place. Then, together they stretched Connover onto it.

"Hurts," Connover muttered. "Hurts like hell."

"We'll take care of you, buddy," said McPherson. Looking up to the women, he said, "Amanda, you tend to Ted. Get some painkillers into him. Catherine, you know more about schematics than I do. Let's get back to that pump and see how badly damaged it is."

Catherine followed Hi back to the right wing and the damaged pump, still standing on the workbench, but looking charred and blackened.

Catherine slid her arms around McPherson and hugged him.

"That's for luck," she said. "We're going to need it."

She saw Ted's notebook computer open on the workbench and peered at it briefly, then slipped on the same goggles Connover had been wearing. "There must be another pair of goggles in one of these drawers," she said to McPherson.

The pump's probably totally ruined, he thought, but he didn't say it to Catherine. Not yet. *Maybe there's still a chance we can fix it.* But he thought that chance must be very slim.

He stood beside Catherine, feeling pretty useless as she poked around inside the pump, glancing at the schematic on Ted's notebook every few seconds.

"You ought to be wearing gloves," he said.

Instead, Catherine lifted her goggles off her head. "If there was any more NaK inside, it would have flashed by now," she said.

Feeling helpless, superfluous, McPherson said, "I'm going to see how Ted's doing. I'll be right back."

She nodded, her attention totally focused on the pump.

McPherson ducked back into the central compartment and saw that Ted was passed out in his hammock, face and right hand bandaged.

Amanda looked up as he approached. "I've given him the painkillers the medical files called for and sent a message back to Houston, along with pictures of his burns."

"Good work," McPherson said.

"Now we have to wait for their reply."

"Yeah." Feeling equally useless at Ted's side, he said, "I'm going back to help Catherine."

"Sure. There's not much else either one of can do here, for now."

Catherine smiled tentatively as he re-entered the workroom. "It's not as bad as I feared," she said.

"Good."

"The flash fire didn't do much more than blacken the components inside the pump. Remember, this thing is designed to operate at over one thousand degrees Fahrenheit. A little *poof* of a flash fire cannot hurt it."

McPherson said, "Great. Wonderful."

"That's the good news," said Catherine. "Now for the bad. We're going to have to remove all the soot inside the pump. It would contaminate the coolant and cause problems."

"Okay," he said. "We can do that."

"And now the worst news. One of the pump blades is badly cracked. I'm surprised it hasn't broken into two pieces."

"Can we fix it? Ted had started the 3D printer on making a replacement blade, hadn't he?"

"I've checked the CAD files that Houston sent up. There's nothing for a replacement blade."

"But . . ." McPherson sagged onto the bench. "But that's the part we need!"

With a Gallic shrug, Catherine said, "We will have to wait for Houston's call."

McPherson was calculating how long it was until sunset. Once the solar panels shut down, they had only six hours of battery power. Not enough to get through the night. And it would be down to a hundred below zero before the Sun rose again.

Catherine and Hi stepped into the central module, where Connover was lying unconscious in his hammock. Amanda was at the desk, bent over her tablet.

She turned as they entered, and got to her feet.

"How's he doing?" McPherson asked.

"Resting quietly, thanks to the painkillers. His eyes are okay, the goggles protected them. But he's got some pretty bad burns on his face and right hand. I'm waiting for the medics back home to tell me what I should be doing."

Waiting, thought McPherson. *That's all we can do: wait. While the Sun gets closer to the horizon.*

It took an hour and five minutes to get meaningful information about the pump from Houston. And another forty-five minutes before the medical team sent advice about Connover's immediate treatment.

The latter was better news than the former.

The image of Ted's personal physician, Pat Church, filled the screen. Normally Church looked cool and confident, but now his lean face was clearly tense, strained.

"Ted's burns are going to be painful," he said, utterly professional, "but they don't look as if there's going to be any serious risk of infection. From what we can tell, the burns on his face are second degree. The one on his right hand might be a third-degree burn and that's the one you'll have to watch. You're doing the right thing by covering it with gauze and giving him painkillers. Let him rest and hopefully you'll be able to uncover his eyes by tomorrow. I wouldn't let him do much of anything for the next several days. We'll reassess his need for painkillers then."

The camera panned to Nathan Brice and another man, with the dark complexion and big liquid eyes of a Hindu, in a white open-necked shirt.

"I am sorry to tell you that I have bad news about the pump," he began, in a lilting, rhythmic accent. "Dr. Clermont is correct, unfortunately. The problem is clearly with the cracked blade, and sadly your 3D printer cannot make a replacement blade that could survive the harsh environment within the pump."

McPherson felt his insides go hollow. He glanced at Catherine, who seemed to be holding herself together. Amanda looked . . . angry, almost.

The engineer went on without hesitation. "Those blades are made in a complex process that cannot be duplicated in a 3D printer. There is no way to do it. It is not like making a hammer or a wrench or even a circuit board. Any blade you make with the 3D printer would fly apart once the pump began operating again."

None of them said a word.

Brice took over again. "Guys, we've got our best engineers on this and I'm sure we'll come up with something, but time is our enemy. You've only got, by our best estimate, another hour before the Sun sets, and then six hours of battery power. It's going to get pretty rough out there. I suggest you get into your excursion suits. That'll give you a few more hours. We'll be in touch."

The screen went blank.

Hiram, Catherine and Amanda stared at the screen for at least fifteen seconds after the image of Brice and the Indian engineer vanished.

"That's it?" Amanda burst. "That's all they can come up with? That's bullshit!" She was clearly near her breaking point.

"Take it easy," McPherson said to her. "You and Catherine get into your suits, then come back here with Ted's and help me get him into it."

"What about you?"

"I'll get into mine after we've got Ted buttoned up."

"But—"

"Don't waste time arguing," McPherson said tightly. "I'm going to power down everything we don't absolutely need to get through the night. We might need some of whatever power remains to pull a rabbit out of a hat."

"If Houston can find us a rabbit," Catherine muttered.

"Or a hat," groused Amanda.

Twenty minutes later they were all in their excursion suits. Connover was lying inert in his hammock and McPherson had powered down the life-support system. All that remained on full power was the communications system, which they needed to get any bright ideas that Houston might cook up to enable them to survive the night.

Hi looked fondly at Catherine and realized how beautiful she was, even with the bulky suit hiding her curves. This was his wife, and he felt the responsibility of doing all that he could to take care of her and save her life. He was looking forward to being a father someday and this was the woman he wanted to be the mother of his children.

He reached out and clasped her gloved hand.

Catherine looked up at him smiled through the visor of her helmet. "We'll get through this," she murmured.

Waiting was the hardest part. For the better part of an hour, Hiram, Catherine, and Amanda moved aimlessly about the compartment, which seemed to grow colder with each passing second. Occasionally one of them would look out the window at the darkening Martian plain. Nothing out there but sand and rocks, and stars dotting the sky. *One of those dots was Earth,* McPherson told himself. *A pale blue dot, so far away.*

He trudged into the workshop area, where the pump stood on the workbench, useless. Then he came back into the central area. Nothing had changed, except the thermometer. They were on a countdown clock, but time seemed to be crawling by interminably slowly. He looked at Ted, still in a drug-induced sleep, and wondered if they should all inject themselves with narcotics when their life expectancies could be measured in minutes. *More peaceful way to go,* he thought. Suffocating inside a spacesuit was not his idea of a good time.

When the communications system chimed, McPherson, sitting in the command chair and encased in his excursion suit, was dozing, drifting in that halfway place between true sleep and daydreaming reverie.

His eyes snapped open and he automatically activated the comm link on his suit so that he could hear the incoming message without removing his helmet. Half-turning in the seat, he saw Catherine and Amanda doing the same.

Now for the news from Houston, he thought, hoping that it wasn't some sort of last rites.

Brice's face looked stubbled, his hair mussed, but he was smiling.

"One of our engineers has an idea that's worth trying," he said, with an eagerness in his voice. "You ever hear of a Tesla Turbine? It's a simple pump that Nikola Tesla built back in—" He glanced over his shoulder and Hi heard a muffled voice.

"Yeah, right," Brice resumed. "Nineteen-thirteen. It's a pump that doesn't have any blades. Rotating disks literally drag liquids using the boundary-layer effect. The specs for those discs are well within the tolerances of what your 3D printer can do. Tesla originally designed it with geothermal energy in mind: you know, geysers. It's relatively simple and you should be able to cannibalize parts from the broken pump and use its outer housing. We're uploading plans so you can feed it to your 3D printer and get started."

Brice motioned for someone else to come on camera, and a young, soft-looking kid with long blond hair, pop eyes and a quizzical smile on his round face came up beside him, holding what looked like a replica of their broken pump. One of its access covers had been removed so that Hi could see its innards.

"Okay," Brice resumed, "as you can see, the Tesla Turbine will mostly replace what's inside the pump's current housing. We're not going to ask you to build a full, high-capacity pump in the few hours you've got remaining. But you can build one that runs at fifty-percent capacity and get it installed, if you hurry. Once it's in place, we can work with you to build a more capable pump. With luck, you can get back up to seventy-percent power. Not the best, but good enough to survive."

The younger engineer carried the pump back off-camera as Brice leaned in closer.

"Given the communications lag, we won't have time to answer specific questions that might come up as you build the turbine. So we've got three separate teams making replacement pumps using the same equipment you have. As they uncover problems or process improvements, we'll shoot the information straight to you."

McPherson glanced at the computer screen and saw that it had indeed received the drawings and instructions for the 3D printer. He motioned Amanda and Catherine to get busy, then noted that the habitat had only about four more hours of battery power.

It was well past midnight when McPherson and Amanda toted their newly constructed pump to the idle reactor. Even in the gentle Martian gravity it had been a chore, especially since they had to walk slowly and avoid stumbling in the dark.

"Just a stroll in the starlight," Amanda said, puffing slightly, as they rested the pump on the ground.

McPherson thought it might indeed be romantic to take a starlit stroll with Catherine. But not until they got the reactor working again.

"No moonlight on Mars," Amanda added, disparagingly. "The planet's got two fucking moons and neither one of them is big enough to shed any light on us."

"But the view of Earth is tremendous," McPherson replied, trying to sound positive.

They had almost depleted the habitat's battery power by running the 3D printer and keeping the lights on as they worked. Now, on the dark Martian plain, they worked by the blue-white light of their helmet LEDs to install the renovated pump back in its place. They hardly spoke at all, grunting with exertion as they worked. McPherson even began to sweat inside his thermally insulated suit.

Better than freezing, he told himself, knowing that just outside the fabric of his suit, the thin Martian air was close to one hundred degrees below zero.

As he replaced the pump's last mounting bolt, he spoke into his helmet microphone.

"Catherine, restart the system and bring her up to five-percent power. Let's go slow and see if this thing really works."

Catherine's voice replied, "You and Amanda need to get away from the reactor, Hi. Once it starts up the radiation level will climb."

"We won't be here long. I just need to replace the outer panel so dust won't get inside and muck things up even more. We can't afford to have anything else go wrong."

"But the radiation . . ."

"We need to get the heat back in the habitat, and get the air circulating again. Start her up. Now!"

McPherson knew that their suits were down to their final half-hour of oxygen, and it would take most of that time to walk back to the habitat. But he had to make certain that the pump would work properly. A slight dose of radiation was a price he was willing to pay to make sure that their jury-rigged repair would do the job.

Still, he jerked a gloved thumb at Amanda. "You start back, kid. I've got it from here."

"No way," she said, defiantly. "I'm staying with you in case we need to pull that contraption out of there again. It's too bulky for you to manhandle it by yourself."

He knew she was right. "Okay. But let's step back a ways before Catherine fires her up. I'm not a big fan of gamma rays and stray neutrons. I feel like I should be wearing lead-lined underwear."

With a smirk in her voice Amanda rejoined, "I'm sure Catherine will be more than happy to check out your functionality once we get this behind us."

Hiram fell speechless. If Amanda was trying to put him at ease, she'd failed miserably.

They backed off about twenty feet, probably not enough to make much difference, but it made them feel better. McPherson stared at the reactor, looking for some sign that it was functioning. But all it did was sit there, gleaming faintly in the light from the stars.

Then Catherine's voice in his helmet speakers, sounding excited: "Hi, we're at five-percent power and all the indicators are showing green. The pump appears to be working!"

He let out a breath that he hadn't realized he'd been holding.

"I'm ramping up to ten percent," Catherine continued. "You two should start back. There's not yet enough power to turn the heat back on, but I'm starting the air circulation fans. The air in here should be breathable by the time you get back. Cold, but breathable. Like Antarctica. Amanda, you should feel at home."

Grinning inside his helmet, McPherson gestured for Amanda to start back.

"Not without you," she said.

"Ramp it up, Catherine," he called. "We'll stay here until you get to the ten percent level without problems."

"I'm throttling it up, but I want you back here with me. Don't be stubborn. If you don't start now, you might not have enough air in your suits to make it, and I refuse to spend the next year or more without you."

Grinning to himself, McPherson said softly, "Just tell us when you're at tenpercent."

Another minute passed—slowly. Then Catherine announced, "Ten percent! Now get back here!"

DECEMBER 20, 2035
MARS LANDING PLUS 45 DAYS
01:00 UNIVERSAL TIME
NEW YORK CITY

It was eight P.M. in Manhattan, and Steven Treadway was desperately trying to piece together all the information that was coming in from the Johnson Space Center in Houston and NASA Headquarters in Washington D.C.

Standing in one corner of the big news desk set, away from the lights and cameras focused on the man and woman at the anchor spots on the other side of the cavernous room, Treadway scanned a report fresh from the computer while listening to the high-speed chatter of Houston's public affairs director in his ear bud.

He nodded as the assistant floor director hurried up to him and held up three fingers. *Three minutes,* Treadway understood. *No time to write anything for the teleprompter. I'm going to have to wing it.*

The makeup woman dabbed his face with a miniature brush, and his two assistants backed away from him. Treadway stepped to his spot in front of the blank green screen as the male anchorman said in his crack-of-doom voice:

"There's been more trouble at the *Fermi* habitat on Mars, where four men and women are struggling to survive in that bitter, hostile environment. Steven Treadway has the latest."

Treadway was suddenly bathed in light. A glance at the TV monitor showed that he appeared to be standing in front of the *Fermi* habitat, alone and alien-looking on the plain of Elysium.

"Yes, Roger," he said, keeping his face solemn, "astronaut Ted

399

Connover was seriously injured when the nuclear reactor that provides much of the Mars' habitat's electrical power suffered a shutdown a few hours ago."

Treadway gave a sketchy account of the reactor problem, then went into the ugly details about Connover's burns.

"But," he went on, breaking into a tentative smile, "Connover's competent teammates have repaired the reactor and doctored the astronaut."

For another two minutes, Treadway outlined what had happened, stressing that there was no leak of radioactivity and that Connover's burns were expected to heal in a week or so. When the floor director signaled he had thirty seconds remaining before they cut to a commercial, Treadway looked directly into the camera and spoke extemporaneously:

"Many people have said that it's too dangerous for human beings to risk their lives in space exploration. It *is* dangerous, there's no doubt of that. But what we are witnessing is that intelligent, dedicated men and women can surmount the problems that they face so many million miles from home. They can adapt, improvise, and overcome the drawbacks of living in that alien environment on Mars. They can survive, and we should be proud of each and every one of them—and the team back here on Earth that supports them.

"Steven Treadway reporting."

Catherine broke into a big, beaming smile as Ted Connover stepped from his hammock to the table where the team was having breakfast.

To treat the burns on his face, she and Amanda were keeping his blistered skin covered in nitric oxide-impregnated bandages while they attached the WoundStim's tiny electrodes to the uninjured skin next to the burn. Developed in India after so many suffered severe burns from the detonation of the improvised nuclear device that devastated Faridabad in 2022, the device reduced the amount of time required to heal from severe burns by at least a factor of three, making WoundStim standard equipment among first responders and, of course, the world's space agencies. The more serious burns on his right hand would be treated the same way, after the wounds on his face were sufficiently healed. The women put Ted's arm in a sling until it could be treated so that it wouldn't contact his body as he slept and moved around the habitat.

"The Mummy from Mars," Amanda said.

"I'm not a mummy," Ted quipped. "I'm a daddy."

McPherson and the women laughed at the the cleverness of Ted's remark.

"How do you feel?" Catherine asked.

"Still a little pain," said Connover, "but I'm glad you cut down on the painkillers. They were making me dopey."

"Dop*ier*," Amanda wisecracked.

"What's for breakfast?" Ted asked.

"You have a choice," said McPherson. "Reconstituted eggs or cornflakes with soymilk."

"Just coffee."

"You should eat something," said Amanda. "Bring up your strength." She pushed her chair back from the table and got to her feet. "Eggs or flakes?"

Ted got up too. "I can get it myself. I've still got one workable hand."

Amanda nodded, but stayed beside Ted as he went to the freezer, pulled out a package of eggs, and slid it into the microwave.

"What's our power level?" Ted asked as the microwave started humming.

"A little over fifty percent," said McPherson, "with the new pump we installed yesterday."

"What are we doing without?"

"Lights and heat, mostly."

Catherine added, "We turn off the lights in areas we are not working in, and we turn down the heat at night."

"Solar panels okay?"

"Yes," McPherson answered. "We get plenty of power while the sun's up." Before Connover could ask, he went on, "And the gardens are doing fine."

Ted nodded as the microwave pinged. "We're going to be all right, then."

McPherson grinned at him. "Like you said, God willing and the creek don't rise."

Bee Benson was sitting in the *Arrow*'s command chair, frowning at the display of their ship's trajectory. To get back to Earth, the *Arrow* was going to have to coast all the way to Venus, where it would loop around that planet and finally approach home.

No big deal, he told himself. *Spacecraft have used these slingshot maneuvers since the 1970s, stealing a bit of angular momentum from a planet to change their own trajectories. Gravity assist. Perfectly orthodox technique.*

Still, he wished they could go straight to Earth without the need to haul out to Venus. *Yeah,* he thought. *Go straight to Earth and go screaming in like a bloody meteor. Burn up in the atmosphere. Haste makes cinders.*

Virginia stepped into the command center. "It's almost lunch time," she said, standing beside him.

He pulled her down onto his lap. "I'm not hungry," he said. "For lunch."

She giggled. "You've fallen under the influence of Venus, goddess of love and beauty."

"You're all the goddess I need," Bee replied.

"Really?"

"Really. Besides, Venus isn't so beautiful, once you see her close up."

"The evening star? Not beautiful?"

"Oh, she looks lovely in Earth's sky. The evening star. Or the morning star, depending on where she is in her orbit around the Sun. But that's because she's twenty-five million miles away from Earth, more or less. When you get closer to her, she doesn't look so good."

"The astronomers call her Earth's twin planet, don't they?"

"Venus is almost the same size as Earth, true enough. But think about it, her atmosphere is almost entirely carbon dioxide. The clouds that make her shine so beautifully are laced with sulfuric acid. The ground temperature is almost a thousand degrees Fahrenheit. The ground glows, it's so hot. Damned planet's more like Dante's Inferno than the goddess of love and beauty."

Virginia heaved a mock sigh. "How romantic you are, Bee."

"I'm a realist."

"But where's the romance, the adventure, the dream?"

"Virginia, the dreamer in me was wounded when we got hit by that rock. It was killed when we lost Mikhail. I can't afford to dream if I'm going to get us back home safely."

She shook her head. "My poor Bee. So much responsibility on your shoulders."

"If it weren't for you, I'd have gone crazy weeks ago."

Virginia smiled sadly. "Ah, love, let us be true to one another," she quoted. "For the world, which seems to lie before us like a land of dreams, so various, so beautiful, so new, hath really neither joy, nor love, nor—"

Bee wrapped his arms around her. "But we have each other,

Virginia. And once we get home, we're going to build a wonderful life together."

Her smile turned warmer. *He said once we get home,* Virginia thought. *Not if. We're going to make it. And he's going to be all right.*

It was approaching midnight in Washington D.C. The black Mercedes sedan stopped at the White House's west gate, where the passengers' credentials were quickly scanned by the guard, then the car drove up to the West Wing portico.

Standing beside the Marine on duty there, Sarah Fleming held her arms tightly around herself. The December night was cold. Past the White House fence she could see the National Christmas Tree, ablaze with colored lights. The city was still buzzing, despite the hour. Most stores were remaining open until midnight to accommodate frenzied Christmas shoppers.

Feels like it's going to snow, she said to herself.

The Mercedes pulled up and two men in dark suits got out, and hurried up the steps to where Fleming was waiting.

"Senator Donaldson," she said, with a heartiness she did not truly feel.

"Sarah," the senator replied.

"Come on in," she said.

As she walked them along the corridor, Fleming said, "The president is waiting for you in the reception room."

"Can you tell me what this is all about?" Donaldson asked, his voice hard, flinty. "A midnight call to the White House sounds pretty melodramatic to me."

Forcing a smile, Fleming replied, "He didn't want any publicity about this meeting. He thought it would be best if you two talked without the ever-present cyberworld watching. I don't think a public figure can go to the bathroom without someone taking a movie, posting it and commenting on their bowel habits."

Donaldson made a sour face; the young aide accompanying him looked shocked.

The reception room was small, quiet, elegant, private. President Harper got to his feet as the three of them stepped in. On the ornate coffeetable in front of the sofa, a small forest of liquor bottles stood waiting. The president already had a heavy-cut crystal glass in his hand.

"William," he said cordially, extending his free hand. "Good of you to come."

Donaldson made the smallest of smiles as he took the president's hand. "What's this all about, Mr. President?"

Harper smiled broadly as he pointed to the array of bottles. "What'll you have?"

"Coffee, please."

"Nothing stronger? Something to ward off the chill?"

"Just coffee."

Fleming went to the phone and ordered a pot of coffee. Harper pointed to the sofa, then sat himself in the armchair at one end of it. Donaldson sat at that end of the sofa.

A butler wearing a dignified white tie came in with a tray bearing a silver coffeepot and three heavy-looking mugs bearing the presidential seal. Fleming poured for the senator and his aide while Harper sat back in the armchair and sipped at his whisky.

"All right, Bob," Donaldson said, letting some crankiness show, "why did you ask me here?"

Harper ignored the deliberate impropriety. Leaning toward Donaldson, he said, "Bart Saxby's had a heart attack."

"When?"

"Earlier this evening. He's in the Georgetown University Hospital, intensive care."

Almost smirking, Donaldson muttered, "Another victim of your Mars program."

Biting back the retort that leaped to his mind, the president said merely, "He'll recover, they're pretty sure."

"Is this why you asked me here tonight?" Donaldson asked.

"No."

"Then what?"

"Bill, it's time for us to talk turkey."

"About what?"

"About the party's nominee for the presidency next summer."

A light glinted in Donaldson's eye, but before he could say anything, the president added:

"And the future of the Mars program."

The light disappeared. "You know where I stand on that," Donaldson said coldly. "Human spaceflight is too dangerous. And too expensive. And I don't give a damn about life on Mars."

Keeping his expression steady, Harper said, "No more dangerous than airplanes were, early on. In fact, spaceflight has a much better record than aviation, safety-wise."

"One of your Mars people died. Another had a serious accident. And now Saxby."

"Prokhorov's cancer had nothing to do with his being on the Mars mission and you know it," said the president. "And Connover's recovering from his burns. I'd say the Mars team has done an admirable job of overcoming the problems they've faced."

"But it's so expensive—"

"It's peanuts, and you know it! Less than one percent of the federal budget."

"It's one percent we could use elsewhere."

President Harper put his glass down on the coffeetable and said slowly, "William, you've got to decide whether or not you really want the party's nomination."

"What do you mean? Of course I want it. I deserve it!"

Leaning back in the armchair again, Harper said, "If you want my support, you'll have to reinstate the funding for the follow-on mission to Mars."

"Reinstate . . . ?"

"*And* promise to continue human missions to Mars and elsewhere."

"No!"

"Do you think you can get the party's nomination without my support?"

Donaldson flashed a glance at his aide, who sat frozen, coffee mug halfway to his lips, his eyes riveted on the president.

Then the senator said, "Yes, I think I could win the nomination without your support."

"Could you win it if I actively opposed you?" Harper asked, very softly, almost in a whisper.

Donaldson's lean face flushed with anger. "You'd tear the party apart over this Mars nonsense?"

"The public is solidly in favor of this 'Mars nonsense,' as you put it. We've confirmed that organic chemicals are there. Some on the team are telling me that there are bound to be fossils too. This is the most important discovery in history and we can't walk away from it. It's too important."

"Fantasy."

"Then let's talk about reality. You'd have a hard time winning the nomination if I opposed you, and even if you got the nod, you'd surely lose in November."

"Because you'd split the party in two!"

"No," Harper countered, "because *you* would split the party in two by your opposition to one of our most popular programs."

"Mars isn't necessary."

"Yes, it is!" Harper insisted. "Don't you understand? We have all sorts of programs for all sorts of needs. But Mars—human exploration of the space frontier—that gives people hope, excitement, something to be thrilled about, something to be proud of. And the technology we develop builds our economy better and faster than all the handouts we offer to the people. Who knows, maybe we'll find out that Mars had more than bacteria in its history."

Donaldson started to reply, then thought better of it.

"I'll support your nomination with everything I've got," Harper promised the senator, "and a united party will win the election in November. If you want the White House, you have to give the voters Mars."

"I can't do an about-face like that. I'm on record as opposing human spaceflight."

"You can become a convert," the president said, with a benign smile. "It's been done before. You've changed your mind on other issues, over the years."

"But . . ."

"You give me Mars and I'll give you the White House."

"I'll lose my core!"

"You can persuade them. Only a small set of fanatics will hold out. They're noisy, but they don't have the votes and the public's getting tired of them." The president leaned forward to tap Donaldson on the knee. "William, this is politics. You have to give something to get something. I'm willing to give you the White House. Seems to me what I'm asking you for is not beyond the realm of reason. Besides, the samples of Martian life will come back while *you're* in the White House, not me."

Donaldson didn't look convinced.

"What if I told you that you'll be able to take credit for creating whole new industries and keeping American biotechnology preeminent for the foreseeable future?"

Donaldson squinted, turned his head to the side, and leaned forward in a clear indication that he wanted to hear more.

Harper filled him in on the NexGenPro analysis of what could come from the Martian organic chemicals.

"What'll keep me from going public with that information tomorrow?"

"Absolutely nothing. Except that I'll withdraw my offer and you won't have my help winning the next election."

Donaldson muttered, "Let me think about it. I'll have to talk to my people, and—"

"No. I need your answer now. Right here and now."

The senator looked away from the president, his eyes scanning the room and settling on the painting of the Yosemite Valley hanging on the opposite wall.

Pointing toward the painting, President Harper smiled and said, "Once that was the frontier, Bill. Wild and dangerous. Men and women died trying to tame it. Now it's a National effing Park. Oh, and do I need to remind you of all the money the robber barrons made by taking advantage of the resources they found as they moved west?"

Donaldson nodded. "I see what you mean." He drew in a deep breath, then said, "All right, give me a few weeks to break this gently. But I'll get my subcommittee to reinstate the follow-on mission."

"And you'll back future human space missions?"

"I guess I'll have to, won't I?" Suddenly the senator broke into a reluctant grin. "Hell, I might even name you as next director of NASA."

Harper laughed. "No. No thanks. Saxby will recover and you'll want some continuity at NASA." Then, his expression turning sly, he added, "a Supreme Court appointment would be good enough."

Donaldson looked as if he wanted to puke. But he kept his mouth shut and got to his feet.

They stood up. Shook hands. The president walked the senator to the door, one arm around Donaldson's shoulders.

"I want to thank you, William. You've made a hard decision, but you've made the right one."

Donaldson looked less than happy, but he managed to mutter, "Thank you, Mr. President."

Beaming his best smile, Harper said, "Next year this time, I'll be calling *you* Mr. President."

Despite himself, Donaldson grinned.

Fleming led Donaldson and his aide out of the room. Harper went to the coffeetable, drained his glass and refilled it.

When Fleming returned, she asked the president, "Well, what do you think?"

"I think we'd better lavish a lot of praise on that sonofabitch once he reinstates the funding for the follow-on. We've got to make sure he stays bought."

Fleming nodded knowingly.

DECEMBER 24, 2035
MARS LANDING PLUS 49 DAYS
23:30 UNIVERSAL TIME
THE *ARROW*

"Merry Christmas, Bee." Virginia was smiling warmly as she handed Benson a folded slip of paper.

They were in the cupola, which they had turned into their private little nest. Beyond the observation ports, the stars hung solemnly in the infinite black sky. One of the points of light was blue and beckoning: Earth.

"Thank you, Jin," said Benson as he carefully opened the single sheet and looked down at the paper.

Virginia had drawn an elaborate scene: a cutaway view of the *Arrow* with a Christmas tree prominently displayed in the galley, bright with lights. At its base, instead of gift boxes, was a scattering of reddish rocks: Mars rocks, he surmised. Standing around the tree were caricatures of the three of them, Benson, Virginia, and Taki. They were actually well done, he thought, looking happy and healthy with broad smiles on their faces. Even Prokhorov was there, floating above them like a Christmas ghost, smiling also.

Feeling guilty, he mumbled, "I didn't get anything for you. I'm sorry."

"You've given me love and joy, Bee. Every day, not just for Christmas."

He felt his cheeks warm.

Taki's voice on the intercom broke into their moment. "Hey, you guys, front and center! We're getting a call from the President of the United States!"

Benson blinked with surprise, then pushed against the cold observation port to move away from the hatch. With a sweeping gesture, he said, "Ladies first."

"The president?" Virginia marveled. "Must be a Christmas greeting."

They floated up to the command center, where Taki was hovering in midair, facing the communications screen. A redheaded woman was saying, "The president will be with you in a minute."

"We're here," said Benson, as he and Virginia coasted up on either side of Taki.

"Relax. They won't hear you for at least half an hour," Taki reminded them.

The screen now showed the presidential seal, nothing more. Taki muttered, "Take your time, Prez, we've got nothing better to do than—"

A male voice announced calmly, "The President of the United States."

President Harper's heavyset, silver-maned form filled the screen. He was smiling, and to Benson it didn't look like the plastic smile of a professional politician. Harper looked genuinely pleased.

"Good evening and Merry Christmas," he said. "I want to give you my personal best wishes and tell you that the whole nation—the whole world—is praying for your safe return home."

Standard political fare, Benson thought.

"I have some good news for you. Bart Saxby is out of danger, and it looks as if he'll make a full and speedy recovery."

The three of them smiled appreciatively.

The president went on, "This is a private message, people. No news coverage, nobody else in the loop. Even the technicians who set up this communication have left the room. Just you folks on the *Arrow* and the *Fermi* habitat. I want to give you all a sort of Christmas present."

President Harper's expression was somewhere between delighted and ecstatic. "I wanted to tell you personally that we're going to reinstate the funding for your follow-on mission. We're not going to leave your teammates stranded on Mars. We're going to go back and rescue them, and we're going to continue exploring."

"That's the important point," President Harper emphasized. "We're going to continue exploring. Your mission to Mars is only the first one. There will be others."

Taki clapped her hands. "Wonderful!"

"I know that you won't be able to reply for another half-hour or more," the president was saying, "but I couldn't resist giving you the good news in person. Merry Christmas to you all! And when you return to Earth, I'll be there to personally shake your hands."

The screen went blank.

For several heartbeats neither Taki, Virginia, nor Bee said a word. Then they all started to speak at once.

Laughing, they finally said together, "Merry Christmas to you, Mr. President. And thanks for the good news."

Ted Connover's bandaged face appeared on the screen. "Did you just hear what I just heard?"

"Yes!" Benson said. "Looks like you're going to get rescued."

The time-lag between Mars and the *Arrow* was less than a minute, but still the seconds ticked slowly.

Hi McPherson poked his bearded face into the camera's view. "Well, I always figured they wouldn't leave us stranded here. At least, I hoped so."

"The president seemed very excited about it," Virginia said, from behind Benson's shoulder.

"His Christmas present to us," said McPherson.

"Damned nice of him to call," Taki said.

"Yeah, it was."

Benson asked, "How're you guys doing out there?"

"We're fine," Connover replied.

Amanda said, "We'll take the bandages off Ted's face in another day or so."

Benson hiked a brow. "Oh, I don't know. I think Ted looks better with part of his face hidden."

"He might at that," Catherine agreed. "It makes him look more mysterious."

"Maybe you ought to cover up the rest of his face," Benson joked.

"Yeah, yeah," Connover groused. "And a Merry Christmas to you, too."

"What do you want Santa Claus to bring you?" Virginia asked.

All four of the *Fermi* team answered as one voice, "Water!"

To McPherson, the novelty of going outside the habitat and walking on Mars would forever be exciting, filled with wonder. Even on Christmas day, he and Catherine had suited up and gone out onto the plain of Elysium.

But there was more than the thrill of adventure motivating them now. They had to find water. The *Fermi*'s water supply was running low, even with their reduced consumption and recycling.

Still, McPherson was especially excited as he and Catherine stepped out of the *Fermi*'s airlock and onto the rusty-colored, rock-strewn sands of Elysium.

"We're going to cross the path that the old Curiosity rover took when it explored Gale crater." He was practically humming with glee.

Pointing to the hills rising in the distance, Catherine said, "It's more than a two-hour walk."

"A long way from here. We'll barely get there before we have to turn around and start back."

They both knew why they were heading out on such a long walkabout. The geology team back at Mission Control had picked that location as the best place to dig for water. According to their latest analysis, there was a shallow crater just to the east of where Catherine and Hi would be crossing the old rover's track. The east wall of the crater had been in shadow for ages, raising the possibility that there might be ice close enough to the surface for their core sampler to reach it.

415

His elation melting, McPherson said, "We won't have much time to look around, let alone drill for ice in more than one or two spots."

Catherine opened the panel in the *Fermi*'s side that covered the core sampler. "It's a shallow crater. We'll carry the mole over its rim and rappel down the inner slope."

"I'll carry the mole," McPherson said, taking the portable rig in his gloved hands. "You take the climbing stuff."

Even in the gentle Martian gravity the core sampler felt heavy. But McPherson hefted it onto one shoulder and started off for the distant hills, with Catherine scampering to come up beside him.

Nearly two hours later they both stopped and stared. Even though they were expecting to see them, actually walking up to the weathered tracks made by the Curiosity rover filled them both with awe.

"Look," said McPherson, letting the sampler slide from his shoulder to the ground. "It's still here."

The ridged tracks made by the old rover were clearly visible.

"After all these years," Catherine murmured. She sank to her knees, inspecting the tracks closely.

"Like the tracks of an old wagon train, out west," McPherson said.

"How far away is the rover?" asked Catherine

"Too far for us to get to it." He pointed toward the hills rising over the horizon.

"*Quel dommage*," she murmured. What a pity.

Hi stretched his hand to her and pulled Catherine to her feet. Then he shouldered the core sampler again and said, "We'd better keep moving. Still got a lot of ground to cover."

Reluctantly, they left the tracks behind them, carefully stepping over the rutted trail so that they wouldn't disturb them. They started a slow descent down a slight grade, heading for the shallow crater that Mission Control had identified. Catherine fell silent, and McPherson mused that even if they found ice in the crater and could liquefy it with power from a set of solar panels, it might be too far from the *Fermi* to pipe the water back to the habitat.

He shook his head. Find the water first. *Then we'll figure out a way to get it to the habitat.*

Following the GPS signals from the network of satellites orbiting Mars, they found the crater about twenty minutes later. It was indeed shallow: McPherson thought they would be able to descend into it without using the mountaineering gear. But he remembered what had happened to Ted with the NaK and decided not to take any risks that they could avoid.

"Catherine, I'll unlimber the mole while you set the anchors for the climbing rope."

"Are you still comfortable going down there with the drill?" she asked.

"As long as you're at the other end of the rope, I'll make it down there and back."

He connected the segments of the core sampler and lifted the ungainly looking rig onto his shoulder once more.

He grinned at Catherine. "I feel like Queequeg."

"Who?"

"The harpooneer in *Moby Dick*."

"Ah," said Catherine. "But there are no whales here."

"No, and this isn't a harpoon," Hi said, as he stepped over the rocky rim of the crater.

"Hiram," Catherine said as she clipped the climbing rope firmly around his waist, "perhaps we should both go down. Together."

"No," he said firmly. "Somebody's got to stay up here and work the winch, in case I fall."

She sighed audibly, but did not argue.

McPherson lifted his left hand to glance at the digital clock set among the instrument cluster on his wrist. *I'll only have about forty-five minutes before we have to start back,* he thought. *Not enough time. Never enough time.*

He reached the bottom of the crater. "Give me some slack," he called to Catherine. "I need to move around."

He unlimbered the core sampler, set it up on the hard-pan ground and unfolded the solar panels that provided its electrical power. With its usual bang-banging noise, the mole dug into the ground.

Ten minutes. Fifteen. McPherson scanned the crater bottom as he waited for the sampler to reach its maximum depth. The motor shut off automatically. Hiram put the motor in reverse and waited for the mole's head to emerge from the rust-red-colored surface.

"Anything?" Catherine's voice made him wince. She was forgetting that she didn't need to shout, despite the distance between them.

Fingering the dust-dry, crumbling dirt that the drill had brought up, Hi shook his head and answered. "Dry hole."

Her silence spoke louder than words.

"It's pretty flat down here," he said. "I'm going to disconnect the rope and head over there." He pointed to a jumble of smallish rocks in the shadow of the crater's slope. "Looks interesting."

"I don't like you disconnecting," Catherine said. "What if you fall?"

"I can do it without falling, dear. Even if I did, do you think you could pull my weight?"

"If I had to," she answered, her voice firm, sure.

He unclipped the rope despite her fears and, hauling the sampler onto his shoulder once more, made his way carefully to the shadowed area.

As McPherson set up the mole again, he saw that its solar panels just caught the sunlight. In another half-hour, as the Sun sank toward the horizon, they would be in shadow and the drill would shut down.

Hell, he thought, *in another half-hour we'd better be on our way home or we'll run out of air.*

He turned on the sampler, fidgeting nervously as it bit into the ground. Not enough time for it to get down to its maximum depth, he knew. *I'll have to pull it out. Give it another five minutes.*

He looked up at Catherine, standing on the crater's rim. Even in her excursion suit she looked taut, strained.

"We've got to start back in ten minutes," she said.

"I know." He stopped the mole, then reversed it.

The sampler head came up. McPherson pawed at the crumbling dirt, pebbles, and . . .

"Paydirt!" he bellowed.

"What?"

Holding several small chunks of ice in his gloved hands, he yelled, "It's ice! Look!" He raised both hands over his head like an ancient gladiator, victorious.

"It's ice, Cath! We did it! We found it!"

Hiram left the mole where it lay, clipped the rope around his middle once more, and hauled himself up the slope of the crater—after carefully placing the ice chunks in one of the storage pouches on his belt.

Once he got back to the rim he grabbed Catherine and the two of them pranced around in a frenzied jig of triumph and joy.

All the way back to the *Fermi* they jabbered with Ted and Amanda about their discovery.

"Don't worry about how far it is," Ted reassured them. "We can cannibalize pipes from the lander, and if that's not enough to reach us, then we'll take out the lander's goddamned tankage and use the tanks as a water dump, close enough for us to get to every day."

"But the tanks are contaminated with propellant," McPherson objected.

"I already checked with Houston. We can open up the tanks and leave them on the ground for a day or two. Any residual propellant in 'em will evaporate."

"Really?" Catherine asked.

"Really."

Amanda was more cautious. "First let's make sure what you found is really water ice."

"Yes, of course."

McPherson called, "Mandy, don't throw cold water on our discovery."

Connover laughed and added, "Yeah. Don't rain on our parade."

It was well past sunset by the time Catherine and Hi got back to the habitat. As soon as they came through the airlock, Amanda reached for the pouch on McPherson's belt.

"Let me see it. I've got to test it."

She opened the pouch and plucked out the three pieces. "Cold enough to be ice," she said as she hurried toward the bio lab.

"It's water, all right," Amanda said, the widest, brightest grin any of them had seen splitting her happy face.

"There's probably some minerals in it, of course. I'm testing for that now." With a giggle, she said, "Maybe we could sell it as the Martian equivalent of Perrier."

McPherson asked, "What about microbes? Bacteria? Viruses?"

Amanda shook her head. "I've got the electron microscope scanning the samples. Should be finished its run in a couple of minutes."

Ted went to the comm console. "Bee will want to know about this."

"And the geniuses in Houston."

Up the chain of command their report went: Nathan Brice at Mission Control, then Robin Harkness and finally Bart Saxby in his hospital room.

"The president will want to know," Saxby said, his face beaming.

"You tell him," Connover replied, knowing that his words wouldn't reach Earth for half an hour. "We're going to celebrate. It's Christmas, after all!"

While they waited for a reply from Saxby, Catherine said, "We should drink a toast."

"We don't have any booze," Ted lamented.

"Ah, yes, that is true. But we have water."

Laughing, Amanda headed back to the bio lab. "I'll pour enough for a toast."

She ducked into the minuscule lab and reached for the sample of melted ice that was being automatically scanned by the electron microscope.

Her hand stopped in midair.

Amanda stared at the microscope's screen, her heart thumping beneath her ribs. She swallowed hard, then slowly turned and stepped back into the central room of the habitat.

In a near whisper, she said, "The water's contaminated."

McPherson frowned at her. "You mean we can't drink it?"

Her voice shaking, Amanda said, "It's contaminated with microbes."

"Microbes?"

Catherine gasped. "Life? Living organisms?"

"Come and see for yourselves."

Connover jumped to his feet, McPherson and Catherine half a step behind him. The bumped into each other at the narrow doorway to the lab, making Amanda giggle.

Crowding the lab, the four of them stared at the microscope screen. Tiny blobs of protoplasm were wriggling and pulsating in the water sample.

"They're alive!" Connover shouted.

McPherson leaned each of his arms around the shoulders of the two women. "It's a Christmas miracle."

Amanda smiled knowingly. "It's Martian life. There must be a whole ecology out there living off the permafrost."

"My God," Connover said, his voice hollow. Then he grabbed Amanda and gave her a heartfelt kiss on the lips. "You did it, girl! You did it!"

Amanda grinned and said, "We did it. The four of us."

"We've found life on Mars," said Catherine, her voice trembling with wonder.

McPherson straightened up. "But this means we can't drink the water we get from the permafrost."

Connover said, "But we need that water."

Her eyes never leaving the microscope's screen, Amanda told them, "We're not going to drink from *this* sample, that's for sure. But there's no reason why we can't dig up more ice and distill the water so it's drinkable."

"But won't that kill the Martians?" Catherine asked.

McPherson said, "Can't be helped. We need the water to survive."

"Better than killing us," said Connover.

Amanda nodded and said softly, "We've got to see how big the permafrost deposit is. I'm guessing that it's big enough to provide us with drinking water *and* plenty of microbes to study."

"From your mouth to God's ear," Catherine murmured.

Even behind his bandages, the grin on Connover's face was obvious. "Come on, let's send word to Houston. Give 'em a Christmas present from Mars."

Later that night, on the dark windswept plain of Elysium, a new sound rose from the alien habitat standing on Mars. Above the sighing wind, four human voices sang:

> "Silent night,
> "Holy night,
> "All is calm,
> "All is bright . . ."

And the stars, in all their glory, continued to shine.

THE END